VISION OF THE
EAGLE

VISION OF THE EAGLE

A NOVEL BY

KAY McDONALD

THOMAS Y. CROWELL COMPANY
ESTABLISHED 1834 · NEW YORK

By the Author

The Brightwood Expedition
Vision of the Eagle

Copyright © 1977 by Kay L. McDonald
All rights reserved. Except for use in a review, the reproduction or utilization of this work in any form or by any electronic, mechanical, or other means, now known or hereafter invented, including xerography, photocopying, and recording, and in any information storage and retrieval system is forbidden without the written permission of the publisher. Published simultaneously in Canada by Fitzhenry & Whiteside Limited, Toronto.

Manufactured in the United States of America

Library of Congress Cataloging in Publication Data

McDonald, Kay L.   Vision of the Eagle.
1. Indians of North America—Fiction. I. Title.
PZ4.M13483Vi   [PS3563.A285]   813'.5'4   77-2579
ISBN 0-690-01491-0

1   3   5   7   9   10   8   6   4   2

For my two very special friends
and two truly beautiful people
Grace P. and Jean W.
whose enthusiasm and support
have meant more than they know

CONTENTS

PART I

1

A B I G A I L

Abigail Whitteker stood on the edge of the wooden sidewalk and breathed the sweet spring air freshly wrung of rain. The whole world seemed to be bursting forth into bloom just for her. With youthful optimism—in five months she would be twenty—her eyes saw her three-block world of Riverwood in upstate New York with bewitchment. Even the farm store, blacksmith shop, and livery stable at the other end of town, two blocks away, seemed fresh and unblemished.

She remembered her errand and turned purposefully to complete it, her small hard-heeled shoes seeming to tap a dance on the damp glistening boards of the walk. She saw the familiar figure of her dearest friend hurrying up the side street on her way to work in her father's store across the street from the Whitteker bank building. Beth was probably late—she usually was. Abigail stepped into the muddy street lifting her skirts and sidestepping a puddle of water, her eyes still on Beth across the street. Beth saw her and waved, and Abigail waved merrily back just as a wagon came wheeling by. Too late she jumped back as the horses and wheels sloughed through the huge puddle in the street, sending a shower of muddy drops as high as her pale golden curled hair and down the pale green dress that picked up the color of her eyes. Gasping in indignation, she looked up to see the driver rolling the wagon down the street toward the other end of town without so much as stopping to apologize.

Beth came rushing up to her. "Are you all right?" Then she giggled. "My! You look a sight!"

Abigail scowled as she lifted her soiled skirt and angrily left the street saying, "It's not funny. Who were they? Did you see?"

Beth shook her head, trying to hold back her smile. "No, but they looked like some of those Irish farmers to me."

"Well, they certainly need a lesson in courtesy, I'd say." She took her handkerchief and tried to wipe the muddy water from the papers she carried, making her angrier still. She looked down the street and saw the wagon stop in front of the farm store. Impetuously she made up her mind. "And I think I'll just give them one. Do you want to come?"

Beth shook her dark head with dismay. "You wouldn't, would you?"

"I certainly would." Green eyes flashed stubbornly.

Beth giggled again, expectancy of adventure lighting her eyes. She was about to say yes but thought better of it and looked at the watch pinned to her dress and sighed. "Oh, dear. I can't. I'm late already and Daddy was in such a mood this morning I'd better not go."

Determinedly Abigail said, "All right. I'll go by myself."

She turned on her heel and drawing herself up to her full, pert, but not imposing height she marched across the side street and onto the next walk, completely forgetting the soiled papers she carried.

She reached the farm store and turned the knob on the weathered door. It resisted her and she angrily threw her weight against it and it swung suddenly inward, catapulting her into the middle of the room where she came to a sudden ungraceful stop. The two men talking to Mr. Lynch, the store owner, turned around to stare at her in surprise, but Mr. Lynch had the most surprised look of all. If Abigail hadn't been so angry she would have seen two square-jawed, obviously related and ruggedly handsome young men, but all she saw was two dirty Irish immigrants smelling of sweat and animals.

"Are you the two men who own the wagon outside?" she demanded.

The older of the two answered, "Aye."

"Didn't you see me standing in the street? Just look what you've done to my dress! You could have stopped and let me cross or gone to the other side of the street. Why didn't you?"

The older man grinned and cast twinkling eyes on his younger brother. "Sure now, Ross, will ye be tellin' her why ye didn't stop for her."

The younger man straightened and his ruddy complexion grew two shades darker as he looked at Abigail. He swallowed and a fierce devilment glowed in his eyes. "Sure now, I thought ye wanted to be splashed, standin' there like ye were, next to that big puddle."

Abigail stiffened, her eyes sparking dangerously. They were enjoying her anger, and there was nothing to be gained by being further humiliated. Looking at all three of the men witheringly she stated, "I think it is a sad day for this town when a lady can't expect a little courtesy and consideration from the men of the community."

Meaningfully she looked Mr. Lynch straight in the eyes, then, turning on her heel, marched stiff-backed to the door and, with a last gesture of anger, pulled it shut as hard as she could after her. She wanted the slamming door to emphasize her anger but it caught with a dull thud instead, making as much impression as she felt her speech had. Frustration added to anger, she stalked back up the street into the town clerk's office, plopped the papers down, and walked out without a word, leaving the clerk to look after her in wonder at why this usually smiling girl, who always had a cheerful word to say, was in such a state.

She went into the bank and slammed the door with some satisfaction, and her father looked up in surprise. He pulled the pince nez off his fine-boned nose and asked, "What in the world happened to you?"

She stormed across the floor and blurted, "Some of those awful pig farmers splashed me with their wagon, and they didn't even have the courtesy to stop and apologize!"

Elias Whitteker frowned. "Well, you can't look like that. Go home and change."

"Thank you, Father. I'll be back as soon as I can."

Abigail entered the large, comfortable, two-story house situated on a side street a block from the bank. It was a fitting residence for the family of the richest man in town, owner of the bank. Abigail found her mother in the elegant parlor, busy with her handiwork.

Lucia Whitteker looked up with shock at the sight of her daughter. "Good heavens, Abigail! What happened to you?"

Abigail explained, and her petite, warmly rounded mother, her hair still a youthful golden color only a shade or two duller than Abigail's, clucked in dismay and immediately took over the task of helping her daughter change.

Abigail returned to the bank and quickly became absorbed in her work as she tried to catch up for the time lost in the morning, almost forgetting the incident that had upset her so. Her father had a local resident in his private office, and Abigail was alone in the front of the bank until the door opened. She looked up, and the anger of the morning came rushing back to her. Entering her domain was the younger of the men she had so angrily chastised, and she glared at him, daring him to take one more step into her presence. Step he did and snatched, belatedly, the cap from his head, loosing a lock of dark chestnut hair to fall over his forehead.

With a shy but serious little smile he stopped before her and offered, "I be here to apologize for splashin' ye this morning. If ye'll be givin' me the dress now, I'll take it to me mother to wash for ye."

Tempering just a little she answered, "Thank you, but it's already taken care of." She turned her eyes downward to her work, hoping he would leave.

She heard him shift uneasily, and after a long silence he said less shyly, "Look, now, I said I was sorry. Can't we be shakin' hands and be friends?"

Her eyes flashed a negative message as she flared, "Why? Why now? The time to apologize was this morning."

The deep brown eyes took on a twinkle and the blarney so near the surface bubbled over with a smile as he said, "Aye, I know I should've but I was seein' the fairest colleen I'd ever seen and what man could be speakin' at a time like that, now?"

Abigail weakened. His flattery was infectious and she smiled in spite of herself. "All right. I will forgive you but that doesn't mean I'll forget, and I hope you don't either."

His smile broadened into a grin and he nodded contritely. "Sure now, I won't." He held up his hand to her and saw as she did that the nails on the long, strong fingers were black with dirt and the palm was streaked with grime. His smile fading, he let the hand drop and turned his cap self-consciously, saying, "Well, good day to ye, Miss Whitteker. Will ye be lettin' me see ye again, now?"

Abigail looked uncertainly into the dark eyes so seriously begging hers for approval. She cast her eyes down in confusion. How could she answer this man? Everything he was was the opposite of what she was, yet she didn't want to be cruel. Under different circumstances she could even like him. He had an attractiveness that was hard to deny even under the dirt. She heard him turn away and walk to the door, and she raised her eyes after him.

Just as he reached the door, Beth came bursting in and without hesitation gushed, "Aloÿsius asked me to the box social Saturday night!" She took time then to see who was going out the door and, staring after the solid, soiled figure, gasped. Quickly she came to the counter. "Is that the one who splashed you this morning?"

"Yes."

She smiled appreciatively. "He's handsome." She wrinkled her nose and added, "But he smells like dirty old pigs."

They both giggled and Beth eagerly pried, "Well, tell me what he wanted?"

"Oh, nothing other than to apologize."

Beth's face fell. "Is that all? Didn't he do that this morning? Are you sure there isn't something more?" She was breathless with expectation.

Abigail laughed. "Yes. He asked if he could see me again."

"I knew it! I just knew it!" Beth shivered in anticipation, her violet-blue eyes large with the thoughts whirling behind them. Beth was an incurable romantic. Every meeting was a romantic encounter to her. "Well, what did you say?"

"I didn't say anything."

"Well, why not?" Beth looked with disappointment at her friend.

"Oh, Beth! You know why not."

Beth sighed, the light going out of her eyes. "Yes, I guess I do. It seems like all the good-looking ones have to have something wrong with them."

"Why, Beth! That's an awful thing to say. Aloysius is nice-looking, and he's asked to take you to the social."

Her eyes lighted again. In her eagerness to build a romance for Abigail she'd forgotten her own good fortune. And good fortune it was. Aloysius was the most eligible man in their small world. His family owned the biggest farm in the community. Even Abigail had hoped Aloysius would ask to be her escort. It was as if being the banker's daughter was a bigger drawback than being from the wrong side of town. She was sure Aloysius liked her more than Beth, but he was afraid of being rejected by her, though she had never done anything to make him think so.

Beth was saying with a giggle, "I almost forgot. Isn't it wonderful!" Then her face fell. "Oh, Abigail, we just have to find someone for you. Do you suppose—?" She let the sentence hang unfinished.

Abigail shook her head. "No, Beth. Even if I liked the idea, which I don't, Father would never approve."

Beth shrugged her shoulders. "Well, it was just a thought. I'd better get back to the store before Daddy misses me. I'll see you later."

She rushed out of the bank and Abigail watched her go, brunette curls bouncing on sturdy shoulders, still thinking about what they'd said and remembering the look in an Irishman's eyes.

Saturday evening Elias Whitteker, tall, portly figure well dressed, silvering hair firmly in place, strolled with his attractive wife and smilingly dimpled daughter to the church down the street for the box social. Abigail had on her new spring gown, delicately flowered and ribboned, and her hair hung in rich, golden waves down her straight back as she carried a box tied in ribbons to match her dress. The church was filled with people and a good share of them were young. Abigail's eyes found Beth and Aloysius immediately and went to where they sat. Beth looked radiant in a muted violet gown that brought out the vibrant color of her eyes. Her round face was flushed with excitement.

"Oh, Abigail, you look so pretty. Doesn't she, Aloysius?"

Aloysius reddened and swallowed and answered a little uncertainly, "Yes. You sure do look nice, Abigail."

Abigail smiled patronizingly at him. "Thank you, Aloysius." She was suddenly thankful he was Beth's escort. She wondered how she could have ever thought him good-looking. His eyes were humorless behind steel-rimmed glasses and his well-scrubbed face was terribly plain. His straw brown hair straight and uninteresting.

Beth, forgetting for the moment that she had Aloysius all to herself, asked, "Won't you sit with us, Abbie?" She blinked as she realized what she was saying and her eyes pleaded with Abigail but it was too late to take back the words.

Aloysius urged, "Yes, sit with us, Abigail."

Abigail was about to decline when Beth's face took on a look of surprise, and she reached for Abigail's arm. "Look!" she gasped.

Abigail looked and was just as shocked as Beth. Coming into the church was the Irishman. She felt both anger and embarrassment sweeping over her. She turned quickly away but not quickly enough. He had seen her and was coming toward them.

"Miss Whitteker, will ye be mindin' if I sit with ye and your friends now, or are ye expectin' someone else?"

Too late Abigail realized she still held her box in her hand and not knowing what else to do she said, "No. I mean, I guess you can."

He saw her box and said, "Sure now, can I be puttin' the box on the table for ye?"

Dumbly, she let him take it and sat down on the bench feeling bewildered. Smiling broadly, the Irishman came back and joined them.

He held out his hand to Aloysius and said, "Me name's Ross Galligher."

Recovering her poise, Abigail finished the introductions. "Mr. Galligher, this is Aloysius Turner and Betheny Axetell."

With a charming smile he said, "Sure now, 'tis glad I am to meet you." He sat down beside Abigail, and she flushed again with embarrassment. "Did your dress come clean, Miss Whitteker?"

"Yes, thank you. It's fine."

Before any more was said the auctioneer called them to attention and the long process of auctioning off the box lunches began. Abigail had a chance to relax and take notice of the man sitting with her. He was freshly bathed and his clothes clean—vastly different from how she remembered her first encounter with him. Even the nails on his broad, strong hands were freshly pared and clean of dirt. He laughed at something that was said and the sound was deep and rich. She looked at his face and his eyes immediately came to hers. She couldn't pull away from the deep-brown, thick-lashed eyes holding hers captive. He was the first to look away as the next box went on auction. It was Abigail's, and he was outbidding everyone for it, as she knew he would. Proudly he went to retrieve it from the auctioneer, and she felt guilty because he'd had to pay such a high price for it and she knew he probably couldn't afford it. The family had only been in the area about a year but everyone knew they were desperately poor, as were most of the Irish families moving into the area. Aloysius outbid the room for Beth's box, and soon they were feasting on the lunches the girls had brought.

Ross was complimenting her with, "Ye fry a good chicken, me girl."

She blushed and murmured, "Thank you, Mr. Galligher."

He smiled at her, his eyes twinkling. "Sure now, I'd feel better if ye would call me Ross."

"All right, Ross." But she made no offer for him to use her first name. If he noticed the slight he didn't let on.

Aloysius asked between mouthfuls, "Got your ground worked yet?"

"We be workin' at it. We got the seed when we were in town the other day, now. Mr. Lynch said there'd be a good price for grain this year."

"Yes, if the weather's good, it should be a good year since the government decided our ships can trade with other countries again."

"You bought the old Standley farm, didn't you?"

The brown eyes came back to Abigail. "Aye."

Aloysius commented, "That's good land. If it hadn't been so far from our place, Paw would've bought it."

"Aye, 'tis good land. We be almost done buildin' the barn, now."

Abigail asked, "But what about a house? Surely you're not living in that cabin?"

"That we are. Sure now, any farmer'll tell ye the barn comes first. Right, Mr. Turner?"

Aloysius smiled, his pale blue eyes crinkling at the corners. "That's right, Abbie."

The brown eyes turned on her again. "Sure now, would ye be likin' to see what we've done? How about me comin' for ye Sunday, now, and ye can see for yourself?"

Abigail flushed and turned her eyes down. "I'm sorry, I've already made other plans."

"Well, now, would ye be free the Sunday after?"

"No, that wouldn't be possible."

"And would ye be tellin' me what Sunday would be possible?"

Beth giggled and Abigail blushed. There was no tactful way to tell him she didn't want to see him and he didn't take the hint. "All right, three Sundays from now."

He grinned and his teeth were dazzling in his dark face. "Fine. I'll be pickin' ye up after church if that be all right?"

"Yes," she answered unenthusiastically, hoping by then she could think of some way to get out of the engagement. The social was breaking up and Abigail rose, wanting nothing more than to leave.

He stood, too, and asked, "May I be walkin' ye home, Miss Whitteker?"

"My parents are with me."

"Will they be mindin', now, if I walk with ye?"

She looked him straight in the eye and said, "Probably."

He grinned down at her in pleasure as if her honesty pleased him more than politeness. His eyes danced devilishly. "Then I'll be walkin' with ye and see."

He held his arm for her to take and she pretended to have to carry the box with both of her hands and he took it from her and still held his arm out to her. She took it hesitantly and he said, "This time it be clean."

She blushed even deeper as she walked with him to the door, her eyes looking wildly for her parents. She saw her father frown disapprovingly from where he and her mother stood by the door. Abigail introduced them and felt even more embarrassed when Ross held out his hand and her father didn't take it but said stiffly, "I expect you home immediately, Abigail."

"Yes, Father."

They followed after her parents and their walk was a silent one until they came to the gate of Abigail's house.

Ross said, "I'll be here to pick ye up three Sundays from now."

She wanted to tell him not to come but couldn't. If he'd been anything but what he had been this evening it would have been easy, but she found herself liking him and answered, "I'll be ready."

He went whistling down the walk and she went into the house to face her parents.

"Well, Abigail, what did he want?"

"He wants me to go for a drive to his home three Sundays from now."

"And what did you tell him?"

"I told him I would."

Lucia Whitteker's face fell. "Oh, Abigail, you didn't!"

"Yes, Mother, I did. I couldn't get out of it. He knew I didn't have any reason not to accept his offer. You don't want me to be rude, do you?"

Elias answered, "To his kind, yes. They won't understand anything else. Now you tell him when you see him again you can't go with him."

"All right, Father, I'll tell him I can't see him, but I can't be so cruel as to break my date with him like that."

A shocked look passed over both her parents' faces. "And why not?"

She didn't know herself why not. "Please, trust me. I'll tell him and make him understand, but let me do it in my own way."

Her father sighed. "Well, all right, but make sure you do, Abigail. We can't have you seen with people like that. What will the town think?"

At that moment Abigail didn't care what the town thought, but she nodded and murmured, "Good night, Mother. Good night, Father," and kissing them dutifully, she went up the stairs to bed.

Three weeks passed quickly and April turned into a lovely warm May. Abigail kept hoping all through church Ross Galligher had forgotten about her and wouldn't be waiting for her, but she knew he would be and she couldn't keep her mind on what the minister was saying. Even less did she know what she was feeling or why she was feeling it.

Church was finally over and they rose to leave. It seemed to take a long time to gain the door as each family paused to speak to the minister, and when they were at last going down the walk from the church Abigail permitted herself to look for his wagon. It was there, waiting in front of her house. Her father frowned as he saw it, too.

Ross got down as he saw them coming and, pulling the cap from his waves of chestnut hair, smiled charmingly at them. "Good day to ye, Mr. and Mrs. Whitteker."

Mr. Whitteker didn't answer the salutation but said, "You have her home as soon as possible, Mr. Galligher, and you had better take good care of her."

Ross nodded affirmatively and smiled. "Aye, that I will, sir."

Before Abigail could help herself his strong hands lifted her into the wagon, and in a few moments they were trotting briskly out of town. They must have gone a mile before he broke the silence.

"Did your father be givin' ye a bad time about me, now?"

Honestly she answered, "Yes."

"Aye, I thought so. But I don't be blamin' him. Ye are like a red-ripe and luscious apple just ready to be picked."

She blushed furiously and gasped, "Mr. Galligher!"

"What? What have I said, now?"

"Those are not words for a lady to hear."

"Sure now, it was a compliment."

"If it was, I thank you, but please put things a little less crudely."

He chuckled. "All right. And while we be on the subject, what did your father find wrong with me?"

For a moment she hesitated but she had already made up her mind to be totally honest with him, even blunt, if necessary, to make him understand she couldn't go with him again. Tactfully she answered, "If you know he gave me a bad time and found you objectionable, surely you know why."

The smile left his face and his eyes took on a strange fierceness, his already square jaw squaring more defensively. "Aye. Well, I be Irish and a pig farmer, and me name be Galligher and I be damn proud of it!"

"Mr. Galligher! You're swearing!"

He looked taken aback. "Swearing?" He laughed. "All right. I be willin' to learn how to talk to a lady. Will ye tell me what I should've said, now?"

"My name is Galligher and I'm proud of it."

He thought about it, his eyes growing devilish. "It doesn't quite have the spirit behind it, does it, now?"

She looked at him, his eyes twinkling at her, and she had to laugh. When she stopped he said, "Oh, no, don't stop. It's like the leprechauns playin' music from the ol' sod."

She smiled at him and shook her head, and he raised his eyes to heaven and blarney flowed smooth as honey from his full lips. "Dear Father in heaven, all this and dimples, too. Sure now, did ye ever see a fairer colleen?"

"Oh, Ross Galligher, you're so full of it it's running out your ears."

He laughed and slapped the reins against the team. "Sure now, and if I don't be gettin' ye home me mother will thrash me for bringin' ye late for Sunday dinner."

"Dinner? You didn't tell me I was to come to dinner!"

"I didn't? Well, ye be knowin' it now."

"Oh, but I couldn't. I've never been . . ." She let her words trail off.

He looked at her and smiled. "Sure, now, I doubt it be much different than eatin' anywhere. We say the blessing and eat. There be nothin' so bad about it, now."

Still uncertain she said, "But I haven't even met her. Really, I shouldn't."

"Would ye be disappointin' me mother now? For four years she's worryin' herself about me not havin' a girl home for dinner."

"Well, all right, but does she know I'm not a Catholic?"

"Aye, I told her."

"And she didn't object?"

He grinned ruefully. "Well, now, she did. But even a Protestant can be converted."

She looked at him in amazement. "You can't be serious!"

She could see by his eyes he was perfectly serious as he said, "Sure now, and why do ye think I'm not?"

"Don't be. Father doesn't want me to see you again."

"Sure now, ye be old enough to make your own decisions?"

"I'll be twenty in September."

"Sure now, that should be old enough."

"Not for me. Father will never approve of you." Suddenly twenty didn't seem such a magic age after all. Quickly she changed the subject. "How many brothers and sisters do you have?"

"Well, now, ye saw me older brother, Sean. Then there's meself, then Mollie, Patrick, Brian, Kathleen, and Eileen."

"Oh, yes. I know Mollie, Patrick, and Brian from school."

"From school? Sure, I know, now. Ye be the pretty teacher Mollie says comes in when Miss Cox be gone."

"Yes."

"Poor Mollie. She's sad to be leavin' school, now."

"Leaving school! But why?"

"Me mother needs her at home when the baby comes."

"What baby? Whose baby?"

"Me mother's."

"Oh." She blushed and looked away for a moment. But the thought of Mollie leaving school brought her back. "Isn't there someone else to take care of your mother? Mollie is such a good student. She could really go far if she had the training."

"Well, now, there would be if Sean's wife wasn't expecting their second one, too."

"Surely there's something you can do. It would be such a shame for Mollie to quit school."

He looked at her and said, "I'll try to keep her in school, now, if I can." And she knew by his eyes he would.

They turned into the farmstead and the children came running to meet them, all giggles and wide-eyed to see Ross's girl. Mollie looked surprised to see her.

"Hello, Mollie."

"Miss Whitteker! I didn't know *you* were Ross's sweetheart!"

Abigail smiled. "That makes two of us, Mollie. I didn't know it either."

The rest of the children took up the chant. "Ross's got a sweetheart!"

He laughed and chased them off with, "Get back in the house, now, with ye and help your mother or I'll be throwin' ye all in the hog trough."

They ran screaming to the house except for Mollie who asked, "When are you coming to teach us again, Miss Whitteker?"

"I don't know, Mollie. Whenever Miss Cox needs me to."

"I wish you would be there all the time. She won't try to answer my questions like you do."

"Well, thank you, Mollie. Maybe she'll retire this year and then I'll be your permanent teacher."

Her large brown eyes looked hopeful. "Do you think there's a chance she might?" She paused and the light went out of her eyes. "It'll be too late. Mother will be needing me at home."

Ross said, "Now, don't ye be worryin' your pretty head about that, Mollie, me girl. Miss Whitteker has made me see ye should be stayin' in school, and if it be possible, ye will."

She clapped her hands together in joy and threw her arms around her brother and then around Abigail, gasping, "Oh, if I only could! I'm going to go say a prayer to the Virgin Mary right now." She gave them a brilliant smile and ran with upraised skirts to the cabin as fast as her legs could carry her.

Abigail looked at Ross with the I-told-you-so look, and he smiled at her. He took her arm and they walked to the cabin door as it opened and the older members of the family gathered to meet her.

"Mother, Father, this be Miss Whitteker. Ye met Sean, and this be his wife, Mary, and their son, Timothy."

Abigail politely shook hands with them and said the appropriate words, feeling for once the outsider. Ross's mother and his sister-in-law were both very big with child, and it only made Abigail all the more uncomfortable. But nothing seemed to bother them and Ross's mother welcomed her warmly in broken English which Ross laughingly interpreted. Mary was more reserved and Abigail wasn't sure if it was dislike or shyness, but it added to her uneasiness. Ross's father was even ruddier than his two older sons and welcomed her with a fermented kiss on the cheek. Uncertain and nervous, she let Ross lead her inside the crowded cabin smelling strongly of cabbage and lamb. She soon saw the reason for the elder Galligher's uninhibited merriment. Mugs of ale stood on the table and he offered her one. She shook her head no and smiled, saying, "No, thank you."

Ross translated for her and took her to a worn settee, the only piece of upholstered furniture in the room. They sat down while the rest of the family scurried around getting in each other's way, laughing and joking until Abigail felt she wanted to run outdoors. Ross drank his ale and Abigail tried not to look disapproving but it was hard.

Self-conscious, she asked Ross, "Is there something I can do to help?"

"No. Ye just sit and stay out of the way, now. Some other time she'll be expectin' ye to help, but not the first time."

She was about to tell him there wouldn't be another time when Sean announced dinner was ready and everyone should find his place. Ross seated Abigail next to himself and the first quiet she knew reigned as they all bowed their heads for the blessing. The prayer was long and mechanical. When Abigail heard "Amen" she raised her head thankfully but, to her dismay, saw they weren't done yet. Ross winked at her from the corner of his eye as they crossed themselves and said the final Amen. The quiet was over.

After dinner Ross took her outside to show her the barn while the dishes were cleared from the table. He was obviously proud of his work and Abigail hoped she said the right things to praise the building, but she knew nothing about barns. They were just about done with a tour of the farmyard when Mollie came for them.

"They're ready to start the music now."

The elder Galligher was already practicing up on an old squeeze box and Sean was filling beer glasses out of a jug to different levels and tuning them with a spoon. He sipped the beer to the right tone, much to Abigail's chagrin. Then the singing started in earnest and the whole family joined in. Ross sang with them and his voice was clear and rich, his brogue thicker singing than speaking. She found herself relaxing and enjoying their happy songs and makeshift music, which was better than she had imagined it would be. A pause came when dry throats had to be wetted with more ale and Mollie whispered something to Ross. Mr. Galligher leaned close and nodded with approval saying something in slurring Gaelic.

Ross translated for her. "Mollie wants ye to sing us a song. Me father wants to know what music ye be wantin' him to play for ye?"

Abigail paled. "Oh, Ross, I can't sing that well."

Mollie offered, "Yes you can. You sing beautifully. Father can play 'Greensleeves.' I've sung it for him, and he can play it."

There was no way she could get out of it, so she said, "All right, Mollie, if you'll sing with me."

The girl clapped her hands and nodded to her father, saying in Gaelic what he was to play for them. The squeeze box wheezed and out came the sweet-sad melody and Abigail and Mollie blended their sweet young voices as the rest of the family smiled with approval. Ross clapped the loudest when they were done.

"Sure now, ye be singin' like an Irish nightingale, Abbie. Can ye be singin' us another?"

She blushed and answered, "Thank you, but I really do think you'd better take me home now." .

"Aye, if that's what ye be wantin'."

Abigail thanked Mrs. Galligher and said good-by to all of them. Ross lifted her into the wagon and they started on the road for town.

They were barely out of sight of the farm when Ross asked, "Well, now, what be ye thinkin' of me family?"

"They were very nice, Ross. I liked them."

"Aye, that's good. Sure now, ye'll be comin' for dinner next Sunday?"

"No. That's what I've been trying to tell you all day. I can't see you again."

"Is that how ye be feelin', or how your father feels?"

"It doesn't make any difference. Our families are worlds apart and religions apart. Can't you see there is no future in us seeing each other?"

"Sure now, I won't be givin' ye up that easily. I don't believe anything be impossible."

She had to turn her face away from his intent gaze. She didn't want to see what was in those compelling eyes, didn't want to know how deeply he felt. She bit her lip. It wasn't going to be easy to convince him and she wasn't at all sure she wanted to, but she knew it was what she had to do.

"If ye won't be comin' to me home, now, where can I be seein' ye? Will your father be allowin' me to come to your home?"

"You know he won't."

"Aye, but where then?"

"I suppose if you really want to see me you could come to church."

"Abigail! Do ye know what ye be askin' of me! Great Father in heaven, forgive me! Sure now, Abbie, 'tis a sin for me to step into another church. Would ye be havin' me sin and suffer the fires of purgatory?"

"No, Ross. I'm just trying to make you see how impossible our seeing each other again is."

He shrugged and a devilish twinkle came into his dark eyes. "Well, now, if I say enough novenas and do penance, I'll be forgiven."

"But I don't want you to go against your religion and I don't want to go against mine. Can't you understand?"

"Aye, I be understandin', and ye better be understandin' I intend seein' ye again."

She had to smile in spite of her exasperation. He was determined to see her, and she could do nothing about it. It was out of her hands now. She would let her father take over. She changed the subject. "How long have you been in the United States?"

"We be here about thirteen years now. Me father came first as a bound man when I was a wee babe. He worked over five years to pay for me mother, Sean, and me to come here. 'Twas almost eight years we never saw him."

"What did you do before you came here?"

"We was workin' the docks of New York until Congress put the embargo on the ships and one by one we was laid off. That's when me father decided to go back to farmin', like he did in Ireland."

"Will you go back to the docks now that the embargo has been lifted?"

"No. Me mother hated New York. She was afraid for Mollie and she wanted Sean and me to go back to school, but once we was started on the docks that was the end of schoolin'. No, she'll never let us go back."

"Were things so bad for you in Ireland that you wouldn't have been better to stay there?"

"Aye. Things were bad for Catholics in Ireland when me father was growing up. England ruled us and the Catholics had no rights —not to worship or even own land. Our government was all Protestant ruled by a Protestant king. Finally the Protestants of Ireland demanded and got control over our government from England and they promised to give Catholics back their right to own land and worship and even take part in politics, but they were slow in comin' and me father grew tired of waitin' and decided we'd be better off here."

"And are you?"

" 'Tis a hard question for me to answer, now, but I'd say we be better off."

"Did you have any schooling?"

"Aye. Some. I be luckier than Sean. He had to work the docks soon after we arrived, but I was young enough me mother wouldn't let me go and I went to school."

Abigail asked no more questions. Everything she learned about him only widened the gulf between them. She felt sorry for him, even liked him, but for all practical purposes their relationship had to end and the sooner the better. The horses trotted on in their silence, the beautiful springtime vista of river and woods passing by in slow panorama of bright green hues. Soon the buildings of Riverwood appeared through the trees and Ross turned the horses down the street leading to her house and pulled to a stop in front of her gate. Without a word he jumped down and came to help her down. She held out her hand but his hands caught her around the waist and lifted her from the wagon easily. Her hands went quite naturally to his broad shoulders for balance as he swung her down and gazed at her with eyes full of laughter and something else she didn't want to put a name to.

He held onto her once her feet were on the ground and said,

"Sure now, I'll be seein' ye again, darlin' Abbie, come hell or your father."

She was about to protest when her father's voice startled them both with its nearness.

"Mr. Galligher, take your hands off my daughter!"

Abigail saw the fierceness come into Ross's eyes as he dropped his hands and turned to her father.

Quickly she defended Ross. "Father, he was just helping me down from the wagon."

Elias Whitteker stopped at the gate and glared at Ross and asked, "Did you make it plain to Mr. Galligher that he isn't to see you again?"

Before she could answer Ross answered, "Sure now, she made it plain, Mr. Whitteker, but I told her and now I be tellin' ye, I'll be seein' her again." He turned away, his back stiff with stubborn pride and in one smooth movement he was in the wagon and sending the horses out of town at a gallop.

Abigail watched him go and then turned to her father's reproachful eyes.

"I will not allow that man on this property."

"I told him as much, Father."

"Then what does he mean he'll see you again?"

"I'm sure I don't know." She passed by her father and walked swiftly up the walk to the house. Lucia Whitteker stood in the door and wrung her handkerchief.

"Are you all right, dear?"

"Of course I'm all right, Mother."

She smiled and looked relieved. "Have you had something to eat? I was getting worried about you."

Abigail kissed her mother gently. "Yes, Mother. Mrs. Galligher had dinner for us."

She went through the door and Lucia followed with Elias, still stiff with indignation, coming with her. "How was it? Could you eat it? What were they like?"

"The dinner was fine. It was boiled cabbage and lamb. They seemed like nice people and they were very nice to me."

"What kind of a place do they live in?"

"A very small cabin. Really only one room and terribly crowded and all the sleeping space must be in the loft above, but it was clean."

"Did they try to convert you?"

"Oh, Mother, please! No, they didn't try to convert me. May I go to my room now?"

Lucia looked satisfied and smiled her consent but Elias still looked upset and not ready to let things stand as they were. Abigail turned away and quickly ran up the stairs before her father could put his anger into words. As she reached her room she heard his voice call after her, "We'll be going to church in a little while. Be ready."

Beth was waiting for her as they mounted the steps to the church. Excitement and curiosity flushed her face even in the dim light of dusk. "Oh, Abigail! I've been thinking of you all day long. How was it?"

Abigail was suddenly tired of questions and the knowing looks of everyone filing into church but she kept her patience and answered, "I had a very nice day. His family was very nice to me."

"Are you going to see him again?"

"No. Father won't permit it."

Conspiracy glowed in Beth's eyes. "Do you want to?"

Abigail looked thoughtful for a few moments. She hadn't had time to decide the answer to that question herself. "I don't know, Beth. I really don't know." She turned away from her friend and hurried down the aisle to join her parents in the first pew just as the minister came to the pulpit. Abigail shut out everything from her mind and tried to concentrate on the words being spoken.

2

THE COURTSHIP

The week seemed to drag by for Abigail. Every time the door of the bank opened she would look up with expectancy and chide herself for doing so. She kept telling herself she didn't want to see him again—couldn't see him again because it could only bring them both trouble, but still she couldn't forget the way he looked at her with the devil in his eyes.

Sunday came and she wondered, as she dressed for church, if he really would be there. It was inconceivable that he would be and still attend his own church services. The nearest Catholic service was held in Albany several hours away. They walked to church and her heart stopped for an instant as she saw him waiting outside. Elias saw him at the same time and she felt his step falter as he stiffened with anger and then continued purposefully on. Abigail didn't dare look at Ross as they went into the church but she knew he came in right behind them. They filed into their pew at the front of the church and Ross smiled down at them.

"May I be sittin' with your daughter, now, Mr. Whitteker?"

Her father's face went red with indignation. "You have a lot of nerve, Galligher. Absolutely not!"

Ross nodded and smiled without warmth, and Abigail saw him step into a pew at the rear of the church. Warmth rose to her cheeks and she wanted to flee, feeling all eyes in church on her. She slid down as low in her seat as she could and bowed her head as low as she dared to try and hide the embarrassment she felt.

The service was over and Abigail rose with her eyes turned downward and held her skirts around her in embarrassment as she filed from the pew behind her father. She bumped into Elias in the aisle and had to look up. He was glaring at Ross and when her eyes met Ross's he smiled at her.

Stiffly, Elias ordered, "Please step outside, Mr. Galligher."

"No, Mr. Whitteker. I came to see your daughter and I'll not budge until I can walk with her, now."

The red crawled up Elias' neck and he gritted his teeth against the words wanting to escape, not daring to make a scene in church. With eyes blazing, he stalked down the aisle with Lucia on his arm in what Abigail knew was a terrible defeat for him, leaving her standing with Ross. Her own face flamed as he held out his arm to her for all the congregation to see. If she took his arm it would mean she accepted his courtship of her and she knew it was against everything she knew to be right and practical. She turned away from him and walked down the aisle, refusing his arm, and he quickly followed her, seemingly undaunted by her denial of him. With flaming cheeks, she ignored the minister standing on the church porch and fled down the steps after her parents. Ross's voice called to her but she ignored him, too, until his hand caught her arm and stopped her. She looked at him with anger and dismay.

"Abbie, wait, now. 'Tis sorry I be for embarrassin' ye."

Elias' voice broke into his words. "My daughter doesn't want to see you, Mr. Galligher. Now will you stop bothering her or I'll report you to the constable."

Ross didn't take his eyes off Abigail's distressed face. "She didn't say that, did ye, Abbie?"

She looked from one face to another and her confusion grew. She didn't want to answer that question. She picked up her skirts and ran down the walk toward her house, not looking back and not stopping until she was inside her own home. She bolted up the stairs two at a time and shut the door of her room, her heart pounding. She was still leaning against the door when she heard her parents come in and her mother come up the stairs.

"Abbie, dear, are you all right?"

"Yes, Mother." But the face staring back at her from her mirror didn't look all right. Her small heart-shaped mouth was tense and her arched brows, which usually made her look perky and interested in everything, only made her look all the more dismayed.

"Come out, dear, so we can talk."

"No, Mother. I don't want to talk now. Please, just leave me alone for a while."

There was a silence of hurt from the hallway, and Abigail saw her eyes become even more confused. Then her mother said, "As you wish, Abigail. We'll talk later."

Later, when she did gain control of her emotions, she went downstairs to face her parents. She entered the parlor and stood before them. "Mother. Father. Please don't tell me I can't or shouldn't see him anymore. I know I shouldn't see him. I know everything about him is wrong for me and I don't want to encourage him and I don't want to go with him, but neither do I want to have happen what happened this morning. Between the two of you you wanted me to make a choice and I don't want to have to choose. So, please, Father, if he comes to church again, don't make a scene or I won't go anymore."

"But, Abigail, we've got to stop this thing."

"I know, Father. But he's stubborn and I think he'll be even more stubborn if you try to stop him. I'm hoping he'll give it up soon. I think his own religion will make it difficult for him to keep coming. Don't you see?"

"Well, maybe. We'll see. I'm sorry things were so humiliating for you this morning."

She smiled at last, feeling relieved. "It's all right, Father."

But the next Sunday Ross was there. He waited beside the walk to the church and fell in beside her, smiling. "Good morning, Abbie."

She didn't answer his greeting but frowned at him. "Oh, Ross, why did you come? Can't you see this is impossible?"

"Sure now, nothing be impossible if I can see ye."

She had to smile.

"Aye, now, that's better. I hope ye are not mad?"

"No, I'm not mad. I just can't understand why you would put yourself through this."

"Is it so hard for ye to see, now? It's clear as the air I breath when I look at ye."

She blushed and stepped ahead of him quickly and up the steps of the church. He sat in the back during the service but came forward to walk with her down the aisle, not offering his arm as he had the Sunday before. She stopped to speak with the minister, hoping it would discourage Ross, but she should have known it wouldn't.

The minister said, "And how are you today, Abigail?"

"Just fine, Reverend."

"And who is this young man? I saw him last Sunday, too, but we didn't meet."

"This is Mr. Galligher, Reverend. Mr. Galligher, this is Reverend Stoner."

Ross held out his hand and smiled. "Sure now, I'm glad to meet you, Reverend."

They shook hands and Reverend Stoner said, "It's always nice to have young people become interested in the church. I'm available for counseling any time you feel the need, Mr. Galligher."

"Thank you, Reverend, but I already be havin' a church."

"Oh? And what church do you belong to?"

With a devilish twinkle, Ross answered, "I be Catholic."

Reverend Stoner opened his mouth in shock and looked as if he had spoken with the devil himself. Abigail fought down a giggle and hurried down the steps with Ross following her.

She turned to him on the walk, not able to suppress a laugh. "Ross, that was awful!"

He grinned at her, his eyes dancing. "He asked me, now, so I was tellin' him straight out."

She laughed. "Did you see the look on his face?"

"Aye. Do ye think he'll be lettin' me come back?"

"I don't know. It would serve you right if he didn't."

They reached the road and Abigail's parents waited to take

possession of their daughter. Beth came rushing up and greeted them. Aloysius was on her heels. Without realizing it, she compared the two men and Aloysius was a poor second. The reserve she had thought maturity in Aloysius was merely self-conscious immaturity compared to the self-assurance of Ross's bearing. Aloysius seemed awkward. Ross was all muscle and graceful strength of coordination. And was it any wonder—he had worked like a man since he was a child. Ross wasn't more than an inch or two taller than Aloysius, but the very power of his personality dwarfed the slighter man.

Ross said, "Good day, Abbie, I'll be seein' ye next Sunday." He swung into his wagon and she returned his smile. Aloysius said good-by and left with his family, and Abigail's parents, feeling their daughter safe now the Irishman was gone, walked away from where the two girls stood watching the departing men.

Finally Beth questioned, "What on earth did he say to Reverend Stoner? The man is positively shaken."

Abigail laughed, remembering. "Ross told him he was a Catholic."

Beth exploded into laughter. "Oh, no! No wonder he looked like he'd been stricken. Is your father letting him see you again?"

"No. Only in church."

"How exciting! Aloysius seems so dull compared to what's happening to you."

"Oh, Beth, be realistic for once. Nothing but sadness can come to both of us if he persists in seeing me."

"But don't you want him to keep seeing you?"

"It's not as simple as that, Beth. Under different circumstances, of course I would. I like him. He's not like anyone I've ever known. He's fun to be with and yet he seems so much older."

Beth shivered with delight. "I wish he'd ask me to go with him."

Abigail looked at her friend in surprise. "Why, Beth! I didn't know you liked him."

"I'm not sure I do but I find him terribly exciting."

Mr. and Mrs. Axetell came to the street and Beth said good-by and Abigail was alone. Slowly she walked home, wondering how it would be resolved or if it could be resolved. Each time she saw him only seemed to make her want to see him more in spite of what she knew to be an impossible situation.

He came to church every Sunday from then on, always sitting in the back, always clean, always polite, always touching her heart with his eyes and going away with a smile she remembered too well.

One day she was working in the bank, her father sitting at his desk in his office with the door open, when Ross came in. He smiled as he came up to the counter.

"Good afternoon to ye, now, Abbie."

"Why, Ross, what are you doing in town?"

"We be bringin' in our crop today and I be bringin' some money to put in your bank."

"That's wonderful! How much is it?"

"Well, it's not much, now, but maybe I can be addin' to it." He laid several coppers on the counter adding up to twenty-five cents.

She blinked in disbelief. She'd never had a deposit so small. It wrenched her heart. She turned away quickly before he saw the way she felt and rummaged for the new account slips. When she was in control she turned back to him. Her father came and joined them.

"What's this, Galligher?"

"I be wantin' to start an account with ye, Mr. Whitteker. Sure now, ye will accept me money?"

Elias Whitteker's face paled and then reddened. Gruffly he said, "We try to serve everyone, Mr. Galligher." He turned away, clearly defeated in the battle of wills.

Abigail handed Ross the paper to fill out and watched as he laboriously printed his name and birth date and the other information called for on the slip. It was the first time she knew he was twenty-three years old. He seemed pleased to have been able to fill out the slip without her help and it was hard for her not to feel sympathy for him and harder yet not to show it. She already knew him well enough to know he wouldn't like her pity.

"There, now, Abbie, is it all right?"

She looked over the slip and smiled. "It's just fine, Ross. And thank you."

"Do ye always smile that way at your customers?"

"I try to."

"Sure now, I can see why your father is the richest man in town. The men of this town be bringin' in their money just to see your smile."

She laughed at him, her dimples deepening even more as she blushed prettily at his flattery. "Oh, Ross! Will you be serious."

"Sure now, and when I am ye run away. But some day ye won't be runnin' away, will ye?"

His eyes pleaded with her but she didn't answer, and Sean stuck his head in the door and called, "Come on, Ross, ye got work to do, now."

"Aye, Sean," he answered. "I'll be seein' ye on Sunday, Abbie."

He left, and silence and dullness returned to the bank. Her father called her and she turned. "Yes, Father?"

"Come in here, Abigail. I want to talk to you."

She went into his office and he motioned her down into a chair. For a long time he looked at her and she looked back. Clearly he was having difficulty saying what he wanted to say. His usually smooth forehead was furrowed and his eyes looked at her with pain. Poor Daddy, she thought, this is more difficult for you than for me, and it's getting harder for me all the time.

"Abigail, I've been thinking."

"Yes, Father?"

"This man Galligher doesn't appear to be the type to give up."

"No, Father."

"I could send you away to your aunt's in Boston."

"Yes, Father."

"But I imagine he'd come after you."

"Yes, Father."

"What do you think I should do, Abigail? You're old enough to know right from wrong in this matter."

"Father, I really don't know. I like him. I'm afraid I like him too much. I look forward to seeing him. I think he's a good man even if he isn't the kind of man I should be seeing."

"You realize marriage with this man is out of the question as far as I'm concerned?"

"Yes, Father."

"You understand, then, that I'll never give my approval nor will you be my legal heir if you do anything so foolish as disobeying my wishes in this matter. Do I make myself clear?"

"Yes, Father."

"Then he has my permission to see you and I sincerely hope by allowing this, against all my principles as it is, you will be able to come to the right decision about this man."

She nodded, too torn by her conflicting emotions to answer. She rose and blindly left the office and stood at the counter not knowing whether to be happy or sad. She wasn't given to crying but tears were close to the surface. The choice was hers to make and it wasn't getting any easier.

Sunday came and Ross was waiting in the churchyard. He said a cheerful greeting to her parents, as always, and gave her his special smile as he fell in beside her. She returned his smile and they entered the small white church. She stopped at the pew in the rear of the church and he looked startled when she entered and sat down. Quickly he sat beside her, not able to contain his grin or the sparkle in his eyes as he looked at her questioningly. She put her finger to her lips and whispered, "Later."

All through the service she could feel the tenseness in him and could see it in the restless way he kept locking and unlocking his long fingers. The moment the service was over he was on his feet. She shook her head and smiled at him, trying to signal him to be patient just a little while longer. They moved with the congregation and stopped and said a brief pleasantry to the minister though it made the man extremely uncomfortable. It delighted Ross and his eyes twinkled with devilment. They moved down the steps and she led him away from the rest of the congregation before she let him question her.

"For God's sake, will ye be tellin' me, now, what's happened?"

She smiled teasingly at him enjoying his perplexity. "You've won, Ross. Father says you can see me outside of church."

He raised his eyes to heaven and said with a deep sigh, "Praise be to God and thanks be to ye, Father. And, sure now, it's about time. I be havin' penance and novenas to do until Christmas." He grinned ruefully. "My priest was about to be stoppin' absolvin' me for me sins." He paused, his smile softening, his eyes hopeful, as he asked, "Can ye be goin' with me, now?"

"Yes. I've packed a lunch. Could we go on a picnic?"

His eyes danced. "Sure now, ye know I wouldn't refuse."

He held his arm out to her and she took it and they walked to his wagon. He lifted her in and drove the block to her house, reaching the gate at the same time her parents did.

"Galligher, I want to make one thing clear to you. I've given Abigail permission to see you not because I've changed my mind about you. I still don't approve of you and I never will. But I'm hoping she'll come to her senses as she realizes how wrong you are for her. And let me warn you, you have my permission to see her but nothing else. The moment you get out of line you lose that permission."

Ross nodded gravely. "Sure now, I be understandin', Mr. Whitteker."

Abigail was glad to hurry in after the picnic basket. Why did her father always manage to cast a dark shadow over her happiness? By the time she returned she once more was able to feel the happy expectancy of being with Ross.

They drove out of town and turned off the main road and drove to a secluded spot by the river. It was a beautiful day. No cloud cast a shadow on the clear blue water running deep and pure between forests of vibrant green trees. Dozens of birds sang and flitted among the trees and to Abigail everything seemed right. She spread the cloth on the ground and set out her lunch. Ross ate without ceremony as if eating were necessary—if you enjoyed it, fine, but if not, it wasn't important. He was about to wipe his hands on his pants, as she was sure he did most of the time, and she quickly thrust a napkin at him.

He grinned at her good-naturedly. "Aye, I'm not used to eatin' with ladies." He wiped his mouth and hands and smiled as he handed her back the napkin. "Do ye think ye can teach me how to be acceptable to your parents, now?"

"Do you really want to learn?"

"Sure now, I wouldn't be sayin' it if I didn't."

"I could probably teach you but I doubt you would ever be acceptable to my father. Remember, your religion would always be against you."

"Aye, I guess ye be right there."

"Aren't there any girls in your church you could court?"

"Aye, there's one or two. There's Maggie Callahan, with the flamin' red hair and a temper to match. Then there's Katy O'Malley, and she be plumper than one of me sows." His eyes looked at her with devilment.

"Ross, you're terrible!"

"Aye, and so are they."

She laughed. "Perhaps you deserve each other then. But, seriously, what do you plan to do with your life? Do you want to be a farmer?"

"Aye. I like the soil. I like to watch things grow. I think Sean likes the docks better. He'd be a seaman if Mary'd say the word, but me, I like the farm. It's somethin' a man can hang onto and say, 'This be mine.' What I be doin', the way I be doin' it, will show. There's somethin' to be proud of, now. I never felt that way unloadin' ships."

"And if you married, where would you live?"

"Sure now, there's no choice at the moment. The money I be bringin' to ye is the first money I've had that didn't have to go back into the farm. But someday I'll be wantin' a place of me own—a house of me own—but it'll be takin' a long time, no doubt."

She frowned and looked out at the water, each ripple singing on its way to the sea. She could never live in his tiny cabin crowded with people and sleep in a community bed. This is what her father had hoped would be accomplished by his allowing her to know Ross better.

The sound of his stretching out on the grass broke into her thoughts. Quietly he said, "Sure now, that's not what ye be wantin', is it?"

Not looking at him she answered honestly, "No."

"What would ye be, now, a schoolteacher?"

She let her eyes turn to him and her heart twisted as their eyes met. He lay stretched full length, his hands locked under his dark, waving chestnut hair, his eyes watching her intently with undisguised invitation. She turned away again.

"Yes. I like working with children. I'm hoping Miss Cox will retire. Of course working with father isn't hard, but I'd feel I was accomplishing so much more if I were teaching."

"How much does teachin' pay, now?"

"Not much. I would get the house on the school grounds and expenses, plus ten dollars a month while school is in session."

"Ye be right, now, it isn't much. And what do ye do for money when school's out?"

"You're supposed to earn your own money when you're not teaching."

"Who be decidin' that, now?"

"Well, my father and the other businessmen in town."

His eyes took on a thoughtful twinkle. "Do ye be supposin' if ye was teacher your father'd see ye got more money?"

"I doubt it. My father is not one to show favoritism."

"Aye, I can see that." He got to his feet and held out his hand to her. "Come on, now, Abbie. Let's be seein' who can skip a rock across the Mohawk."

They skipped rocks, laughed, and walked along the river bank. And when they got hungry they finished what was left of lunch. The sun was sinking dangerously low when they picked up the basket and cloth and he swung her into the wagon and drove at a fast trot into town.

He escorted her to her door but seemed restless and reluctant to leave. She asked, "Would you like to come in?"

He smiled. "Aye. I never was in a rich man's house before."

Her father heard them and came out of his library at the end of the hall. "It's a little late to be bringing her home, Galligher."

Abigail interjected, "It was such a lovely day, Father, we lost track of time. It wasn't Ross's fault."

The frown on her father's face told her he didn't quite accept her explanation. "Well, I'll not have you keeping her this late again. Now it's time to go to church, if you'll excuse us."

Ross looked dismayed. Mrs. Whitteker came down the stairs and said, "Oh, there you are. I was beginning to think you weren't going to get home in time for church. Now run along and comb your hair or we'll be late."

She looked at Ross and his eyes pleaded with her silently. She shrugged her shoulders and said, "I'll be just a minute," and dashed up the stairs.

He walked with her to church and there was a strange tenseness about him. She knew there was something on his mind but he said nothing. He stopped at the church steps and said, "I'll have to be goin', now, but I'll be comin' for ye next Sunday." He turned away before she could answer and strode with quick, frustrated energy back to where his wagon stood almost lost in the last light.

He didn't wait until Sunday to see her again. Monday evening there was a knock on the door and Abigail went to answer it. Ross stood before her, his cap clenched tightly in his hand, his hair still damp from the bath he had taken before he came.

"Sure now, I be needin' to talk to ye, Abbie. Can I come in?"

She stepped aside. "Of course, Ross. What is it?"

"Do ye need to ask, me darlin' Abbie?"

She tried to quiet him with a look and whispered, "Please, Father will hear."

Her mother came from the parlor with her embroidery in hand. "Oh, it's you. How are you, Mr. Galligher?"

Ross smiled and, briefly, his tenseness was hidden. "Good evening to ye, now, Mrs. Whitteker. I'm fine. Do ye be mindin' if I speak with Abbie?"

Mr. Whitteker came down the hall and answered, "Yes, I mind, Galligher. I'll not have you taking up all her time. And I'll not have her out after dark with you."

Abigail tried to smooth the conflict between the two men with, "Please, Father. He came a long way to see me. I'm sure he can say what he has to say in the parlor, if that's all right with you?"

Elias looked like he knew very well what Ross had come to say and he didn't like it. Abigail's heart was choking in her throat as she waited for her father to answer.

"All right. You can use the parlor this once, but you put a hand on her, Galligher, and you'll not be seeing her again."

The two men measured each other silently. At last Elias said, "Come, Lucia. We'll be in the library."

Abigail watched them disappear into the library and then turned into the softly lighted parlor where she and her mother had been so quietly busy just minutes before. Abigail's handiwork still lay on the settee.

Ross saw it and picked up the delicate work. "Sure now, is this yours?"

"Yes."

He looked at her with admiration. "It be fine work. Ye can cook well and do handsome handiwork. Ye can figure sums and teach. Sure now, ye be makin' some man a fine wife, Abbie."

"Is that what you came to tell me?"

"Aye. And more if ye be lettin' me."

She sank down on the settee feeling a strange warmth flush not only her cheeks. "I'll listen to what you have to say."

He sat down beside her, his dark eyes deep and molten in the lamp light. "Sure now, I was wantin' to say this last night. I couldn't wait 'til Sunday. I wanted to ask ye what I would have to be for ye to accept me?"

She looked away from those intense eyes. How terribly he must want her to be willing to do anything she asked. How could she answer him? All this time she had refused the truth about his feeling for her, hoping it would fade and die. But it hadn't and now she had to give him an answer. Oh, why couldn't they have just gone on like they were?

Hesitantly, she started to speak. "Oh, Ross, how can I tell you? I don't want to hurt you, but you must understand I can't marry you. I know nothing about farms and animals. I couldn't live in your family's cabin, never having a moment's peace and quiet or privacy. I would never leave my faith for yours." She paused, searching for the right words, and continued in anguish. "Oh, Ross, can't you see the man I marry has to live and work in town—has to be able to give me a house, however small, has to be a man I can go to church with on Sunday?"

"Ahh, me darlin' Abbie, I accept your proposal and I be promisin' to do all that and more for ye."

In exasperation she faced him. "Oh, Ross! Be serious."

"Sure now, I be serious. I'll be doin' whatever ye want me to do."

She saw he was serious, terribly serious. She looked away from those eyes—eyes that frightened her with their intensity. What could she possibly say now?

"Abbie, look at me, now. Can't ye be seein' what ye are doin' to me?"

"No, Ross. I don't want to see. I can't see because it's not possible."

"It be possible," he whispered and took her hand and she sat motionless, her heart pounding, afraid to look at him, knowing one look would be devastating to her resolve. Before she realized what he was doing he placed her hand against his body and even through the rough cloth of his pants she could feel the heat and hard swelling life throbbing against her hand.

She jerked her hand away and jumped to her feet crying out, "Don't!"

He rose with her and placed his hands on her arms and held her against him, and she could feel the shaking tenseness of his body and hear it in his voice as he whispered against her hair, "Oh, Abbie, me darlin', I love ye. I've loved ye from the first moment I saw ye and I will be anything ye want of me if ye only be marryin' me."

Her father's voice cut across his words sharply. "Leave this house at once, Galligher!"

His hands slowly released their strong, almost bruising grip on her arms and she turned as he turned, her eyes wide with shock and confusion. His breath was heavy and fast with the emotion he was feeling but his voice was steady and his eyes stubborn as he faced Elias, his wide jaw set with determination. "I just be askin' your daughter to marry me, Mr. Whitteker, and now I be askin' ye. Will ye give me your daughter?"

"No!" Elias fairly shouted it. "Now get out and don't come back! And don't come to church or I'll have you thrown out."

Ross turned his eyes on Abigail but she couldn't speak, didn't dare speak. Her heart was at once pounding and stopping. He gave one last fierce look at her father and left the room, passing Abigail's mother, who was clutching the ornate archway molding for support. The slamming of the door as he left released Abigail from the trauma of the moment and she went after him.

Her father yelled, "Where are you going?"

She yelled back a little hysterically, "I've got to tell him!" with the sudden revelation of how she really felt about him and, more important, why. He was a man. While the boys she had grown up with still teetered on the brink of manhood, vacillating in their wants and desires, Ross knew what he wanted and he had the determination to get what he wanted. And it was little wonder he had the maturity of an older man. His childhood had been spent in religious oppression in Ireland before he had been brought to the United States and, once here, he had had to take on the job of a man when most boys his age were still catching frogs and dipping girls' braids in inkwells. She fully realized his faults—his quick temper was fully capable of violence, and while his determination was a good quality, the stubbornness embellishing that determination might prove difficult to deal with at times, as it was now. But just as his anger was quick, so were his smile and his laugh and his pure, honest love vibrating from every inch of him, which she felt and wanted to respond to. All this she wanted to tell him but he was gone by the time she reached the door. All she heard was the wagon rocketing away as he whipped the horses into a gallop. She shut the door and leaned against it.

Her father stood before her, his face stiff with anger. "Tell him what?"

Calmly, she said, "That I love him."

3

THE ELOPEMENT

Days passed and she didn't see Ross again. Her birthday came and though she tried to feel what she had felt a few short months ago, she couldn't. There was no joy in being twenty. There wouldn't be joy in anything until she saw Ross again. School started and Miss Cox didn't retire as much as Abigail had hoped and prayed she would. More than she had ever thought possible she wanted to be on her own, and the teaching position would at least have gotten

her out of her father's bank, if not out of his home. There had been
little said since that night, but the night was not forgotten. Several
times she saw Ross go by the bank but he never came to see her, and
she was torn between pride and the desire to see him.

Miss Cox took ill the last Thursday in September and Abigail
was called to take over her teaching duties until she recovered. She
was overjoyed at the thought of seeing Mollie and having the
opportunity to ask about Ross, but the more she thought about it
the more she knew she should not encourage their relationship by
sending him even the smallest message. It was most difficult for her
to pretend there was nothing between them. Every time she looked
at Mollie she thought of Ross, but she made it through the first day
without breaking her resolve.

Friday passed more easily. The last lesson was given for the day
and she dismissed the children. With noisy enthusiasm they scrambled for the door and she was left alone, cleaning off the blackboard. She was almost done when the door opened and she
thought it was the Parker boy bringing in the erasers he'd been
given to clean outside as punishment for talking in class.

Without looking around she said, "Thank you, Billy. Put them
on my desk and you can go." But the footsteps on the floor
sounded too heavy for Billy's and she turned around and gasped,
"Ross!"

He stopped a few feet from her and smiled faintly. "Aye, Abbie.
Can we be talkin' now?"

"Yes, of course."

"Sure now, I'm sorry for what happened. Ye know I didn't
mean to be scarin' ye, don't ye?"

"I know."

He wrung his cap nervously as he spoke. He was fighting hard
to keep his feelings under control, but it wasn't possible and he
exclaimed, "Damn it, Abbie, I can't be hidin' what I feel for ye! I
love ye and I want to be marryin' with ye. Can ye be givin' me an
answer?"

There was such terrible pain in his eyes she reached out to him
in despair. He took the few quick steps separating them and held
her in his arms, his lips covering hers with a kiss that left her
breathless. She clung to him, her heart beating so rapidly she was
dizzy with the ectasy of his embrace.

At last he drew away from her enough to look at her and
whispered with strained emotion, "Oh, Abbie, me darlin', sweet

Abbie. Do ye have any idea how much I be wantin' ye? Can ye no feel it, too?"

Resolve destroyed, she breathed softly, "Yes, Ross. I wanted to tell you that night but you were gone before I could. I love you, Ross. I love you!"

He held her close again and kissed her and she was a torch consumed by flames spreading like wildfire through her. Billy Parker came into the room and they separated in embarrassment. He grinned wisely at them and, dumping the erasers on the desk, ran back down the aisle between the desks and shut the door with a bang. Abigail giggled and tried to recover her composure. Ross perched on the corner of her desk and looked at her with eyes that left no doubt in her mind what he was thinking. Shaking yet, she took the erasers and lined them up on the blackboard and wondered wildly what had happened to her self-control. He didn't say anything for several long moments but she could feel him—feel the burning intensity of his presence—and it was impossible to calm her own pounding heart.

Finally he broke the silence. "I have a job in town, Abbie."

She turned in surprise, her arched eyebrows arching even higher as she asked, "Where?"

"Sure now, it's not much to be buildin' hopes on but I be workin' at the livery stable cleanin' stalls and then I be swampin' the feed store after closin'."

Her heart sank, but he wasn't through.

"I've been workin' for a month now and I was paid today. I made arrangements last week, Abbie, if ye be agreein'. I went to Albany to see a magistrate and he said he'd marry us, now. I've spoken for a room for the night at an inn on the way. Sure now, I know it's not what ye be plannin' and it's not what I be plannin' either, but I can't be without ye. We can be leavin' right now and be married tonight."

Her heart stopped beating. "It's impossible, Ross. I just can't run off and get married."

"Why, Abbie? What's to stop ye?"

She looked around uncertainly. He was right—there was nothing to stop her. She could go with him and marry him right now, but the suddenness of the proposal and the consequences of the action frightened her, and she could only say helplessly, "It's just not possible."

"Sure now, it's possible. I'm askin' ye, now, to be me wife—to marry me today, as soon as possible. Can ye not answer me, now, before it be too late?"

She felt faint. "But what about your church?"

"It'll be there when I be wantin' it."

She closed her eyes and slowly nodded her head. She heard him leave the desk and she leaned against him as he took her in his arms. He led her out the door, grabbing her shawl as he passed the coat hooks. He lifted her into a buckboard which had the stable's name emblazoned on it and slapped the team into a trot. They didn't have to go through town, for which Abigail was thankful, but that was the only rational thought she had on the long, dreamlike ride to Albany as Ross kept the horses going at a fast pace.

They reached the magistrate's house at dark and he opened the door. Ross introduced himself and the man replied, "Oh, yes, Mr. Galligher. I remember you. Come in. And this is the bride-to-be?"

"Aye, your honor."

The papers were filled out and the magistrate's wife and daughter stood as witnesses. The ceremony proceeded smoothly enough until the magistrate asked for a ring.

Ross looked at Abigail, pleading forgiveness as he explained, "Sorry, your honor, but I don't be havin' a ring, now."

The ceremony continued and they were married. Abigail felt a dullness of unreality settle over her and she barely found voice to thank the couple as they left.

Once on their way again, Ross told her, "I be sorry about the ring, Abbie, but I don't be havin' enough money for it, too. As soon as I be able to, I'll buy ye one. Can ye forgive me, now?"

She nodded dumbly, not taking her eyes off the road ahead, seeing nothing but blackness, as they traveled back over the road to Riverwood.

Ross stopped when he reached the inn he had selected for their wedding night. Even in the dark the place had a run-down, over-grown appearance and Abigail was depressed even more, but she was too much in shock to say anything. Ross led her into the shabby tavern and the unshaven inkeeper gruffly accosted them, while his few customers watched curiously as they sipped their ale.

"You need something, friend?"

"Me name be Galligher. I spoke for a room to ye the other day."

"Righto. I remember now. Honeymooners you said you was. Got just the room for you. Got fresh straw in the mattress just last month."

There was a series of guffaws from the onlookers. Abigail

couldn't believe what was happening. She wanted to protest but couldn't. They followed the disheveled innkeeper up dingy steps to the room he held for them. He opened the door and set the lantern on the table and proudly said, "There, now, girl, this is the best in the place."

Abigail looked around the room in dismay. The bed was narrow and the floor unswept. A small square table and crude chair completed the furniture in the room. The bedding consisted of one soiled pillow and a ragged blanket. Not even a wash bowl or pitcher of water was anywhere to be seen.

Ross said, "Thank ye, Mr. Tillett. We'll be down for a bite to eat after a bit."

The innkeeper winked knowingly and backed out of the room with a lascivious grin.

Abigail found her voice, "Oh, Ross, it's terrible. Do we really have to stay *here*?"

He looked around the room as if trying to see it with her eyes. "Aye, ye be right, it be pretty bad, but, Abbie, it be all I could afford. Ye know I would be gettin' ye better if I could, now."

"I know, but this is—" She couldn't finish. She snatched up the dirty and ragged blanket. "Just take a smell of this. It's filthy!"

He took it and looked bewildered. "I'll be gettin' a clean one for ye, now."

He strode to the door and she heard his feet thump down the steps. She sat down at the table and put her head on her arms and cried. She was still crying when Ross came back, not realizing he was there until his hand gently touched her shoulder. She looked up at him and tried to wipe away the tears.

He pulled her to her feet and whispered against her ear, "Oh, Abbie, sure now, I be sorry. I shouldn't be doin' this to ye. Come, darlin', I'll be takin' ye home, now."

With his arm around her he led her down the stairs and out of the stale inn into the fresh night air and helped her into the buckboard. Reluctantly he turned the horses on the road to River-wood, holding her close to him to shield her from the chilled night air. Clouds raced across the sky and hid the moon and stars and distant lightning streaked from the sky followed by the dull roll of thunder. Halfway to Riverwood the thunderstorm caught them and torrents of water lashed them from the sky and wind hurled branches at them, making the horses skittish. When Ross saw a lighted farmhouse he turned into the lane and sent the horses galloping through the rain. He carried Abigail, wet and shivering,

from the buckboard and set her feet on the wide porch and
pounded on the door. A light moved to the curtained window of
the door and the door swung open.

An elderly man and his wife peered at the bedraggled couple
and the man asked in surprise, "Where did you come from, boy?
What in the world are you doing out on a night like this?"

The woman, short, plump and motherly, her face sweetly pleasant, said, "Oh, for heaven's sake, Henry, you can ask them questions later. Come in out of that storm. Come in!"

They went in, dripping and chilled, Ross smiling his thanks.
"Me name's Galligher and we be on our way back from Albany. We
didn't expect to be out in the weather but—" He didn't finish.

The woman immediately grasped the situation and said, "Henry, you take care of their horses while I get them into something
dry. I'm Hannah Beal, and this is Mr. Beal. Now, don't you worry
about a thing. I've got dry clothes and you're welcome to spend the
night."

Abigail protested, "That's very kind, Mrs. Beal, but really we
must get back to Riverwood. We can go as soon as the rain stops."

"Nonsense, child. Look at you. You're shiverin' out of your
shoes. Now come by the fire and I'll find you something to wear."

Abigail was too tired, too emotionally drained, wet, and cold to
protest farther. She went to the fire and Ross went to help with the
horses. When he got back Abigail was cozily dry in a voluminous
gown and warm robe belonging to Mrs. Beal.

He came soaking wet to the fire and smiled down at her. "Are ye
all right, now, Abbie?"

With more certainty than she felt she answered, "Yes."

Mrs. Beal came in with a dry garment for Ross. "You can use
one of Henry's nightshirts, Mr. Galligher. Come into the kitchen,
dear, while he gets out of those wet things and we'll get some nice
hot tea."

Abigail meekly followed the round figure into the kitchen and
stood by the fire on the cooking hearth and took the tea Mrs. Beal
handed her, hoping she didn't look as distraught as she felt.

Mrs. Beal asked, "Can I ask a question?"

Abigail turned uncertain eyes on her hostess and nodded.

"Is he your husband?"

Before she thought Abigail answered, "No," then quickly cor-
rected, "I mean yes. We were just married. We were on our way
home."

"I see. Well, don't worry about a thing. We've got a spare

bedroom. All our children are gone from home but I keep a bed made up just in case."

Abigail turned her dismayed eyes back to her tea.

Mrs. Beal cleared her throat and Abigail raised her eyes from the steaming cup. "You ain't been to bed with him yet, have you?"

Abigail whispered, "No."

"No wonder you look so scared. Well, if you don't mind a nosy old lady givin' you a bit of advice, I'll tell you just what I told my children before they got married. No need me tellin' you what to expect. You probably already heard all about the bad side of it. I'm not going to tell you those things ain't going to happen. Most likely they will, but it probably won't be as bad as you expect it to be. At least not the physical side of it. The worst of it'll be afterward when you have second thoughts about it. I know I did. Plenty of 'em, too, until the idea dawned on me one day that if I was ever going to have the kind of love I'd pictured on havin', I was going to have to do something about it. Now it stands to reason that most respectable, God-fearin' men don't know any more how to love us than we know how to love them. How could they? Where is they to learn and still be God-fearin' and respectable? That's the day I knew I had to teach Henry how to love me and I had to learn how to love him, and you can do the same.

"Now everything's going to be all right and if it isn't, all you have to do is call me. Just remember what I told you and tomorrow or the next day when you've had time to get used to your man, you can tell him how to please you and if he's the kind of man he appears to be, he'll be more than willin' to do whatever you ask of him. Now, if you're ready we'll get you two off to bed. No use waitin'. The longer you wait the more scared you'll be."

Abigail nodded, not sure she was ready at all.

Henry Beal stuck his head through the door and announced, "We're ready for that tea, now, Mother."

Abigail followed them into the sitting room and Ross was standing before the fire, the slender Mr. Beal's nightshirt straining to cover his well-muscled body. He took the steaming cup and blew at it before taking a swallow.

"That be good tea, Mrs. Beal. Thank ye."

She smiled. "You're welcome, young man. Mr. Beal, it's this young couple's wedding night."

Henry held out his hand to Ross. "Well, congratulations, young man. You've sure picked you a pretty little bride."

Ross looked at Abigail and she saw pride fill his eyes. "Sure, and don't ye know I be knowin' that, now, Mr. Beal."

Mrs. Beal continued, "Do you know how to treat your bride, son?"

Ross looked uncertain. "How do ye mean, now?"

"I mean, have you been told how to treat her the first time?"

Mr. Beal looked pained. "Hannah! It ain't none of our business."

"Mr. Beal, we raised six kids and if I hadn't made it my business, you never would've. This young couple has got the right to know that what happens tonight is going to affect their life together. I wished someone'd had the good sense to tell me." She turned back to Ross. "You just remember to be gentle with her, son. She'll forget the pain quickly but she won't forget how you treated her. If you want her to love you, you think of her ahead of yourself. Do you understand, Mr. Galligher?"

Ross smiled. "Aye, Mrs. Beal, I be understandin'."

Mrs. Beal stood up. "Well, now, it's getting late and we all best be getting to bed. Good night, children." She bustled out of the room leaving Mr. Beal standing dumbly. He mumbled an embarrassed good night and followed his wife into their bedroom.

Abigail looked uncertainly at Ross and he set his tea cup on the mantel and came to where she sat, touching her still damp hair, his eyes dark and tender. "Will ye be comin' to bed with me, now, Abbie?"

She looked at him, frightened and small. Speechless, she nodded yes. He lifted her in his strong arms and carried her into the clean room that was to be their bedroom for the night. He gently placed her on the crisp, clean sheets and covered her and went to blow out the lamp. She felt his weight on the bed and he turned to take her in his arms, kissing her gently. He stroked her hair and whispered soft Gaelic words she didn't understand in her ear and soon she relaxed under his gentle touch, responding as she had much earlier to his kiss until the all-consuming passion that had brought her to this place with him rose up and engulfed her, erasing all fear. With trembling hands he helped her from her entangling gown and pulled the narrow nightshirt from his own smoldering body. There was nothing between them but the heat of their impassioned bodies. She cried out as his body united with hers in one passionate, tearing thrust. But the pain was gone as quickly as it had come as the driving force of his body died inside her. She felt an unaccustomed sensation, aftermath of the conjugal embrace, and pulled from his arms, afraid she was bleeding.

He rose to follow her, his voice shaking. "Abbie, I'm sorry. I didn't mean to be hurtin' ye. Let me be helpin' ye now." He fumbled with the lamp trying to light it.

Abigail pleaded, "Please, don't light it."

The room filled with light and she quickly retrieved the gown from the floor and put it on and quickly took the washcloth from the bowl and ministered to herself. Ross struggled to get his nightshirt on behind her. She brought the cloth away and was surprised to see only a small amount of red. Ross was beside her, the tight nightshirt straining over his chest and arms.

"Are ye all right, Abbie?"

She finished rinsing the washcloth and wrung it out. He touched her arm and questioned softly, "Abbie?"

She put the washcloth down and turned to him and looked at his anguished face. He had been gentle except for the one brief moment and even that hadn't been as bad as she had expected. It would take awhile to know just what she felt, but she couldn't blame him. That would be unfair. He was all she had now and she must not let him know her disappointment. She bent to blow out the lamp and put her arms around him and felt the tension leave him with her acceptance of him. She shivered as lightning illuminated the room briefly from a distance, followed by a muted rumble of thunder. Ross picked her up and carried her to the bed and gently got in bed with her and held her in his arms. Soon his even breathing told her he was asleep. For a long time she lay watching the lightning grow fainter and farther away until it disappeared altogether and she slept too.

Abigail awoke with a start, forgetting where she was and who she was with. She sat upright as if awakening from a nightmare and Ross stirred sleepily and opened his eyes. When he saw her he smiled tenderly at her.

"Sure, now, it is true? Are ye really in bed with me, darlin' Abbie?"

She lay back, the turmoil of the night's thoughts eased by rest and time. He moved to take her in his arms and she let him. Things she had accepted by dark made her blush in the morning light, especially when he sought to remove her gown. He laughed and teased her, kissing her, touching her, tantalizing her out of her modesty until she could close her eyes to the sun and help him discover the sensuous secrets of her body. The unlocked passion of her being came swiftly once she let it, but still there lurked the fear of pain she was sure would come and when there was little discomfort she knew a moment's disappointment as she wondered if it was over. But the control he had lacked the first time didn't fail him and when she thought she could never have enough of him, the sweet, magic moment slipped away from them and she lay clinging to him, trembling with the wonder of what she had felt. Her lips caressed his neck and shoulder as he held her, quiet and loving.

The tranquillity slowly dissipated and the curiosity to know the body of this magnificent man who had delighted her beyond her wildest imaginings overcame her shyness. She pulled from his embrace and sat up, abruptly throwing the covers off them in a moment of complete abandon, and saw for the first time his strong, hard-muscled, compact body, so near the perfection of a Greek statue she had seen in a book on ancient civilization Miss Cox had given her to read as she furthered her education. She remembered all too well how she had turned the page unknowingly and blushed furiously at the picture. She had read the page quickly and never turned back to it, but she hadn't forgotten it; and now this reincarnation of Apollo was lying at her side.

"Hey!" he exclaimed and reached for the covers in the cool room.

She kept them away, giggling as he struggled with her, feeling the strength of him and luxuriating in it. He held her away from him and appraised her with open and undisguised delight. She blushed.

"Aye, ye be as I said—red-ripe and luscious."

She countered with, "And you're beautiful."

He laughed and threw the covers over her. "Beautiful! Father in heaven, what manner of woman have I wed with, now?"

She giggled and they laughed until they could laugh no more. Then they held each other, reveling in the sweet intimacy of kisses and caresses until the smell of breakfast filtered into their room and brought them back to more immediate needs. Neither of them had eaten since early the day before and now hunger drove them from their marriage bed. Modestly gowned, they blushingly entered the kitchen.

Mrs. Beal turned from the fire and smiled at them. "Good morning, children. Did you sleep well?"

Ross smiled at Abigail, and the smile was not lost to Mrs. Beal's alert eyes. "Aye, very well, Mrs. Beal."

She smiled with satisfaction and returned to her cooking, saying, "Breakfast will be ready in a bit. You have time to dress."

They returned to their room and dressed. Abigail combed out her tangled hair with a comb on the dresser and Ross stood behind her, watching, his face strangely thoughtful.

"What's wrong, Ross?"

"What's wrong is we have to be facin' your father soon."

Her own feeling of content slowly drained away and she lay down the comb and turned to him, putting her arms around him. "I'm afraid of what he might do."

"Aye. But don't be forgettin' our marriage be consummated. Permission or no, we be legally wed. Now kiss me and promise you'll be lovin' me after your father has told ye how bad I be."

She kissed him and answered, "That's one promise I won't have to worry about breaking. I love you enough to withstand anything Father might do."

He smiled down at her. "Good. Now we'd better be eatin' breakfast. 'Tis starved I am."

They drove toward town silently, clinging to each other with unspoken desperation. Just once did Abigail break the silence to warn Ross, "Promise me you won't lose your temper, Ross. Let me talk to Father. I think he'll listen to me better than he will you."

He frowned, but consented. "All right, Abbie, I'll be tryin', but your father rubs me the wrong way and I don't be knowin' if I can hold me temper."

"I know, but please try."

He nodded, his jaw set at the thought.

The constable of Riverwood met them at the edge of town. "Sure am glad to see you, Miss Whitteker. Are you all right?"

"I'm fine, Mr. Hooker. Is there something wrong?"

"Not nearly so much as was a while ago before I saw you, but I've got to arrest this man for abduction and possible—" He stopped and cleared his throat nervously. "Well, we'll talk about that later. I'd better get you home to your father."

Ross, his face stiff with anger, questioned incredulously, "Arrest me?"

Abigail said firmly, "You can't arrest him. He's done nothing wrong."

"Not according to your father. According to the Parker boy, Galligher was molesting you in the schoolhouse."

It was Abigail's turn to be shocked. "That's a lie! Mr. Galligher and I were married last night."

Constable Hooker looked embarrassed and a fine film of perspiration sprang across his forehead. He mopped his brow and clapped his stained hat back on his head. "Do you have any proof of that?"

With unyielding jaw, Ross pulled the marriage document from his coat and handed it to Constable Hooker. "You consented freely to this marriage, Miss Whitteker?"

"Yes."

"Did you have witnesses?"

"Yes. The magistrate's wife and daughter were witnesses for us."

He looked uncomfortable and shifted uneasily in his saddle. "I mean do you have witnesses that the marriage was— uh—consummated?"

The question was too much for Ross and he exploded, "Enough of your damn questions! We be legally married and that's all ye need to know." He grabbed the paper from the constable and stuffed it in his pocket and slapped the reins against the horses and galloped them into town with the constable trotting self-consciously after them.

They pulled to a halt in front of Abigail's house and there was a crowd gathering from out of nowhere. The door opened as Ross swung Abigail down from the buckboard. She could see the dis-traught face of her mother and the ashen, enraged face of her father. As she clung to Ross's arm, they met on the walk between house and street.

"Why isn't this man in jail, Hooker?"

"Ain't done nothing wrong, Mr. Whitteker. Got papers to prove he married her legal."

"Legal!" Elias stormed. "She had no approval. She needs my consent to marry *anybody*." '

"Got the paper to prove it and she done it willing."

"Willing and be damned, Hooker! He abducted her."

Abigail interjected her voice loudly between them. Ross was too angry to speak calmly, his square jaw pulsing with the dangerous pounding of his blood. "Stop this at once! I married Ross Galligher because I love him and because I wanted to marry him. We are legally married and you can't change it, Father."

Elias turned angry eyes on her. "You get into the house, Abigail. I'll talk to you later."

"Father, I don't live here anymore. I live with my husband."

"Not without my consent!" he shouted.

Before anything more could be said Ross did the last thing he should have done. He stepped forward and grabbed Elias Whitteker by the coat front and if Abigail hadn't been still holding on to his arm, he was sure her father would have been on the ground but she hung on tightly and all Ross could do was shake Elias Whitteker in his rage.

Elias yelled, "Hooker, arrest this man!"

Hooker belatedly grabbed Ross and pulled him with Abigail's help away from her father. Men in the crowd of onlookers outside the gate rushed to help and Ross was soon held on both sides. Abigail was helpless. Everything had gone wrong. If Ross hadn't lost his temper nothing could have parted them. Now he was physically in the hands of the constable and could be put in jail for attempted assault. Anxiously she looked about for one person to help her but there was none. She was alone and defeated.

Her father straightened his coat and said, "I'm pressing charges, Hooker. Put him under arrest."

Ross glared and struggled to get free but even his strength was no match against the three men who held him.

"Ross, Ross," she cried. "Don't fight them. You'll only make it worse."

He realized the truth of her words and she watched with dismay as the men marched him off to jail.

She turned on her father. "How could you! How could you do that to him!"

She had no other place to run except to her own familiar room and she ran with unforgiving rage to the one sanctuary she knew. She closed the door and locked it and fell across the bed and wept in uncontrollable, terrified anger.

Much later she opened the door. She had changed her clothes and rectified the swollen, tearstained face, and with quiet determination she went downstairs. Her mother confronted her at the foot of the stairs, her face as ravaged as Abigail's.

"Oh, Abbie. Dear, dear, Abbie. I'm so sorry. Why did you do it?"

Stiffly, she said, "I thought I made it clear outside."

Her mother sobbed. Abigail reached out and touched her in a gesture of sympathy. "I'm sorry, Mother, I didn't mean to hurt you or Father, but I love Ross."

She let her hand fall from her mother and went for the door.

Her mother asked anxiously, "Where are you going?"

"I'm going to see my husband."

Lucia moved quickly to block her daughter. "No, Abigail. You mustn't. You must give up this terrible man. It'll be easier if you never see him again."

"Get out of my way, Mother. I'm going to see him."

"He's in jail and your father has given Mr. Hooker orders not to let you see him. Now be reasonable. This thing will pass and you'll come to your senses."

Before Abigail could protest the doorknob turned behind Lucia and she moved aside as Elias came in. Father and daughter glared at each other across an ever widening gulf of hostility.

Elias spoke first. "Where are you going, Abigail?"

"To see my husband."

"I've given Hooker orders that you are not to be permitted to see him. Now, I have a few things I want to say to you. I didn't want this to happen but you have left me no choice, Abigail. You have a name in this town and position. I thought you were mature enough to make the right decision about this man but you didn't. Now I must undo what you have done. How far has this thing gone?"

Through clenched teeth Abigail whispered, "What do you mean?" knowing very well what he meant but wanting to hurt him by the embarrassment she knew the subject would cause him.

His color deepened, as she expected, and he stiffly asked, "Did you sleep with this man?"

"Yes, Father, I slept with him and I loved him. Beyond my wildest dreams, I loved him."

Abigail heard her mother gasp at her words. Her father blinked and said, "Very well, then, you'll remain here until we see if you bear any fruit from this union and then we'll start annulment proceedings."

She laughed, suddenly finding the whole scene ridiculous. All at once she felt victorious. They could jail Ross but not for long. If they dissolved her marriage she would marry him again. She matter-of-factly told him, "Don't waste your money, Father. Ross is the man I intend to be married to and whatever you do, I will go to him when he's released from jail."

Elias smiled a small self-assured smile and replied, "We'll see, Abigail, we'll see."

4

ESCAPE

Abigail fought her parents no more. A veneer of normality returned to the Whitteker household. It was as if Ross had never existed, but he did exist and Abigail carried his existence with her constantly. She saw him in her mind's eye everywhere she went, and in everything she did she heard his laugh, the endearing lilt of his Irish brogue, felt his touch, and most of all saw those magical eyes filled with devilish, twinkling lights. At night she longed to kiss his full, sensuous lips, treasuring the one moment she remembered when he had awakened her body to unknown delight. She worked at the bank again, and every opening of the door brought her head up with expectancy. Her father made it clear she would not be able to substitute at school, and the hope she had held of communicating with Ross through Mollie was dashed.

Beth, the one person she needed to help her through this most difficult time, seemed to avoid her. At first it hurt deeply that Beth would desert her, but she soon realized Beth's parents were concerned about Beth's reputation and had most likely forbid her to see Abigail. Two months passed in which she went to church and appeared as a repentant prodigal. The scandal soon died without more fuel to feed it and Abigail felt the town once again accepted her as one of its own even though her father still viewed her with guarded skepticism. Even Beth came to see her a few days before Christmas, bringing her a present as she had done all the years of their friendship.

They talked and giggled almost as if nothing had happened, but there was an unspoken curiosity in Beth that punctuated her every word and look. Abigail knew she would have to undergo a quizzing but she didn't want it to be done where her parents could hear. She was afraid they would discover how very close Ross still was in her mind. On the pretext of showing Beth her Christmas gown, the two girls went upstairs and Abigail very quietly shut the door to her room. Beth turned to her with eyes pleading for forgiveness and they went into each others arms, all pretense of lightheartedness gone.

Beth sniffed and wiped her eyes. "Oh, Abbie! Father wouldn't let me come see you. It's been horrid. He was afraid Aloysius wouldn't ask me to marry him if I was your friend."

"I don't blame you, Beth. I knew something like that was the reason. Has Aloysius asked you to marry him?"

Her eyes filled with unconcealed happiness. "Yes. We're to be married in the spring. Isn't it wonderful?"

Abigail hugged her friend again. "Yes, Beth. I'm so happy for you."

"I want you to be my witness, Abbie, will you?" She looked uncertain.

"Of course, if no one objects, you know I will."

Beth bit her lip. "It isn't that. It's—" She faltered. "It's—if you'll be able to."

Abigail laughed. "You mean am I pregnant?"

Beth nodded, her face coloring.

Abigail squeezed her hand. "No, silly, I'm not."

She looked relieved. "I've been dying to talk to you. Weren't you scared to death?"

She smiled, remembering how afraid she really had been. "Yes. It was perfectly awful."

Beth plopped down on the bed in an attitude of rapt attention. "Tell me about it. I want to hear everything. Was he really molesting you in the schoolhouse like they said?"

Abigail stretched out on the bed on her stomach and Beth did the same, as they often had in bygone times of childhood, whispering confidences. "Of course not. He came to tell me he had a job in town and he wanted to marry me and if I would go with him he'd made arrangements for us to be married and had even spoken for a room at the inn for us. What Billy saw was Ross kissing me, not molesting me."

Beth shivered with expectancy. "How was it? Was it as bad as we've heard it was?"

"What? You mean his kiss?"

"No. You know what I mean. When you went to bed with him."

Abigail smiled faintly, remembering. It all seemed like a dream now but a very detailed dream. "Well, the first time was awful because I didn't know what was going to happen."

Beth looked shocked. "You mean you did it more than once?"

Abigail placed her chin on her folded arms and closed her eyes. "Yes," she murmured, her body tortured with the memory.

Beth mistook her misery for regret and reached out to touch her friend. "Oh, Abbie, how awful."

Abigail heard the sympathy in her voice and opened her eyes, a smile touching her lips. "No, Beth. How beautiful. I wouldn't trade that one hour with him for anything in the world."

"Do you suppose Aloysius and I can feel that way, too?"

Abigail sat up feeling restless and wanting to be alone. "I don't know, Beth. Perhaps. A lot will depend on how quickly you can forget about modesty and learn how to please each other. It was easy for me because Ross was so wonderful. If Aloysius is like Ross then you will know what I mean." Abigail went to the door and opened it, ending their sharing of confidences. Beth looked at her strangely and rose and walked ahead of her down the steps.

Abigail's parents were in the sitting room and if Beth had anything more to say she didn't say it then. They said their good nights and Beth left her with a still curious look of questioning awe on her round face. Abigail's mother stopped her before she could return upstairs to the sanctity of her own room.

"And what were you two girls talking about, dear? Something secret?"

"Yes, Mother. Aloysius has asked Beth to marry him and she wanted to know if I could be her witness. Is it all right with you?"

"I don't see why not, do you, Elias?"

Her father studied her for a long moment and said, "I guess not."

The weeks passed slowly for Abigail but they were made more bearable by Beth's presence and her increasing excitement about her marriage. They would sit for hours on Abigail's bed making Beth's trousseau and when they were stitching Beth's nightgown and robe Abigail suddenly had tears spring to her eyes and run down her cheeks right in the middle of their happy chatter.

Beth put down her sewing and took Abigail in her arms. "Dear Abbie, you are in such misery, aren't you?"

"I miss him so," she sobbed.

"Have you heard from him?"

She wiped her eyes and answered, "No. Is he still in jail? I don't even know. It's not like him not to try to see me. Surely you have heard why he doesn't come for me?"

Beth patted her and looked thoughtful. "I'm not supposed to say anything but I just can't be silent when it's so obvious you love him. They let him out of jail with the understanding he wasn't to come into town or he would be put in jail again."

The tears came again. "Oh, Beth, what am I to do? I can't go on like this!"

Beth didn't say any more but Abigail saw a look come into her eyes she had never seen in her frivolous friend. Something deep and mysterious was going on in Beth's mind, and it worried Abigail.

She didn't have long to worry. The next time Beth came to sew she was more bubbly than usual. She fairly shoved Abigail upstairs into the privacy of Abigail's room and closed the door. She unfolded the garments she had brought to be worked on and handed Abigail a piece of paper tucked inside. Abigail's heart nearly choked her as she unfolded the paper and Ross's printed words greeted her eyes. She hurried to the lamp to see better and sat down feasting on this first message from him since she had last seen him months before.

The letter read, "Darling Abbie, I love you and miss you. I can't write good but will try with Mollie's help. I have been wanting to see you so many times but I will be jailed if I come to town. I am hoping and praying to the Father that you still love me. Ross."

Abigail looked up at Beth and whispered in a trembling voice, "How did you manage this?"

She giggled with delight. "You know I sometimes have to deliver things to Miss Cox, and of course I see Mollie once in a while. I just happened to mention that if she left something in that old hollow tree on the schoolyard I'd check it every day. And this is what I found."

Abigail's face fell even while her heart was nourished by the words she held. "Oh, Beth, we can't do this. It's too risky. If Father found out it would erase everything I've gained."

Beth sighed in acknowledgment. "I suppose you're right. But don't you want to answer him first and tell him not to write anymore? Surely we can get one more letter through without discovery."

She was taking a chance but she wanted so much to let him know she still was waiting for him and loved him. While Beth sewed she wrote: "My dearest Ross, Words can't tell you how happy I was to get your letter. These months without you have been bearable only because I am looking forward to the day when I can be with you again. I love you so very much and would give anything to see you or hear from you again but it is too dangerous. Please don't write again or do anything to upset Father. Just be patient and remember that no man can put us asunder. I love you, my darling. Yours forever, Abigail."

The fear she lived with all the next day that they would be found out came to a head at dinnertime. There was a knock on the front door and Abigail forced herself to remain calm while her father went to answer the door. One look at him when he came back into the dining room was all she needed to know she had been betrayed.

He waved her letter at her and shouted at her angrily, "What is this, Abigail? How long has this been going on?"

Bravely she faced him, trying to remain calm, "It's a letter to my husband—the first one I've written."

"I dare say, and the last one, too. He will not be your husband long. I've started annulment proceedings. You disappoint me, Abigail. I had hoped you would come to your senses by now. I will not let you ruin your life with this scum. The day after Beth's wedding I am sending you and your mother to Paris. It was your wish to go to school there and now you will. As soon as I can find a suitable chaperone for you, your mother can come home but you are going to stay in Paris until you forget this man or marry a man suitable to your station. Is that clear?"

Abigail rose to her feet, her face white and her hands shaking from the anger she felt. "I don't wish to go to Paris and I don't wish to marry another man. Can't you understand! I love Ross and there is no way you can make me go to Paris and forget him."

He shouted at her in rage, "You will go! You will go and forget this man or you will never be welcome in this house again!"

She smiled coldly. "That suits me fine." She walked stiffly to the door and turned to throw one last barb. "If you had let me go to Paris three years ago when I wanted to go, I might have lived up to your high standards." She paused meaningfully, then continued, "But not now. Do you think someone of your high standards will want to marry me when I tell them I've been bedded by an Irish pig farmer?"

Elias turned red with rage and her mother, already white with shock, swooned with a strangled cry. Abigail didn't wait to see what happened, she fled upstairs two at a time and closed the door of her room and locked it and flung herself across her bed. Somehow she must escape before they sent her to Paris. In one short month she had to work out a plan. She had to see Ross or let him know, some way, what had happened. Beth was the only one she had to help her if they allowed Beth to see her again.

But Beth was of little help in the next week. Abigail's mother was given strict orders not to let Abigail be alone with anyone. Too well her father knew her, it seemed. They had to stay in the parlor and do their handiwork. They were working on the last of Beth's linens when it came to Abigail how she could let Beth know what had happened. She embroidered her message on the hemstitching of a sheet, one letter at a time, disguising it with flowers and knots but pointing to each one at a moment when her mother wasn't looking. Beth understood and the look of a conspirator lit her eyes. By the time Beth went home that night she had a message she could read across the top of her sheet when she was alone.

That Beth had deciphered the message was apparent the next time Abigail saw her—her look was eloquent enough, but there was no way Beth could tell her what she might be trying to do for her. She would just have to have faith that Beth would get a message to Ross. Anxiety took its toll on her in the following days. She couldn't sleep and she didn't feel like eating but she forced her food, knowing she couldn't take a chance on not being strong enough to flee with Ross if he came for her.

The night of the wedding rehearsal came and it was the first time she was able to have a few quick, private words with Beth as they waited their turn to walk down the aisle.

Breathlessly Beth told her, "The night of the wedding Ross will be waiting for you. At the reception afterward I'll try to keep everyone's attention. When you get the chance you're to slip out and meet Ross at the side of the church where the horses are tied. He said to try and get some clothes to me if you can, warm ones, and anything else you'll need."

Before she could say anything, Beth's father joined them and it was time for Abigail to begin her slow march down the aisle as Beth's attendant. She could hardly stand still as they practiced the wedding ceremony, every word wrenching a cry from her heart as she heard Ross's voice instead of Aloysius' repeat the vows with Beth.

Abigail had been making a quilt as her gift to Beth and it provided the means of sneaking a few things out of the house the day before the wedding. When Beth came for the last time to see her, she handed her the wrapped gift which weighed strangely heavy. She winked at her friend and nodded to the cumbersome package and Beth nodded in understanding.

The evening of the wedding a serenity settled over Abigail which seemed unbelievable under the circumstances. From somewhere outside herself something was giving her fortitude she couldn't understand—only be grateful for—as she, with more normality than she would have believed possible, smiled her way through the ordeal of Beth's wedding. When she kissed Beth in congratulations after the ceremony they both knew it was a kiss of good-by and the tears sprang to their eyes. She knew she would have to leave as soon as possible. Lucia Whitteker was an unwitting ally in this instance. She protested when Elias wanted to leave immediately after the ceremony and Abigail sent up a prayer of thanks and watched for her chance.

True to her word, Beth went out of her way to keep things in a turmoil. She flitted around the reception hall, diverting everyone's attention with her squeals of laughter. She pulled the grand coup when she upset her wedding cake. Abigail quickly disappeared out the side door of the church into the darkness. Blindly she ran for the place where the saddle horses were usually tied and ran squarely into something. For one awful moment she feared she was discovered until his arms closed around her and a voice she had heard only in her memory whispered, "Abbie, Abbie, me darlin'. At last ye be here. Come, now, we must be hurryin'."

He guided her without further hesitation to a horse waiting for her and lifted her into the saddle. Quickly he mounted another horse and led her into the night. For hours they rode without stopping, without a word, until the weariness in their mounts made them slow down and then Ross dropped back and rode close to her, his arms going around her, and she clung to him, devouring his lips with her own until their horses, guideless, stopped and stamped inpatiently and whickered into the unknown night. He held her and caressed her until an owl dove at something crossing the road ahead and the horses shied apart, almost unseating Abigail.

"We'd better be goin' on, now, Abbie. As much as I want to be holdin' ye, we'd better be goin' on."

He turned his horse back into the road and they rode on. Abigail didn't wonder where they were going or what they would do. The only thing she could think of was they were together and she cared little for the moment beyond that, but as the weary miles dragged on and every step of her horse brought agony to her body, unaccustomed as it was to riding, she became aware of what could lie ahead for them. But even that was forgotten as her exhausted body fought to cling to the saddle. At last Ross turned off the road and led them into a thicket in some unknown woods. She was too numb to dismount and he lifted her from the saddle. The weariness the brutalizing hours had bestowed on her claimed her and she slept in his arms as he carried her to a soft, sheltered place under a tree.

How he had managed to make them a bed she didn't know but when she awoke hours later he was holding her to him under some warm blankets. She felt cramped and sore, and when she tried to shift to a more comfortable position a thousand aches enveloped her in pain. She moaned and Ross awoke and blinked sleepily at her.

The sight of her brought him fully awake and he smiled. "Sure now, I thought for a moment I was dreamin', but I'm not. 'Tis really me darlin' Abbie lyin' by me side. Are ye all right, now?"

She grimaced at him and answered, "I hurt all over. I haven't ridden a horse since I rode Aloysius' pony around the schoolyard nearly ten years ago."

He grinned at her and asked, "Where does it hurt the most?"

"Everywhere." She tried stretching an aching leg and it cramped painfully.

She moaned and clutched at her leg. He sat up and put his hands to the tightly knotted muscle in the calf of her leg and rubbed it vigorously until the pain eased. He didn't stop with her lower leg but rubbed her feet and on up her other leg to her thigh. She shivered at his touch and he looked at her, the devils doing a dance in his eyes.

"Be I rubbin' the right spot, Abbie?"

She pulled him down to her, not caring that it was daylight, nor caring that they were miles from home and undoubtedly being hunted. Their union was brief but desperately intense, like a shooting star—brilliant but quickly burnt out. He held her close for a little while afterward until hunger and worry drove them from each other's arms.

For days they traveled at night following a wilderness track along a narrow river valley, seeing little in the forested darkness, avoiding the settlements and people when at all possible. Abigail was continually cold or wet or both, and aching in the blustery March weather. By day they hid in some well-concealed spot to sleep and eat the meager provisions Ross had brought for their flight, wary and breathless at every sound that threatened to come near and discover them. It was hardly the honeymoon Abigail had visioned in her mind, but Ross was everything she had dreamed he would be. With loving and tender concern he welded her heart to his and, as miserable as their fugitive flight was, she never once thought of going back to the comfort of her home.

Their food finally ran out and Ross decided to chance trying to obtain what they needed during daylight. They reached the good-sized settlement of Harrisburgh situated on the bank of the river they had followed through the mountains. Abigail's spirits lifted just to see good solid homes again and the white-spired cupola of the courthouse standing out against the dark, forested mountains they had just left. She thought surely Ross would let them rest for a few days but she was wrong, and the disappointment only added to her fatigue and the worsening cold she was fighting. They crowded onto the river ferry with other travelers and ate eagerly the fresh bread and milk Ross had acquired. To Abigail it seemed the whole population was on the move. Besides wagoneers and packers with their horseloads of wares, there were numerous families on their way west in wagons, carts, or on foot. Some were well equipped and some, like themselves, had little but what they carried. Once across the Susquehanna they again looked for a secluded place to spend the day sleeping.

5

PITTSBURGH

The ride to Pittsburgh was a nightmare of mountain ridges and stream-filled valleys on dark and sometimes treacherous roads. When they climbed the last hill on a miserable road up from Turtle Creek, Abigail was sick with fever. At dawn they overlooked Pittsburgh and the surrounding lush bottom lands watered by two broad rivers that joined at Pittsburgh to make the Ohio River. Ross encouraged her to try to hang on just a little longer. She doggedly turned her horse after his and they rode closer to the settlement that had been their goal. Here they felt they would be safe.

Abigail was beyond caring where Ross was leading her, and little noticed when he left the improved streets to find a less frequented inn at which to stay. They passed several that looked shabby and gray, as every building in Pittsburgh looked from coal soot. When he finally turned under a sign reading Black Forest Haus, she was too sick to notice the well-scrubbed appearance of the building. They rode their horses into the stableyard behind the building, and a stocky middle-aged man came briskly from the stable.

"Goot morning. You need room?"

"Yes. Me wife be ill with a fever, but I don't be havin' much money. Ye don't happen to be needin' help in exchange for food and lodging until she be well now, do ye?"

The round face looked thoughtfully at them. "Vell, could be. Just could be. You vait here just one minute." He went to the door of the inn and called, "Frau Wenzel. Come, please."

In a few moments a crisply clean little woman came through the door. Her bright blue eyes immediately fastened on the ailing Abigail, and she questioned her husband rapidly in German.

He cut her off with a sharp, "*Nein*. This is my wife, Frau Wenzel." She gazed at them impassively while he went on to explain, "They need a place. Can ve use some help in pay for room and board?"

Suspiciously Frau Wenzel asked, "Vat's wrong with the voman?"

Quickly Ross explained, "We be travelin' for days in the wet and cold. She's taken cold and fever. With good care she'll be well soon, now."

Frau Wenzel's doubt disappeared instantly. "Vat you stand there for, Gustav? Bring the poor child in. With Greta and Rudy in their own place now and Wilhelmina married, of course ve need help."

Ross lifted Abigail from the saddle, his smile of relief and gratitude augmented by, "God bless ye."

Abigail was carried up three flights of steps into a spacious attic room with a large feather bed and light streaming in from four brightly curtained dormer windows.

Frau Wenzel turned back the bed explaining, "This vas my Greta and her husband's room. Ve don't rent it out. People don't vant to climb so many steps. Now I take care of her. You go take care of your things. *Ja?*"

In a week's time Abigail was able to be out of bed. Her fever was gone and the color was coming back into her cheeks. She stood at the window enjoying the warmth of the bright spring sun and looking for Ross in the stableyard below. She hadn't seen much of him. He had not shared her bed and had only brought supper to her each day and eaten with her, telling her all he was learning about their new surroundings.

She saw him come out of the stable with a wheelbarrow full of manure from the stalls and swung open the window to wave at him but he didn't look up and disappeared around the stable. She pulled the slipper from her foot and, as he came back around the corner, threw it down at him. It landed just ahead of him and he lowered the wheelbarrow and went to pick it up and looked upward until he found her waving at him. He needed no more excuse to run to the house. She heard him coming up the stairs two at a time and stood flushing with expectancy until he burst into their room.

"Did me lady be losin' her slipper, now?" he asked with a grin.

She put her arms around him, smelling the sweat and earthy odor of horses and manure on his clothes and hugged him.

He kissed her and said, "Aye, it be good to be seein' ye feelin' better. Do ye be wantin' a bed partner tonight, me darlin'?"

"Only if you take a bath first. Have you been sleeping with the horses?"

He laughed. "Ye noticed, finally! I figured if ye could be smellin' me again I could be movin' back in with ye. But back to bed with ye now, before ye get too tired." He swung her up in his arms and carried her the few steps to their bed and lowered her gently, saying, "Aye, it'll be better holdin' ye than that four-legged filly I've grown fond of."

She giggled and he kissed her again before he covered her with the feather comforter. "Save your strength, Abbie."

She watched him disappear out the door and lay back, contented.

In a few days Abigail was well enough to start helping Frau Wenzel and their remaining daughter, Helga, who was only a few years younger than Abigail, around the inn. It didn't take long for the word to get around that Wenzels' had a pretty new serving wench and business became more than brisk. Abigail soon was on the receiving end of pats and pinches of appreciative men, looking for a willing partner to spend the night with. She tried to tell them she was married but they would grab her ringless hands and laugh at her. She didn't dare tell Ross her problem, knowing his temper.

Their days were not all work. On the glorious spring afternoons, Frau Wenzel insisted Ross take Abigail for walks to bring back the color to her pale cheeks. And on one such lovely, warm day only a few weeks after their arrival in Pittsburgh, Ross took her to a goldsmith shop and bought her a ring with all the money they had. She questioned inwardly the wisdom of spending all their money, since they made so little in addition to their room and board at the Wenzels' but she held her tongue, seeing his obvious joy in being able to buy her a ring.

He smiled as he placed the golden carved and engraved band on her finger, saying, "Now, me darlin', they'll no more be doubtin' ye be married."

She looked at him in surprise, "How did you find out?"

"Aye, and how could I not be findin' out? Your name be on the lips of every man leavin' his horse in my care."

She put her arm through his and held him close, looking at the ring, twisting it to see the hands, hearts, and flowers so intricately worked around it. "It's beautiful."

Pittsburgh was a busy town as jumping-off place into the wilderness, and Ross and Abigail always ended up walking along the river to watch the many boats being built to carry the increasing tide of people and supplies constantly going downriver. They discussed the possibility of having to go downriver themselves, but Abigail would hesitate, saying, "Not so long as there is no need to. I've had enough wilderness travel. Couldn't we settle here?"

A little uncertainly, Ross replied, "Aye. I can be lookin' for a place if ye want to. The land be rich here. A farmer could do well."

But Abigail knew he was not certain yet of their safety and she did not insist. For the time being they were happy with the Wenzels and now that they both were working full time, they would be able to put away more money for the farm Ross dreamed of. She almost felt guilty about the ring, knowing how dearly Ross wanted a farm, but they would save more.

They returned from just one such walk when all the fears Ross had been trying to repress came quickly back to them. The laughter on their lips vanished when Herr Wenzel called them anxiously into the stable.

"Herr Ross, I think I have bad news. There vas a man here today looking for two people. The father of the voman he looks for gives big reward for her return. I think this man look for you, *ja?*"

Ross paled visibly. "Aye. I suppose he is. Did ye be tellin' him we be here?"

"*Nein*. The voman they look for vas taken against her vill. How could such a voman be as happy as this one if she vas taken against her vill? Vat you think you should do?"

"I don't know, Herr Wenzel. I suppose we be havin' only one choice, now, and that be downriver."

"*Ja*. Dat's vat I figure. You take your vife to your room now and stay there. Gus take care of things for you but he not like it. You and your pretty vife goot here."

Ross smiled. "Thank ye. Ye don't know how much we be appreciatin' your help."

Herr Wenzel held out his hand and Ross took it warmly. "Don't need thanks from goot man. You go now before someone sees you here."

For two days they stayed in their attic room with the Wenzels bringing them their meals and Frau Wenzel and Helga nearly crying each time thinking each meal would be their last with them. When Herr Wenzel roused them early one morning they knew the time had come to leave. With food and bedding they huddled together in the back of the Wenzel wagon, covered by canvas. To anyone about at that early hour it was just Herr Wenzel going after a load of coal for his inn, only this morning the wagon went along the river where the boats were waiting to cast off downriver.

The wagon stopped by one of the waiting flatboats and the driver quickly climbed down and turned back the canvas to let his passengers out.

"Quickly, now, before you are seen."

Hurriedly, they gathered up their few possessions, already more than doubled with the things the Wenzels had provided, and quickly they followed Herr Wenzel onto one of the large, rectangular flatboats straining at its ropes to be off downriver with its load of people and livestock.

They were met by a tall, thin man. "Herr Claypool, this is Herr Ross and his vife. They go downriver vith you."

Claypool stretched a laconic hand toward Ross. "Howdy."

Abigail wasn't sure she liked the man and her feelings became even more certain as the rest of the Claypool family began to gather about them.

With a quick, regretful handshake, Gustav Wenzel said, "Vell, I leave now. Good luck and take care."

Abigail took his hand and said with a catch in her voice, "Thank you for everything."

He waved away her thanks and with quick steps retreated to shore and his wagon.

All the Claypools were gathered around them now and Abigail could see there were two families of them as introductions were made. The elder Claypool brother was Horace, his wife, Elvira, and their three boys, the oldest one Abigail's age. He looked at Abigail with such undisguised interest that she blushed. The younger Claypool was Clifton, his wife, Bertie, and four younger boys and girls.

Abigail, feeling all eyes on her, said, trying to mask her confusion, "Thank you so much for letting us go with you."

Elvira Claypool smiled patronizingly back at her. "No need to thank us, Mrs. Ross, extra hands are always helpful."

Ross interrupted the uncertain silence with, "If it please ye, Mr. Claypool, we'd be puttin' our things where ye be wantin' us, now."

Claypool motioned Ross to follow and they gathered up their things with the rest of the Claypools standing and staring at them without any offer to help. Abigail hid her anger and embarrassment behind a load of blankets and followed the lanky elder Claypool to what was, to Abigail's further chagrin, the livestock shelter. The large shed near the front of the big flatboat was for the Claypools. A corral of sorts with an open shed housing horses, cows, and an assortment of chickens, pigs, and goats took up the larger portion of the boat. Claypool escorted them to the back of the animal shelter where the feed was stored and said, "This'll be a good bed. We're shovin' off, so's soon as you get your things settled we'll be needin' you to pole."

He turned on his heel and left them standing. Abigail was livid with anger. "Who does he think we are?"

Ross put his arms around her. "Abbie, Abbie, me darlin'. Don't be upset, now. 'Tis the only way, now, we can be makin' it. Herr Wenzel did the best he could for us."

"I know that. And I'll bet he paid them, too, but they're treating you like a hired man and I don't like it."

"Sure now, they have every right to our help."

"Of course they do, but don't demean yourself so, Ross. You don't have to be beholden to them."

There was anger in his eyes when he retorted, "I don't be demeanin' myself. 'Tis the way we Irish be gettin' by. Ye'd best be learnin' that, Abbie."

She bit her lip and pressed herself against him. "I'm sorry, Ross. To me you're not an Irishman or any other man. You're my man and I love you and I won't have you belittled in my eyes."

His voice was softer when he said, "It'll be all right, now, Abbie. We won't be havin' to put up with them for too long. I don't think we'll be needin' to go farther than Louisville to be safe."

6

DOWN THE OHIO

Abigail soon found out what Mrs. Claypool meant by helping hands. They were barely in the current when her duties began. She hardly had time to take in the beauty of the passing landscape, glimpsing only briefly the farms along the cultivated river bottom and a lovely island home just below Pittsburgh. While the men guided the boat around the island and through the rapids at McKee's Rocks, Abigail peeled potatoes in preparation of the next meal. Her days at Wenzels' had given her much needed experience at feeding a group of people and the poise to handle any task given her. In moments of bitterness she wished she knew nothing, but it was a quirk of fate that the Claypools recognized good breeding when they saw it and as soon as she let it slip that she had taught school she had another job added to her regimen.

To the happy-go-lucky Claypool women the trip was an adventure equal to a picnic on a Sunday afternoon. And why not? With Abigail doing the greatest share of the work, they had plenty of time to enjoy the scenery and be lazy, as Abigail had imagined they were from the very first day. She hated her slavery, as she began to think of it, more with each day, and could only look with despair at what lay ahead of her and regret the folly of defying her family to marry Ross. She wondered how she would survive, not realizing that the hard work she was doing was invaluable conditioning for what she would yet go through. All bitterness and regret vanished at night when they were alone and she held Ross's tired and aching body against her own and the soft lilt of Irish phrases caressed her ears as his hands, roughened from guiding the huge boat sweeps, gently caressed her body until they slept united in love and physical exhaustion.

Every day the boat stopped to procure feed for the animals on board. Even though Abigail didn't always get the pleasure of exploring their surroundings with the Claypool women, she still enjoyed these stops. Usually they would pull close to some uninhabited island with a lush growth of grass to let the animals graze, and when the boat was cleared of all the Claypools Abigail could relax, although she always was left with some chore to do. But she took time then to look at the river and the view along it, enjoying the solitude. As the days and miles slipped by, she was surprised that there were settlements, farms, and taverns all along the river. A ferry or a floating mill near some river tributary meant civilization near by. Even more fascinating was the amount of traffic on this wilderness river. Keelboats loaded with cotton from downriver plantations would pass them poling upriver to Pittsburgh or other boats just as loaded going downriver. Nor were they the only flatboat on the river. They didn't need to see them to know by the evidence left at the places they stopped what went on ahead of them and would just as surely come behind.

On one such warm summery day the boat stopped and Abigail, feeling tireder than usual, stayed on board and went to lie down when the boat was at last quiet. She lay curled on her bed of straw in the sun with her eyes closed, hoping her sick feeling would soon pass. A shadow fell across her and she opened her eyes, smiling at the thought of Ross being able to join her. But it wasn't Ross. It was the oldest Claypool boy, and his eyes gave her reason to feel uneasy.

"Howdy, Mrs. Ross, or can I call you Abbie like your husband does?"

She sat up, feeling too vulnerable in any position before his intent eyes. "No. I think you'd better continue to call me Mrs. Ross."

"Well, all right, if you say so, if you're sure that's your name?"

She felt a growing apprehension. "Of course it's my name. What makes you think it isn't?"

He squatted down to peer at her with narrowed eyes. "I just

don't understand why a lady like you is travelin' with one of them damn weaselin' Irishmen. He got somethin' on you?"

"Of course not." Her voice was sharp. "I think you'd better leave now."

He stood and grinned down at her. "I will for now. But I'll be back when you ain't bein' womanly." He leaned over her in an insinuating way and whispered, "Howsomeever it's encouragin' to know you ain't pregnant."

She jerked her head away from him feeling the rush of blood to her face as she tried to control her anger and embarrassment, thankful he had misread her condition. He chuckled and left her alone. When her anger subsided she wondered just what her condition was, with more than a little anxiety. She only hoped Ross hadn't seen him bothering her. She knew too well his temper was just as devastating as his smile.

Later in the day they passed a floating merchandiser and, true to Claypool fashion, they had to turn the cumbersome flatboat out of the current and investigate this latest river oddity. Even Abigail was infected by this newest adventure and, as intrigued as the Claypools, had to explore the floating store. Ross bought her a length of ribbon for her hair and she was as thrilled as any girl. Supplies were purchased even though they had only the day before stopped at the last large settlement.

The climate was warmer and the mosquitoes were beginning to be bothersome but still the beauty and ever changing hills and forests as the river carried them slowly southward never failed to lift Abigail's spirits when she had the chance to enjoy it. She decided it was safer to go with the Claypools when they grazed their stock and gathered feed on the islands and bottoms along the river. She would start out with the women and children and when out of sight of the men she would find a way to be by herself to sit and watch the river. One day she found a patch of wild strawberries and was gathering her apron full when the Claypool boy found her.

"Well, there you be, Mrs. Ross. You couldn't be tryin' to avoid me, could you?"

She glared at him and frankly stated, "Yes, Mr. Claypool. And I want to keep it that way."

"My name is Elton, Abbie. I don't know why you want to avoid me. I'll be awful nice to you. Nicer'n that Irish papist."

"The man is my husband and I warn you not to anger him."

He moved toward her and she backed away but he grabbed her

wrist and the berries rolled from her apron. "I can take care of him
and I can take care of you, too, green eyes."

"If you don't let go of me, I'll scream."

He dropped her arm and looked at her in amusement. "Not if I
don't want you to, you won't. You see I've got an idea you two are
runnin' from something and when I find out what it is, you'll be
beggin' me to take care of you."

"You're wrong, Mr. Claypool, if you think we're not married."

"Prove it then by showin' me your marriage paper."

Before she thought she retorted, "Ask my husband to show it to
you."

He grinned in triumph and said, "I'll let you get back to your
berry pickin' now, Abbie. I'll be around to take care of you later
and, besides, I sure don't want to miss strawberry shortcake for
supper."

She looked after him in dismay, hearing his licentious laughter
and seeing the lustful eyes in her mind as she realized she'd let him
know there was a paper with them he could get information from.
She knew he wouldn't stop until he found it and she was torn with
indecision whether to tell Ross or not.

Ross came after her in a short while and she was still kneeling on
the ground picking the plump, juicy berries.

"Aye, 'tis a pretty sight ye be, me darlin' Abbie."

He kneeled beside her and lifted her chin in his hand when she
didn't smile at him. "Sure, now, what be troublin' ye?"

She mustered a smile. "Nothing. I just hate to go back to that
boat with those awful people."

He grinned at her. "Would ye rather be stayin' here and be
makin' love to me?"

That brought a genuine smile to her lips. "Oh, Ross!" She
giggled. "You know we can't do that."

He kissed her and breathed against her responding lips, "And
who be sayin' we can't?"

The berries rolled from her apron again as he took her in his
arms and lifted her away from the fragile berries to a secluded
thicket nearby.

The Claypools were on board and waiting for them when they
got back and only for the fact that Abigail had an apron full of
strawberries were they forgiven for being late.

Until they stopped again Abigail watched their belongings carefully, and when she could do so without Ross's suspicion, she
searched for their marriage contract. She knew Ross didn't carry it

on him. There was too much chance of its getting soiled or wet. When she found it she was faced with the problem of where to conceal it on herself. Ross would feel it if she should pin it to her underclothes. She finally chose to sew it into her cloak collar and quickly pulled loose the stitching and inserted the paper. Relief swept away her fears once the paper was hidden, and she went about her work more calmly.

The days turned to weeks and they finally reached Kentucky. Abigail grew more tense as the days passed, waiting for Elton Claypool to accost her again. She tried to stay on the boat as much as possible without Ross's becoming suspicious so no one could search their things, but once in a while she had no other choice than to go with Ross. At the last large settlement of Gallipolis they'd all gone ashore for supplies, but mostly she was contented to watch the brilliant parakeets that filled the forests or listen to the redbirds that sang so beautifully or gaze with wonder at the cotton fields in the clearings along the river.

They stopped at the renowned Salt Licks and all went ashore to see the salt works and purchase much needed salt. Abigail could only imagine the great herds of buffalo that had once passed through the area by the wide trace left from the now vanished herds.

Below Maysville the river was cleared of dangerous obstructions like the ones that had plagued them on the upper river and they sailed on without the delays of working the heavy flatboat off bobbing sawyers and submerged trees. Abigail grew more hopeful each day that they would reach Louisville without Elton Claypool's bothering her again, but she was wrong. They stopped to let the livestock graze in a lush bottom along the river. The Claypool women took their buckets to pick berries and Abigail was left to wash clothes for the whole family. It was very hot and still as she sweated over the tubs of water scrubbing the clothes on a washboard which was little better than a rock.

From out of the south a threatening black cloud came swiftly and silently across the Kentucky hills and without warning the sun was blotted out and the sky filled with lightning and thunder. The men frantically were trying to get the animals back on board when the first steamy drops of rain fell, but two of the horses bolted and they all went in chase. Abigail sought shelter in her bed and watched as lightning lashed at the hilltops and the rain drummed the roof over her head.

Elton Claypool found her before she knew he was there. He

squatted down in front of her, the rain plastering his long brown hair against his narrow face. "Thought I'd forgot about you, didn't you? Well, I ain't. Now just where did you hide that paper, Abbie? I know you hid it on me."

"You have no right to search our things or to see anything belonging to us, Mr. Claypool."

"All right, I'll give you a choice, Abbie. You produce that paper or I'll start tearin' the clothes right off you."

She started to get up but he caught her and held her. She screamed but the thunder drowned out her screams and his mouth came down hard on hers as he pinned her down with his body and started to tear her dress. She felt the wild power in him and knew she couldn't fight him.

When he released her mouth she gasped, "All right! I'll show you."

"Where?" he demanded hoarsely.

"In my cloak. I sewed it into the collar."

He shifted his weight from her but not before his mouth and hands bruised her again and his eyes told her she was only buying time and nothing more. He ripped the collar of her cloak and unfolded the paper still keeping a hand on her wrist. When his eyes left her to glance at the paper she sank her teeth into his arm and jerked free of his hold, rolling to her feet. He grabbed for her dress, swearing obscenely. She felt her skirt caught in his grasp and lunged to free herself and fell against Ross as he came around the corner of the shed. Instantly he was on her attacker with the fury of a wild man. She hid her face as his powerful fist smashed the lustful look from Elton's face. The younger man was tough and wiry enough to withstand the blow and even as he fell he kicked at Ross. Ross, with the ease of a man skilled at handling cumbersome weights, grabbed the thrusting legs and heaved the lighter man over the side of the flatboat just as the Claypools arrived to witness the fight.

"What the hell's going on here?"

Mrs. Claypool screamed from the bank, "Oh my God! Somebody save him! He can't swim!"

Quickly they raced to extend a pole to the thrashing boy. Abigail looked wildly for the paper and found it as Ross turned to see if she was all right.

His face was still tight with anger when he asked, "Did he hurt ye, Abbie?"

"No, no. I'm all right. Hadn't you better help them get him?"

He looked in the direction of the struggling Elton as they hauled him back onto the flatboat, his face still dark. " 'Twould be better if he drowned."

As soon as Elton was judged unhurt, except for the bruises he'd received, the Claypools surrounded Ross and Abigail.

"You'd better explain why you threw my boy into the river, Mr. Ross."

"You can be lookin' at me wife and be answerin' your own question, Mr. Claypool."

Elton coughed, spat out some water, and choked. "It was her fault, Paw. Look at her! Can't you see what a hot little bitch she is?"

Ross was on the boy before anyone could stop him. It took the four older Claypools to pull him off, with Abigail pleading for him to stop. They all looked at Abigail accusingly.

"You know that isn't true. All of you! Better than I, you know what kind of a man he is and you know in your hearts what I say is the truth."

"Maybe you'd better tell us the truth then, Mrs. Ross."

"All right, if you must hear it. He has been bothering me. I have refused his advances. He has been trying to find out if Mr. Ross and I are really married in order to blackmail me into submitting to him and today while you were chasing the horses, he came back and threatened me if I didn't show him our marriage certificate. I was trying to get away from him when my husband came to my rescue."

Horace Claypool studied his son thoughtfully and Abigail felt he knew all too well she was telling the truth. But Clifton Claypool, grasping more of the situation than his older brother and seeing the possibility of some advantage, asked, "Maybe we'd just better see that paper, *Mrs. Ross.*"

Abigail didn't like the way he emphasized the "Mrs. Ross" but she saw no other choice than to let him see the paper. She reluctantly took it from her pocket and handed it to Mrs. Claypool. She and her sister-in-law looked it over carefully and Elvira commented, "They's married all right but their name ain't Ross, it's Galligher. Now why do you suppose they didn't tell us their right name?"

Seeing they clearly had the advantage, they released Ross and Horace asked, "What you got to say to that, Galligher?"

Ross, still angry, said hotly, "I say it be none of your damned business, Mr. Claypool."

"Could be, unless you're wanted back where you came from.

We'll sure as hell find out at the next settlement and guess you can just plan on sittin' tight 'til then. Elvira, you and Bertie keep the woman with you and we'll watch him. I figure we can't be too far from the next settlement. We'll keep goin' 'til we get there and then we'll find the truth to this."

7

C A P T U R E

They reached Cincinnati late the next afternoon. Abigail had not been allowed to speak with Ross and she was exhausted and feeling even sicker than usual from worrying about what would happen to them if word of a reward for her return had reached this far into the wilderness. A lesser worry was how she could explain to Ross why she had kept silent about Elton's advances. Like criminals, they were herded up the double-stepped bank into the large, orderly-looking settlement. They soon found the town constable in his office and Claypool told his side of the story.

Ross looked grim during the telling and as soon as Claypool finished he asked, "Now be ye listenin' to me side of the story, sir?"

A little skeptically the constable agreed with, "I reckon that's only fair. Speak your piece."

"The reason we be leavin' Pittsburgh and the reason I be not tellin' these people me real name is me wife's father. He didn't want us to be married. He took her from me once before and was keepin' her prisoner for near six months before we could get away. He's the only man that be lookin' for us, I swear on the Virgin Mary. All we be askin' from the Claypools is our belongings and we'll be goin' our own way, without pressin' charges against their boy for molestin' me wife."

The constable looked a little more interested and turned

thoughtfully from one to the other, finally resting his gaze on Abigail. "What do you have to say about it, little lady?"

"My husband speaks the truth."

Claypool asked impatiently, "Ain't you even goin' to check your wanteds?"

The man opened a drawer of his desk resignedly and said, "Check 'em yourself. I been through 'em enough times to know I ain't got one for these people."

Abigail felt weak-kneed at the statement and looked quickly at Ross. The tense lines of his face softened and she could see his whole body relax. The Claypools looked disappointed but they were not done yet.

"Well, they may not be wanted but they owe us passage money and I reckon we'll just have to keep their things in payment."

If Abigail hadn't grabbed Ross when she did she knew he would have floored Horace Claypool right in front of the constable. The constable didn't miss the flair of anger and asked Abigail, "Is that true, Mrs. Galligher?"

"I really don't know. Herr Wenzel of Pittsburgh arranged for our passage. I'm sure he must have paid for us and even if he didn't, we have both earned our way by working for them the whole trip. You can't let them put us off without what belongs to us. It's only our clothes and a few blankets, but it's all we have."

Mrs. Claypool sniffed disdainfully.

The constable turned to her and asked, "You got something to say, ma'am?"

"Well, just that she may a called it work where *she* comes from, but you can tell she ain't done much work in her life."

Abigail had to tug on Ross's arm to keep him from raising his hand against Mrs. Claypool. The woman stepped back quickly before the anger in his eyes. His voice shook as he denied her statement. "The woman be a liar! They all be liars and a pack of thieves at that, now." He thrust Abigail's work-roughened hands under the constable's nose. "Do these look like the hands of a woman that be doin' no work at all?" He spread his own strong, lean hands before the man, displaying calluses and peeling blisters from handling the sweeps and poles. "Do me own hands look soft, now, man? Mother of God! Can't ye be seein' they be lyin'?"

The constable stood up and hitched up his belt decisively. "Well, it's plain to see you haven't exactly been idle. Mr. Claypool, I think you'd better turn this couple's things over to me. I'll send my deputy back to your boat to get them."

The Claypools, finally left with no other choice, left quietly. The constable sat back down and motioned Ross and Abigail into chairs. "Where were you bound for, Galligher?"

"Louisville."

"Well, that's not too far to go. You got a trade?"

"Aye. I be figurin' to farm but I was raised on the docks of New York."

"Wouldn't be too hard for you to stay here. They could use a good man on the dock that knows something about ship loading."

"We be appreciatin' the offer, but we heard Louisville be the big shipping port."

"That's true, for the time being, but we'll catch up. How you plan on gettin' there?"

"We'll be walkin' now. We don't be havin' much money."

"I wouldn't advise walkin'. The Indians are getting a little troublesome and they might run across you walkin'. I could maybe get you on another boat."

Ross shook his head stubbornly. "I'd rather be walkin' than get in the Claypools' path again. Sure now, I be hopin' they'd be well past Louisville when we get there."

The deputy came in with their belongings and the constable had them make sure they had everything. When Abigail was satisfied everything was there, they thanked the constable for his help and went to the inn he had told them would put them up and feed them for the best price.

They ate their meal quietly, Abigail afraid to say anything that would arouse Ross's temper in public. His eyes searched hers questioningly, as if trying to discover the answers without asking, but she looked away, trying to put him off until they were alone.

No sooner had the door shut on their room than he asked, "Why didn't ye be tellin' me, now, that cur be botherin' ye?"

She sat down on the bed in weariness. "You know why, Ross. You would've lost your temper."

Impatiently he came and sat beside her. "Damn right I'd be losin' me temper. If I'd been knowin' all I know now, I'd be hittin' him a damn sight harder than I did the dirty—"

Abigail put her fingers to his lips to stop the expletive and he closed his mouth and took her hand in his and kissed it. "Sorry, Abbie. But the thought of another man touchin' ye makes me blood be boilin'. I still can't get over their lyin' and the way they was usin' us."

She felt the anger building in him again and put her arms

around him and pulled him down on the bed beside her. "It's all over now. We're safe and we're not wanted here. Let's not spoil what few hours we have by even thinking of those dreadful people again."

He smiled at her and bent to kiss her neck and whispered, "Aye, ye be right. Tomorrow we won't be havin' a bed." His mouth covered hers and all worries were lost in the warmth of his embrace.

Unwillingly, they left the clean, comfortable bed well past sunup. Leisurely they enjoyed a large breakfast and, with directions and warnings fresh in their minds, they took the westward road out of Cincinnati. The walk was a delightful change from the labor of the flatboat, and they were enjoying the countryside and warm summer morning. Everyone they passed spoke to them and wished them well on their journey, and all thoughts of danger were quickly forgotten.

They came to a large river late in the day and were ferried across by a disgruntled ferryman who charged them double because they declined to stay in his untidy tavern even though Abigail was long since willing to stop. But one look at the crowded and noisy tavern was enough to give her strength to go on. They came to another, smaller river near dark and knew they could go no farther until the next day. They went upriver a short distance and found a small grassy campsite next to the river and quickly spread out their blankets in the last fading light and sat exhausted watching the sky grow dark through a canopy of trees. Stars came out while they ate buscuits and berries gathered along the way. Abigail was asleep the minute she lay down and didn't wake until morning.

When she did awake, Ross was already cooking something over the fire he'd built, and the smell was filling her with a voracious appetite in spite of the slight queasiness she had grown used to. She wasted no time getting up and taking care of her early morning necessities. She was washing her face in the river when she heard a sound slightly different from the rhythm of the river. She looked up, her eyes widening with fear as a number of canoes filled with Indians paddled toward her under the overhanging shadows of the trees. They saw her at the same moment she saw them and the first Indian pointed her out without missing a stroke with his paddle. Abigail rose, white-faced and trembling, and scrambled through the brush lining the river to warn Ross.

Instantly he saw her fear and set down the pan of bacon and eggs as the first Indians landed their canoe and broke through the

thicket and into their midst, a fresh scalp hanging from the waist of
the leader. Ross was not to be taken easily and reached for the hot
frying pan and hurled it, the hot grease and food splattering the
nearest Indians. Abigail would have screamed but a foul-smelling
hand closed over her mouth and she was roughly imprisoned in a
strong grip. Ross was on his feet and fighting furiously, the
strength of his blows staggering more than one of their attackers.
He was quickly subdued by several Indians and Abigail couldn't see
what happened to him. She was bound and gagged and was carried
to the canoes fighting as best she could to little avail. She saw with
some small relief, before she was shoved into the bottom of a canoe,
that they hadn't killed Ross and were carrying him, unconscious, to
another canoe.

Long hours later they stopped in the shroud of darkness and
made camp of sorts. Ross and Abigail were tied to trees several
yards apart from each other and she couldn't see how badly he was
hurt. The Indians ate hungrily of whatever they had with them and
then removed Ross's gag and offered him some food. He ate what
they gave him and when he was finished they replaced his gag and
came to Abigail and removed her gag. She was terribly hungry but
the smell of their food turned her stomach and she turned her
head away. The gag was replaced and she was left alone. Soon the
Indians lay down to sleep, leaving two of their number as sentries.

In the morning they again offered Ross food and water and he
doggedly ate what they offered, even though his expression clearly
told Abigail he was having difficulty doing so. When it was her turn
she drank the water but the sight of the food they offered was even
more revolting in daylight. She refused it again and the Indians
said something to each other and laughed. Too late it occurred to
her that she should try to eat. She would need strength if there was
any chance of escape. She vowed she would eat no matter what the
next time food was offered.

It was night before they stopped again. Abigail was so hungry
she didn't need to force herself to eat, but the unfamiliar food
didn't agree with her and she spent a miserable night. When
morning came and more food was offered she had to force herself
to eat the greasy substance and promptly vomited. Her captors
laughed and without further hesitation dragged her and Ross off
to their canoes.

They paddled for only part of the day and stopped. Abigail's
fear redoubled as she wondered what this midday stop meant, but
they only hid their canoes and in a few minutes they had retied her

and Ross and set off at a fast pace into the woods. Abigail was so weak from hunger she could not keep up after the first few hundred yards and fell. The rope around her neck bruised her as her captor yanked on it in impatience. There was a commotion behind her and she looked quickly while struggling to her feet and saw Ross being beaten viciously. The rope tightened on her neck in a hard yank and she was almost pulled off her feet again before she could regain her balance and trot breathlessly after her leader.

In a short time she fell again and this time a stick was laid across her shoulders. She heard an echoing thud behind her and knew Ross's temper was causing him to be beaten, too. Valiantly she tried to keep her feet, not only to save herself but to save Ross, too. But it was impossible. The branches whipped her face and tore her dress and finally tore the gag from her mouth, but she was oblivious to that until she collapsed again and felt the bruising blows of the stick across her back. Her will to resist vanished when a violent pain began in her lower body and ravaged upward. When it passed she heard but did not feel the blows and wearily opened her eyes. Her captor stood above her looking at the men behind him. Abigail raised until she could see what he was seeing and cried out, "Ross! Ross! Don't fight them! I'm all right." She hardly recognized the bruised and bloody face of her husband as they subdued him.

The rope yanked her up and with a great effort she got to her feet and stumbled after the Indian again, feeling a strange heaviness in her and a liquid warmth slide down her legs. In the first lucid thoughts she had had for hours she knew what was happening. She was long overdue and she was miscarrying.

What was happening to her soon became obvious to the Indians behind her, and one of them called to the Indian leading her and the procession stopped. Quickly they assessed the situation and for reasons unknown to Abigail they untied Ross, except for the rope leading him, and with gestures and threats they let him come to her.

He tore the gag from his mouth and sobbed, "Mother of God! Abbie! Oh, Abbie. Why didn't ye be tellin' me?" A reminding yank on his neck cut off his words but not the tears blurring his eyes as he picked her up. The leader spoke harshly to them and wrapped the rope around his hand in warning. Immediately Ross moved forward and the leader turned and set off once more at a slightly slower pace.

Within an hour they reached the Indian village. Abigail was in no condition to take in her surroundings thoroughly, but she was

aware there were at least two dozen huts arranged in a small
clearing among the trees, and it seemed everyone was crowding
around to see the returning warriors and their captives. The leader
spoke and the men immediately backed away and two older women
came forward. The leader motioned that Abigail was to go with the
women and Ross reluctantly let her down and she clung to him,
knees weak and feeling dizzy.

Ross protested, "She's sick. She needs to be taken care of. If ye
have any mercy at all, ye'll be lettin' me take care of her."

His answer was a sharp yank on his rope pulling him away from
Abigail. The two Indian women took hold of her and, both speaking at once, they dragged her away, through the crowd to a hut
smaller than the others. Willingly she collapsed on a woven mat
and let the women work on her. She was beyond caring what they
did and only hoped she would die quickly.

Somehow the women kept her alive and even induced her to
eat. She got used to the thin, greasy soup and the cornmeal mush
they brought her, and in a few days her bleeding stopped and the
women pulled her from the hut and led her between the larger
structures until she stopped, a cry of disbelief escaping her throat.
The nearly unrecognizable figure slumped against a stake in the
middle of a hard-packed area looked up at her cry and moaned her
name through swollen and bruised lips. She was dragged roughly
to the other stout stake a few yards away and likewise tied by the
neck with enough slack to enable her to sit or lie down, but her
hands were tied behind her. As terrible as the sight of him was,
Abigail couldn't take her eyes off Ross. He'd been beaten and
tortured until he was a mass of bruises, welts, and oozing cuts. His
hands and feet were particularly gruesome, with every nail torn
away.

"Ross! Ross! What have they done to you?"

When the question was hardly finished she knew. A stick was
brought down on her shoulders for daring to speak and she
opened her mouth to protest, but Ross shook his head to silence
her. In a barely audible whisper he cautioned, "Don't speak. It only
gives them an excuse to be beatin' ye."

And beaten he was for his warning. Abigail couldn't watch and
closed her eyes and turned away, a terrible dread choking her.

For the rest of the day the women and children of the village
brought wood in and stacked it near and around them, taunting
and tormenting Abigail in fiendish delight—thrusting snakes at
her or placing spiders in her hair. At nightfall the nightmare of

torture came to a stop and even their guard left them to go to his hut. For the first time since she had been brought to the stake, Abigail turned so she could see Ross. He was sitting slumped against the stake as she had first seen him and she eased herself toward him as far as the rope around her neck would permit.

Softly she called, "Ross, Ross."

His head raised slowly and he looked around intently before he crawled toward her. "Abbie, darlin'. Are ye all right, now?" His voice was almost unintelligible.

"Yes. Oh, Ross, I can't believe this is happening to us. Do you think they're going to burn us?"

"Aye." He paused and his body shook with anguish. "Mother of God, what a fool I be for bringin' ye out here. I prayed ye'd die, Abbie, and not have to be goin' through this." His voice broke momentarily and he fought to control his emotions before he said, "If God be willin' to forgive me sins and be savin' us, I will take ye back, Abbie. I be a fool and a selfish one at that, to think we could be escapin' your father and God, too. Can ye forgive me now, Abbie?"

"Ross, don't blame yourself. No matter what happens, I love you and I want to be with you, not with my father."

Before they could say more they saw another guard coming toward them, and Ross crawled away from her and Abigail crept back to her stake, afraid and hungry. But the hunger didn't last long. The guard brought food and untied Ross and when he had eaten the guard came to her. She couldn't imagine why they would feed her if they planned on killing her. Her hopes rose and the renewed hope allowed her to sleep.

In the morning they were fed again and Abigail wanted to encourage Ross with her interpretation of the Indians' consideration of them, but she didn't dare with so many of the Indians gathering around. Their presence and the fact that they were arming themselves with clubs and knives began to contradict her high hopes. Her hopes were completely discarded when they untied Ross and led him to the head of a double line of cheering Indians. She felt sick and cried out in horror as they pushed him between the two lines of weapon-wielding Indians. How he found the strength to run she didn't know, but somehow he managed to, staggered and reeling at times from the blows rained upon his bare body. He managed to escape a few blows but dozens fell upon him, and Abigail had to turn away before he was near the end of the row of yelling savages. When the yelling stopped she mustered courage to look again and saw Ross on the ground, bleeding and battered but still alive. The Indians were pouring water on him and, when he was able, they once more slipped the noose over his head and led him back to his stake. He was mumbling something in a pleading, desperate voice and though she couldn't understand what he was saying through the laughter and jeers of the Indians, a cold dread began to fill her. When they left Ross and turned to her she knew what he had been pleading for.

A sudden shout from outside the crowd silenced them. Abigail saw a runner come in and the chief of the village arose from his place of honor overlooking the scene and listened intently to the Indian's news. The chief in turn dispersed the crowd and, with a look of apprehension apparent on his face, walked toward the place where the trail entered the village.

In a few minutes a dozen more Indians appeared and greetings were exchanged. Even from a distance Abigail could sense an air of authority about the man the chief was escorting into the village. The chief seemed nervous and acted as if he was trying to keep the visitor from noticing the two captives in their midst, but their presence was not easy to hide and the visiting Indian saw them and stopped. He questioned the chief and moved closer, giving Abigail a better chance to see the visitor and his party. The rest of the men looked like Indians but the man stopping a few yards away appeared vastly different. In spite of the muggy summer heat, he was entirely clothed in a plain, belted buckskin shirt falling to his knees. He wore leggings and moccasins and had a woolen turban on his dark hair. Even his skin and eyes were lighter than those of the Indians with him, and her heart beat with renewed hope. She strained at her rope to get as close to him as possible and pleaded, "Please help us."

The guard picked up a nearby stick and stepped in to beat her, but the man stopped him with a word, and no one questioned his authority. Abigail looked beseechingly at this one and perhaps only chance to escape certain death, but he turned away from them without another word and moved away with the rest of the Indians following, leaving Abigail and Ross alone.

The Indians stayed inside the chief's lodge for hours and Abigail watched first Ross and then the chief's lodge with nearly unbearable anxiety. Ross lay as he had lain since the beating and had neither spoken nor looked at her. If it hadn't been for the slight rise and fall of his ribs she would have thought him dead. The sultry heat was draining the moisture from her body and she was desperate for a drink and knew Ross must be even more desperate. Her heart ached to tend him and bathe his battered body.

Near evening she heard the village sentinels call again and she struggled to her feet to see better. A runner came in and went straight to the chief's hut. In a matter of moments all the Indians filed out of the lodge and stood waiting in silence for the new arrival. He came between the outer huts in a few minutes and Abigail's breath caught in her throat. Truly God had answered Ross's prayers and hers, too. The man coming into the village was a priest.

Abigail called to Ross, "Ross! Ross! Oh, Ross, please wake up. A priest has come."

Slowly, Ross's blood-encrusted head rose from the ground and his eyes found the black-robed figure coming toward them. He struggled to his knees and made the sign of the cross with his head and in a tortured voice cried, "Father! Father!"

The priest heard Ross's anguished cries and, ignoring the Indians waiting for him, came to Ross. A gentle hand rested on Ross's head and Ross said something in a language Abigail couldn't understand. The priest made the sign of the cross over his head and held the crucifix to Ross's lips. Abigail was still on her feet and the priest looked at her and said something in what she was sure was French but she still didn't understand and shook her head.

Ross spoke again and Abigail heard tearful anguish in his voice. "Father, I have sinned. Be hearin' me confession."

The priest shook his head sadly and said something in French, made the sign of the cross again, and turned away. The look on Ross's face was too pain-wracked for Abigail to bear. She kept her eyes on the priest and watched him greet the Indians. They eventually went inside the chief's dwelling again and Abigail kept watching the hut and hoping, paying little attention to the increased activity going on about her.

Total darkness came and the cooking fires were lit and what amounted to a feast was prepared. Even Abigail and Ross were treated to a choice of fully cooked meats and plenty of water and fresh fruits. The dancing and singing in honor of the guests lasted half the night and even when things were relatively quiet Abigail couldn't sleep. All night she watched the flicker of the fire and the silhouettes inside the chief's lodge as the Indians and the priest talked.

In the morning Abigail could feel the whole mood of the camp was different. There was a hurry in the morning's activities and she

was filled with expectation. Ross was strong enough to be aware of
what was going on and his swollen eyes watched the chief's lodge
along with hers. When the Indians finally came out of the chief's
lodge Abigail stood in anticipation. The visiting dignitary and the
priest came toward them, along with the village chief. Abigail and
Ross were cut loose and Ross immediately rose to his knees in front
of the priest and kissed the ring on the priest's hand. The priest
helped him up and kept a hand under Ross's elbow and motioned
Abigail to help. She passed the slender, regal figure of the other
man and paused momentarily to look into his attentive face.

Softly she said, "Thank you."

The hazel eyes softened briefly and a quick smile lighted his
face. She was sure he understood her but he said nothing and she
turned to help Ross dress. The priest said something in French to
the Indians, and with Ross between them they made their way out
of the village. Abigail and Ross were full of questions, but the priest
would only shake his head and answer them in French. He offered
them some food the first time he stopped to let Ross rest and
Abigail hoped he would make camp until Ross was stronger, but
the priest urged them on.

They made the river by nightfall and still the priest wouldn't let
them rest. He found the hidden Indian canoes and by motioning to
them with the paddles they understood he meant to go downriver
in the dark. They got into the canoe and Abigail fully intended to
try paddling the long craft with the priest, but Ross took the
paddle, saying, "I be all right now, Abbie. Ye lay down, now, and be
gettin' some sleep. Too soon ye'll be gettin' your turn at it."

She started to protest but the priest touched them and held his
finger to his lips and she did as Ross wanted and curled up in the
bottom of the canoe. But she slept only fitfully and finally Ross let
her paddle when he was too exhausted to keep his balance.

Morning found them many miles downstream, and when a
good-sized stream entered the river, the priest pointed to it, turned
the canoe into the smaller waterway, and beached the craft in a
secluded spot. They ate again from the small pack of food the
priest carried, after he had blessed it, and then he motioned for
Abigail and Ross to rest and he kneeled to pray. Ross kneeled with
him and repeated some of the prayers the priest recited until the
priest indicated he wanted Ross to rest again. Ross lay down next to
her and took her hand in his and held it against his bruised lips.
Before she could say anything he was asleep.

It was afternoon when they awoke and Abigail sat up with a

start, dreaming they had been abandoned, but the priest was still there, kneeling as he had been kneeling when they had gone to sleep. He smiled at Abigail when he finished his prayer and in a soft voice asked her something in French. She shook her head and he shrugged and pointed to the food. Ross awoke, too, and the three of them ate and the priest prepared to leave.

Ross didn't move and when the priest motioned to him Ross shook his head. "Father, please be tryin' to understand me now. I can't be goin' any farther without ye performin' absolution for me. Do ye be understandin', Father?"

The priest shook his head, his gray eyes seemingly perplexed. Ross was determined and tried to show the priest by pointing to Abigail's ring and to Abigail and then to himself that they were married but Abigail was not Catholic and their marriage was not legal in the eyes of the church. The performance was both amusing and pathetic. Abigail had not realized how much Ross's faith had meant to him nor the terrible burden of sin he felt from marrying her without church sanction. When it seemed the priest understood all Ross was trying to tell him, he took from his pack the few vestments of the church he carried, and in a secluded glen on a river unknown to them, in an unknown territory, a Catholic priest heard Ross's confession, administered communion, and married him to Abigail in the eyes of his God. When the marriage mass was over Ross turned to Abigail with tears in his eyes and kissed her, the emotion in his voice making his words almost unintelligible as he held her to him.

"Now we be truly wed, me darlin' Abbie, and I promise ye I'll be takin' ye home now."

It wrenched her heart and she held him tightly. She couldn't say anything just then. Too much of her wanted to go home. Too much of her wanted the safety of her familiar things and the easy life she didn't think she would ever know again, but even more of her didn't want to give Ross up and she knew her father would never let her live with Ross now.

The priest's insistent urgings in French broke into their embrace and they hurriedly departed their haven and were once more on the river. Ross was stronger and the large canoe sped along and they made many miles before dark fell and many more afterward, stopping around midnight to rest and sleep.

They were awakened in the morning by the priest. He handed them the packet of food and they ate after he performed the blessing and then he and Ross kneeled together and prayed. The priest sat back relaxed after their devotion and smiled at them.

"My friends, we will soon be to the Ohio and I will have to leave you. In a few more days you should reach Louisville."

Abigail and Ross exchanged startled glances. Ross was the first to recover and asked, "Sure now, Father, ye haven't been deceivin' us?"

The man smiled and nodded, "*Oui*. But, God forgive me, I couldn't let them know I understood you. But now I think we are safe."

It was Abigail's turn to ask, "You mean they followed us?"

"*Oui*. We were watched until last night, I'm sure."

Ross frowned. "I don't be seein' why. Why would they be lettin' us loose and be watchin' us?"

"Tecumseh wanted to make sure we got away safely."

Abigail asked, "Was he the man in the turban?"

"*Oui*."

"Well. I be thankin' God ye came to save us, Father. Sure now, I was not havin' much hope left."

The priest smiled again. "I'm afraid I can't take the credit for saving you. It was Tecumseh's order. I could have done little but administer last rites for you and myself, too, perhaps."

Ross looked at Abigail and paled. "It's beginnin' to make less sense the more ye say, Father. Who be this Tecumseh, now?"

"A Shawnee Indian of no little influence. He is trying to unite the Indians against the United States. If he succeeds there will be war."

"Then why did he be savin' us if he wants war?"

"Tecumseh's war is with the government of the United States. He wants to fight an army, not torture and kill captives. But I am afraid not all Indians hold the same belief."

Abigail asked, "That's something else I don't understand. Why did they feed us as if they cared about our well-being, yet they tortured Ross and I'm sure they would have me, too, if Tecumseh hadn't come?"

"*Oui*. But it is simple to comprehend when you know them. They do not wish you to die the quick death." He stood then, a small man, looking even smaller and terribly vulnerable. "Come now, my friends, we must be on our way."

They traveled downriver until nightfall and again made camp. In the morning the priest fed them and prayed with Ross before he told them, "We are near the Ohio now. I will leave you the canoe and what money I have. Use it to buy lodging at night. No more sleeping out to be captured by the Indians, eh?"

Abigail protested, "We can't take your money, Father, you have done too much for us already."

"But I insist. I have no need for the money. Always someone is willing to salve their conscience by feeding and lodging a priest."

Ross suggested, "Come with us now, Father. I would be feelin' better if I was knowin' ye be safe, too."

"Thank you, my son, but I have much work yet to do here."

"Father, surely now, ye can be savin' souls in Louisville as well as any place?"

"*Oui*, but that is not all of my work." He paused and sighed. "I have not been completely honest with you. Part of my work is to keep track of Tecumseh for my government."

Ross was visibly shaken. "Mother of God! Ye mean ye be a spy?"

"*Oui.*"

The color came back to Ross's face slowly as the two men looked at each other and Abigail saw Ross's crestfallen look change slowly into a smile, then into laughter as he shook his head in disbelief. "I knew it was too good to be true when God sent me a priest that could not understand me confession and was absolvin' me of sins he had no idea of. And now ye be tellin' me ye be not a priest at all!"

The slighter man chuckled with Ross and laid a comforting hand on his shoulder. "My son, I did not say I was not a priest. I am a priest, of that you can be sure, and I understood your confession, but because I can move freely among the Indians, the British have asked me to keep track of what is happening between the Indians and the United States. Someone is fomenting this war, and the English want to know who."

"But we have heard the English be armin' the Indians."

"*Oui*. In a sense that is true, but they arm them only to keep them self-reliant. If the Indians can not eat they can not catch the furs. It is a matter of economics. The English do not want war. The Indians can not be fighting and bringing in the furs, too."

"Then where do you go now?"

"To Vincennes and the meeting Governor Harrison has called with Tecumseh."

"Then go with God, Father."

"And you, too. But that reminds me. I have not given you your penance to do for your sins, have I?"

Ross grinned and shook his head and the priest smiled. "I will not be hard on you. Will doing a novena work a hardship on you?"

Ross smiled and bowed his head. "No, Father."

The priest stood and made the sign of the cross over Ross and Ross again kissed the ring on the priest's hand. Then the priest turned to Abigail and made the sign of the cross over her. "May God always bless you, my children." He took Ross's hand and dropped a few coins into it and pressed closed Ross's fingers and taking up his sack wished them "Bon voyage."

They watched him walk away, and when he disappeared Ross came to Abigail and put his arm around her and said, "We'd best be goin' now, Abbie. I think we can be makin' the last settlement we was in by nightfall."

"Aren't we going to Louisville?"

"No. I promised ye I'd take ye home if God'd spare us, and I be not about to break me promise now."

"But what if I don't want to go home?"

A slow smile spread over his face and he kissed her. "Well, now, I didn't be promisin' when I would take ye home, did I?"

She laughed at him and love for him filled her heart to overflowing. He picked her up and swung her into the canoe and each of them took a paddle and guided the craft into the main current.

They found their abandoned campsite and stopped to gather their belongings. The animals had scavenged what food had been in their pack and had managed to scatter their clothes and soil what they left, but they managed to find enough clothing to change into which was far more presentable than the torn and bloodstained clothing they wore. Abigail wanted to suggest they take time to bathe but the ordeal they had just suffered was too fresh to ignore the possibility that they could again fall into Indian hands. The total impact of what she had been through fully descended on Abigail when she saw the bloodstained skirt of her dress. She, who had been the tower of strength the last few days in spite of everything, suddenly felt weak-kneed and sank to the ground emitting a despairing gasp.

Ross was immediately at her side. "What is it, Abbie? Be ye ill?"

She looked at him, seeing all too clearly the bruises and scars of his torture on face and body. She put her arms around him and hid her face against his welted and discolored chest. "I'll be all right. I think I'm just now going into shock. Just hold me."

She trembled and he held her, stroking her tangled hair. "Aye, and it be no wonder. Have ye not been through the worst kind of hell? And losin' our child, too. Sure now, it'll be all right soon, Abbie, me darlin'. Soon now, we'll be safe and we can be startin' that baby again."

8

L O U I S V I L L E

Their first sight of Louisville not only gladdened their hearts but their eyes as well. The town was elevated above the river on a plain. A creek coming in from the southeast, combined with several islands abreast of the town, made a quiet harbor. Many of the houses bordering the creek and river bank were large, two-story homes with wide, full-length riverside piazzas hung with colorful and fragrant flower gardens. They landed the canoe and eagerly climbed to the top of the bank to take in the town they hoped would be their permanent home. It did not disappoint them. The town looked prosperous and busy with numerous shops along the main street, and a new brick courthouse rose resplendent on the town square.

Ross saw it and suggested, "Do ye think we'd be wise to go first to the courthouse and see if anyone be lookin' for us?"

Abigail hesitated a moment, then answered, "I suppose we should. At least it would ease our minds for the present, and maybe they could tell us where we could find work and a place to stay."

They walked arm in arm on the wooden sidewalks—extensive in this frontier town because of the abundance of planks from abandoned flatboats and necessary because of the boggy ground. They took in everything, becoming more pleased by the minute with the town, its huge, lovely trees, purposely left to enhance the

town, and the many shaded ponds scattered throughout it. They
found the constable's office and entered.

A corpulent man in a sweat-dampened shirt looked up from his
work and asked, "Anything I can do for you?"

Ross cleared his throat nervously and stated, "Yes, sir. Our
name be Galligher and we be just arrivin' from the state of New
York. We thought to ask if someone be lookin' for us or maybe
there might be mail for us."

The man scratched his balding head and looked thoughtful. He
opened a drawer in his desk and went through it and then swung
his chair around to go through another drawer, then turned back
to them. "Nope. Don't find a thing here with your name on it."

"Did ye look through the wanted posters, now?"

The man's eyes widened, then narrowed as he took a closer look
at their disheveled appearance. "You mean you're wanted?"

Ross cleared his throat again and Abigail could see his ears turn
dark red, but his voice was glib as he answered, "Sure now, there
might be someone wantin' to find out if we got here bad enough to
pay for the information."

The man grunted and pulled a stack of posters out of another
drawer and, licking his finger, methodically went through them.
Abigail shifted from one foot to the other in suspense. When the
man at last looked up and shook his head, she breathed a sigh of
relief.

"Nope. Ain't nothin' here, either."

Ross smiled. "Well, guess they be not worried about us as much
as we was thinkin', now. Ye don't be knowin' where the missus and
me can be findin' work and a place to stay?"

"Depends on what you can do, mister."

"Well, I be lookin' for a farm but I have no money. I was workin'
on the docks in New York and I be a fair man with a hammer. Me
wife worked in a bank and she be a schoolteacher, too."

The jowled face radiated interest. "Well, you'll have no trouble
fitting in here, Mr. Galligher. We got a damn sight more things to
load on boats than we got people who can load them and as for your
missus, we sure can use a schoolteacher. If the town council finds
her qualified, they'll sure 'nough give you a place to live. Now you
go down to the docks and you can ask anyone down there who to
see, and when you get back I'll have the council rounded up and
we'll see what we can do for your wife."

With light hearts and even lighter feet they walked to the river
and in less than an hour Ross had a job. Then they returned to the

courthouse, and Abigail was interviewed by several of the town's councilmen. She begged them to forgive her appearance and told them briefly what they had been through. She had their sympathy from the beginning and without too much trouble she became a schoolmistress in Louisville.

With a loan toward her wages and a house to live in, they went on a shopping spree and arrived at their cabin full of enthusiasm that was dampened only slightly by the spectacle of the home they would share. They opened the plank door and stepped inside the one-room cabin, piled their purchases on the shaky table and laughed at the sorry sight of the place. The cabin had been built of planks from a flatboat before they had had time to dry. Drying had warped and shrunk the boards until daylight streamed profusely through every crack. Town legend had it that the cabin had been built by Squire Boone, brother to the famed Daniel Boone.

Ross shook his head and chuckled. "Sure now, there be no two boards as I couldn't throw a pig between."

Abigail giggled. "But think how much air will be able to come in on these hot, muggy nights."

"Aye. And just think of the show people passin' by will be seein' when I take ye to bed, me darlin' Abbie."

She hit at him playfully and he caught her and pulled her to him in an embrace that quickly became filled with desire. He kissed her passionately, his hands caressing her, and she forgot all the terror, pain, and uncertainty of the past weeks.

But Ross hadn't, and he restrained his desire and breathed, "Ah, Abbie, I want ye so much but after what ye have been through I think ye should see a doctor."

"You know we can't afford a doctor."

"We can, if he'll be willin' to let me do work for him, now. We'll go tomorrow to see one. I'll not be touchin' ye till we find out and I be swearin' it to God."

She could do nothing less than agree with him. He was stubborn enough to hold to his promise and she knew it, but she couldn't resist tempting him and everything they did was a temptation for two people who had not had a moment together free from anxiety for days. The cabin cleaned and their bed made by dark, they carried in water to bathe and it was Ross who showed the greatest will power and determinedly stood by his promise even though he couldn't resist the pleasure of helping her bathe or resist the wanton way in which she helped him bathe. The experience was made even more enjoyable by the fact that they had to keep the cabin dark and giggled all the more when they wondered what passersby would think if they heard them. But their enjoyment didn't last long. They soon became prey of the scourge of the pond-filled town—the mosquito. To find relief from the buzzing pests they had to cover themselves completely with a blanket and suffer the heat, vowing to find something to use for netting in the morning.

Abigail suffered her visit to the doctor only because she knew Ross would not go back on his word. The doctor found nothing to indicate that she could not carry on as she had before the miscarriage, since she so obviously had recovered without difficulty, and blamed the incident on the trauma of the events coinciding with it. She spent the rest of the day sewing together netting for their bed and cooking a meal to celebrate their good fortune and the delayed reunion. But when darkness fell and Ross still had not come, she began to worry and paced the small, dirt-floored cabin. When he finally did come home her dinner was ruined and he was so tired and miserably sticky from the long hours and heat that he wanted nothing but a cool bath and bed, not even asking her what the doctor had told her. He was asleep the moment his head hit the pillow and she lay seething with anger and desire, feeling the only good thing the day had brought was the netting that protected them from the hungry mosquitoes.

In the cool early morning gloom Abigail was awakened by the caresses of her husband's work-roughened hands and turned to him without anger.

"Abbie, me darlin', I be sorry about last night. Can ye be forgivin' me?"

She kissed him and whispered, "You know I do."

He pulled her closer and returned her kiss, not stopping with her lips but tasting every inch of soft, pulsating skin on her face, neck, and shoulders. Then he remembered and pulled away from her. "I be almost forgettin', now. Tell me, what did the doctor say?"

"He said there was nothing to worry about but I—we should proceed with caution until we know if I will be hurt or not."

He pulled her close again and hugged her. "Then it is careful I'll be. Like a hummingbird sippin' nectar from the fairest flower, I'll be. Abbie, me darlin', ye won't even know I'm there."

She giggled as his hand touched her, exciting her until she was desperate to receive him. But Ross remained gentle and it was Abigail's frenzied desire that finally conquered them both, surprising herself as much as it did Ross.

"Father in heaven," he breathed against her tousled hair, "what kind of wild temptress have ye given me? The doctor said we were to be careful. Did I hurt ye, Abbie?"

Abigail blushed beautifully, the smile of contentment deepening the dimples in her cheeks. "No. I guess I just wanted you too much to worry about anything. I'll try not to be so improper again."

"If ye do I'll practice abstinence until ye are, now. A man dreams of such a woman, Abbie. It be the thing a man's fantasies be made of."

She blushed even deeper and scrambled out of bed, saying, "Well, you can't eat a fantasy, Mr. Galligher, so I'd better get your breakfast or you'll be late for work."

There was not much Abigail could do to the cabin to make it any more livable and, being the accomplished seamstress she was, it didn't take her long to finish making a dress for herself and a new shirt and pants for Ross from the material they had bought. With time on her hands she decided she might as well work until the school year started. Donning her newly created dress and combing her thick golden hair back and tying it with a bright ribbon, she set out to find a job. And before the day was through she had a clerk's job in the dry goods store.

Ross came home on time that night and she was bubbling with excitement. After dinner she wouldn't let him rest, feeling so full of joy at their good fortune she made him take her for a walk. Louisville at night, Abigail thought, was just about the most romantic town in the world. The huge poplars and sycamores towered over the town and the many ponds were alive with the concerts of frogs and a host of night insects. The night watchman greeted them on his rounds, patrolling the town, and they finally came to the river and sat down on the dock to listen to the rush of the rapids beginning just below Louisville and known as the falls of the Ohio. They didn't stay long. The mosquitoes finally drove them back to their cabin and after a cool refreshing dip in their washtub they lay quite content under the protection of the mosquito netting and thought nothing could be more wonderful.

Before the week was over they discovered there was a Catholic church as well as a Protestant church of Abigail's faith in the town. On Sunday they attended services in both churches and Abigail's joy with life was complete, her happiness and love for Ross growing daily as he remained the loving, considerate husband, totally uninterested in joining the mainstream of the townspeople in the drinking, brawling, gambling, and horseracing that seemed to be the lifeblood of the town.

But this paradise, just like the first paradise, had its drawback and in a little over a fortnight their joy was tarnished when Abigail awoke in the middle of the night with chills and fever. Her violent shaking awoke Ross and he lit the candle and brought it close.

"Abbie, me darlin', what is it?"

"I don't know," she moaned, "I'm so cold. Hold me, Ross, please hold me."

He held her, pulling the blanket over them and after a while the chilling subsided only to be followed by a more severe siege of fever, headache, and nausea. Ross reached for his clothes. "I'll be goin' to get the doctor. Ye stay in bed and don't be movin', now."

She felt too ill to do anything but stay in bed and was still flushed and feverish when Ross returned with the doctor. It didn't take him but one look to know what was wrong with her.

"It's the fever, Mr. Galligher. A lot of the people suffer it here. The only medicine I have that seems to help is ground bark from a tree in South America, called cinchona. It'll relieve her but, unfortunately, it won't cure it."

"Thank God ye can at least be doin' something about it. Do ye be knowin' what causes it?"

"Not for certain. Some claim it's the foul air rising from these stagnant ponds. I don't rightly know if they're correct, but that's the only thing we can lay it to, so far. Bring me a glass of water and we'll give her a dose."

He took a bottle from his bag and measured some powder into the water Ross brought him and held it for Abigail to drink. She took it eagerly, wanting anything that would relieve her suffering. The first swallow of the bitter liquid was almost worse than the illness and she gagged and tried to decline the rest, but the doctor wouldn't let her.

"Come now, little lady, you have to drink it all or it won't help."

She drank the rest of it and shuddered. "Will I have to take any more?"

"Yep. As long as you keep having attacks. I'll leave you the bottle and you take a glass whenever you feel the fever comin' on. This illness seems to ease off within a few days for most people, but it never goes away completely. You'll have to keep a bottle of this on hand all the time and if you should have a baby, remember, it may affect your milk and make the baby sick."

She nodded weakly and closed her eyes. "Thank you, Doctor."

Ross added, "Ye know I be appreciatin' ye comin' in the middle of the night like this, Doctor. What can I be doin' to repay ye for it, now?"

"Well, I still have firewood to cut up any time you have time to work on it."

"Thank ye. I'll be comin' over the first night I be gettin' off early enough."

By the time Ross was back in bed Abigail could feel the fever subsiding a little and before long she was able to sleep.

Abigail felt well enough to go to work in the morning but by the time she got home that afternoon she was more tired than usual and lay down on the bed to rest until it was time to fix Ross's supper. She fell asleep and didn't hear Ross come in until she felt his hand on her shoulder.

"Oh, Abbie, ye poor thing, now. I should have taken ye home like I said. Is it the fever again?"

She smiled away his concern. "No. I was just tired. I must have fallen asleep. I'll have supper ready in a bit."

"No. Ye lay there and rest. I'll be gettin' supper if ye tell me where things be."

She let him fix supper and came to eat with him, feeling somewhat better for her nap.

"Did ye have another attack today, Abbie?"

"No. And I certainly hope I don't have another one. That medicine is awful."

"Be it really that bad a tastin' stuff, now?"

"It's terrible. I'll give you a taste."

He laughed. "No, thanks. I thought maybe ye was keepin' somethin' good from me and I didn't want to be missin' out. Do ye be realizin' how long it be since I've had a real good brew?" He got up from the table and continued, "I best be gettin' over to the doctor's place and be gettin' some of that wood cut. Will ye be all right, now, if I be leavin' ye, Abbie?"

"I think so."

"I'll be stayin', now, if ye be wantin' me to."

"No. You'd better go tonight and I'll go to bed and catch up on my sleep and by tomorrow night I promise I'll feel better and I'd rather you were home with me then."

He grinned and came to kiss her. "Aye, ye be givin' a man somethin' to look forward to."

She smiled back at him and he started for the door. "Ross." He turned. "Stop by the tavern and have yourself one good brew on the way home."

He blew her a kiss and was gone. Abigail forced herself to scrub the tin plates and tidy up the cabin before going to bed and promptly went to sleep the minute she lay down. Ross came in some time after dark, waking her. He smelled of smoke and ale and she knew he had stopped at the tavern. He lit the lamp and, stripping off his sweat-stained clothes, washed quickly in the cool tub of water and came to join her, stretching out on the bed naked and flushed with the ale and full of news.

"I be hearin' news in the tavern about the Indian, Tecumseh. He didn't be agreein' with Governor Harrison's terms and the governor be callin' up the troops. They be askin' for volunteers and a lot of men'll be goin'."

She frowned with concern. "I hope you're not planning on going."

"Sure now, I wouldn't leave without ye being well. Ye know that. And I'd not be so sure I'd want to be fightin' against a man who's saved me life."

"It might come to that if there is a war."

"I know, but I'll be stayin' out of it as long as I can. Does that please ye, now, Abbie darlin'?"

She smiled at him. "Yes. And it would please me even more if you'd blow out the lamp and go to sleep. Every time you open your mouth I think I'm in a tavern."

He chuckled and patted her lovingly before he turned to put out the lamp and in a few minutes he was sound asleep.

School started and Abigail soon fell into the role of teacher. Happiness with her position, Ross, and their life in general speeded her recovery from the fever, and it was soon forgotten. The news of troop movements from Vincennes to the main Shawnee town at Tippecanoe brought on a rash of patriotism Ross was unable to escape. He didn't want to leave her any more than he wanted to fight the Indians, but neither did he feel he could withstand the label of coward if he didn't go.

In the week following his departure, Abigail knew uncertainty and loneliness. But she didn't let the condition last long. Work was the answer and she immediately began tutoring students needing extra help after school, volunteering for all church charity projects, and working Saturdays in the dry goods store until she hardly had a minute that wasn't filled or a day without being at someone's home for a meal. At night she was too exhausted to spend much time missing Ross and would try to think with satisfaction of the extra money she was earning and how surprised he would be when he returned. Why, they might just have enough to be able to move onto the farm he wanted.

She fell asleep thinking just such happy thoughts on a clear moonlit night near the first of November and was startled out of her sleep by a sound so loud and shrill her heart stopped from fear. The noise came again, piercing the night, and this time she was awake enough to realize it sounded like some sort of a whistle. Dressing hurriedly, she went to her window. Other people were up and moving rapidly down the walk to the river. She threw on a shawl and followed.

Cavorting in the wide waters of the Ohio like some strange sea monster was the most amazing boat Abigail had ever seen. Lit like a fairy castle with a huge paddle wheel dashing the water until it frothed and sparkled in the moonlight, and deafening the ears with its whistle, was the steamship *New Orleans*. Here was a vessel that could make the trip from Pittsburgh to Louisville, which had taken Ross and Abigail weeks, in just days. No more were they in an isolated wilderness safe from her father's influence. She returned to her cabin and securely bolted the door and lay awake the rest of the night worrying about how soon someone would come looking for them or, just as bad, someone would recognize them and report back to her father in order to get the reward she was sure her father had offered for her return.

9

TRAVEL INTO TERROR

The Kentucky volunteers returned home and with them came Ross. He appeared at the schoolroom door and stood waiting for Abigail to turn away from the blackboard. The giggles of the children soon brought her attention away from the lesson she was writing and when she turned to scold them she saw Ross and dropped her chalk, shrieked with delight, and ran down the aisle to kiss her husband. She paused long enough to dismiss school for the day and once the children were out of the room and the door shut against intrusion, she allowed herself the abandonment of kissing and hugging Ross until she was faint.

Ross finally broke their embrace and said with a sigh, "Ah, now, Abbie, it be good to see ye and hold ye, but I'm sure, now, we'd better save the rest 'til we be gettin' home."

She blushed and brought her wild emotions under control. "Oh, Ross, I've so much to tell you. What happened? I heard some rumors but I didn't know if they were true or not. Did you get hurt?" and she began to examine him for wounds.

He caught her hands and laughed. "Whoa, now, Abbie. I be all right, me darlin'. Gather up your wrap, now, and let's be goin' home. I'll be talkin' a lot better over a plate full of supper."

Quickly she gathered up her things and locked the schoolroom, and they walked briskly through the chill December air to their cabin. Abigail prepared supper while Ross washed the mud and dirt of days on the trail away.

"Was Tecumseh there?" she asked.

Between mouthfuls, Ross answered, "No. After his last meetin' with Governor Harrison be went south to visit the Creek Indians."

"Good. I'm glad you didn't have to fight against him."

"I be, too. I think if I'd seen him I'd've walked away and be damned."

"Tell me from the beginning what happened."

"After we got to Vincennes we marched up to the Shawnee town at Tippecanoe and made contact with the Indians. Tecumseh was gone but his brother was there, and he and Harrison held a meetin' together. Harrison had us make camp in one place and then he moved us to another place. This made the Indians suspicious and they came sneakin' out early the next morning to see what Harrison was up to. Someone fired a shot and all hell broke loose then. I think it was what Harrison wanted. They was no match for us and finally they even fled their town. Harrison had us burn it then, before we left. It be a dirty business, now, and I be glad it be over."

"Then you wouldn't object to moving and staying out of the war, if it comes to that?"

"Move? Why?"

"While you were gone a steamboat came down the Ohio and stopped here. It only took a few days to make the trip. Do you realize what that means? Someone could go upriver now easier than we came down and in far less time. Someone is bound to come eventually who knows us. Father could get the news we were here and be after us in a matter of days."

He looked at her and the weariness of the days just past caught up with him. He looked very tired and very uncertain, and Abigail went to him and held him in her arms. He stroked her pale hair and said with a sigh, "Father in heaven, will we never be free?" He was quiet for a long while, just holding her. Finally he said, "All right. Tomorrow I'll be seein' if I can be gettin' us passage downriver."

In two days they boarded a keelboat loaded with supplies bound for St. Louis in the Louisiana Territory. The captain hadn't wanted to be responsible for passengers, but when Ross offered to sleep aboard the boat at night, so the boat crew could all spend the night at the taverns along the way, the burly captain agreed, much to the satisfaction of his hard-visaged, hard-drinking crew.

The day they left Shippingport, the small community flourishing at the bottom of the rapids downriver from Louisville, it was cool and drizzling. Abigail took a last backward look at the little settlement, now looking as gloomy as she felt without the colorful hanging gardens and lush-foliaged trees of summer. For once, she thought, they had a few possessions to help keep them comfortable on the trip and to furnish their new home, wherever it might be.

They would have to use some of their hard-saved money to buy most of their meals as the crew ate at the settlements along the way, but at least they would not have to pay for lodging and they would be quite alone in the little cabinlike room ahead of the cargo box on the keelboat at night.

For the most part Abigail stayed in the cabin. There was no room on the deck for walking on the narrow catwalk along each side of the cargo box where the crew trudged back and forth poling the boat away from snags, submerged logs, and sandbars. They were a rough, uninhibited group and their language was too crude for Abigail's ears so she didn't mind seeing the landscape from behind dingy windows. But it did bother her that they seemed to be constantly watching her until she felt like a goldfish in a bowl and more than one covetous glance caught her eye until she was apprehensive as well. Ross, however, fitted right in with the crew and enjoyed listening to their adventures. At night after they had returned to the boat and were warm and contented in their bed he would tell her some of the tamer stories suitable for her ears.

In a week's time the keelboat entered the broad, turbid Mississippi. The force of the Ohio extended to the middle of the river and from there the boatmen had to use all the strength and skill they possessed to keep the boat from being swept downstream. Their goal was the landmark across the river known as Bird's Point and from there they would pole, row, or pull by rope the heavy-laden craft against the powerful Mississippi current to St. Louis. With luck they might even be able to sail, if a wind came up. Abigail watched from first one window and then the other in nervous apprehension as the cursing, straining boatmen slowly brought the keelboat into the eddy at Bird's Point.

It was cause to celebrate, and no matter what time of day they reached Bird's Point, the rest of the day was spent in livening up the settlement and getting roaring drunk in the process. Ross joined them, much to Abigail's displeasure. It took several attempts to get him to eat supper and then he ate very little. She asked him to take her back to the boat at dark and when he willingly went with her she was relieved. But her relief was short-lived. He saw her safely inside the cabin and turned to leave.

"Ross, where are you going?"

"Sure now, Abbie, ye wouldn't mind if I be havin' a drink with the men?"

Sharply she said, "You've been drinking with them all day."

The smile faded from his face. "Aye, and I'll be drinkin' with them all night, now, if it suits me."

More softly she pleaded, "Ross, please don't leave me alone."

"Ye don't have to be alone. Ye can be comin' with me and visitin' the other ladies."

"I've visited all afternoon with them. Now I want to go to bed and I want you to go to bed with me."

He smiled again. "That'd be soundin' like a bribe, Abbie. Is it?"

She knew she'd lost him and bit her lip. "Yes. I don't want you to go back with those men and I don't want to be left alone."

"I'll not be bribed, Abbie. I be goin' to have another drink and if ye don't want to be comin', then ye'll have to stay alone, now."

She turned away from him fighting back the angry words welling up in her, knowing they would only anger him more. She heard the door shut and when his footsteps left the plank she went to the door and barred it. She worked on her fancywork for a while and, getting cold, she got ready for bed. Leaving the hanging lamp lighted, she crawled under the blankets, her anger growing and making sleep seem impossible, but in spite of it, she at last dozed.

She was awakened by a banging on the cabin door and, sleepily, she crawled from the bed. The lamp was still burning and she was surprised that she had slept at all. She went to the door and unbarred it without pausing to put on her robe. The door swung open and she gasped at the foul-smelling, rumpled figure and tried to slam the door shut again but the man was not to be shut out and heaved against the door and sent Abigail staggering off balance across the tiny room. She stood against the rough plank wall in terror as he shut the door and barred it and then took a mouthful of whiskey from the jug he carried on one finger.

"Well, now, little lady, if you ain't the prettiest thing ol' Joe ever did see. Ain't you goin' to ask ol' Joe to sit down?"

Abigail didn't know what to say. She decided to try and humor him. "I'm sorry, but I'm not dressed for company. Could you come back later?"

He laughed. "You're dressed just right, little lady." He settled his tall, massive body onto the bench by the table. "Now you just come here and talk to ol' Joe."

"Please go. My husband will be back any minute."

He laughed again and eyed her with a crafty look. "There's few men that tremble me, ma'am, and your husband ain't never goin' to be one of 'em. 'Sides, ol' Joe done drunk 'em all under the table. Now you relax and come here."

Abigail shivered as much from fear as cold and looked about quickly for an avenue of escape.

"Ah, you be cold, ain't you?"

Abigail answered, "Yes," and sidled sideways to get a blanket from the bed but with surprising quickness for such a big man, Joe was off the bench and grabbing the blanket. He held it spread out and said, "Now, you jus' let ol' Joe wrap you up in this."

Abigail reached for the blanket with no intention of getting any closer but Joe grabbed at her arm and caught the sleeve of her nightgown. Abigail jerked away and the sleeve tore from her shoulder. Joe moved to catch her again and Abigail ducked and eluded his grasp for only a moment before he caught her and pressed her against the slivery wall, grinning down at her lustfully. "Now, you ain't goin' to play hard to get, are you?"

Abigail lunged against him with all her strength but he only laughed at her efforts. She knew it was no use. He was the biggest of the boatmen and she didn't doubt he was the strongest and, from what she had seen of him, the wildest. He placed his forearm across her neck holding her against the wall, stepped away from her, and with his free hand grasped the neck of her nightgown and tore it from her body. She struggled violently, kicking and flailing at him with her fists. He struck her with his hand, the blow stunning her into inactivity for a few seconds.

He held her at arm's length and ran hungry eyes over her body. "My, my! Ain't you somethin'. I sure don't understand why your husband would want to spend the night drinkin' with you warmin' his bed."

He fumbled with his free hand at his pants and Abigail made another desperate attempt to free herself, kicking and twisting and sinking her teeth into his arm. He slapped her with the flat of his hand and sent her sprawling across the bed. She scrambled off the bed without stopping as Joe tried to kick off his pants. She reached the door and had the bar in her hands as he came at her. She whirled with the bar, trying to knock him down, but he caught it in his hands and hurled her onto the bed with tremendous force, breaking her grip and knocking the breath from her. He barred the door and came to the bed and stood looking down at her with wild, hungry eyes.

Abigail looked about desperately for a weapon but it was no use. He was on her forcing her legs apart while he bruised her with his mouth and hands. He weighed more than twice what she did and beneath his weight she was helpless as his body plunged painfully into hers. She tasted blood and moved her lips trying to free them and felt only his wet mouth against her teeth. She opened her clenched teeth and bit down as hard as she could on his thick unshaven lip until she tasted his blood and released her grip. At the same instant he used his battering ram body in vengeance and she cried out in pain. His hands bruised her cheek, and she tried to scream again but he covered her mouth with his hand. She wrenched her head, sinking her teeth into the fleshy part of the palm under his thumb. He swore at her just as she thought she heard someone pounding on the door. She screamed Ross's name twice before Joe's fist slugged her senseless.

When Abigail awoke she rolled her head and opened her eyes, moaning with the pronounced throb the movement brought. She raised her hands to her head and tried to remember what had happened. She saw four men seated at the small table. One of the men was Ross and she closed her eyes against the sight of him. He looked almost as bad as he had when the Indians had released them. One eye was almost swollen shut and blood was drying from a cut at the corner of his mouth.

The captain said, "You better see if she's all right."

Abigail opened her eyes again and saw Ross rise painfully from the bench and move toward her hesitantly. She closed her eyes and turned her head away.

His hand touched her and his voice sounded strained as he asked, "Abbie, are ye all right? Do ye hurt anyplace?"

She slowly moved her head once back and forth and remained faced away from him. She heard him go down on his knees next to the bed and both of his hands took one of hers. His voice was sobbing when he spoke. "Abbie, Abbie. Me darlin' Abbie. I'm sorry. Mother of God! I'm sorry!" His voice broke and he cried, the tears wetting her hand where he held it against his swollen lips.

She heard the men move uncomfortably at the table, and the captain said, "We'll go on outside. You see to her and then come on out. We got to get movin'."

The men left the cabin and she heard voices outside and felt the boat move. She felt Ross rise and sit down on the bed.

"Abbie, they've gone. Ye can tell me, now, what happened?"

She answered him with silence.

"Please, Abbie, ye got to be tellin' me where ye hurt, now. I can't be helpin' ye unless I know."

When she still didn't answer, she felt him move to take down the blanket covering her, and she cried fiercely, "Don't touch me!"

For long, tense moments his hand held the blanket and then he finally released it. "Abbie, I said I be sorry. I be sorrier than ye'll ever be knowin'. I can ask ye to forgive me but I'll not beg it of ye, now. Your father was right. I be not good enough for ye. Whatever it be ye want of me, just ask. If it be to take ye back to your father, I can hardly be blamin' ye, now, and as soon as we be gettin' to St. Louis, I'll be findin' some way to be takin' ye home, if that's what ye want."

She said nothing and in a few moments he stood up and she heard him cross to the door. He paused and she could tell he turned to face her again. "Joe won't be botherin' ye anymore, Abbie, and neither will I. I killed him and God will be punishin' me. I be prayin' that ye can find it in your heart not to be punishin' me, too."

Abigail heard the door open and close and she cried—bitter tears of agony and anger that drained her of every emotion and left her numb enough to sleep.

When Abigail awoke it was dark. Someone had lit the lantern and a plate of food was on the table. The sharp throb in her head was gone but her face felt swollen and her whole head ached dully. She felt wretched and soiled and looked for the bucket of water. It was in its usual place and she slowly climbed out of bed, looking to see if the windows were covered. But she needn't have worried, Ross had thought of that, too. She barred the door, then bathed and dressed and combed her tangled hair before she sat down to eat. The boat was quiet and she knew the men were gone for the night, just as she knew Ross was still on the boat. All she had to do was call and he would be there, but she didn't want to see him. She didn't even want to see herself.

She spent the hours after supper alternately praying and trying to sort out her thoughts and emotions. Ross's words weighed heavily on her heart and on her mind. Even though he had asked her forgiveness, his question indicated she was not entirely blameless, and she knew he was entitled to an explanation of why Joe had been allowed into the cabin.

Her thoughts were interrupted by a low, distant rumble and she wondered if a thunderstorm was breaking. But the thunder didn't diminish and she saw no lightning flash through the darkness. As the rumble built to a swelling roar, Abigail rose to her feet in unexplained apprehension. She heard a series of loud cracking noises as the boat began to rock with sudden and increasing violence. She was flung against the cabin door and she clawed at the bar screaming for Ross in unreasoning panic. She sprawled on the floor with the bar crashing against the other cabin wall. The door whipped open and Ross stood for an instant clinging to the doorway and then was catapulted down beside her. With a tremendous tearing thunder, the river bank collapsed and huge, whole trees reeled into the river, adding to the crescendo of noise. The cleats holding the boat lines yanked free, ripping up boat planks, and the boat was propelled into the river away from the collapsing bank. Above the terrible thunder of noise a higher-pitched din rose around them as flocks of waterfowl screamed in terror, the panicked beat of wings adding to the frightening roar.

After what seemed like an eternity, the thunder subsided but the river remained wild for several more minutes in which Abigail and Ross clung together, unable to speak or even to cry out in their terror. Only when the boat came to a hard, wrenching crash against a sandbar and all was quiet for several minutes did Ross break the silence. He freed a hand and crossed himself and prayed loudly and earnestly, stroking Abigail's hair as he did.

When his prayer was over he asked, "Are ye all right, Abbie?"

"I think so. Are you?"

"Aye. Father in heaven! I've never been through anything like that! Do ye think it be the end of the world?"

"No, I don't think so. I think it was an earthquake. We read about them in school."

"Aye. I be hearin' of it once. Do ye think there'll be another?"

"I don't know."

"I'd better be seein' if I can see the captain. Ye stay here a bit 'til I be gettin' back."

Gingerly, he rose to his feet and went to the door. He was lost from sight in the overwhelming darkness and she waited breathlessly for his return. He came back in a few minutes and sat down beside her.

"I can't be seein' anything out there now. It's like the inside of me cap—a smotherin', smoky blackness. I can't even be tellin' where we be, but I don't think we be in the water."

"What should we do?"

"Nothin' to do, now, but wait for the captain or daylight—whichever be comin' first."

She said nothing more and they sat in tense, sleepless silence, waiting, breathing the strange sulphury smelling air and praying silently, desperately, as the minutes and hours dragged by.

Another deep rumble interrupted their prayers and within a

heartbeat the violence of a few hours ago repeated itself, but to a lesser degree. The river again boiled but not enough to dislodge the boat. The moment the rumble subsided Abigail knew she couldn't wait any longer to tell Ross what had happened the night before.

"Ross, I thought it was you coming to bed last night. I heard someone knocking on the cabin door and without thinking I opened the door. When I saw who it was I tried to close it again but he was too strong. I should have known better than to open the door and I'll never be able to forgive myself for what it caused you to do."

He took her in his arms and held her gently, his lips moving against the swollen bruise at her temple. "I know. Mother of God, I know. There's not been a minute passed that I haven't cursed meself for not bein' with ye instead of selfishly drinkin' the night away while he . . ." He couldn't finish and she felt him tremble with emotion as they clung together in despair.

Within the hour another less violent shock occurred and after it every few minutes for the rest of the night the earth moved and the river capped as the shocks came and went. At dawn another more severe shock shuddered the boat and, as much from fear for their lives as curiosity, Ross and Abigail dared leave the cabin. Stepping out of the cabin was like stepping from reality into unreality. The boat was not mired on a sandbar but had been stranded high and dry on the west side of the river. From their vantage point on the boat deck they could see more clearly the devastation of the earthquake. The hills were still prominent in the near distance but all that lay between was totally unfamiliar. The valley was scarred with fissures and vents from which choking vapors arose. A grove of trees lay shattered into kindling wood and a yellow haze cast an eerie light on an already eerie scene. Nor had the hills escaped disfigurement. They, too, were crumbled and fissured and, as they watched, they heard the warning rumble and saw the earth heave and roll unbelievably as a new convulsion shook the land and dust rose from the hills as new slides were perpetrated. They closed their eyes against the horror and reached for each other and waited until the tremor passed.

Ross crossed himself and in a stricken voice said, "Father in heaven! I don't see anything I recognize. Where be the captain? Where be the inn? Mother of God! Where be we?"

"We must have drifted farther away than it seemed. Maybe if we walk a little way we could find someone."

"But which way? Sure now, we can't be goin' upstream, but look now at the way the boat lies."

"Then let's try both ways. Surely we'll find something."

"Aye. 'Tis the only way. Let's be gettin' some food and water. No tellin' what we may come to."

They gathered some provisions together and emptied one of Abigail's reticules to put them in. Their next problem was how to get off the boat and, in case they needed to, get back on. Ross found an ax to cut pieces of planking and, using the long poles, made a ladder and lowered it over the side of the boat. They started upriver and made slow progress with detours around fissures and broken groves. They sat down to rest on a large downed tree at the edge of a grove some distance from the boat and Abigail reached into the bag they carried for what would pass as breakfast this day, when a low, ominous rumble warned them of another quake. Ross leaped to his feet and looked in panic for a safer place but there was clearly no place to escape to. Abigail sat frozen with fear. Ross sat back down and straddled the tree just as the ground began to heave and wrapped his arms around Abigail. A rending boom not unlike a clap of thunder deafened them and the earth a few yards away began to heave apart, gobbling trees into the opening maw like some giant monster.

Ross yelled, "Swing your leg over the log and hang on, now."

Without hesitation Abigail swung her leg over the log and hung onto a broken limb stump as the fissure opened beneath them and they were engulfed in a cloud of choking dust.

It was over almost as quickly as it had begun and Ross, still clutching the stump in front of Abigail, breathed a prayer. Abigail said her own prayer, as her eyes fearfully looked down into the narrow fissure beneath them. Ross released her and scooted backward along the tree trunk, and Abigail followed with difficulty, her skirt catching on the rough bark. Ross reached to help her and she clung to him, feeling weak-kneed and faint. Their bag of food was gone—swallowed up into the earth.

"Do ye think we should go on or go back?"

Abigail looked around uncertainly. Her eyes caught movement on a hilltop and she thought she heard something like singing coming from the same direction.

"Look at the top of the hill just upriver there. Do you see anything?"

Ross followed her pointing arm. "Aye, I see it now. What do ye suppose it be?"

"I'm not sure but I thought I heard voices. Maybe we should see what it is."

"Well, it be not far. Maybe someone can be tellin' us where we be."

They threaded their way around the fissure that crossed their line of travel and scrambled over downed trees, finally reaching the base of the hill. Now they could definitely hear the voices of people singing. They rested a moment and looked toward the river and could see the wrecked settlement buildings. Another tremor rolled across the land and one of the wrecked buildings tumbled in. When the shock was over they continued up the hill, almost reaching the top before the group of people saw them and stopped their frantic hymn singing and waited, still kneeling, for Ross and Abigail to approach them.

One of the kneeling men greeted them. "Welcome, friend. Where you from?"

"We don't be knowin'. We be lost. Maybe ye can be helpin' us. We was aboard a keelboat and moored for the night. The crew was on shore at a settlement but me wife and me was on board when this quake hit. We be tryin' to find the crew now."

"Ain't seen nobody like that here. You know whose place you was at?"

"No. But we was just passin' an island and comin' around a big loop."

"If that be so, mister, then you're upriver from where you was."

Ross cast a doubtful look at Abigail but said, "Sure now, we thank ye. Then St. Louis be on upriver that way?" He gestured northward.

The man nodded and asked, "Surely you ain't goin' to try to get to St. Louis?"

"Aye."

"Don't be a fool, man. Better stay with us and pray for your deliverance from this evil that is come. The end is near!"

"I thank ye for the offer, but we be tryin' to find the rest of our people. If they be downriver from us here, we got to be goin' back, now."

"Guess we can understand that, but maybe you should leave the missus with us. You both look like you been pretty badly bruised."

Abigail's hand flew to her face. She'd forgotten all about the way both of them looked. She paled with the memory and was grateful to the earthquake for one thing.

Ross quickly picked up the excuse and carried it. "Aye. We was inside the boat cabin and was banged about pretty bad, but nothin' be broken."

Abigail recovered and added, "Thank you for wanting me to stay, but I couldn't let my husband go without me. I want to be with him, no matter what happens."

The man nodded. "Don't blame you, ma'am. Good luck and we'll pray for you."

"Thank ye and God be with ye."

They started down the hill and the desperate praying began behind them, increasing to hysteria as another quake staggered them. Abigail clung to Ross's arm, feeling a terrible sense of foreboding settle over her as they looked down on the devastated landscape being wracked by another wave of destruction.

They reached the boat and Ross helped Abigail up the ladder. The last severe tremor had made the vessel list slightly and Abigail didn't feel safe aboard it. Another hard shake and it could slide down the bank into the river. Again they gathered up food and climbed down from the precariously balanced boat before stopping to eat.

They ate in silence until Ross asked, "Did ye mean what ye told that man on the hill?"

Honestly she answered, "It was the first thing I could think of to say. I didn't want to stay with them."

"But ye didn't want to be comin' with me either, now, is that it?"

She saw the pain in his eyes and looked away. "Please, Ross, I don't want to have to think about it now. Too much has happened and I can neither think nor sort out my feelings just yet. I need time. And I need to be safe and secure and not worried about whether I'll be alive in the next minute."

He nodded his head. "Aye. I can't be blamin' ye for that. Sure now, it must not be easy for ye to even look upon me, much less be with me." He rose and she put the food back in the bag and followed him. He took the bag from her and the sadness of his look touched her heart.

"I'm sorry, Ross."

He waved away her words. "No, now. God knows ye have every right to feel as ye do. I left ye alone when ye begged me not to"—his face twisted with anguish—"and it be because of me that ye were raped and made adulterous in God's sight. And now ye have to be in the company of a murderer."

He wheeled away from her abruptly and strode off quickly and Abigail had to run to catch up with him. She caught his arm and he stopped. "You're not a cold-blooded murderer. You were protecting your wife from an uncivilized brute."

"Ye think that'll be makin' any difference to the judge in St. Louis? No, Abbie, I be a murderer and I, no doubt, will be punished as one."

"Then let's not go to St. Louis. No one needs to know what happened to us. Let them think we're dead."

He appraised her thoughtfully. "Your words be givin' me hope, Abbie, but I have to be makin' sure we won't be hunted. I have to be makin' sure, now, that the captain and his crew won't be lookin' for us."

"Don't be a fool. They'll think we're dead."

"Abbie, I be their prisoner. They was goin' to turn me in at St. Louis. I was damn lucky they didn't be killin' me on the spot, but the captain stopped them. If one of them be alive they'll be lookin' for us. If they be dead, now, at least I only need to worry about punishment from God."

Abigail could do nothing less than agree. They had already known the anxiety of being wanted for too long. "All right, Ross. Perhaps it is best to know for sure. I'll come with you."

He gave her a thin smile. "Thank ye, Abbie. I should've been tellin' ye sooner, but I didn't want to be pilin' any more on ye now."

She followed him over the broken terrain littered with the dust and rocks of subterranean strata, avoiding vents where steam, fumes, or fountains of water sprang. They were near the river when another, more severe tremor rolled across the earth, heaving the ground in waves like an ocean. They reached for each other and were thrown to the ground. Ross crawled to Abigail and they watched while hills crumbled and trees fell. The earth beneath them suddenly sank and a well of water burst forth from a new vent, soaking them with its pressurized force, creating an instant pond as they struggled to their feet and scrambled to higher ground.

Abigail cried in desperation, "Oh, God, will it never end!"

Ross held her and quieted her as the earth grew quiet again and, taking her arm, they forged on, almost passing the place they were looking for because there was little that looked familiar left. The smell of smoke hung over the place, quite different from the sulphurous fumes of the vents. They discovered the ruins of the tavern room in a fissure sunk the depth of a well below the surface. The rest of the building was a pile of smoldering beams overlayed with still burning trees.

Ross led Abigail away from the scene and seated her on a downed tree. "I'll be doin' the lookin', now. Ye stay here and rest."

She watched him poke through the ruins looking for any signs of the crew or their corpses. Abigail turned away, feeling a sickness rise in her. She closed her eyes and prayed.

She jumped when Ross touched her shoulder. "Are ye all right?"

She nodded. "Did you find anything?"

He looked pale even under the ugly bruise. "Aye, there be some of them there all right, but God knows how many."

"What do you think we should do now?"

"Go back to the boat and be gettin' some sleep and food. In the mornin' I guess we best be startin' for St. Louis."

They reached the boat at dark and saw that the last tremor had caused the boat to slide backward, making it now impossible to board it without having to crawl. No surface was without a slant, and undoubtedly another tremor would send it into the river. Ross hauled everything out of it they thought they would need, and they huddled together around a small fire as the night grew chill and strangely quiet with no sound from bird or insect. They dozed only fitfully, leaning against each other, yet far apart and alone in their terror and guilt.

Long before dawn they were awakened by another earthquake, and a strange phenomenon occurred. The animals unseen the day before had come out of hiding, and as soon as Ross built up the fire several pairs of eyes appeared in the protective circle of firelight. Ross and Abigail sat silent and apprehensive in the midst of their unwanted guests but presently, as unobtrusively as they had come, the animals left.

The dawn broke pale and yellow, tinged with the same roar and shaking of the earth as the day before. When it was over they ate in silence and Ross watched the now sunken boat with a troubled look. At last he stood up and kicked dirt over the fire and once again stood looking at the boat.

"Ye know, I'll never be understandin' how that boat brought us upriver against the current. As long as I be livin' that will be puzzlin' me."

"I think I know how if you'd like to hear it?"

"Ye know I would. Out with it now."

"I read it in one of the books at school. They explained an earthquake was like someone dropping a pebble into a calm pool of water and watching the ripples spread. An earthquake has a center, like the pebble dropped in the water, and the ripples, or shock waves, move out from that center. If the center of the earthquake was downriver from us, then the waves would move away from the center and, if it was strong enough, it could have created enough force to reverse the river's flow."

His smile broadened into a grin as he absorbed the solution and found it logical. For a moment the happy-go-lucky, golden-tongued Irishman she married returned. "Father in heaven! Sure now, 'tis a wonderfully smart and beautiful woman ye have given me." Then the memory of the past forty-eight hours returned and the smile faded. "Well, come now, we best be goin' before another one of them pebbles be droppin'."

They stopped to visit with the members of the settlement they had spoken with on the hill the day before. They had returned to their cabins and were in the process of salvaging what they had so hurriedly abandoned and erecting shelters. Two nights on the hill had not brought the end of the world but the realization that until the end did come they needed food and shelter. Again they asked Ross and Abigail to stay and Ross seemed mildly surprised when Abigail declined and followed him away from the settlement, but he said nothing.

Another severe, unusually long shock rocked them after leaving the settlement but no more than slight tremblings were felt the rest of the day and Abigail was becoming inured to the movements. By nightfall they had stopped clinging to each other at every rumbling and had settled into a quiet, grim acceptance of their situation and surroundings. They stopped at dark to make camp and eat in silence and crawled under the same blankets, as they always had, but without any other desire but to sleep. And sleep they did for a short while until another tremor startled them awake. But it soon passed and they were too exhausted to worry about it and slept again.

The next morning brought a repeat of the previous day's early arousal by quakes. It ended sleep and they ate what was left of their food and waited for dawn to begin travel again. They found a wrecked boat near noon on the river bank and helped themselves to the provisions and sat down to eat when another long and violent quake made them scramble away from the river turned suddenly wild by the agitation. The banks caved in and what trees were left standing fell with tremendous noise into the capping water. For a few minutes all the terror of the past days returned, and they clung to each other until the shock passed.

They weren't aware they had partners in fear until they turned to go and Abigail gasped, "Look!"

Cowering nearby were three wolves who apparently had been scavenging for food among the boat cargo, just as they had. Ross held Abigail still and they waited until the wolves, assured that the tremor was over, rose to their feet and glided noiselessly into the tangle of broken timber along the river bank.

Another mile or two upriver they came upon another wreck, marked by the wheeling of vultures, and Abigail stayed back from the river, unwilling to see what the vultures were feeding on. Ross went down alone and it seemed like a long time before he came back, but when he did he was loaded heavily with supplies and appeared happy.

He set down the loaded bags he carried and opened them, showing the store of food he had found, and with a grin reached into his pocket and pulled out a handful of coins to show her, saying, "And I be findin' these, too."

"Ross! That's money!"

"Aye."

"But you shouldn't have taken it!"

"What be the difference if I be takin' money or food?"

"It just isn't right to take money off a dead person."

"I didn't be sayin' where I be gettin' it."

"But you did take it off a dead body, didn't you?"

"Aye."

She shuddered. "Then you are stealing from the dead."

"Do ye think the next person along will be lettin' that bother him? I say we be needin' the money as well as the food, now."

Stubbornly she argued, "But the money doesn't belong to us."

His jaw set with anger as he answered, "Aye. And neither do the food be belongin' to us, but who's to be claimin' it, Abbie? No one be claimin' it except the animals and the vultures or other people that be in need like us. If it be wrong, then ye be lettin' God punish me or ye can be stayin' here to turn me in to the next thief to come along. And while ye be at it, ye might remember that stealin' be not the worst of me sins. And ye might be rememberin', too, that we be leavin' as much or more than this behind us. Now be ye comin' willin' and no more be said about it, or be ye stayin' here?"

She stood up and fought back the hateful, hurtful words flashing through her mind. For the moment she had no other choice. She lifted one of the bags and trudged away from him in silence, feeling weary and depressed.

10

ST. LOUIS

In the following days they found no more wrecks, and the tremors they felt had little effect as they traveled ever northward into less devastated country. They found an inn to stay at a few miles' travel from St. Louis and, with their food all but gone and Abigail showing signs of exhaustion, Ross insisted they spend the night. Abigail didn't argue. She was too near physical and emotional collapse to care what he did, saying little about anything.

That night she was awakened in the middle of the night with the onslaught of chills and fever marking an attack of the illness she had almost forgotten about in the trauma of the past days. There was no medicine. It had disappeared with the first bag of provisions into the earth days ago. She had no choice but to suffer. By morning the chills and fever had passed, and she was wringing wet from the last stage of the attack. She felt weak but greatly relieved. When Ross woke at dawn she had no doubt that she could continue, but Ross quickly saw her condition when she had trouble keeping her feet.

"Mother of God, Abbie! What be wrong with ye? Ye be soakin' wet."

"It's nothing. I'm all right now." But even her voice betrayed her weakness.

He perceived it immediately. "Is it the fever, now?"

"It was, but I'm fine now. Really. As soon as we eat I'll be ready to go on."

But she had difficulty keeping up with him and he had to assist her to the edge of St. Louis. He immediately inquired where a doctor could be found. With directions, they walked along the street lined with walled courts built in the style of the French settlers who had built the town, and soon found the sign on the gate of one of the walled yards where the doctor lived. Ross opened the gate and with Abigail leaning heavily on him, they reached the door.

The doctor's wife answered his knock and didn't hesitate to ask them in. "Come in, please. Sit down here and I'll call the doctor."

They sank to the bench in the wide hall and the doctor came in a few moments, followed by his wife and two young and curious children, who kept their distance in the far doorway.

"Hello! What do we have here? How long has she been like this?"

"It be startin' last night, Doctor. But she be havin' it before in Louisville. The doctor there be givin' her bark from a tree to take but we be losin' it in the earthquake. Do ye have something for it?"

"Yes. There's a lot of the same illness here, too. Were you on the river when the earthquake struck?"

"Aye, about a day away from Bird's Point. We've been walkin' ever since."

The doctor frowned. "Then you don't have a place to stay?"

"No. Can ye be tellin' us where to find a place now? I be havin' a little money."

"Sorry, there's no room that I know of in town. But she shouldn't be out with a fever or she'll catch her death." He turned to his wife. "Do you know of any place, Nettie?"

Abigail turned hopeful eyes on the still young-looking, attractive woman, a fitting companion to the equally young, dark-haired and mustachioed doctor.

"No. The town is so full of people that everyone has every room full. How about your office, John? We could move your things out here into the hall for a few days. It's the holidays and no one will be bothering to be sick for a few days."

Abigail smiled as best she could. "Thank you. You're more than kind."

"Aye. Thank ye. And I'll be glad to pay ye, Doctor. We'll be stayin' here a while and I be intendin' to find a job, too. Can ye tell me where to start lookin'?"

The doctor smiled. "Best place to start looking is at one of the warehouses on the waterfront. But don't worry about that now. Let's get you a room made up and some hot food into you both. We can talk business later."

The next few days Abigail spent most of her time in bed fighting the effects of the fever, exhaustion, and the uncertainties caused by all that had transpired. Ross found a job without difficulty and was gone long hours every day, giving Abigail more than enough time to think, but she could resolve nothing. And Ross didn't try to force a decision from her, for which she was grateful. He came in late and tired and smelled like the soured furs he worked with. She got up long enough to prepare him a bath and then would wash his clothes and fix his supper from food he bought with the money he had found. By the time she had washed his dishes and straightened up the doctor's kitchen, Ross would be asleep.

The medicine and rest soon had her physically better and she was able to help the doctor's wife with the household chores and helped the doctor start a bookkeeping system and a patient file. It was a pleasant diversion being able to work with the doctor and his wife and she soon came out of her depression. She quickly fell into a routine and ignored the possibility that it might change. For now things were as she wanted them. She could avoid Ross and the decision she knew she must eventually make.

The first indication that things would not remain as they were came after Ross had been working over a week. He was still awake when she came into their room and she was immediately defensive but instead of the questions she expected, he handed her a brown paper package tied with string. She was both surprised and touched by the gesture.

"Ross, I don't deserve this."

"Abbie, ye still be me wife and nothing that be happenin' can change the love I be havin' for ye, now."

She sat down on the chair near the bed, feeling as embarrassed as if she were being courted again. But more than embarrassment, she felt a deep shame and guilt for not having faced her feelings about him. "But I've nothing to give you in return."

His eyes were very tender as he answered, "Ye do, Abbie— probably more than any man, especially me, be entitled to."

She couldn't look into those eyes any longer and turned to the package, taking all the time she could in opening it. His gift was three pieces of material—one a warm flannel for a new nightgown, another a sturdy calico for an everyday dress, and a beautiful, wispy flowered organdy for good. "Oh, Ross! They're lovely. Thank you very much." She dared to look at him then and her heart wrenched at the sadness in his eyes. She knew he had expected more from her but she couldn't give it—not yet—maybe not ever.

He smiled with more gaiety than she was sure he felt and said, "Happy New Year, me darlin' Abbie." He turned away from her and pulled the blankets over himself and she sat clutching the material and fighting back tears until he was asleep.

The next day she made up her mind to start actively seeking a place for herself and Ross. She knew nothing could be resolved by evading a confrontation with him and with her feelings, and she could do neither hampered by her dependence on the doctor and his wife. But the doctor was called out early and his wife went to help on a church charity project, leaving Abigail alone to work on her material.

She was just fixing herself a midday lunch when the doctor came in. He was tired and hungry from being gone since early in the morning to deliver a baby, and Abigail immediately enlarged her lunch to include him. They sat eating in silence until Abigail got up her courage to ask, "Have you heard of any place my husband and I could rent yet, Doctor?"

"No. But I'll start inquiring a little closer if you're sure you're ready to leave."

"I'm fine, now. At least I thought I was. Is there something I don't know?"

"No. But I have the feeling there's a lot I don't know."

His keen eyes appraised her and she had to look away. She busied herself with clearing away their dishes self-consciously. He sat smoking his pipe until a pounding on the front door broke their strained silence. He rose to answer it and Abigail felt relieved until he urgently called her name.

"Mrs. Galligher. Come here, please."

She hurried with apprehension to the front hall and was confronted by a group of men surrounding a badly bleeding and moaning man. The doctor was on the floor, intently examining the victim. Her stomach turned but she stood steadfastly. "Yes, Doctor."

Without looking at her he said, "I'll need some blankets and cloths out of your room and some water put on the stove to boil. Are you up to it?"

"Yes. I'll get the things. Where do you want me to spread the blanket?"

"On the kitchen table. Have you ever assisted a doctor?"

"No."

He looked at her then with the same keen eyes of only minutes ago. "I'll need help. Do you think you can handle it?"

She squared her shoulders. "I'll try."

She went into the room and gathered up the blankets and cloths and carried them to the kitchen, where she spread the blanket on the table. The men carried the wounded man in and laid him on the blanket, and the doctor began cutting away the clothing around the wound. Abigail built the fire up in the stove, set water on to boil, and came to stand with the cloths.

Intent on his work he ordered, "Place the cloth over the wound and press it down firmly. We've got to stop the bleeding."

She did as she was ordered and asked, "What happened to him?"

One of the men standing at the foot of the table answered, "He got shot, ma'am."

Abigail asked no more questions but watched with interest and did as the doctor ordered, quickly and efficiently, even to the point of anticipating what he needed before he asked. When the doctor was finished the men carried the now unconscious man away on the blanket. She brought water for the doctor to wash with and set about scrubbing the table. The doctor sat down in a chair with a cup of coffee and watched her.

"You did a right admirable job, Mrs. Galligher. Have you ever considered becoming a nurse?"

"No. I'm a schoolteacher."

"I see. Well, St. Louis can use a good teacher, too. Are you planning on staying?"

"I don't really know yet. Until spring at least."

"I know it's none of my business, but you don't seem like the usual sort of frontier woman. If you need help in any way, I'd be glad to do what I can."

"Thank you, but there is nothing you can do."

Before he could say more the front door opened and Nettie and the children came in. Abigail stayed only long enough to exchange pleasantries and listen to the doctor recount their emergency before she went to her room and lay down, feeling tired and troubled by the doctor's questions. She hadn't realized it was so obvious they were having difficulty, but now that she thought about it, it was easy for anyone to see, even without the doctor's keen perception, that all was not right between them. Ross had been nothing less than the solicitous, considerate husband to her and the grateful, cheerful guest. He had kept his promise not to touch her, for which she was thankful, but she had been so concerned with herself that she had made no effort to return the concern and consideration, to the point of cool aloofness. When she had felt well enough to resume normal activity, she realized she still had pretended their problem, and even Ross himself, didn't exist and he had become increasingly tense and strained, his smiles forced and his words few. Things could not go on like they were. It wasn't fair to Ross. When he came in she would suggest they try to find a place of their own.

When Ross did come in it was late but she dutifully had hot water ready for him. She fixed his supper while he bathed and as he ate she washed his clothes in his bathwater and hung them to dry behind the stove in the kitchen. She decided she would wake him if he was asleep when she was done cleaning up the kitchen. She returned to their room and was surprised to see Ross still awake.

"Abbie, are ye well enough now to be helpin' me do some decidin'?"

"I think so. What did you want to decide?"

"I think ye be knowin' that, Abbie, but I'll be explainin'. I be havin' enough money now to find us a place if ye be willin' to stay with me, or I'll be makin' arrangements to take ye back home if that be what ye want."

"I've had enough winter travel. I'd like to stay until spring, at least, if it is all right with you. I feel quite well enough to keep house for you."

Like magic the strain and tension was replaced by a relieved smile. "Aye, I be glad to hear that, now. And I be havin' a place to show ye but it be outside the town, on the hill, and I don't be wantin' to leave ye alone there. If ye be willin' to stay, I think it be best if ye be goin' to work, not for the money so much as to be keepin' ye safe from the riffraff that be here. Do ye think ye be up to it?"

Again she saw the deep concern in his eyes for her and she had to look away from those earnest eyes. "Yes. In fact I look forward to it. I've had too much idle time."

His smile grew even broader. "Tomorrow be Sunday and I'll be findin' a church to take ye to and afterward I'll be showin' ye the cabin, if ye like?"

She smiled at him. "Yes. I'd like that very much."

The next day they went to church and then to see the cabin overlooking the town. It was at least a tighter cabin than the one they had shared in Louisville, and they went back to retrieve their few things at the doctor's house and move into the cabin. Abigail was reluctant to leave the comfortable security of the doctor's house but knew it was the only way to face her problem. She spent the rest of the short afternoon making a list of provisions while Ross cut wood for the fireplace.

In the morning he took her to see the members of the school board, and before the day was over she was teaching school. From that day on their life took on a pattern of normality again. Ross would take her to the school every day and come for her each night. She was never alone and her anxiety began to fade away. The happy man she had married returned a little more each day as he enthusiastically talked about his job at the Chouteau warehouse and the people he met there—the fur traders who were beginning to open the way to the west and the men backing them—and once in a while he would say something that led her to suspect he was making plans to settle.

Spring came and the cargo boats began arriving from the east with the goods that would supply not only the town but the wilderness outposts. It was necessary for Ross to work longer hours to load and unload the boats, but he would take long enough to see her home and eat with her and make sure she was safely behind a barred door with a loaded gun, which he had shown her how to use, before he would return to the dock and work until dark. Abigail found she missed him and the feeling surprised her. Soon she would have to give him her decision, and she was beginning to suspect it wasn't going to be as easy as she thought. She hadn't believed she would ever forget the trauma of being raped nor had she believed she could ever feel about Ross as she once had, but a strange thing was happening to her. The emotional scars were healing. She was beginning to discover all over again the things that had drawn her to Ross in the first place and she actually looked forward to seeing him and being with him. And when she thought of the long, arduous trip back east and the reprisals, shame, and guilt that would be heaped on her, the thought of returning home became less than attractive. And she began to care about what leaving Ross would mean to him. He had shown her in every way that he loved her and as the time had passed she had become more convinced it wasn't just his guilt he was trying to compensate. With the first boat that had come from the east his demeanor had become increasingly anxious.

When he came to take her home on the last day of school he was even quieter than the previous days. She didn't question him. She knew he was ready now to hear her decision and he would ask her in his own good time. She prepared their supper while he sat fidgeting. Three mouthfuls into the meal he laid down his knife and waited for her to look at him.

"Abbie, I be hearin' there's a steamboat comin' to St. Louis. When it be leavin' here it'll be goin' up the Ohio. I could have ye home in a matter of weeks. Do ye want me to buy passage on it?"

Quite simply she answered, "No."

He blinked and asked, "What?"

"I said no. I don't want you to buy passage on the steamboat."

Still not understanding he protested, "But it'll be the fastest and best way I can be gettin' ye home now, Abbie. It'd be like the honey—" He stopped and swallowed. "It'd be like one of those holidays the rich people be takin', now. Sure now, ye'd like that, wouldn't ye?"

"Yes, I'd like it very much. But I don't want to go home. I want to stay with you."

He looked at her with utter disbelief and then all the agony he felt over the thought of losing her twisted his face into a mask of pain. "Don't be doin' this to me, Abbie. Don't be torturin' me with your promise of stayin' if ye don't mean it."

She rose and came around the table to him, voluntarily touching him with her hand for the first time in months. "I mean it, Ross. I want to stay with you if you want me to."

He looked up at her and his voice choked. "Mother of God! Want ye to—" His voice was lost as he took her in his arms and pressed his face against her. She didn't pull away and felt his tears soak through her dress. Her hand rested on his thick chestnut hair and traced the waves she had loved so well and now knew she loved again. After a few minutes he released her and, once more in control, got up. "Well, now, it be back to work I have to be goin'. Ye bar the door, now, and don't let anyone in."

She smiled. "I won't."

He grinned back. "But me?"

"But you."

He went out the door and she heard his voice singing as he strode down the road to the warehouse. She barred the door and leaned against it in nervous expectancy of what his return home that night would mean. She longed for his kisses and caresses but the brutality of her rape still filled her with revulsion and she was uncertain if she could resume a physical relationship. By the time he came home, she was so tense her hand shook as she unbarred the door, but Ross acted as if nothing were changed between them.

He bathed and went to bed, and when he didn't take her in his arms, she was both surprised and disappointed. She would have to make the first move and the thought of it made anxiety and anticipation wage an unresolved war in her.

He was strangely quiet in the morning and she knew exactly what his thoughtful looks meant. She pretended not to notice. Instead, she asked, "Will you go with me while I look for another job today?"

"I was thinkin' of makin' a change. What would ye think of startin' that farm I be wantin'? It would mean hard work for ye, but we would be together and it would be a place of our own."

"I know how much you want a farm, Ross, but don't you think it best to wait and see if there's going to be a war or not?"

He looked crestfallen. They both had heard stories of Indian depredations on the outer settlements, and if war was declared the Indian threat would become much worse. "Aye, I suppose it would, but the fact that people be leavin' because of it makes the land easier to be gettin' now, with a cabin and land cleared. I know it be a lot to be askin' of ye after what ye have already been through, and I won't be forcin' ye into it if ye don't want it."

The thought of a cabin away from people and exposed to Indian attack was frightening to Abigail, and she didn't want to go through any more of that kind of terror—she had already had too much. Yet she knew Ross would never be completely happy unless he had the chance to farm. He had always considered her, just as he was doing now, and she could do no less for him. She had to give him the chance and hope he would decide, after all, he was not a farmer. She didn't speak of failure but the thought lurked in her mind, too. That gave her at least two chances to hope that by winter they could move back to St. Louis.

"All right, Ross. I'm willing to try it if you'll promise me we'll move back here if things don't work out."

His smile was glorious. "Abbie, me darlin', ye be wonderful! As the Father, Son, and the Holy Ghost be my witness, I promise ye if things don't be workin' out and you're not happy, I'll bring ye back to town."

11

SNOW CLOUD

In a few days time Ross had found a farm to his liking with the help of none other than the renowned Daniel Boone. Boone was an old man in his seventies and grown stout with idleness but his deep blue eyes were still alert and his movements those of a much younger man. He had been in the Missouri Territory for a number of years, and the land he told Ross about was land he had once claimed under the Spanish government that had subsequently been taken away by the United States government because he had never filed a deed for it. He lived near Le Charrette with his wife in a cabin on one of his son's farms and was often a visitor to St. Louis and adviser on the land and Indians to many.

The highway to their new home was again water. In the company of trappers, traders, and other settlers on their way upriver, they set out on the Missouri for their new home, sight unseen, in the wilderness, more than two hundred miles away. Looking calmer than she felt, Abigail became once more the unwilling traveler. But the river soon worked its magic, and Abigail forgot her apprehension as each mile brought new and spectacular scenes. Limestone rocks sparkling with quartz crystals lined the north side of the river and, after passing an abandoned settlement, they came to a landmark known as Tavern Rocks, where boatmen before them for years had used the cave and painted and written on the walls.

They spent nights at settlements along the way and the contact with other settlers and the large, comfortable homes and prosperous farms of some of them encouraged both Abigail and Ross. Yet when it came to talk of Indians apprehension returned.

They reached the area known as Boone's Licks and, with the aid of one of the families settled in the area, they were soon taken by wagon to their new home. They reached it by nightfall and Ross was not disappointed at the first look of his new farm. A timbered creek bordered the farm and a good spring provided water for the cabin. A few acres had already been cultivated before and a small shed would hold a cow and a horse temporarily. Their neighbor spent the night with them and promised to send over other close neighbors for them to meet and to put the word out that they needed to buy a horse and a cow.

The first month in their new home often left them too exhausted to eat at night. For Ross there was the cultivating and seeding of his land and the cutting of wood for cooking and building fence for the animals that had been bought within a week of their arrival. For Abigail it was the gathering and drying of the first fruits of summer and the meat Ross brought in. One of their neighbors offered to trade Abigail a pair of chickens for the making of a dress, and she agreed without hesitation. When she had spare time she helped Ross clear the land, carrying away the many stones they uncovered. She soon had enough to start a stone fence around her yard.

It was a killing pace and they both knew one day it would have to end, just as they both knew the reason they drove themselves to the brink of exhaustion. After one especially long day of carrying rocks Abigail ached in every bone of her body. She dutifully cooked supper for Ross but instead of eating she lay down on their bed and, without intending to, fell asleep. Ross woke her and she groaned as she tried to get up but the effort wasn't worth it.

Ross shook his head with concern. "Ye really be worn out and 'tis me fault for lettin' ye drive yourself so. Let me help ye, now, to undress and I'll be givin' ye a rub."

She didn't protest and once her clothes were off she collapsed again on the bed, not caring that she didn't have on her nightgown. Ross began to rub her back and shoulders working down her arms.

She turned her head and looked at him through heavy-lidded eyes and his dark, deep, intent eyes met hers with warmth. "Ye remember when I be doin' this once before for ye, now?"

Huskily she whispered, "I remember," beginning to feel a hunger for him she thought she would never feel again.

He smiled at her tenderly. "And do ye, now, be rememberin' what be happenin' when I rubbed your legs, Abbie?"

With breath almost stopped, she whispered, "Yes."

"Do your legs ache, now, Abbie?"

"Yes."

"Do ye want me to rub them, too, now?"

"Yes."

With slitted eyes and barely breathing she saw him swallow hard and turn his attention to her aching legs. He finished presently massaging the backs of her legs and with pulses pounding she turned over. His hands trembled as he touched her thighs and Abigail could no longer deny her need for him. She pushed herself up and encircled him with her arms.

"Ross, please, *please* love me. I want you so much. I love you so dearly, my darling. Please love me."

He took her with all the care of a man who takes something very precious and fragile in his hands and dares not crush it because he knows it cannot be replaced. The tender lilting words of love she had missed caressed her ear, almost incoherent so great was his emotion. But Abigail was not a fragile piece of glass and she needed not only his gentleness but his strength and her body vigorously demanded him to conquer her and when he did, she lay crying in his arms, pouring out all of the misery accumulated by months of anxiety and heartbreak. They fell asleep in each other's arms.

Their first visit by Indians brought terror anew to Abigail. They turned out to be friendly and pleased with the food they were given and vowed their friendship, but that didn't help Abigail's peace of mind at all and she was able to relax only when they had been gone more than a day. She had been sure they would come back to rob and kill them in the middle of the night. When they did show up in a week's time with their families, she had an even greater fear they would become permanent fixtures on the farm. They spoke a little English and were able to make Ross understand they were on their way south to visit other Indians. Abigail was able to smile in her relief and treated them to homemade bread and milk, generously lacing the bread with honey from a bee tree Ross had cut down.

The hot, humid weather brought on another attack of fever and Abigail used the last of her medicine. Ross made her stay out of the fields until she was better but she didn't get better. The heat overpowered her, leaving her capable of little more than her household chores, robbing her of her strength and even the newly reborn wild enthusiasm for their most intimate embraces. The morning she woke up sick to her stomach and had to dash outside to vomit she knew there was something terribly wrong.

She crawled back into bed and Ross awoke and asked sleepily, "What is it, Abbie?"

"Nothing. Go back to sleep."

He looked at her white face and sat up. "Do ye want me to send for the doctor or be gettin' one of the women to come?"

"No. I'll be all right. It must be the aftereffects of the fever. I'll get over it soon."

And by noon she did feel better and she thought surely she would be better, but for the next three days the same sickness launched her out of bed every morning. The fourth morning when she came back to bed Ross was propped up on one elbow and grinning at her. She lay down weakly and said stonily, "I don't see what you find so amusing. I feel terrible."

"Sure now, ye do. But I be knowin' what be wrong with ye, Abbie darlin'."

Sarcastically she retorted, "And since when did you become a doctor?"

He pulled her into his arms and laughed, burying his head against her breasts and kissing them until she wasn't mad any longer. She pulled on his hair until he looked up at her. "Are you going to tell me or not, Dr. Galligher?"

"Sure now, I don't be needin' to be a doctor to know that ye be pregnant."

"Pregnant!" she gasped. "Are you sure?"

"Sure now, I be seein' me mother carry on enough times just like this."

She sank back into the pillows in a state of shock. Too well she remembered the time she had been pregnant before. She hadn't realized it that time either and she hadn't been sick like this. Ross remembered, too.

"From now on I don't want ye to be doin' any heavy work like packin' rocks or cuttin' wood and packin' it in. I be doin' that from now on for ye. I don't want to be losin' this baby." He got up and pulled on his pants and turned back to her as he buttoned his shirt. "And when the harvest be done I be takin' ye back to St. Louis until the baby be born."

Her heart made more room for her growing love for him. "I love you, Dr. Galligher."

He sat down beside her and kissed her. "Ye stay in bed now and I'll be comin' in for lunch."

"What about your breakfast?"

He grabbed a hunk of bread and a handful of fruit. "This be doin' me fine."

When the sickness eased Abigail got up with a light heart and set about making bread and a pie from the berries she had gathered the day before. The pie was in the oven and she was kneading her bread dough when she heard a horse gallop into the yard. The door was open and she saw a glimpse of the horse and rider. It looked like another Indian and she went on with her kneading, confident Ross would be there to handle this latest visitor.

A shadow fell across her table and she looked up, her hands going to her mouth as her eyes saw the horrible blackened and bloody figure in the doorway, something familiar swinging at his side. She screamed as she recognized her husband's chestnut-colored hair and kept on screaming as she sank to the floor, fainting with shock.

When consciousness returned, her first sensation was one of extreme discomfort. She tried to move and relieve the ache in her arms and legs but found she was restrained. Her eyes opened and all the terror returned. She was tied securely with her arms stretched over her head to the bed leg and her legs were spread and tied each to a table leg by the ankle. Her skirt was bunched around her waist and her underclothes had been cut away. The Indian squatted beside her, the blackened, inhuman face demoniacally evil. She saw now that the blood on his body was his own and came from a number of slashes over his chest and arms. The little finger of his left hand had been severed at the first joint and hung grotesquely by a flap of skin. She shuddered with horror and closed her eyes. She didn't need to be told what would happen next. He moved and she felt his body cover hers, the smell of him gagging her and causing more nausea in her already uncertain stomach. She knew by experience there was no use struggling but strove desperately to protect herself from his thrust by pulling with all her strength on the table until she could brace her heels on the dirt floor and move with him. She endeavored to pray out loud as calmly as she could as the Indian brutally took her.

"Dear, sweet Lord," she gasped, "hear my prayer and have mercy on me. Forgive me my sins and prepare me to enter the gates of heaven. Jesus, my Savior, I am ready for you to enter my heart and make it pure to serve you. Make my death quick and merciful. Oh, God!" she cried, "Let me—!" Her eyes flew open as the sharp point of his knife nicked the tender skin of her neck and closed them again just as quickly upon seeing his face so close to hers. She waited for the final stroke that would end her life, her lips still moving in prayer as she tried to ride out the fury of his body. He pressed the sharp edge of the knife against her throat with increasing strength until she could think of nothing but the steel cutting her and her prayer was lost in apprehension and expectation. The blade was removed when she stopped praying and she thought that it was possible he had wanted her to stop praying. She started to pray out loud again, hoping it would anger him into killing her. Instead he slashed her cheek, and she gasped in pain and surprise as he savagely thrust against her, increasing her pain as she struggled to push away from him. Knowing she could not stand many more brutal thrusts she coolly chose to end it by bringing him to a climax as soon as possible. By the time he realized what she was doing it was almost too late and even though he held her to inflict more pain, it was over and he rolled from her breathing heavily.

Abigail lay unmoving, barely daring to breath with her eyes closed, waiting for him to kill her. He moved and she stopped breathing altogether. He untied her from the table legs and bed and pulled her to her feet. Wildly she thought of her other captivity and knew she had to make him kill her. Now. She jerked away from him and ran for the door, screaming as loudly as she could. He caught her in the doorway and knocked her to the ground and dragged her to the corral and tied her hands and feet to a post.

The cow, visibly upset, came bawling to the fence. The Indian went to his horse and, stringing his bow, shot the cow through the heart and she fell convulsing at Abigail's feet to die. She looked in desperation toward the field where she knew Ross lay, unable to keep from looking, and could see nothing because their own horse stood blocking her view. He had dragged the plow to the gate and stood waiting to be let in. The Indian went to him and cut most of the harness from him and brought him into the yard and tied him. The Indian returned to the house and found the flour sacks Abigail was embroidering and ransacked the house, filling them with food and whatever caught his eye. She was surprised when he didn't set fire to it and then knew why he didn't. The smoke would have been seen too quickly and would have alerted the other settlers of trouble.

Her two embroidered and grass-stuffed bed pillows were brought to make a saddle and pad of sorts for the horse and as soon as he had them tied in place and the other sacks slung over the horse, he came to her and untied her and placed her on the horse, tieing her feet beneath the horse's belly and tieing her hands in front so she could grasp the reins and mane. He slipped a noose with a long length of rope over her head and she knew it made no difference to him whether she rode upright or hanging upside down and she could make it as easy or as difficult as she wanted on herself.

They didn't stop until dusk and it was all Abigail could do to keep from sliding beneath the horse's belly. She ached in every muscle and bone of her body and the tears rolled down her cheeks as she thought about Ross and the hopelessness of her situation and the fact that Ross would never again rub the soreness from her body. The Indian pulled her from the horse and tied her to a tree. She was too numb to think clearly but knew she had to. She had to escape or make him kill her. It was obvious he was not going to kill her now and she doubted she could anger him into killing her before they reached where he was taking her. Her only other chance was to escape.

He brought her food and, having decided escape was her only means of salvation, she knew she had to eat to be strong enough to get away from him. It was her own food and she ate eagerly all that he gave her. He gazed at her intently and Abigail didn't like what she was seeing in his eyes. It meant only one thing. As soon as she was finished eating he retied her until she lay on her back on the ground and she knew there was no way she could protect herself from him this time.

She begged him, "*Please*, give me some slack."

He silenced her with a slap and she gasped in pain as he forced his body into hers, praying silently as he brutalized her. Then as if in answer to her prayers she realized this would be a way to die. If he ruptured her womb and she miscarried, she would soon bleed to death and she prayed for him to tear her apart and bring her death. She waited in tense agony, when he was finally through with her, for her abortion to begin but even this was denied her and eventually the ache caused by the abuse of his body eased and she slept.

She was sick in the morning but it was only her morning sickness and she was disappointed to find she had not started to hemorrhage. She couldn't eat and vomited, but this didn't deter her captor and he raped her again. Oh, God, she thought, how low she had become when she could accept such treatment without outrage and even strained to meet his brutal attack, wanting the pain and glorying in it as a means to her end.

Without concern he again tied her to her horse and led her onward, always following the river though he led her along the top of the bluffs that stood back from the river, riding on a vast, wind-rolled prairie of grass. It looked empty of life except for the wind rippling the golden grass in perpetual waves, but as they rode she constantly saw deer and antelope leap out before them and flocks of birds of bright plumage would skim over the grass, undulating with the waves. The heat became unbearable on her bare head and forgetting propriety she pulled her skirt from beneath her and draped it over her head. She was terribly hungry and even more thirsty now the morning sickness had subsided. But her captor never stopped and she suffered in silence trying to decide when she could best escape.

After a few more days of the same grueling dawn to dusk riding Abigail began to despair of ever escaping. He was always on the alert and his eyes were constantly studying her. He never failed to tie her just as he never failed to rape her night and morning. And if she did escape she could never make it back without the horse and the food he carried but with him she was as visible as a tree in this featureless prairie. She prayed for guidance.

Again she felt her prayers had been answered when their food ran low and he began killing game. He built no fire to cook the meat and she couldn't even look at the raw, oozing morsels he brought her and gagged when she saw him consume flesh or organs without discrimination. Starvation was then her answer. When she was too weak to stay on the horse he would have to kill her or leave her to die. Starving in the morning was easy but by noon she was ravenously hungry and thought she could even eat raw meat. But in a couple more days starvation too became bearable.

She was to the point of delirium when they rode into an Indian camp and through her dizzy weakness she believed her journey was over. She expected torture and burning and was ready and eager for it, knowing her life would soon end, but instead she was taken to a lodge and laid upon a soft bed of buffalo robes. Water was forced between her parched lips and grease spread on her sun-burned face and cracked lips. She smelled the delicious aroma of cooking meat and her hunger returned as her stomach rebelled against her imposed starvation. Hallucinating, she saw herself in a battle with the fetus she carried over a piece of meat. The baby, looking very much like her dead husband, was crying and hanging onto the meat with one hand while trying to stick his thumb in his wailing mouth, and she was pulling on it with all her strength trying to wrench it from his grasp. She tried to pray but it was difficult to think and each time she tried one of the ten commandments kept interrupting her flow of thoughts until it was impossible to think of anything except *Thou shalt not kill.*

She awoke sometime in the middle of the night. The lodge was dark and quiet but outside the cacophony of an Indian village at night was distinct. Her mind was clear and she felt rested, though weak. She thought of Ross and all the happy, tender moments they'd shared together and tears filled her eyes. She relived every day since she'd first seen him and the last day of his life with her was so vivid she felt the touch of his lips against her breasts and pressed her hands over her heart clasping the sensation to her. With reverent awe she realized her husband was not dead but lived inside her. The child she carried was alive and God had chosen to save it and her, too. She could not die or she would kill her baby. A peace of mind came over her and she knew this was what God wanted. If her child lived, Ross would live, too.

In the morning, she awoke still at peace. Her stomach so long denied food did not have anything to regurgitate and she lay quietly taking in her surroundings. This dwelling was entirely different from the hut she'd known on the Ohio. It was circular in form and made of long poles in a cone shape and covered with large hides sewn together. The equipment placed in neat arrangement around the perimeter was beautifully decorated and the bed she slept in was more comfortable than most she'd known in the months since she'd left home. The squaws attending her saw she was awake and brought her water and food and she ate hungrily. When she had finished, the squaw serving her hurried out and in a few minutes her captor came in and looked down at her. He was still covered with dried blood and blackened hideously and Ross's scalp still swung from his belt but none of that seemed so upsetting now.

For two more days she rested and was fed, with her captor coming in to check on her several times a day. The third day he came he gave her his first command. She sat uncomprehending on the bed and he motioned to the door of the tipi and repeated the word. She was afraid and didn't want to go with him, not knowing what unspeakable things waited outside. He came to her and grabbed her wrists and yanked her to her feet, repeating the word again and dragged her outside.

Her horse waited with his and she was placed on its back. She was in better condition to appraise the Indians gathered to see her leave and found them to be generally taller than the Indians she had seen on the Ohio, with no articles of white clothing among

them and very few guns. They seemed untouched by the debilitating contact of the white man and had an air of proud strength and
boldness. The beautifully wrought designs on their skin garments
intrigued Abigail's discerning eye and she marveled at the indi-
viduality of each one as they passed through the camp.

Then they were alone again on the vast prairie, riding ever
northwestward, passing increasing herds of deer, antelope, elk,
and buffalo. When they stopped at night he cooked meat and when
he was finished eating he brought her what was left on the point of
his knife. She shuddered to think what that knife had touched but
she was too hungry after a long day of riding to refuse it. She
reached for the meat with her tied hands and he held it just out of
her grasp and, pointing to it, named it. Several times he repeated
the word, and when she wouldn't say it he cuffed her, bowling her
over on the ground. She determined she would have to learn his
language or not eat, and she repeated the word, feeling the com-
forts of civilization slipping farther out of reach and reality.

By the time they came in view of his village, she knew several
words. They stopped on a hilltop overlooking the Indian village
camped in a grove on the banks of a fair-sized stream. He pointed
to the camp and named it, and she repeated it several times for
him, not knowing at all what the word meant in English as she had
the other words she had learned. Much to her surprise he didn't
ride into the camp but led her back out of sight of the lodges. She
watched in fascination as he meticulously added more black to his
face from color he carried with him and now added stripes of color
to his face and took Ross's hair from his belt and fastened it to the
point of his lance. When he had completed his rituals, they rode
back to the top of the hill where he began yelling insanely and
galloping the horses in an oval on the crest of the hill. Abigail could
do nothing but hang on for dear life as he raced the horses back
and forth.

At last he plunged the horses down the hill and Abigail saw
people crowding around the lodges as he rode breakneck and
whooping into camp. He was cheered as they entered but Abigail
was the target of stones and whips and she thought surely he would
let them kill her. He stopped in front of what appeared to be the
biggest lodge and the best decorated and when an elderly squaw
came out he handed her a medallion Abigail had not noticed
before. Immediately the woman began wailing terribly, with other
women taking up the cry, and soon the whole camp was in a state of
chaos.

Her captor took her to the next lodge and untied her from the horse and set her into the midst of yelping and snarling dogs. She was already bruised and bleeding and expected to be torn apart by these vicious-looking animals, but he pulled her inside the lodge and she collapsed on the earthen floor, the dogs following to sniff and lick at her as she cowered in fear and distaste, hiding her head. He spoke to the stolid, heavy woman inside and, with a gleam in her eye, the woman picked up a stick and pointed to what Abigail thought looked like a cow's stomach. After several painful prod-dings with the stick, Abigail understood she was to pick up the ugly vessel and follow her new mistress. Once outside the tipi, she was again stoned and beaten as she followed the squaw to the river and filled the flesh bag with water and returned to the lodge. Her captor was gone, and Abigail wondered if her lot could have been any worse with him than with this cruel woman master.

Before the day was over Abigail learned she had three more sadistic mistresses. The squaw had three daughters, the oldest girl near twelve and the youngest about six. They delighted in being mean to Abigail, contriving to trip her at every opportunity and laughing heartily when she fell, and calling her in Indian what Abigail suspected was close to clumsy idiot in English. They quickly had Abigail doing their tasks, too, and enjoyed beating her as much as their mother. And as the days went by, they terrorized her by hiding insects or snakes in her bed or in whatever they knew she would have to use. She quickly learned to watch closely where she was going to avoid falling into their traps and to shake her bed and open any of the storage containers carefully. And as if the long, brutally exhausting days weren't bad enough, the nights were even worse. Sleep was a virtual impossibility to one uninitiated to camp life. The inhabitants seemed never to sleep but spent nights wailing to the monotonous and nerve-wracking throb of drums, and people came and went from lodge to lodge in utter disregard for privacy. Eventually Abigail became accustomed to the noise and slept in spite of it.

The squaw, unlike Abigail's captor, didn't try to teach Abigail the Indian language, using Abigail's ignorance as another excuse to beat her. It made Abigail all the more determined to learn in order to avoid the beatings. It wasn't easy, as the woman was either mumbling or screaming at her in fury, and the daughters were no better. Then, as if someone had thrown a switch, the camp changed from the wailing and weeping Abigail correctly guessed was mourning for someone—she didn't know who, only that they

somehow seemed to blame her for the person's death—to an air of
expectancy and excitement. An abundance of meat was brought in
by the hunters and the women gathered wild grapes and other
fruits in preparation for a feast of huge proportion. With the
change in attitude in the camp the people of the camp became too
busy to bother Abigail. Even the children ignored her, all except
for the family in whose tipi she was still slave and scapegoat.

She little understood the rituals, dancing, and singing taking
place but was allowed to watch what looked to her like the election
of a new chief. The man looked fairly familiar to her and with
increasing interest she decided the new chief was the man who had
taken her captive. Without the blackened face and blood-crusted
body, he looked quite different and had a certain dignity and grace
Abigail had been too terrified to see before. He was perhaps an
inch or more taller than Ross, with his black hair carefully dressed
in Indian finery of feathers and fur. He had high cheekbones and a
prominent nose and looked every inch a leader. On his broad chest
hung the copper medallion she had seen the day they arrived.

It was a few more days before the camp returned to normal
and, to Abigail's surprise, the new chief was the husband of her
mistress. She looked upon his return to the lodge with apprehension, remembering the many days he had used her mercilessly. His
return proved to be a mixed blessing. He immediately showed
favoritism for her and Abigail feared for her life at the hands of a
jealous squaw but, surprisingly, she suffered less because he kept
the squaw in her place and even beat her when she unjustly treated
Abigail. Even his daughters became immediately respectful of her,
and the malicious tricks ceased.

The next day the camp was broken, and Abigail gained some
respect for the Indian society. The dismantling started out looking
like mass confusion, but somehow, in a matter of minutes, the
lodges were down and made into travois, the leather boxlike containers they stored all their goods in were tied securely on top with
their robes and other household equipment, and under directions
from a mounted group of men, the caravan started to move.
Fortunately Abigail's morning sickness had started to subside and
she felt only a slight queasiness in her stomach in the mornings,
allowing her to eat heartily. Her strength was once again almost
normal. She thanked God it was, for they marched for days across
the endless sea of sunburned grass, getting sunburned herself and
grudgingly having to protect her skin with the grease the Indians
used.

They crossed the Missouri and seemingly headed for the black-looking hills now looming in the distance. They finally reached the bizarre outcropping of bluffs, spectacularly colored and hosting groves of deformed cedar, and made camp in a cool canyon. The atmosphere now was one of leisure and relaxation. The women went on foraging trips and brought back an abundance of berries while the men hunted, but there were days they stayed in camp and her master spent hours lounging on his couch and teaching her his language. She learned his name was Snow Cloud, his wife's name was Slow Water, and her name was to be Little Yellow Bird.

After several weeks of comparative vacation, the camp moved once more back across the plains to begin what Abigail was to learn was the fall buffalo hunt. By the time the buffalo herds were located, Abigail was more than glad to set up a semipermanent camp. But that was only the beginning of what proved to be an exhausting experience for her. She never believed such a quantity of meat could possibly be preserved before spoiling but she learned quickly cleanliness was to be ignored for the sake of the most important object of getting the meat cut in strips and onto the drying racks.

The robes were not allowed to spoil either, and as soon as the meat was drying, the distasteful task of tanning the buffalo robes was undertaken. The first few times Abigail tried to rub the hides with the mixture of buffalo brains and urine, she vomited and was beaten by Slow Water. It was all she could do to smell the vile mixture, let alone touch it. It was Snow Cloud who came to her rescue. He always made sure she was not mistreated excessively by his wife by examining Abigail each night. Finding her covered with bruises and welts, he questioned his wife, and Abigail was able in a limited way to tell him the tanning mixture made her sick. He ordered Slow Water to get something for him and when she brought him the embroidered pillowcases, Abigail was surprised and then terribly heartsick at the sight of things from her home with all the memories of Ross they invoked. Snow Cloud was questioning her and she finally understood he wanted to know if the embroidery was her work. When she said it was, he immediately had Slow Water bring her a tanned robe that had been aged and worked until it was soft and pliable. She was given sinew and awls to use and she understood she was to duplicate the pattern of the pillowcases on the robe. It would be no easy task, but Abigail welcomed it in exchange for the drudgery of tanning hides.

The weather had been increasingly cold with the approach of

winter. Fierce winds howled across the vast, unbroken landscape and Abigail had no choice but to wear a buffalo robe like the rest of the Indians to keep warm. Her dress was getting much too tight for her as the baby she carried swelled her body and with the robe arranged over her, she could wear the dress unbuttoned, much to her relief. Since Snow Cloud had set her to work embroidering on the robe, she had had few beatings, and now that he was in camp most of the time and knew everything that went on, he had quit examining her and her condition had escaped his notice.

When the first snow whitened the plains, the Indians moved into winter camp in a sheltered valley along a good-sized river. With leisure heavy on his hands, Snow Cloud spent more time in their lodge and taught her while she worked. It became all too apparent to Abigail that this closeness was increasing his desire for her, but with Slow Water and his daughters ever present there was little opportunity to satisfy his desire. This was just as well as far as Abigail was concerned. Yet his obvious modesty at taking her in front of the others mystified her. As she comprehended more of their language and life-style, she was aware of their constant preoccupation with all things sexual. Even the women, at times, talked and gestured obscenely. Still they observed rigid standards of modesty, when it came to expressing love before others; but let a maiden be caught alone without a chaperone and she was fair game.

The day came when her embroidering was almost finished, and the design was so beautiful on the soft buffalo robe even Abigail was pleased with it. Snow Cloud came in from being with the other men of the village and came to examine her work. By the smile on his face, Abigail knew the robe pleased him and his hand touched her hair and rested on her shoulder. His face became solemn as desire for her filled him. He ordered Slow Water and the girls to go cut wood, even though there was plenty of wood outside the lodge. Not daring to disobey, they put on their heavy robes and left the lodge.

Abigail held her breath as he laced the door of the lodge shut and turned to unfasten her robe, his eyes seeing the gaping dress with her stomach pushing through. He touched her belly and she wanted to draw away. She kept her eyes downcast, as was required of women in men's presence. He undressed her and examined her thoroughly. As resigned as she was to this moment—when she would have to accept his body—it was still impossible for her not to flinch at his touch, and the idea of his hands going over her, touching what was to her a sacred gift with hands that had killed her husband, was still unbearable.

His voice was gentle with awe as he remarked about her pregnancy. She realized he believed the child to be his and when she had to answer him she didn't deny it. He took her to his bed then, and she almost thought a different man was with her. The brutal animal passion was gone. He spoke to her softly, though his words weren't words of love as she knew them, but jests and obscenities that grated on her, no matter how tenderly they were expressed. His hands caressed her not with the gentleness of her husband's, but with almost bruising heaviness, as if wanting her to feel his strength and dominance over her. There was even less consideration in the rest of his use of her and when he was through with her, he left the lodge and she resumed her work, close to tears as she recalled a love she would never have again.

12

A CHILD IS BORN

Immediately a feast was announced and Abigail became the center of attention. She didn't at first understand what was going on, but she soon was aware of the complete change in her position. No longer did Slow Water order her about, and the day of the feast she was dressed in a beautiful dress of soft deerskin like the other women wore. She had no choice but to sit still for her hair to be braided and greased and her face painted, and that night, at a lavish feast and what to Abigail seemed an instant divestment of months of work on her and Slow Water's part, Snow Cloud proceeded to squander gifts on the whole village, even giving away some of his most valued horses. When Abigail finally understood she had been made Snow Cloud's wife, she felt weak. The chances that he would ever give her up now, if she were somehow found or escaped, were even more remote than before.

The compensations of being wife instead of slave more than made up for the anxiety she had felt. She still had work to do but it was her own work and Slow Water no longer intimidated her. It was obvious Snow Cloud favored her and she usually wound up the winner in any tattling sessions on the part of the three daughters. She guarded carefully against giving Slow Water any opportunity for vengeance, feeling the woman couldn't help but feel jealous and angry. Always Abigail remembered she must practice the golden rule and remain a good Christian, though at times an irresistible malice for the woman who had treated her so cruelly reared its head.

Winter swept across the prairies with a cruel and harsh hand. Hunger and cold were not unknown to the camp, and whenever weather permitted, Snow Cloud would lead the men on a winter hunt to replenish supplies of those who needed food. Their own food had been severely depleted by the wedding feast, and Abigail still bridled at the thought of such mismanagement. She never thought she would be reduced to eating dog, but after suffering from hunger for several days and becoming concerned about what that hunger was causing to her unborn child, she ate dog and any other thing that was brought in and forced herself to keep it down.

March came and with it the first letup in the icy grip of winter. In the next few days game began to appear and when the ice started cracking on the river, fish were once again obtainable. The complacence Abigail had felt all winter as her child grew and filled her was now replaced with near panic at the thought of delivering a baby at best with one of the old women of the village to help her. The baby dropped ever lower and the pressure increased as did her panic. Abigail was nearing her time and a separate lodge was prepared for her in expectation of the impending birth. When the first labor pain racked her body she went to the confinement lodge to wait for whatever God's will brought. Several women of the village had become her friends during the winter and they constantly attended her, offering advice and comfort, but when the pains indicated she didn't have much longer to go, a steadying calm descended over her. Somehow she was able to collect her thoughts and realize the birth of this child should not be witnessed by the other women. Their keen eyesight and penchant for scandal and gossip were not unknown to Abigail.

They were unwilling to leave when Abigail pleaded with them to go and only when in desperation she resorted to yelling and throwing things at them did they abandon her, leaving the dyes they had been using to dye the sinew thread and quills while they kept her company. With enough knowledge of their art after a winter of learning, Abigail was able to mix a dye that when applied to her skin turned it a hue more nearly that of the Indians. If they saw her child before she was able to disguise its pale skin, they would know Snow Cloud was not its father.

Frightened and gasping for breath in the few moments between pains, Abigail squatted before the round post planted for the purpose in the lodge and clung to it desperately, her forehead resting on its smooth surface between contractions. She felt a chill breath of air as the door flap was raised and opened blurring eyes upon the intruder. It was Wind Woman, Snow Cloud's mother and the village's highly respected medicine woman. Her appearance was every inch one of royalty. She was taller than most of the women, with a look of strength instead of stoutness. Her face was unlined and her movements regal and dignified, with only the color of her hair betraying her advanced years. Even since the marriage she had continued to befriend Abigail, although custom dictated that wives and mothers-in-law should avoid each other. Abigail didn't know if Wind Woman still considered her a slave or felt the custom irrevelant in Abigail's case, even though everything indicated the latter. She was the last person Abigail wanted to witness the birth of her child.

"Do you need help, daughter?"

Abigail shook her head torturously. "No. Yellow Bird thanks you, but this is something I must do myself to prove myself strong and brave enough to bring honor to your son."

A smile lighted the older woman's face. "Wind Woman understands and is proud. No one shall enter until you call. The Great Spirit is pleased and will give you a son."

Wind Woman left the lodge and Abigail collapsed against the post as the next contraction overwhelmed her. She had little time to relish her quick thinking as she closed her eyes against the pain. Panting and panic-stricken, with tears running down her cheeks as she tried to muster enough strength to resume the unfamiliar birthing position and bitterly resenting the circumstances that had brought her to this crude state of dropping her child like an animal, she felt her water break. Abandoning the post, she crawled to a mat and lay on her back and pushed with all her strength as the contractions came swiftly. A terrible, insistent pain tore at her and her shaking hands clawed at the soft cradle pelts nearby to scream into. One last violent contraction and the baby's head broke through and instantly all pain was gone. Diminishing contractions quickly pushed the rest of the child from her body, and Abigail lay weak and shaking but triumphant.

Breathing deeply to control the incapacitating trembling of her body, she slowly raised herself to a sitting position and felt another contraction as she compressed her body and forced the afterbirth from herself. She sat dazed, looking at the still form between her legs covered with blood, and slowly her mind began functioning as she wondered what to do next. Reason returned with a rush and she gingerly picked up the lifeless form and turned it over. Her child was a boy. Instinctively she used her fingers to check its mouth and nose and, remembering the only thing she could about having babies, she lifted it by the heels and swatted it hesitantly until the child sputtered and gasped its first breath of air and wailed lustily. Working quickly and more assuredly now, Abigail tied and cut the umbilical cord. Warm water was close at hand near the fire and she bathed the child and lay it on the clean, soft pelts and proceeded to take care of herself.

As soon as she had washed herself and rolled up the bloody mat, she took up the dye and gently spread it on the still red and wrinkled little body while her son wailed in anger. She soon realized she was smiling and talking softly to the kicking little body, and when her task was complete she took time to examine her baby thoroughly, her heart filling to capacity with the totally new sensation of mother love. She was delighted in every way with him, not only because he was hers, but because he was beautiful and perfect and, she knew beyond question, the image of his father. Feeling very tired and growing cold, she added wood to the fire and, cradling the child in her arms, covered the two of them with a warm, soft buffalo robe and lay back and closed her eyes.

It was dark when Abigail awoke and she was terribly hungry. The child stirred next to her and she smiled lovingly at the tiny form. She got up and with careful movements added wood to the fire and went to the lodge opening.

"Wind Woman may come in now."

Instantly the lodge flap raised and the older woman entered. Her sharp eyes looked for and found the infant and she stepped close to peer down at the child she thought was her grandson. She smiled and remarked, "The Great Spirit has truly smiled upon us. This child will bring much pride to his father and to all of the Follow the Wind people. Now I will make something for you to eat."

Abigail felt she had truly done something special and the surprise could not be kept out of her eyes. Wind Woman, being the
most esteemed member of the village next to the high-ranking
members of the band, never had to cook anything for herself. She
was an honored guest at someone's tipi almost every day or the
recipient of the choicest of morsels from all who wished her special
ministrations in their behalf. Abigail murmured an appropriately
awed, "Yellow Bird is honored beyond words."

Abigail was further surprised when the meal Wind Woman
served her was better than she had expected from a woman who
seldom had to cook. She also insisted upon examining Abigail and
the baby and took the necessary steps to make certain Abigail
would recover quickly and with little discomfort. Abigail was relieved when the wise old woman finally left and she and her baby
could sleep undisturbed.

The baby awoke Abigail early with its whimpering and she
quickly got up to throw wood on the fire and warm the broth
Wind Woman had left for her to feed the baby. Before long the
baby was howling and Wind Woman hurried into the lodge,
frowning.

"He must not be allowed to make noise like that. Our enemies
would find us if we were trying to hide."

Abigail was at a temporary loss. Before she could hush the
child, Wind Woman had picked him up and, sticking her finger in
the congealed fat still floating on top of the cooking bladder,
immediately stuck the greasy finger in the child's mouth. Instantly
there was quiet as the baby sucked the greasy finger. The older
woman smiled and cooed to the baby. The broth was soon ready
and Abigail dipped some into the makeshift bag with its ugly teat.
She was soon feeding her baby.

Wind Woman watched and then said, "Sweet Grass will come to
give him his next feeding."

Abigail nodded. She had almost forgotten the custom practiced
by the Indians of not feeding their infants on their own mother's
milk for a number of days after birth.

"When your milk comes do you want one of the old toothless
ones to take it from you?"

Abigail shuddered visibly at the thought. "No. Isn't there some
child?"

The older woman shrugged her shoulders hopelessly. "I will
ask again. They are afraid."

Abigail spent the rest of the day resting and working on her

quilling to pass the time, glad there was no more important work to
do than to dye the porcupine quills and work them into a design on
a soft skin. She knew how lucky she was not to have borne a child
during the busy time and for now was perfectly content to care for
the baby and sing softly in English to him. Her contentment fled
when Sweet Grass came to nurse her child and she watched resent-
fully. She dreaded even more Snow Cloud's coming. She knew he
would examine his son with utmost care, and even after Sweet
Grass left her contentment did not return.

At dusk Wind Woman announced, "Your husband comes."

Abigail sat tense with downcast eyes as Snow Cloud's imposing
presence filled the small lodge. He stopped before Abigail and
said, "You have honored me with a son and I in turn honor you.
Today I am a proud and happy man. Though I will die my seed
shall live on."

Abigail couldn't help but raise her eyes. He had never spoken
thusly to her even though she knew he was capable of eloquence
from hearing him address the village in general. Quickly she
dropped her eyes again before he saw, but she needn't have feared.
Already he was engrossed in the baby, and she watched with
growing amazement at the tenderness and gentleness he exhibited
as he examined the child. Satisfied that his son was at least perfect
in body, he left the lodge and Abigail could relax.

Sweet Grass came for the last feeding and when she left the
baby was asleep and Abigail was alone with only the crackle of the
fire to disturb her thoughts. She looked at the sleeping child
trussed securely in his cradle board and lay back herself, too tired
to dwell for long on the past or on the future.

By morning her own breasts were beginning to ache and she
was anxious for Wind Woman to pay her morning call. She was
already beginning to feel it was worth risking disapproval if she fed
him and not at all convinced her milk would make the baby ill. The
thought of being nursed by one of the toothless grandmothers of
the village was abhorrent to her.

Wind Woman broke into her thoughts and she almost spoke
her mind before the other woman could speak, but she held her
tongue, only the look on her face betraying her anxiety.

"Be without concern, daughter. I have found a child who needs
you as much as you need her. Yesterday Slow Water's niece was
brought to our village. She has been terribly ill with the white man's
disease which has killed her parents and most of her band."

"How old is she?"

"She is four winters but small for her age. I will bring her to you."

Wind Woman left before Abigail could protest and she tried to steel herself against the inevitable. A four-year-old child was not too much different from a grown person in Abigail's mind. Wind Woman returned in a few minutes with the child cowering meekly behind her. Wind Woman took her tiny arm and pulled her out in front of her and held her. Abigail's heart immediately went out to the little girl. That she had been ill was evident. Her skin was a sick, muddy color and her face terribly thin, making her large eyes look even larger. The dress she wore of Slow Water's youngest daughter dwarfed her even more.

Abigail smiled and said, "Welcome. I am called Yellow Bird. What are you called?"

The dull eyes blinked and raised hesitantly to Wind Woman's face. Wind Woman gave her a little urging forward but the child resisted and tried to turn away. Wind Woman held her fast.

"She is called Spotted Fawn."

Abigail smiled again. "That is a very pretty name. Have you eaten yet? I have plenty."

Again the girl tried to shy away but Wind Woman ignored the pleading look. Just then the baby began to stir and make little whimperings. Instantly the child's eyes were drawn to the cradle board and Abigail took advantage of the apparent interest.

"This is my baby. He and I would like very much if you would be our friend."

This brought no response except the continued watchful interest of the baby.

Abigail offered, "Would you like to see him better?"

The girl took a hesitating step forward and Abigail unfastened the wrappings of the cradle board and held the baby for the girl to see. She came close and looked with wide eyes at the wriggling little body.

"Would you like to help me take care of him?"

She looked at Abigail for a long instant and then back to the baby and nodded just once.

"Would you stay here with me and help me? I need someone to take my milk until it is safe for him to take."

Again the long hesitant perusal of Abigail and then the short nod of assent.

"Thank you, Spotted Fawn. Now if you will bring some water we will heat it and you can help me bathe him."

Without hesitation the child picked up the buffalo stomach that served as a water container and left the lodge.

Wind Woman smiled. "You have done well by her. It will be good. I will come later to see how you are."

Abigail returned the older woman's smile. "Thank you for bringing her to me."

Wind Woman left and Abigail was alone. Happily she picked up the kicking baby and nuzzled and kissed his soft, warm body, filled with so much love for him she was afraid it was unnatural. Spotted Fawn came in and Sweet Grass followed shortly to nurse the baby. Abigail's own breasts ached even more intensely as she watched her baby nurse, and she was torn with the desire to take Spotted Fawn to her own breast in front of the other woman and too self-conscious to do so. Spotted Fawn watched curiously, her eyes going from one to the other.

As soon as Sweet Grass left, Abigail knew she couldn't wait longer. Already she could feel a dampness on her dress. Uncertainly she asked, "Would you like to take my milk now, Spotted Fawn?"

The girl just stood there, watching her, making it even more difficult for Abigail. Desperately Abigail suggested, "Come. Lie down on the bed with me." She laughed nervously. "I've never done this before. You'll have to show me how."

Abigail lay down on the soft lounge of robes and unlaced her dress waiting with held breath. Slowly Spotted Fawn came and looked down uncertainly at her.

"Don't be afraid. I need your help, Spotted Fawn. Please."

Slowly the child lay down beside her and Abigail closed her eyes, too self-conscious to want to see the grotesque picture she knew she and the child made, feeling suddenly unclean and depraved. Silently she prayed for forgiveness as she waited tensely for the child to nurse. She felt the small cold hand brush her as Spotted Fawn uncovered her breast and drew in her breath as the lips touched her and began tentatively sucking. Abigail's breath escaped as the pressure was relieved, and she prayed even harder as she found herself relaxing and relieved by the child's fierce nursing. She opened her eyes when the child stopped and looked down briefly and found the big, black eyes looking at her patiently. She realized the first breast was empty and turned over and, not even praying now, she closed her eyes and waited for the blessed relief as Spotted Fawn's lips found her.

The next few days were the most pleasurable Abigail had yet spent since her capture. She tried not to think about the day when she would have to return to Snow Cloud's lodge and determined to ask him for a lodge of her own. It was relatively easy to accomplish her subterfuge by sending Spotted Fawn on an errand, but how much more difficult it would be to keep her son dyed in the presence of so many was a problem she hadn't quite resolved.

The day finally came when Wind Woman declared her ready to return to her husband's lodge, and Abigail knew better than to protest. She had had more than three weeks of relative privacy which only made her long for more. Dejectedly she entered Snow Cloud's lodge and was surprised to find Snow Cloud waiting to receive his son. With delight he took the baby and unlaced him from the cradle board and lounged on his bed, playing with the child, while Abigail put away her few belongings brought from the maternity lodge. Slow Water showed no interest in the baby besides a brief, stolid look, but her girls were more curious and watched with giggles and exclamations as their father played with the baby. Not even when the baby grew tired of all the attention and started to whimper did Snow Cloud lose patience but gently cajoled the fussing baby, cradling him in his arms. Finally when the whimperings became howls of displeasure, Snow Cloud brought the baby to her.

"Quiet him. He must not be allowed to cry."

"It is time for his feeding." With renewed self-consciousness Abigail took the child and prepared to nurse him while Snow Cloud looked on, commenting with delight on his son's lusty nursing and joking with her until Abigail was embarrassed. It became even more important for her to get his permission to have her own lodge. When the baby was finally full and asleep, Snow Cloud returned to his couch and began working on a new bow. Abigail made the baby secure in his cradle board and came to stand before Snow Cloud and waited for him to acknowledge her.

Finally he looked up from his work and said, "Little Yellow Bird has something to say?"

"Yes. Now that I have my own child and Spotted Fawn has come to live with you, I would like to have my own lodge."

He continued wrapping sinew around the bow for several moments before he answered. "No. A man does not scatter his possessions if he wishes to keep them safe."

Forgetting herself, she raised her eyes and her mouth hardened with protest. He glanced obliquely at her and said, "Do not forget your place, Little Yellow Bird."

She knew well what he meant and turned away dejectedly, wondering how she would now accomplish what she wanted.

13

MOON OF CHERRIES

BLACKENING

Abigail had no more than become used to living again with Snow Cloud and his family and taking care of her baby when it was time to break camp and start the spring hunt and food gathering. A winter's work and an addition to her family had brought belongings that she was responsible for and merited her her own horses to pack at moving time. When she had been Slow Water's slave she had had little time to learn how to load a travois and now she was at a complete loss. She was just about to give up and ask Slow Water for help, knowing she would bear ridicule either way, when Spotted Fawn came to her rescue. Silently, the little girl directed her until one of Slow Water's daughters ordered her back to help them.

The camp was moving and Abigail still wasn't ready to go. She saw Spotted Fawn being pulled up behind the oldest of Slow Water's daughters just as the camp police came to harangue the stragglers. Right or wrong, she finished tying on the last of her decorated skin boxes called parfleches and mounted her horse with her baby strapped to her back like the rest of the squaws. She lost track of Slow Water completely in the confusion of moving horses, yelling squaws, and barking dogs, with the policing braves cracking their whips to hurry them along.

It was quite some time later when Abigail caught sight of Slow Water and the three girls riding with her. She stopped in consternation as she realized Spotted Fawn was not with them. Immediately one of the men in charge of keeping them moving galloped to her, yelling, "Keep going! Keep going!"

She waved in desperation at him and he brought his horse beside hers and asked, "Why do you stop? It is not time."

"Slow Water's niece is missing. Do you see her with them? I'm afraid they have left her someplace behind us."

"Keep going. I'll ask about her."

He rode ahead and she saw him catch up with Slow Water. Abigail could see he was getting nowhere with her or the three girls and her heart filled with anger and concern for the lost child. She turned her horse and started back along the trail. Another watchful policeman came charging up to her and grabbed her horse.

"Get back with the others. It is not time to stop."

"A child is lost. I'm going back to find her."

"No. If what you say is true, it is up to us to go back."

Before she could reply the first Indian came riding up. She asked him, "Did you find Spotted Fawn?"

"She is not with Slow Water. They do not know where she is. They said she was with you."

Abigail forgot herself and looked up, her eyes flashing anger. "They took her from me or she would have been with me. Tell Snow Cloud I go to find her."

They looked away at her unbecoming manners, and the second Indian said, "No. I will tell Snow Cloud, but you must stay with the others. Then we will look for her."

"It may take too much time to find Snow Cloud. It will be too late soon to find her before dark. Take my travois to one of the others and I will look for her."

It was clear they didn't know what to do with such a rebellious squaw and, not wanting to chastise a chief's wife, they chose to do as Abigail wished. One of them took her travois and the other went with her, riding at a gallop back along the broad route of travel, looking for Spotted Fawn.

Miles back they found her following their trail. She stopped when she saw them coming and her large black eyes mirrored fear and reproach. Abigail slid from her horse and took the slight figure in her arms and felt the trembling of relief.

"Spotted Fawn! What happened?"

"I fell off and Face of Moon wouldn't stop."

"Come ride with me."

The camp soldier with her urged, "Hurry, we are getting too far behind."

Abigail lifted the child onto the horse and for once was grateful for the awkward, uncomfortable saddle, for without it she wouldn't have been able to mount. The Indian circled her impatiently and, the moment she was mounted, turned his horse after the dark smudge on the distant horizon, across the featureless sea of green prairie grass, that was the Indian camp on the move.

Hours later they caught up with their band as they were making camp for the night. Slow Water gave them a sour look and, as much as Abigail wanted to question her about letting Spotted Fawn get lost, she held her tongue, trying to remember to remain Christian in thought and remembering even better that no amount of questioning or accusing would do any good. Her only recourse was to talk to Snow Cloud and see if he could at least let Spotted Fawn be in her charge since it was so obvious Slow Water was indifferent to the child.

The moment Snow Cloud came in the lodge she knew he had heard about the incident. She could feel his eyes on her as he questioned Slow Water about what he had heard. Abigail remained silent and seething as the other woman defended herself and her daughters. A long silence prevailed while Snow Cloud ate but Abigail could feel he was not satisfied. She finished nursing the baby and put him in his cradle board for the night. Snow Cloud was finished with his meal and she came to eat.

"What does Little Yellow Bird have to say about this thing?"

"Many things, but I do not wish to say them here. I did not see what happened. I only saw when she was missing and I went back for her."

He laughed at her show of tactful displeasure and asked, "Would Little Yellow Bird like to walk with me?"

She stood up abruptly. "Yes."

He led the way out of the lodge and she followed as he left the circle of lodges and signaled the watch that they were going outside the camp. Away from the firelit lodges it was dark and Snow Cloud waited for her and took her arm until they were out of hearing of the camp guards.

"Now will Little Yellow Bird speak?"

"Will you put Spotted Fawn in my care?"

"She is in your care now and Slow Water's, too."

"That isn't good enough. You can see how they act toward her.

Slow Water didn't care what happened to her today. The child needs someone who cares for her."

"And you care for her?"

"Yes."

He chuckled softly. "So! What the man cannot win, the child does."

Impatiently she asked, "Will you give Spotted Fawn to me?"

"I will ask Slow Water if she wishes it."

"You know she'll refuse but you can order it and she will obey you."

"I do not wish to cause trouble in my lodge."

"There is already trouble in your lodge, only you refuse to see it. If you allow your daughters to treat your son the way they treat Spotted Fawn I will leave your lodge."

The mocking tolerance fled his face and his voice became even more guttural with anger. "White witch! I have misnamed you. Have you not learned your place yet?" His arm was quicker than a whip as he unfolded it from across his chest and struck her full force with the back of his hand. Abigail lost her balance and sprawled on the ground. Indignation brought her quickly up but he was already on the ground beside her and with powerful arms forced her back to the ground and covered her with his body. She saw the flash of his knife and felt the cold edge against her throat.

"Know, Little Yellow Bird, that if anyone had witnessed your disrespect I would be compelled to use this on you or be considered a fool among my people. But I have another blade I would rather use on you, white bitch."

He returned the knife to its scabbard and, pulling her dress out of the way, found her body with his and she cried out with the pain it brought her still tender flesh. He withdrew from her and left her lying in the grass, fighting tears of anger and outrage. She heard the ominous howl of the prairie wolf and knew she couldn't stay where she was any more than she could escape. She rose to her feet and saw Snow Cloud waiting for her a few yards away, arms crossed imperiously over his chest and looking with utter disdain at the sky. She clenched her fists in impotent fury at him and thought wildly of the possibility of escape. Anything would be better than suffering his dictatorship. Only the thought of her baby prevented her running headlong over the vast moonlit sea of grass. In utter dejection she walked toward the tall, broad-chested figure waiting for her. Meekly she followed him into camp, her mind a morass of unvoiced epithets and impossible plans.

As she lay wide-eyed and sleepless, she sorted through the half-formed thoughts and knew everything was hopeless. In the end there was only one thing worth fighting for, and that was her child's heritage. Only a miracle could free her, but her baby, her Ross, was a man and he would be allowed a freedom she would never have. It was worth giving her life for if she had to. Her son must have the choice of his two worlds and she knew how to give it to him. She would fight for nothing more for herself, but for Ross she would dare to incite Snow Cloud's wrath.

In the morning the camp prepared to move again. Abigail had no choice but to load her own horses again. Spotted Fawn was being run ragged by Slow Water's daughters as she did most of their work for them. Abigail seethed in silence, unaware for a long while they were being watched by Snow Cloud. Her baby was fussing and she was torn with the need to hurry and her desire to quiet him. If only she had Spotted Fawn to keep him occupied she could pack without interruption. Ross's whines became an unhappy wail and she had to stop and pick him up and it was then she saw Snow Cloud watching her. He moved his horse through the confusion and stopped between where she and Slow Water were packing.

In a voice loud enough for them all to hear he ordered, "Spotted Fawn, you are to go with Little Yellow Bird."

Abigail's eyes flew up to his face but he wasn't looking at her—he was looking at Slow Water and she followed his gaze. The stolid Indian squaw hesitated only momentarily at the order and then resumed tying a pack to the travois. Only when Snow Cloud rode on did Slow Water's eyes follow him with a curious gaze and then come to rest on Abigail with a noncommittal look. Abigail turned away from that look, afraid a flicker of triumph would pass over her face. Spotted Fawn came to her with a shy smile and Abigail handed the squirming baby to the little girl, who sat on the travois and began bouncing him on her spindly knees and singing to him.

Nothing more was said in Abigail's presence about Spotted Fawn being in her charge, but from that morning on it was apparent that that was the case. She was grateful for the little girl's help but she would never give Snow Cloud the satisfaction of thanking him and adding to his already inflated arrogance.

The days passed in a tiresome succession of travel until the scouts found the first buffalo herd of the season. Camp was set up and the first fresh buffalo meat of the year was brought in. The camp gorged themselves until Abigail thought they would all burst from the vast quantities of meat that were consumed. Everywhere children were competing with the camp dogs to keep the entrails the Indians considered a delicacy. It gagged Abigail to see Spotted Fawn chewing with relish on a lapful of the revolting fare and trying desperately to push away the dogs, who were always underfoot and into everything. Always, Abigail was shoving a dog or two off her bed and shuffling about the lodge to keep from stepping on one of the flea-ridden beasts or kicking them away from the cooking bladders. Abigail cut a hunk of meat from the mass and hurled it and a dog, tenaciously hanging onto it, ran outside with the rest of the pack following, and Abigail closed and secured the flap.

After a night of gluttony, the arduous task of preserving what was left began. The days passed with exhausting swiftness as the camp moved from one place to another on its food gathering until midsummer, when under a waxing moon, called by the Indians the moon of cherries blackening, they moved to a new campsite without any apparent reason. Abigail soon began to understand what was going on when other bands of Indians began joining them until the immediate prairie was transformed into a huge village of tipis. It was a time of reunion and celebration and most important of all, as Abigail was eventually to learn, the time of the most sacred of all religious ceremonies, the Sun Dance.

To Abigail it seemed like a transportation back in time to the first pagan people of history as she watched with growing curiosity the preparations being made. She little understood the dances and purification rites and was even more confused when a cottonwood tree was cut with much ceremony and carried with all the pomp of an idol back to the center of camp. More purification rites were completed in the sweat lodges and the tree was raised and a large structure of poles was built around this center tree, which stood like any other pole to Abigail.

When the people of the huge camp gathered after days of preparation for the climax of the celebration, Abigail went with them. All the people were outfitted in their finest dress. The men of importance were resplendent in trailing eagle feather headdresses adorned with mink tails and feet. Arms and chests flashed with adornments of shells and claws. Abigail felt a glow of satisfaction as she saw Snow Cloud wearing the robe she had made for him. In her hate for him she had never considered him attractive but, seeing him moving regally among his own kind, she compared and found him impressive indeed. The crowd soon settled down

and the drums and chanting began. Abigail soon gathered it was a
religious ceremony but she was totally unprepared for the cul-
minating act of the young warriors who allowed themselves to be
slashed on chest and back and their bodies skewered with thongs
and tied to the sacred center pole while they danced in manic
dedication with eyes fastened on the sun. Abigail, barely able to
keep from retching, left the frightening scene and fled to the safety
of her lodge.

Pale and shaken, she busied herself with her baby and lay down
to nurse him, involving herself totally in him to block out what she
had witnessed, but there was no escaping the low throb of the
drums or the chanting voices. She shuddered to think her own
child might someday be required to undergo the same gruesome
ritual, and she prayed to her God she would not live to see it and
continued to pray with eyes closed until she felt someone watching
her. She opened her eyes slowly. The Indian standing at the entrance of the lodge was a stranger to her. He was young and powerful and the look his eyes held left her no doubt as to his intent.

In one quick, instinctive movement she rolled from the bed of
buffalo robes, screaming as loud as she could, her hand frantically
pulling at the knife fastened in her belt as the Indian leaped across
the fire pit and onto the bed above her. She tried to scramble
underneath the rolled-up cover of the lodge, but he grabbed her
dress and held her, trying to pull her back into the lodge. She held
onto one of the lodge poles and screamed incessantly as she tried to
slash at her attacker underneath the edge of the thick hide lodge
covering. The Indian suddenly released his grip on her and fell
across her legs. She kicked free and scrambled to her feet not
knowing whether to run or to try and save her baby. People were
coming now to see why she had been screaming, and she motioned
them to hurry and, assured of help, ran to the front of the lodge.
Wind Woman stood in the doorway holding the baby in her arms.

"Is Little Yellow Bird all right?"

"Yes. What happened? Where is the man?"

Without a flicker of emotion Snow Cloud's mother answered, "I
have killed him."

A dozen people now were crowded around and Wind Woman
threw open the door cover for all to see. The dead Indian lay where
he had fallen behind Abigail's couch, with Wind Woman's knife
plunged deep in his back.

The color drained from Abigail's face as she whispered, "Yellow Bird is grateful Wind Woman was near."

Abigail took the crying baby from Wind Woman's arms and turned away, wondering where she could go to get away from the gathering crowd. Snow Cloud blocked her way.

"What happened?"

"A man came into the lodge. Wind Woman killed him."

"Did he hurt you or my son?"

"No. We're all right."

Snow Cloud turned to some of the men crowded around. "Who is this man? Take him to his people."

After several of the gathered people had gone in to look at the dead man, one finally recognized the young brave and went to find the members of his band. In a few minutes some of the Indian's people came and carried the dead man away followed by his wailing family.

Snow Cloud turned to his mother. "Stay with her from now on and I will have two of our braves watching." Without further comment he strode away.

Wind Woman took Abigail's arm. "Come inside now and quiet the child."

Abigail carried the frightened baby into the lodge and sat rocking him until he was quiet enough to resume nursing. Wind Woman sat down across from her as the people left them in quiet to rejoin the Sun Dance ceremony which still permeated the lodge with drums and chanting.

"I told my son you would bring trouble."

Abigail looked up, startled by the frankness of Wind Woman's statement. She had the uneasy feeling that perhaps Wind Woman wasn't her friend after all.

The older woman smiled. "Do not let my words disturb you. This trouble I have seen in a dream. Even if I had not dreamed it, anyone who knows the hot blood of the young braves could see that men will desire you. Was it this way among your own people?"

Abigail almost shook her head no but stopped as memories she had almost forgotten returned vividly to her mind. Among the people she considered her own—the good Christian people of her home town—the answer was no, but she had met others, white people whom she had not considered her kind, and she had to answer honestly, "Yes."

"Beauty has its own curse. Of all men my son knows this, yet he brought you to his people. This time the Great Spirit has smiled on him and given him life instead of death."

Abigail changed the baby from one breast to the other and lay

back. Wind Woman's words increased her curiosity as she was sure
they were meant to do. In her polite Christian society gossip such as
this would be a vice to be shunned, but she had been with the
Indians long enough to know there was nothing they loved more
than to relate everything there was to relate about a person, unless
it was to gamble.

"If your son desired beauty why didn't he choose the most
beautiful of his own people to be his wife?"

Wind Woman flashed a knowing smile. "He did. He was once
loved by the most beautiful maiden in all our villages."

"Then why didn't he marry her?"

"She was Slow Water's younger sister—the sister between Spotted Fawn's mother and Slow Water. Her father saw all too well the
advantage of including in the bride price the condition that any
man wanting to marry the one had to marry both. My son loved
Night Song so dearly he readily paid ten horses for Slow Water first
in the agreement of getting his beloved as soon as he could acquire
ten more horses. Before he had ten more horses Night Song was
killed when buffalo stampeded through the camp in a terrible
white fire storm."

Abigail felt a pang of sympathy for Snow Cloud. Here was a side
of him she hadn't known or understood, and she felt a little guilty,
too, because of the feelings of hatred she harbored for him. Still it
was hard to consider him capable of human feelings even though
her Christian rearing kept reminding her he was human. She was
now accustomed to the smell of him and her surroundings—in
fact, had learned soon after her arrival at the Indian camp that the
Indians themselves bathed with surprising regularity, when the
weather permitted, and it was the rancid grease and paint they
used to protect their skin from sun or cold which was offensive. She
even performed the painting, greasing, and attiring of herself like
the other Indian women now for the same reasons and had become
immune to the smell and even looked forward to the almost daily
bathing when she could do so in the company of women without
men present. It was her bitter resentment of him that had never let
her grow accustomed to his use of her.

At sundown the climax of the Sun Dance was reached and the
religious ceremony of the past several days was over. Everywhere
in the camp the religious fervor was being replaced by hearty
ribaldry and gambling. Snow Cloud, Slow Water, and their daughters came in with Spotted Fawn in tow, and Wind Woman departed
the now crowded lodge. Eagerly they consumed the contents of the

cooking bladder Abigail had prepared. Slow Water and her girls left as soon as their appetites were sated and Spotted Fawn sat playing with the baby, but Snow Cloud stayed on his couch, leaning against his back rest and smoking thoughtfully. Abigail could feel his eyes on her as she ate, standing, as usual, to keep the dogs from grabbing her food. When all her chores were completed it was time to nurse the baby again and put him to sleep for the night. When the baby was sleeping at last, Spotted Fawn went outside to watch the dancing and Abigail sat down with her quilling, intensely aware of Snow Cloud's presence and what his remaining in the lodge meant while the rest of the camp became one big party, unrestrained and undisciplined to extremes.

He finished his pipe and came to where she sat. She ignored him and he reached down and took her work from her hands. She didn't raise her eyes or protest, knowing he might slap her for being disrespectful, but sat still, resisting silently.

"Now," he commanded.

Abigail lay down on her bed and Snow Cloud lay down beside her, his hand reaching to pull up her dress. Abigail turned her head away and closed her eyes as his body moved to take hers.

A voice intruded into their intimacy and Abigail's eyes flew open as Wind Woman berated her son, "Does my son forget the teachings of his people?"

Still covering Abigail, his jaw set and his voice grating and guttural with anger, he replied shortly, "I forget nothing."

"Then you should not be lying with this one but with Slow Water if your body desires a woman."

Snow Cloud removed himself from Abigail and stood to face his mother. "Does a man ride his poorest horse when he has a better one to choose?"

"He does if he wants the foal of that horse to have full benefit of its mother's nourishment."

The mother and son glared at each other briefly, and Snow Cloud stalked from the lodge. Wind Woman settled herself on the couch across from Abigail and shook her head. "Sometimes I do not understand my son. He knows it is the duty of all men to leave their wives alone until their babies have lived more than two winters. There must be an evil one at work in his mind. I shall have to pray to the Great Spirit to uncloud his mind."

Abigail straightened her dress and found her handiwork, too embarrassed to reply to Wind Woman in any way. There was so much she didn't know about the Indians yet. She hadn't been worried about learning any more than she had to, but a new thought crossed her mind. If she was to teach Ross she would have to know as much as possible or she would not be able to show the difference between the two cultures. Already the custom she had just found out about seemed a wonderful blessing to her. Surely there were more, and she needed to know them all to protect herself and her child.

14

THE WINTER OF
WOUNDS HEALING

The next morning the camp broke up. It was time now for the serious hunting and food gathering, and it was not unusual for two or more of the bands to go together in search of the buffalo meat that would sustain them through the winter. The meat taken now was the sweetest, juiciest, and tenderest and dried the quickest and most thoroughly in the heat of July. Fruits and nuts were also gathered and dried as they traveled after the great herds of buffalo in an exhausting, almost frenzied preparation for winter.

Even with the wilderness experience she had already had, nothing quite prepared Abigail for the intense heat, the dirt, flies, and the grueling labor from dawn to dusk without rest, and it was inevitable that the dreaded fever would strike at this time. She woke in the middle of the night shaking violently with chills and nausea. She called weakly to Spotted Fawn and the little girl brought her the cool water she wanted.

Snow Cloud awoke as did everyone in the intimate confines of the lodge. "What is it? What troubles you, Yellow Bird?"

Weakly she explained, "It is the fever. I have had it ever since my husband and I came down the Ohio River. There is no cure for it, but the doctors among my people have a medicine that makes it bearable. How near are we to a white doctor?"

"Many sleeps. Wind Woman will know what to do. I will call her."

He left the lodge and came back in a short while with Wind Woman.

"My son tells me of your sickness. What is the medicine you need?"

"It is made of bark from a tree in South America called cincho-na. It reduces the fever. Can you make something like it?"

"I do know of something that will work like it, but it is not found here."

Snow Cloud asked, "What is it you need? I will go for it."

She motioned him away. "Come to my lodge and I will tell you what I need."

Abigail looked with feverish eyes at the retreating figures and before her vision blurred altogether she saw the bright black eyes of Slow Water watching her with unconcealed malice.

The next several days and nights were the most difficult Abigail had yet experienced. Every other day for almost two weeks the fever would strike in the middle of the night. By midmorning she would be weak but able to resume her work. Each attack left her more exhausted, and her milk began to fail along with her strength.

By the time Snow Cloud returned Abigail's attacks had run their course and she was feeling stronger. It was time now to move camp to cooler climes, and the band began the long trek to the Black Hills and a relative time of vacation until the fall hunt began. In the shaded, stream-coursed canyons and high, multihued cliffs they gathered the sweet succulent berries that were the equivalent of dessert for the Indians while the men cut new lodge poles and hunted something besides buffalo. It was a time of rest and recu-peration for Abigail, and by the time they broke camp to return for the fall hunt on the golden plains, she felt almost normal. She soon found she wasn't normal as the long days of travel wore her out. The buffalo herds were located, camp set up, and the arduous task of preserving more meat and rending vast quantities of fat to make the mixture of dried meat, berries, and bone marrow into pemmi-can began. The latent fever took full advantage of her exhausted and weakened condition and struck with a vengeance. She went to bed with a violent headache and woke vomiting and shaking with cold. Wind Woman was called immediately and brought her mysterious medicine and Abigail took it—would have taken anything, in fact, to relieve her anguished body. Her stomach rebelled against the vile medicine, and she was forced to weather the attack through without relief. When the last stage of the attack began she could at last keep the medicine down and was able to sleep while the rest of the camp worked. She only woke when Ross needed nursing and then slept again while Spotted Fawn and Wind Woman stayed with her and took care of the baby.

She continued to take the medicine Wind Woman had made for her the next day. When the next attack was due to commence it was far less severe and by the third scheduled appearance of fever she had no symptoms at all. But as she continued to take the medicine and feel better, the baby became increasingly irritable and when she fed him he would fuss and act as if he didn't like her milk and shortly after his latest feeding he began to howl in distress and finally vomited.

Snow Cloud watched with frowning concern as she tried to soothe the unhappy child. "Is the child sick with your illness?"

Abigail hadn't remembered until the baby retched what the doctor in Louisville had told her about the cinchona bark medicine and wondered if the same thing could be happening with this medicine. "No. The doctor who treated me did say the medicine might make a nursing child ill. I will feed him soup until I am sure the attacks are over."

"How long?"

"It will be eight more sleeps at least, and then it will take a few more sleeps before the effects of the medicine will be gone."

"You will lose your milk."

Abigail hadn't thought of that. She looked at Snow Cloud in despair. "It would make Spotted Fawn sick, too."

"Then one of the old ones will have to take your milk."

Abigail looked away in distress, holding the crying child to her and rocking him. "If it is what must be done." She shrugged in resignation.

Wind Woman entered the lodge and surveyed the situation. "What is wrong with my grandson?"

Snow Cloud answered, "Yellow Bird believes the medicine is making him sick through her milk."

The older woman nodded in agreement, "Yes, it is possible. Will the sickness last as long as the last time?"

"Yes. I could stop taking the medicine and perhaps the fever will not return."

"No. I will fix you more medicine, and then I will find Sweet Grass to nurse the child and find an old one for you."

Sweet Grass came and with a sympathetic smile on her round, pleasant face took the baby and sat down to nurse him and at last he quieted and slept. Abigail ate as soon as Snow Cloud was done eating and she, too, lay down and slept.

Wind Woman came in the morning with more medicine but there was no old grandmother with her. Abigail was not yet in agony, so her relief was greater than her concern as she asked, "Wouldn't one of the old ones come?"

"No. They are afraid. Someone has told them they will become sick if they drink your milk and they will die."

"But they don't need to drink it, just take it and spit it out."

"I have told them this but they have heard their mouths will burn and they won't be able to eat and they will die."

"But who could have told them that?"

Wind Woman shrugged noncommittally and let her eyes glance briefly in the direction of Slow Water who sat eating stolidly. Abigail caught the implication and knew it was true.

By nightfall Abigail was in misery. Snow Cloud sat eating ravenously while she spooned broth into her infant's eager mouth. If Wind Woman didn't come soon she would go to her lodge. She had to do something. She had to find someone brave enough to take her milk. She was even ready to ask Wind Woman if she would. She finished feeding the baby and he lay gurgling contentedly on her couch of buffalo robes while she washed his tiny horn spoon.

Snow Cloud said, "Bring him to me."

Abigail picked up the happy baby and placed him in Snow Cloud's big hands and saw his proud smile. She ate her supper and watched Snow Cloud and the baby. Slow Water's daughters, jealous of the attention the baby was getting, crowded around their father and began to join in the tickling, poking game until Snow Cloud sent them from the lodge when the baby cried out from too much touching. Snow Cloud laid him on the couch beside himself and let the baby kick in complete freedom.

Wind Woman came at last with the news that she hadn't been able to convince the old women they would not die from Abigail's milk. Abigail shot a quick look at Slow Water. Her face remained stoic but Abigail was sure there was a look of triumph in her black eyes. Snow Cloud picked up the baby again and Abigail turned her eyes to him. He held the baby gently in his strong hands. In a protective gesture he cradled the child in his arms and, looking fondly at the infant he believed to be his son, said, "I will take her milk."

Abigail suppressed a gasp, but the howl that Slow Water voiced would have drowned out any lesser sound.

"You must not! You will die!"

"Silence!" Snow Cloud commanded. "If I die it is so my son can live."

Abigail watched the woman suffer under her husband's stern look and it was her turn to smile, but Abigail's smile faded as Snow Cloud stood up and came to her.

"I am ready."

Slow Water threw down her food and rushed from the lodge wailing as if in mourning.

"Tell her to stop or I will cut out her tongue." Abigail looked up at his angry face and knew he meant what he said.

Wind Woman knew, too, and hurried after Slow Water and they were alone except for Spotted Fawn and the baby. Abigail held up her hands for the baby and placed him in his cradle board and tied him securely.

"Spotted Fawn can take him to Sweet Grass."

Snow Cloud nodded and the little girl came to Abigail, her large eyes looking from one to the other of them as she let Abigail strap the baby on her back. The moment she was gone Snow Cloud laced the door flap shut and came to lower himself to the floor robe in front of her. Her heart stopped beating as he unlaced the opening of her dress and cupped a swollen breast in his hand. She looked away and gasped as his lips touched her and she jerked involuntarily. His hand grasped her arm and held her still as he proceeded to relieve her, spitting each mouthful of the fluid into a wooden bowl in his lap.

When he was done Abigail sagged in relief and whispered a grateful, "Thank you."

He grunted and rose to his feet and rinsed his mouth with fresh water and left the lodge. She sat for a long while with downcast eyes while the shame and degradation overwhelmed her and tears coursed down her cheeks. Her distressed mind asked her God why, but no answer came. One of the dogs got up and came nosing around the bowl of fluid and lapped at it hungrily. Abigail watched in fascinated disgust which soon turned to anger and she chased the dog from the lodge and took the bowl and threw its contents outside the lodge.

Spotted Fawn came with the sleeping baby on her back and

Abigail unstrapped him from the tiny back and put him down for the night. She felt very tired herself and went to her own couch and Spotted Fawn, without a word, curled next to her. Wanting to hold something, needing some comforting contact, Abigail put her arm around the little girl and held her close and at last slept.

In a few days Abigail stopped taking the medicine and had no more attacks of fever. After another few days without the medicine she resumed nursing the baby. From then on the days flew by as one after another the hides were finished and Abigail added another black dot to the handle of her scraping tool according to custom. She even felt a flush of satisfaction the day she had ten black dots and could make a red dot on her tool, denoting that she had tanned enough hides to make one lodge cover. Before she realized it, it was time to move to winter camp. She looked forward to the less strenuous work of making clothing articles out of the old lodge cover, now properly smoked and softened by a year of use. She would have more time to spend with Ross, too. He was beginning to make more sounds every day and she wanted to start teaching him his first words. Every chance she had she talked to him in English and sang him the songs she knew, especially the song she loved so well, the memories of which brought tears to her eyes—"Greensleeves."

By the time Ross was one year old she had him saying Mama. He was now allowed to explore the confines of the lodge in the evenings and, much to Abigail's dismay, she wasn't allowed to restrain him in any way. He was fascinated by the fire and she constantly had to pull him from it until Snow Cloud ordered, "Let him touch the fire."

"But he'll be burned!"

"How else is he to learn? You are to help him be a man, not shield him from what he must learn."

She watched tensely as the crawling child aggressively headed for the dancing flames. She was ready to grab him but the heat from the fire on his face was enough to slow him down. He grabbed at a licking flame and howled as the flames singed his hand. Abigail was quick to plunge the small hand in cold water, but the tears still rolled down the child's cheeks while Snow Cloud and his daughters laughed in delighted ridicule which Abigail and her son would learn was one of their most effective forms of censure.

Spring came and with it the opportunity Abigail had been waiting for—to be alone with her child so she could start teaching him to talk in English. She managed always to wander the farthest away on their food-gathering trips. She would, contrary to Indian custom, make Ross stay with her and have him repeat words in English. Only Spotted Fawn was allowed to witness her teaching, and the little girl was soon coaching the boy, too, so quickly did she learn Abigail's words.

All too soon it was time again for the gathering of the bands and the Sun Dance ceremony. With mixed emotions Abigail helped set up their lodge among the hundreds gathered for the annual reunion.

Snow Cloud announced to her the first night, "This year my son must watch the Sun Dance, and both of you will have your ears pierced and be tattooed."

Stunned, she questioned disrespectfully, "But why?"

Between patient puffs on his pipe he told her, "It is our belief that no one can enter upon the spirit trail if he has no tattoo. These things are necessary for my son to have a complete life. I desire it for both of you."

Abigail bit her lip to keep from protesting. She had seen the tattoos on the foreheads and chins of most of the gathered bands, but most of Snow Cloud's band were marked on the wrist. That she could tolerate, but the way the Indians pierced their ears all around the outer rim she could not.

"My eyes do not find the tattooing and piercing of ears beautiful as yours do. If I and my child must have it done, it is my wish that we be tattooed on the wrist and only the lobes of our ears be pierced just once."

She felt his eyes on her but kept her own down respectfully, not wishing to anger him at this moment especially.

"I have heard your request."

He rose and left the lodge, and Abigail was enveloped in the ridiculing laughter of Slow Water's daughters. She gave them a scathing look and returned to her supper. Slow Water and the girls were too anxious to join in the reunion with friends and relatives to spend much time ridiculing Abigail, and they quickly put away their eating bowls and left her. Wind Woman joined her in a few minutes.

"My son asked me to come stay with you."

Abigail looked surprised that he would still remember and be concerned for her safety. "And are we guarded, too?"

The older woman smiled. "Yes. Did you think he would forget?"

"I should have guessed he wouldn't."

"Now, what would you learn, daughter?"

"What have I not learned?"

"You have asked little about your husband. Is it not important that you know about the father of your child?"

"Yes. I'm sorry I have not been able to show more interest in him, but the memory of my reason for being here is still painful."

"Because he killed your husband?"

Abigail swallowed and their eyes met briefly and were cast down again. "Yes. He had no reason to kill my husband. I can never forgive him for that."

Wind Woman nodded in understanding. "Yes, just as he can never forgive your people for killing his father."

Abigail looked up again. "But why my husband? Why didn't he kill the man who killed his father? That I could forgive."

"In war who knows who kills whom."

"War? What war?"

"The Shawnee, Tecumseh, fights against the whites. He called for a meeting of all the Indians to ask them to fight with him against your people. My husband, my son, and some of our bravest warriors went. My son was the only one to return."

Abigail said nothing while she let the information take shape in her mind. War between the Indians and English against the Americans must have finally been declared. It was strange they hadn't gotten the news, but it was possible. They were far from civilization on the farm. "Does the war still go on?"

Wind Woman shrugged. "I don't know."

"Why didn't Snow Cloud stay and fight?"

"As the last left alive, it was his duty to bring back the news. And then his father was chief—this too, brought him home."

"Then he became chief because his father died?"

"No. The elders' council decides who is to be chief. It is not always the son of the chief, but the man best suited to be chief."

They worked in silence for a while until Abigail asked, "Then my child will not be chief unless he proves himself worthy to be chief?"

"Yes."

Ross, who had been entertaining himself with a puppy, grew tired and crawled over and pulled himself up on Abigail's knee, saying, "Mama, Mama."

She put aside her work and picked him up into her lap. He pulled at the lacing on her dress and she let him open her dress and nuzzle her breasts, finding a sinful, sensual pleasure in the feel of his hands and mouth as he caressed her. He nursed himself to sleep, and she laid him down tenderly on the couch and fastened her dress. Snow Cloud came in, and he and his mother talked of what the elders of the council had discussed. Spotted Fawn came in, tired from playing with the other children of the camp, and lay down beside Ross and was soon asleep. Wind Woman left and Abigail was alone with Snow Cloud and the sleeping children.

"Will you have my mocassins ready before the Sun Dance?"

"Yes. I am almost finished."

"Good. Let me see how they look."

She held one out to him and he took it, holding it to the light coming from the smoke hole. "It is good, but it is getting too dark to see now. You can finish tomorrow."

She put away the beads and quills and lay down next to the sleeping children.

"Come share my bed tonight."

She dared to look at him and saw the intense look in his black eyes. "Does Snow Cloud forget the need of his child?"

"No. But the child's father also has a need. Come."

She went to his couch obediently and found her heartbeat strangely quickened. With horror she wondered if she could actually be desiring his touch and fought against the idea. Dutifully she lay down beside him and tensed at his touch. His body filled hers, and she felt the desperate wild need she had known with Ross. She tried to remember she hated him but her body's need swept away the hate and her mouth blindly sought his, remembering too well the clean taste of Ross's lips and breath. She pulled her head away in distaste at the grease of this man's lips and the acrid smoke of his breath, her eyes opening just as the figure of Snow Cloud's daughter came through the door of the tipi. The girl backed out quickly and Abigail could hear her giggling voice as she drew her friends away and became part of the laughing, barking cacophony that characterized the reunion of the bands.

The fire of her body was effectively quenched by the girl's intrusion and she became once more the passive partner. If Snow Cloud knew of the interruption it didn't bother him, and in spite of her complete change of response he finished with her and grunted in satisfaction, his hand resting in a momentary tender gesture on her hair before he raised his body from hers. Abigail returned to her couch and lay frustrated and angered at her body as much as she was mystified and moved with expectation by his show of tenderness.

Abigail somehow managed to endure the experience of the Sun Dance and the ensuing tattooing and ear piercing and felt relief when it was finally done and the camp was breaking up to go separate ways. The buffalo were found soon afterward and the whole camp settled down to the drudgery of drying the meat for winter and tanning robes. The fever came in the sweltering heat of August and Wind Woman was prepared for it. Abigail hardly lost a day so quickly was the medicine administered. She didn't worry about losing her milk. Ross was devouring almost everything offered him. He was a happy, healthy child, growing by the day and walking strongly and beginning to talk in sentences. She was afraid Snow Cloud might object and was relieved when he didn't. The emotional bond that was created by the replica of his father during the intimacy of nursing was one Abigail felt should be broken. She was relying too much on her child for the physical satisfaction that should belong to his father, and Abigail was growing increasingly frustrated because of it, praying desperately against the sin of incest.

The first night was the hardest when he came to her tired and ready for the relaxing panacea of her milk and the comforting warmth of her body. He whined and whimpered but she remained firm and tried to explain her milk would make him sick from the medicine she had to take. She was ready with warm broth as a substitute and held him in her arms until he finally slept and with trembling hands put him to bed, feeling the break more deeply than he ever would.

The next day they started their journey to the Black Hills and the adventure, all new to Ross, was the exact compensation for the little boy. The excitement and the new experiences distracted him enough so that he little missed the comforting closeness of nursing. Once in the spectacularly featured mountains so startlingly different from the wide open prairie, he was too busy investigating his surroundings with wide-eyed amazement to be bothered with sitting still long enough to eat, much less the time-consuming act of nursing. By the time they were back on the plains for the fall hunt, the weaning was complete for Ross, if not for Abigail.

All signs pointed to a hard winter. The horses had thick coats long before the warm weather was entirely gone and the buffalo rapidly moved south, ending the hunting season weeks ahead of time. They moved constantly as the nights grew colder, looking for buffalo or any game to fatten their parfleches, but there was little left on the vast frozen and windswept prairies between the Red

River and the Missouri. Tired and uncomfortable, with icy winds
blowing in from the vast northern plains, they turned dejectedly
toward the river bottoms, looking for a well-protected winter
camp.

They were barely settled in their camp when a band of maraud-
ing northern Indians driven south by the cold and hunger raided
their horse herd, stealing and scattering more than half the herd.
Snow Cloud proposed immediate and swift retaliation, and in a
matter of days the warriors, led by Snow Cloud, were on the trail of
the raiders.

Abigail hadn't realized the tension she lived under in his presence until he was gone. She tried to blame it on her fear that he
would discover her teaching English to her child and more than
that, even, she feared someone would discover her dyeing his skin
and cause suspicion that the child was not Snow Cloud's. She still
had to be careful to do these things out of Slow Water's presence,
but the woman accommodated her by spending long hours away
from the lodge with her friends, taking her handiwork and her
daughters with her and leaving Abigail alone with Spotted Fawn
and Ross. Spotted Fawn was learning as much as Ross. She could
speak quite well to Abigail in English and delighted in doing so,
and somehow her aptitude helped Ross learn more easily as he
imitated his playmate more readily than he did Abigail.

Abigail was shaken out of her complacency when the warriors
returned with two of their group missing, and the mourning wails
filled the camp as the relatives mutilated themselves over their
dead young men. She lay awake while the women wailed under a
cold moon and wondered what would happen to her if Snow Cloud
had not come back. She only then began to realize how dependent
her existence was on him. If he died she was sure Slow Water would
not tolerate her and would throw her out of the lodge. If another
Indian took her she might fair far worse, for she knew most of the
men beat their women unmercifully when their changeable moods
dictated. The thought of all that was possible if Snow Cloud didn't
return was frightening. It was hard for her to be grateful that she,
after all, was his, but there was a small relief in the security he
offered and apprehension against the time when he might leave
again.

And leave again they did. The diabolical raids and retaliations
continued until the first snow. Abigail thought at last it would stop
but she was wrong. Snow Cloud led his men on what he hoped
would be the final retribution against the northern marauders,

gambling against weather and luck that he could strike hard and escape and that his escape would be covered by a snow deep enough to end all raiding.

Each passing day, Abigail's worry increased. A heavy snow fell after several days and Abigail knew something was wrong when more days passed and still Snow Cloud and his warriors didn't return. Subtle changes began to take place in her feeling for Snow Cloud as she waited for his return and became increasingly fearful he wouldn't return. She began to realize his desire for her was not something that could not be changed. In her hate for him she had totally ignored the possibility he might change his mind about her and kill her. It was possible he kept her after she was obviously pregnant only to see if she would bear him a son and now that that son was old enough to live without her, her position was tenuous at most. How long would he give her to respond to him in the way she now realized was his only reason for keeping her before he would grow tired of her resistance and find a more willing partner?

She came to the conclusion that if she desired to raise her son the way she wanted him raised, she would have to try to be the wife Snow Cloud obviously wanted of her. Surprisingly, she didn't find the idea too repulsive to accept. She now knew she could respond to him without the love she had thought was necessary. Her body had betrayed her often enough to know it was possible.

Snow Cloud and his warriors returned after being gone for almost three weeks, and as Abigail had feared, the inevitable had happened. Snow Cloud had been wounded and his braves carried him into the lodge and laid him on his couch. He was weak from loss of blood and days of eluding the Indians hunting for them, and being caught in a blizzard without food or the proper attention had given infection time to set in.

Wind Woman and the village medicine man were called at once. For two days and two nights Abigail watched as the medicine man performed his rituals. Still Snow Cloud didn't improve. His fever increased until he was in a state of delirium. Abigail felt little better off having had no sleep since the shaman stayed in constant attendance performing his noisy and useless ceremonies. She felt increasing contempt and dismay for their superstitious belief that everything that happened was due to good or evil spirits, and their prayers to birds and animals as friends or foes she found just as ridiculous. She could stand by no longer. Her experience with the doctor in St. Louis had given her enough knowledge to know what needed to be done and the confidence to do it.

"Enough!" she cried in desperation. "Can't you see your medicine is not helping? Now leave and let me take care of him."

Wind Woman gasped at the effrontery of her daughter-in-law. "Yellow Bird! Have you gone crazy? Do not anger the shaman or my son will die."

The tribal medicine man looked at her angrily. "How dare you interrupt. The evil spirits will surely take the chief now. There is nothing more I can do. His death is on your head."

It was Abigail's turn to gasp, but she didn't say anything. It was all too clear now that the shaman had given up hope. She had interfered at the opportune moment and would now be the scapegoat if Snow Cloud died.

Wind Woman looked appalled and Slow Water let out a keening wail that sent shivers down Abigail's back. The wails were echoed by the three daughters; her own two charges looked frightened and Ross began to cry. "Be still, all of you! He is not dead yet and I will need you to help me if he is to live. Slow Water, I want you to heat water until it boils. Wind Woman, I will need a very thin and very sharp knife and I will need something like my fingers, only longer and thinner, to remove whatever causes the wound to be infected. Do you understand?"

Wind Woman nodded uncertainly and hurried out of the lodge. Abigail turned her gaze back to Slow Water, who still sat stubbornly, but silently, on her couch watching Abigail with a look of suspicion. Her daughters' eyes were no less suspicious. "Do you wish to help Snow Cloud live?"

In her deep, guttural voice the woman answered, "Yes, but I am afraid."

"Why? If he dies you can blame me. If he had not come back at all, would it be any different?"

"No."

"Then we understand each other. Please get the water—and hurry! And you girls can take care of the little ones. Feed them and keep them quiet. I must have absolute quiet!"

Slow Water picked up the buffalo stomach containers and went for the door where she was greeted by the elders of the village who had been aroused by the death wail and had come to see their dead chief. They filed in respectfully and exclaimed when they found Snow Cloud still breathing.

"What is this? He still lives. Why was the death wail sounded?"

Slow Water hung her head, clearly reluctant to admit anything.

Abigail answered, "Slow Water thought he had died. It was a mistake."

"But the shaman has gone. He would not leave unless the chief had died."

"He left because he doesn't think there is any more he can do for Snow Cloud."

Grunts of dismay echoed among the circle of men, and much to Abigail's dismay they settled in a circle around their chief to wait for his death. Wind Woman returned, bringing the things Abigail had asked for. She motioned the woman out into the snow and cold out of hearing of the elders.

"Can you get them to leave?"

"It will not be easy."

"I can't do what must be done with them watching."

"I will try."

Abigail pressed the older woman's hand and they ducked back into the warm interior of the lodge.

Wind Woman announced, "I have taken over the care of my son. He is not beyond my help but I must be allowed to work my medicine in secret, otherwise it will be of no use."

Glances were exchanged. They had too much respect for her to question her request and silently rose and filed from the lodge.

Slow Water returned with the water vessels and the tough organs filled with ice water were hung over the fire. While Abigail waited for the water to heat, she, with the help of Slow Water and Wind Woman, removed Snow Cloud's bloody legging, cutting it with a knife from the hip past the hole where the spear had pierced his thigh until they could remove it and the dirty bindings that covered the wound and were now stiff and adhering to it. Carefully she lifted them, peeling them from the hot and swollen flesh. Abigail's stomach churned precariously at the sight of the ugly wound revealed but she couldn't give up now. There was too much at stake.

Slow Water moaned and turned away, and Abigail had to command her, "Hold the torch steady."

Wind Woman stood staunchly by and murmured, "It is bad. Are you sure you can do anything?"

"I have no other choice."

The wound was oozing from the removal of the bindings and Abigail turned away to find some small pliable scraps of skin to use as cloths to catch the discharge. This done she tested the water and found it warmed enough to use and, bringing out her precious but crude soap made from ashes and animal fat, she washed her hands and the makeshift instruments she would have to use and placed two broad-bladed knives in the fire to heat. Since Wind Woman would have to help her she asked her to wash, too, and the older woman didn't hesitate to follow her instructions.

With the thin knife Abigail opened the festering wound and cleaned away the infection released from the swollen flesh. As she worked she could imagine what had happened. In the fury of combat an enraged warrior had driven his spear at Snow Cloud with all his weight behind the thrust. Snow Cloud's war shield had deflected the weapon downward into the thick muscle of his leg and the force of the thrust had driven it to the bone. Snow Cloud had undoubtedly killed his assailant and pulled the spear from his leg, but before he had had time to bind it he had lost quite a bit of blood. When they had at last eluded their pursuers at night, his braves had probably seared the wound and bound it, but in the harrowing circumstances it hadn't been cleaned thoroughly and something had been left in the wound to cause the infection.

Abigail continued carefully opening the wound, Wind Woman sponging away the blood and Abigail cauterizing. The knife scraped bone and Abigail gently spread the wound with her fingers. "Hold the light closer so I can see into the wound. Wind Woman, take up the blood."

Quickly Wind Woman soaked away the blood and briefly Abigail glimpsed a black sliver next to the bone. The spear point had broken, leaving a splinter. Quickly she reached for the makeshift forceps and, with Wind Woman cleaning away the blood and searing the wound with a white-hot knife, Abigail was able to grasp the fine chard of stone and remove it from the wound. She checked again to make sure the wound was clean and, satisfied she had done everything possible, she took her finest fishbone needle, threaded with the thinnest of sinew, and sewed together the gaping wound.

Wind Woman sighed deeply. "If the Great Spirit wills it, he shall live and sing your praises, Little Yellow Bird, and I will do you honor as a medicine woman greater than I."

Abigail smiled tremulously, feeling the trembling release of taut nerves. "Thank you, but don't be singing any songs yet. He has lost a lot of blood and the infection has spread through his body. You pray to your Great Spirit, Wind Woman, and I will pray to mine, and if our prayers are answered, he will live."

Wind Woman left, and Abigail and Slow Water finished cleaning up the lodge. Ross and Spotted Fawn were long since asleep, and Abigail, equally exhausted from the sleepless nights during the shaman's rituals and drained by the tension of the past hours, crawled willingly under the fur robes and slept instantly.

Snow Cloud remained comatose for several days without showing any sign of improvement. Abigail tended his wound and prayed. The whole camp waited in foreboding silence for Snow Cloud to die. No threats were made, but the elders of the band came daily and Abigail would allow one to come in and survey Snow Cloud's condition. No word was said to her, which made it all the more ominous, and her tension mounted.

The storm that had kept them from venturing far from their own lodge blew over, and Slow Water, bundled against the cold, took her daughters to visit another lodge in camp. Abigail and the two little ones were left alone with the still figure of Snow Cloud. Abigail was busy quilling a new pair of mocassins when Spotted Fawn called her attention to Snow Cloud. She thought she had seen him move, and Abigail went to his couch and placed a hand on his forehead, fearing his fever was rising again. But his head was cool and his eyelids fluttered at her touch. She took his hand and said his name. "Snow Cloud, are you awake? Can you hear me?"

Slowly the black eyes opened and stared at her blankly.

She took hope and smiled at him. "How do you feel? Are you hungry? Do you want something to eat?"

In a weak, faraway voice he answered, "Yes."

Ross came close and looked with uncertain eyes at the reclining figure. "Father," he said tentatively.

The black eyes turned to the child and a weak smile briefly crossed his face. He moved his hand toward the child and Ross grasped it and beamed happily. "Father well now?"

Abigail stirred the heating bladder and answered, "We hope so, but it will be a while before he'll feel like playing with you. You'll have to be patient for a few sleeps."

Abigail spooned the broth from the meat she had cooked into Snow Cloud's trembling lips until he shook his head and she let him rest.

"Tell me what has happened."

"You were very sick. A piece of the spear broke off in the wound and caused infection. I removed it."

"You?!"

She saw the wonder in his eyes. "Yes."

He said nothing more and she resumed her work, feeling his eyes on her for a long while before he slept.

At dark Slow Water and her girls returned, and Snow Cloud awoke when they came noisily into the lodge. They stopped, stunned momentarily, and then crowded around him, touching him in disbelief.

Slow Water turned to Abigail and said, "He lives."

Abigail nodded. "Yes."

Slow Water rushed from the lodge and Abigail could hear her shouting as she tramped through the snow announcing that Snow Cloud had spoken to her. Soon the lodge was full of people and Abigail was afraid Snow Cloud might have a relapse and ordered them from the lodge. Her order was obeyed instantly. No one would dare question her authority now, and it gave her a feeling of security and peace she hadn't felt in some time.

When the lodge was empty of everyone except Wind Woman and Slow Water and the children, Slow Water said, "Your medicine was good, Little Yellow Bird. You have my respect."

"Thank you."

Wind Woman added, "Mine, too, and more, Little Yellow Bird. Your praises shall be sung and you shall be medicine woman over me."

"I don't wish to be medicine woman. I know nothing of all the things you do. All I did is what I saw done when I lived with a white doctor. You saw what I did and you can do as I did, now. I will be glad to teach you anything I know, but I don't want to take your place."

The older woman smiled gratefully and said, "I respect you as my equal and I will consult you often."

"I will be honored to assist you whenever you need me. Now, please, stay and share our food and maybe your son will be able to talk with you."

In the ensuing days Snow Cloud recovered quickly. The infection gone, his starved body demanded food often, and with each meal he seemed to double in strength. Soon he was able to join the elders and discuss the affairs of the band, and with nothing strenuous to do in the cold winter weather, he had no trouble except for a slight limp, which Abigail felt sure would disappear in time.

The winter weather didn't let up and the camp was running low on food. Several weeks after his recovery, Snow Cloud took a hunting party out. They returned in the middle of the night, unsuccessful, in the midst of a snowstorm. As the days passed their situation became grave. Abigail tried to ration the food out but her Indian companions would have it all or none, and though she tried to keep herself and Ross from eating more than necessary in order to conserve, she soon found that what she didn't eat the others did. She squirreled away food under her couch when the rest were gone from the lodge and kept herself and her two children on short rations. Snow Cloud continued to lead the men in futile hunts until there was no choice in the village but to kill its dogs. She let her son and Spotted Fawn eat the dog, but she could not quite enjoy the food as the others did and ate very little. The food she had hidden helped to keep her going but she could tell she was losing weight, and then the fever came. She had little reserve to battle it, and Wind Woman's medicine was less effective with her own resistance weakened.

Snow Cloud did everything to ensure a successful hunt, and after the purification ceremonies and other religious rituals were performed with great exactness and the Great Spirit beseeched in earnest prayer, he led the strongest of his men out to hunt, vowing not to return until he could bring meat for his hungry people.

Days passed before his return, and Abigail grew concerned that he and his men had perished in the terrible storms sweeping the region since his departure. She lay in her bed, terribly cold and too weak even to attempt anything to occupy her hands. She heard a shout from the camp guards and knew someone was coming in. She sent up a silent prayer that it was Snow Cloud and that he had meat. Trembling with expectancy she waited, watching the lodge opening. When he came carrying a leg of elk in she could have cried. Slow Water and her daughters began tearing at the meat and would have devoured it entirely raw if Snow Cloud had not ordered them to cook it. Snow Cloud came to Abigail and looked down at her pale, drawn face.

"Soon you will eat, Little Yellow Bird, and grow strong again." He turned to Ross and caught the child up in his arms. "And you, my son, your father has not failed you. You will eat well tonight."

Ross put his arms around Snow Cloud's neck and said happily, "Eat tonight. Eat tonight."

And eat they did in the way they always did after an enforced fast, consuming everything.

Abigail cautioned, "You should save some for tomorrow."

Snow Cloud laughed. "We will go again tomorrow and bring more."

"And what if there isn't any more?"

He shrugged eloquently and Abigail lay back, too weak to
argue. But the camp was lucky and Snow Cloud and his men
brought in more meat, enough to feed the band for several days.
They feasted and fasted in such fashion for another two months.
After Ross's second birthday the weather began to warm, and soon
the game became plentiful as the herds began moving once more.
The camp returned to a more normal state of existence, with food
no longer a major concern. It wouldn't be long until the snow was
gone and they would leave their winter camp, and the men spent
most of their time together, finishing bows and arrows and other
weapons that had been delayed by the intense search for game.

Abigail had been slow to regain her strength and still suffered
from cold and stayed inside the warm lodge. She spent quite a few
hours alone while the children went sledding on their buffalo-rib
sleds, taking advantage of the snow before it was gone, and Slow
Water usually was visiting some other lodge. On just such a day she
was alone and surprised when Snow Cloud came into the lodge. He
turned to lace shut the lodge opening, and her heart stopped
beating momentarily at the implication. She continued with her
work, her emotions ranging from dread to desire. She had
dreamed more than once since the day her body had almost betrayed her, of being in Ross's arms and being fulfilled with his love.
She knew she couldn't deny the insistence of her body much
longer, but the thought of responding to this man was still abhorrent to her.

Furiously she sewed on the skins she was fashioning into a dress
for Spotted Fawn until Snow Cloud's hand touched her shoulder.
Without looking up she laid her work aside as he stretched himself
out on her bed and pulled her to him. She closed her eyes against
the sight of him as he removed her clothing and covered her with
his body. His hand turned her face to his and his mouth covered
hers. She expected to be repelled again by the smoke and taste of
grease, but there was no grease and the smoke was faint on his
breath. There was no controlling her desire. Desperately she returned his kiss and strained to satisfy the demands of her body.
Her need fulfilled, she lay in Snow Cloud's embrace, horrified at
her abandoned response. She turned her head away in shame as
tears slowly coursed down her cheeks. Snow Cloud's hand turned
her face back to his.

His voice was gentle as he asked, "Have Little Yellow Bird's
wounds finally healed?"

With eyes still closed she answered, "Only the wounds of the body and mind. My heart still remembers the man you killed."

His hand caressed her hair and cheek. "Where the body and mind go the heart will follow." He paused and she felt his eyes on her and she opened her eyes and looked into his black, probing gaze. "You could have let me die. It would have been revenge for your husband."

"I was afraid of what would happen to me and my son if you died."

"But if I had died from your medicine my people might have killed you."

"It was a chance I had to take."

He laughed as if she had just told him something terribly funny. "I would not let anything happen to you or my son. Wind Woman would have given you a place in her lodge and protected you. But perhaps it is better you did not know this. You would have let me die, would you not?"

Angered by his words she answered forthrightly, "Perhaps."

"Perhaps? What is this perhaps? The answer is either yes or no."

"I can't answer yes or no because I don't know if I could just watch a man die if I knew I could save him, even you. My God does not teach revenge as your Great Spirit does. My God is a God of love. Those who believe in Him believe in doing for others as they want others to do for them."

He laughed again and got to his feet. "Your God would not live long here. And from what I have heard and seen of the white man, there are not many who believe in Him. Is this not true?"

Abigail had to answer, "Yes. I'm afraid it is all too true."

He was silent and she sat with eyes downcast, lacing her dress. His hand touched her hair and he said in a soft voice, "This time I am happy you believed in your God."

15

AS THE TWIG IS BENT

Near the end of April the camp started on its summer of food foraging. Abigail spent every minute she was alone with Ross teaching him English. It was easier for her to remove herself from the women as her food-gathering knowledge and skill now equaled theirs. The task of tapping box elders for sugar was one of the best methods of being by herself, and whenever she could get him out of eyesight she would darken his skin with dye. It was hard for her not to let him know she worshiped him and harder still not just to sit and hold him, hugging him to her as he talked to her in her own language, smiling, laughing, with his father's waving chestnut hair and thick-lashed brown eyes. His lips, as wide as his father's but with the fullness and heart-shaped qualities of hers, were accented by a set of adorable dimples, which Abigail knew were replicas of her own. It was Spotted Fawn who gave Ross his Indian name for the dimples constantly on display in his happy face. To the whole band he became known as Holes in Face.

Snow Cloud was a more frequent visitor to her bed now, and while she didn't love him, her acceptance of her position made it easier to let him fulfill the need she had for him as a man. More than that, she could now respect him and he was good to her and a loving father to her son. She endeavored to respect his wishes completely, knowing one day she would have to question his authority when he discovered his son was being taught the white man's ways as well as the Indian way. It wasn't always easy for her to be silent. The total lack of discipline inherent in Indian character was particularly upsetting to her, and when she and her child were alone she tried to temper the effects of this lack.

By the Sun Dance gathering Abigail knew she was pregnant

170

again. She didn't want another child but it was inevitable. The fever came with the exhausting work and heat of summer and Abigail aborted the fetus she carried. Twice more in the following months she suffered spontaneous abortions. The winter Ross was to turn five she was again carrying a child, and this time she carried it through the critical time and gave birth before the camp left its wintering grounds. The child was a boy.

That spring Abigail saw her grasp on Ross begin to slip. It was only natural that he was attracted by the older boys and would begin to imitate them, following them onto the prairie or into the thickets as they hunted small game and birds with miniature bows and arrows. As soon as he began to fashion his own bow out of twigs, Snow Cloud made one for him. Abigail was desperate to keep him with her, afraid she wouldn't be able to teach him all she wanted him to know, but he was not yet ready to cast off all ties with her and Spotted Fawn and when the older boys left him behind he would return to Abigail and his schooling continued.

In two more years Abigail bore Snow Cloud a daughter. She was a lovely, tawny child and filled a needed place in Abigail's life. Their family circle had changed drastically in the passing years. Snow Cloud's two older daughters had married into other bands and Abigail suffered the seemingly idiotic grand giveaway that was so much a part of Indian culture. Even when she knew generosity to the point of impoverishment was regarded as the greatest of virtues among these Indians, she still couldn't accept it, though she had long practiced the gift giving on a smaller scale which was perpetual among members of the closely knit band. With the departure of the older girls and their influence, Spotted Fawn and the youngest of Snow Cloud's daughters had finally become friends. Spotted Fawn was becoming capable in every way and was as slender and beautiful as Snow Cloud's daughter was stocky and placid. That she would be betrothed early Abigail had little doubt, for there was none prettier in Snow Cloud's band.

Another even subtler change was taking place in their way of life. White traders now visited more frequently among the bands of Snow Cloud's tribe, but Snow Cloud would not let the traders come close to his camp. Abigail had heard gossip that white men were in the area but the thought of escape or rescue didn't cross her mind now. She only longed for the day when she would see her son a man, capable of the thought and reason she was trying to instill in him and able to talk intelligently to her of the world as she knew it.

Abigail continued Ross's schooling, teaching him to do sums

and to print, more than pleased with his quick mind and aptitude for learning. She longed to spend more time with him, but instead saw more and more of his time being spent with his peers. He was old enough now to sit for long hours in the presence of the elders of the band listening to the teachings of the tribe. As the two cultures made their impression on him, he became increasingly thoughtful and quiet, and the happy child Abigail knew was replaced by a solemn boy. She became worried about the effect the conflicting heritages were having on her son, but when she discovered his solemnity was due more to the ridicule of his peers about his dimples than her teaching, her anxiety disappeared. She devised every possible means to have him help her on errands away from the camp so her schooling would not be forgotten in the long sessions with the camp elders, knowing full well he would eventually have to return to the elders, and cramming every minute she had with him full of her knowledge.

It wasn't long before Snow Cloud learned Holes in Face was not attending the elders' training sessions often enough and one day he came looking for his son. He found them near the river a little way from camp. Ross was lying on a sunbathed rock with a stick in his hand, writing sentences in the sandy stream bank.

"What is my son doing here?"

Abigail hadn't seen him come, and Ross was spelling out loud for her in English as he wrote, his total concentration on the difficult lesson. Abigail gasped in surprise and knew the time had come for logic and cool determination, and she willed herself to be calm and sure.

Before she could answer, Snow Cloud saw the lettering in the sand and with an accusing glance at Abigail asked, "What is this you are teaching my son?"

Abigail stood up and faced him. No shy, modest, retiring Indian squaw now but a strong-minded white woman. "I am teaching my son the language of my people."

In one angry movement, Snow Cloud grabbed away the stick from Ross's hand and destroyed the sand writing with his foot. "My son is not a white man. He does not need to know the white man's language. He needs to know the things of his father's people—the people he should be learning to be chief of!"

"Listen to me for a moment! I know you wish him to become chief and so do I, because I know with what you can teach him and what I can teach him he will be the best man to lead your people."

"He needs no white man's language to be that."

Stubbornly she retorted, "Yes he does. Are not the white traders already here among your people? If they are here you can be sure the rest of my people will not be far behind."

He cut her off haughtily. "Then we shall kill all the white traders. We and our brothers the Nakota, Dakota, and Lakota will make war upon the whites."

"Be reasonable, Snow Cloud. You saw the white man's army. Surely you know in your heart there is no stopping the white man. But there is a way you can deal with the white man if you know his ways and can speak his language so you can understand all the white man says. This is the only way you can save your people. And this is the man who will be able to do this."

"Do you think I am fool enough to believe what you, *a woman*, tell me?"

"You will be a bigger fool if you don't believe me. Only you can make the decision. Would you dare to be wrong? Would you dare deny your people the only man who will have the knowledge to save them?"

Snow Cloud threw the broken stick he held to the ground and whirled away, stalking angrily back to the village.

Abigail watched him go with a small feeling of hopeful triumph. Snow Cloud had not forbid the boy to stay nor had he demanded he go with him, but she was wise enough to know that right now was not the time to defy him farther.

She turned to her son. "I think you had better go to the elders now."

He jumped down from the rock, lean and lithe and naturally brown from long hours in the sun. He turned thoughtful eyes on her. "Is what you said true?"

"Yes."

"Do you think he will let me learn your language anymore?"

She smiled. "Yes. I think he will as soon as he realizes what I have said is true. Now run along. We'll study again tomorrow."

He nodded and ran after Snow Cloud, and Abigail walked leisurely back to the camp, carrying the water skins as if nothing unusual had occurred.

The next day Snow Cloud took Ross with him and Abigail despaired that she had not won but later in the day, when the two returned, Snow Cloud told her, "I have been teaching him my ways. Now it is your turn to teach him your ways."

Abigail lived to do nothing else, and while Ross dutifully studied with her, she saw all too clearly the greater influence was the Indian influence and realized her own teaching might, after all, be fruitless. He could talk English only with her or with Spotted Fawn to a limited degree, and even less to his half-brother and sister who picked up very few words because Abigail chose to teach only her white son the language of her people. A feeling of hopelessness haunted her, wearing her away subconsciously along with the intermittent attacks of fever and miscarriages she suffered. All that kept her going was their sessions together and the love and pride she had for him as he reminded her more and more of his father.

To make each session with him more intimate she began leaving the two younger children with Spotted Fawn, intensely aware her time with Ross was growing short. Soon he would have duties to perform for the band and his manhood training with bow and arrow would take more of his time as he hunted with boys his age, perfecting their skills.

She hadn't realized the pressure was becoming almost as great on him as it was on her until the day she was testing him on what she had been teaching him. He was having difficulty spelling a word and finally threw down his stick and looked at her in frustration. "How long must I do this?"

Surprised, she answered, "As long as we can. Too soon you won't have time, so we must make every minute count. Now start over and try again."

Stubbornly he protested, "But why?"

Irritably she snapped, "Because it's important. Now, you're wasting time."

He looked at her with those disarming eyes, unblinkingly, and said, "You haven't told me why I must learn this. Why I should learn and my brother and sister don't have to learn? What makes me different? Why do you dye my skin and call me a name no one else knows? I want to know why!"

She had never thought he would question her and wasn't prepared now with any easy answer to gloss over the question. She suddenly realized she wanted him to know and know it all, and just as quickly realized she couldn't tell him all. Carefully she chose her words.

"I have raised you differently because you are different. Snow Cloud thinks you are his son but you are not. Your father and I lived hundreds of miles south of here near the big river we cross when we go to the hills. Snow Cloud, his father, who was chief of this band then, and some of their warriors joined other Indians and the British in a war against the United States. Snow Cloud's father and the rest of the men with them were killed by the Americans. On his way back to his people, Snow Cloud sought revenge for the death of his father and his men. Your father was the victim of that revenge and so was I. He doesn't know he is not your father and I have never told him. I used to be afraid he might kill us both if he found out. Since your brother was born I no longer think it would matter, but I would rather he didn't know."

She hoped her explanation would satisfy him and they could return to their studies but his eyes were alive with curiosity. She could have demanded they not speak of it but she didn't, more eager now to talk of it than he was. She waited for his questions to come and come they did, tumbling from him in rapid succession.

"Then Ross is what my father's name was?"

"Yes."

"What did he look like?"

She smiled. "Very much like you."

"What kind of a man was he?"

"He was a good man. I loved him very much. He was strong, terribly stubborn, and not afraid to fight, but he was also very gentle and tender. He was the kind of man I hope you will be."

"I can understand strong and not being afraid to fight, but I don't understand gentle and tender. How can a man be gentle and tender and be a man? That is being a woman."

Thoughtfully, she tried to explain it to him. "Gentle and tender are marks of a real man. Only a man unafraid for his manhood can be gentle and tender."

He shook his head in confusion. "But how would a man show gentle and tender?"

She laughed, remembering all the things Ross did that had endeared him to her. "You know the meaning of gentle as opposed to being rough—tender as to tough. This is how a woman likes to be treated—kindly, without fear of being beaten, talked to in soft tones of love, not in anger. Someday you will understand when you find the one you love. And when you do, don't be afraid to show her your love by doing things for her. Things other men might laugh at you for doing, but if you are a real man, sure of your strength, sure of your manhood, you need not fear what others think and the one you love will love you all the more. Your father was like that."

He was silent, assimilating what she had told him. At last he said, "Snow Cloud does not do these things."

She smiled again. "Not in the same way. But he did let us continue this schooling, and when I was sick he made the trip to gather the things Wind Woman needed to make the medicine for me. He has been kind to me in other ways, too, and he is a good father to you. It is just not the Indian way to consider the woman first."

"Is it the white man's way?"

She frowned and answered honestly, "No. Not with most white men, but it is my God's way."

"Then if my father was a man of your God and not afraid to fight, how is it Snow Cloud was able to kill him? He must not have been as great a man as Snow Cloud."

Abigail was distressed and showed it. It was only natural and very Indian to question a man's power by whether his god protected him. She tried to answer without anger. "I know it is difficult for you to understand, but believe me when I say your father was as capable as Snow Cloud. He once killed a man with his bare hands, who was much larger than he was, because the man had hurt me. Many things I could tell you to prove this. I don't know why Snow Cloud was able to kill him, but I suspect it was because he didn't realize Snow Cloud meant him harm. We tried to be friendly with all the Indians. Why our God didn't save him I don't know."

"Then I will never believe in your God. The Great Spirit is much more powerful."

She looked at him squarely, sternly. "Remember that when the Great Spirit fails you. All men live or die according to the plan of God. Some he chooses to save—others he lets die. No one knows why."

He dropped his bold gaze and sat in respectful and thoughtful silence for a few long moments while Abigail stared at him with growing anxiety, well aware he could have lost respect for everything she had told him because it contradicted his strong Indian identity.

At last he asked, "Are your people very far away?"

"Yes. It took your father and me several months to reach the place where he was killed."

"Could we go some day to see these people?"

Abigail's heart almost choked her but she had to answer, "No. They wouldn't know us anymore."

"But how can this be? If they still live they would remember, wouldn't they?"

"Yes." She paused, wondering just how much she should tell him. "But you must understand we are different now. They would not know me as I look now, like an Indian. They wouldn't be able to understand all that has happened to me. They wouldn't be able to understand the Indian way, and it would be hard for you to understand them. It would only cause us both a great deal of unhappiness to try to go back now."

"Will you show me how you looked before?"

"If you want me to. But it will have to be tomorrow when I can bring my soap and wash the grease and paint from my hair and face."

Abigail stood up. It was time they were getting back. Ross delayed her with, "You still haven't told me why I must learn all these things of the white man, especially since you say we can not go there."

"It is because I want you to be a white man, not an Indian, but the choice will be yours. I am giving you the knowledge to become a white man if you want to be a white man. The same knowledge will help you to protect the Indians against the white man if you wish to remain an Indian."

"Are the white men that bad?"

"Not all of them. But a white man needs to own the land as the Indian owns his horse or his bow. He will take the land from the Indians by buying it or driving the Indians off of it if he wants it bad enough. If you understand this then you will be able to deal with the white man."

"I don't think I understand."

She put her arm around him and hugged him. "You will some day. That is why I want to keep teaching you. There is so much you must learn in order to understand."

The next spring Holes in Face began the training that would yield a warrior and eventually a chief if Snow Cloud had anything to do with it. He was invited to accompany the warriors of the village on their first horse-stealing raid of the summer. Abigail felt pride that he was becoming a man but an even deeper anxiety that he would face danger unnecessarily for the first time. When he came back the proud possessor of his own horse captured in the excursion, she was happy for him. He now had his turn to sing of his deed and Abigail attended the dances eagerly to hear her son's song. She was more than pleasantly surprised when his voice showed promise.

Spotted Fawn, sitting next to Abigail, smiled in delight. "Listen, Yellow Bird, how Holes in Face sings."

Abigail smiled with pleasure. "I didn't realize he could. It will probably not be so good when his voice changes."

Spotted Fawn wouldn't be discouraged. "No. It will be beautiful then, too. After all, have you not sung to us and is not your voice beautiful? His will be, too."

Praised for his vocal talent, Ross now took time to practice in the lodge. Those with the best voices were chosen to sing at special ceremonies and no man turned down that kind of recognition. It was the medicine Abigail needed—to have him close again, even if it was only for a short while. And even more gratifying, he asked her for help and she gladly taught him what she knew about music. Most of it didn't apply to Indian music, but it thrilled her to listen to his clear, sweet voice singing the songs she knew. Even Spotted Fawn would join them, often forsaking another man's courtship to listen to Ross. Abigail wondered about her indifference to the men who wanted to marry her. Snow Cloud's daughter had been gone two years but still Spotted Fawn refused Snow Cloud's efforts to marry her to one of the promising warriors of his band. When Abigail would question her she would only say she was waiting for the man she loved.

The summer brought much growth and glory to the boy known as Holes in Face and while Abigail had an abundance of motherly pride in her son and his accomplishments, it meant more and more of his time was spent away from her, widening the gulf that separated him from her and her culture. Anxiety and depression were constant companions, and when the fever season came she had little desire to fight it and little determination left to do so. Wind Woman's medicine was little help, and Abigail's desire to die became stronger with each attack. What she needed was her son but he was hunting. She was sleeping when he returned to the lodge, exhausted from a night of the fever, but she awoke when his strong young hand took hers.

"Ross," she said in English, caring little if Slow Water heard.

He answered her in English. "Mother, they told me you were sick. Wind Woman says the white doctors have a medicine that helps. Tell me what it is and I will find the white traders and get it for you."

Her heart rejoiced that he cared and she answered weakly, "Cinchona bark. But the traders won't have it. They'll have to get it from a white doctor. I don't know if you'll be able to get it."

"I will try. I'll leave in the morning."

"If you find a white trader who will bring it to you, have him bring you a straight-edge razor, too."

"Why?"

She smiled at him. "You will soon be a man, my son, and you will grow a beard like a white man."

He rubbed his chin and nodded as if he didn't quite believe her.

The next morning he came to tell her he was leaving, and she wished him success, hoping against hope that he would be able to obtain her medicine. Snow Cloud and a handful of warriors went with him to locate the trader and insure his safety. Hope gave her the strength to keep fighting the fever, and by the time Ross and Snow Cloud returned the attacks had subsided and she was feeling better.

Ross's smile as he came through the lodge opening was additional balm to her heart. He came to her side followed by Snow Cloud and asked, "You are better now?"

"Yes." She smiled. "The fever has finally run its course for now. Did you find the white trader?"

"Yes. He said he knew where there was a white doctor and for a large number of furs he will see if he can bring you some."

Abigail frowned. She had forgotten there would be a charge for so great a service. "Is it possible to give him what he wants in payment?" She looked to Snow Cloud, fully aware his people were not trappers.

"If it is what we must do, we will have to do it."

It was perhaps the nearest thing to declaring how highly he regarded her she was likely to hear, and she lowered her eyes to hide the emotion she felt.

Winter came and the white trader had not come by the first snowfall. Abigail knew he would not come until spring, if at all. She didn't have another attack of fever but the long, cold winter was just as hard on her as if she had suffered the fever. She stayed close to the fire working on clothes for her growing children with Spotted Fawn helping her and playing with the children. She felt guilty that she didn't love these two as dearly as she did her firstborn, but she tried very hard not to let it show. Brown Hair, as her second born was called, would be seven in the spring and the girl, so beautifully named Morning Star by her father, would be five not long afterward. They were both good children and she wondered if she had been wrong not to teach them English, too. They knew a few words and she knew they both would be capable of learning as easily as Ross, but somehow, now, it was too much effort to try to teach them.

The winter was ideal for trapping and the men who helped Snow Cloud and Holes in Face did well. By spring they had more than enough pelts for the trader if he came. When the snow began to melt Ross was gone constantly looking for the trader, never daring to tell Abigail if he thought the trader would not come.

Abigail heard the whistle of the camp guards one day late in April and knew, before he arrived, the white trader was coming with her son. She stood anxiously awaiting this first glimpse of a white man she had seen since the morning her husband had left her and had died at Snow Cloud's hand. Holes in Face came into the lodge first and the trader after him, followed by Snow Cloud. Several other men of the camp crowded in with them.

In English Ross said, "This is my mother."

The man stepped forward and held out his hand. "Malcolm McDonnell at yer service, ma'am. I didnae know whether to believe this young man of yours when he came to me with his story of a white woman needin' medicine. Now I'm glad I took a chance he wasnae lyin' to me."

"Thank you for coming, Mr. McDonnell. Were you able to get the medicine?"

"Aye. I knew where to find a doctor. I've got it for ye in my pack."

"I'm so relieved. But I'm forgetting my manners. Please sit down. I haven't talked to a white person for years. Can you stay for a while and tell me the news of the country?"

"Well, that'd be fine with me, but the boy told me the chief didnae want me stayin'."

Abigail looked at her son and he nodded. She spoke to Snow Cloud in his tongue. "Is it all right if this man stays to talk with me?"

"No. He must leave quickly."

"Just for a little while? What he can tell me may help me teach your son how to deal with the white man better. It is for the good of your people."

"No. If you are reminded of these things you will want to return to the whites. I would not let him come at all except for the medicine. Already he is planning to bring others to take you away, and I will not let anyone take you from me. He must leave now."

"Believe me when I say I have nothing to go back to. You killed the only thing that mattered to me in the white man's world. All I have is right here. You fear needlessly."

He looked at her for a long moment and finally said, "I will let no more come here alive. Tell him that."

Abigail nodded and turned back to the stocky Scotsman who sat patiently smoking his pipe and rubbing his muttonchop side-whiskers. "He will let you talk with me but he is afraid others will come and want to take me away and wants you to know he will kill any other white men who come here."

"Well, now, I have been thinkin' that was a good idea. How long ye been here?"

"Over twelve years."

"Great God! And ye haven't seen a white man in all that time?"

"No."

"Where was ye taken from?"

"My husband and I had a farm on the Missouri about the time the war started. My husband was killed and I was taken captive."

"Do ye want me to send the soldiers in after ye?"

"No. I have nothing to go back to. My life is here. My son is here."

"But what about other family members? Surely someone has been lookin' for ye?"

"Not anymore. It would be impossible to go back now. No one could understand what has happened to me."

"Aye, I suppose not, but I would be glad to send word to any family members if ye wish it. I can do that much for ye."

"No. It's better this way."

He shook his head. "So be it, but it is hard for me to understand ye not wantin' to go back."

She smiled apologetically. "It doesn't matter now. Will you stay and eat with us?"

He glanced sideways at Snow Cloud's threatening form. "If ye are sure he'll not kill me."

"I don't think he will. He does care about me and if I need this medicine to live I'm sure he will let you bring it. How much were you able to bring?"

His face dimmed. "Not much, I'm afraid, but I did bring ye the straight edge and some other things I think the chief will like in trade for the furs I asked as payment. Do ye think ye can get him to set down here and trade?"

She addressed Snow Cloud. "This man has brought my medicine and other things he would like to trade with you for the furs you trapped. I believe him to be a good man and honest, and he is willing to bring me more medicine if he is treated as a friend."

"Tell him we will trade with him."

Abigail relayed the message, and Snow Cloud came and sat in his place and the other ranking members of the band settled themselves around the fire. The pipe was passed and, with Abigail and Holes in Face translating, the furs were shown and approved. The trader's packs were brought in and untied. Abigail gasped as the trader showed Snow Cloud and the others guns. Immediately the Indians' interest doubled. Guns were almost nonexistent among Snow Cloud's people because he hadn't allowed trade with the white men.

Before the evening was over several warriors were the proud possessors of guns, Ross and Snow Cloud among them. Abigail had mixed feelings about the transaction but knew it was inevitable and if guns had to come it was best they come from a man she thought was honest and respectable. McDonnell had been right when he had said he hadn't brought much medicine, but she was pleased with the razor he had brought for her son. They talked into the early hours of morning, with Ross sitting beside her and Snow Cloud looking on long after the others had gone back to their own lodges. She was doubly pleased with her son's attention and his ability to ask questions when he didn't understand what they were saying. It was a better learning experience for him than anything she could have devised. She learned the United States had won the war and John Quincy Adams, son of John Adams, who had been president when she was a schoolgirl, was now president of the United States. Of the territories created in the past years, Louisiana, Indiana, Mississippi, Illinois, Alabama, Maine, and most surprising to Abigail, Missouri, had become states. Fur traders and trappers were reaching in ever increasing numbers to the Pacific Ocean, and Abigail was more than ever certain it wouldn't be long until Snow Cloud's people would have to face the white man, win or lose.

Even more interesting because it concerned her own home state of New York was the news that a canal was being built along the Mohawk River between the Hudson River and Lake Erie to handle the boatloads of people and supplies going to the fast-growing west. She envisioned how the canal would look, with memories flooding her as she remembered the time she and Ross went to the river and talked, surrounded by the river's peaceful beauty. She blinked back tears and concentrated on what the well-informed Malcolm McDonnell was saying. When every scrap of news and information was wrung from the talkative trader, they gave him a bed and finally went to sleep in the early hours before dawn.

The trader left after eating with them in the late morning, giving Abigail a promise he would return in a year with more medicine for her, and Abigail watched him ride away with a strange sense of loneliness settling over her. Snow Cloud stood at her side, silent, as he had been for most of the trader's visit. When the man was gone from sight Abigail said quietly to Snow Cloud, "Thank you for letting him stay."

He grunted noncommittally and asked, "What did you learn?"

"A great deal, and none of it will bring much good to the people of Snow Cloud. The white people are coming faster than I had thought. The place where you took me captive is now a state. Soon it will be necessary to deal with the white men."

He grunted again. After a moment of thoughtful silence he asked, "Did my son learn anything?"

"I'm sure he did. You would have been proud of the questions he asked of the trader. I am very pleased with the wisdom he showed."

"That is good. He will do well."

Abigail smiled happily. It was one of the rare times when Snow Cloud deigned to praise either one of them and her heart filled with pride for her son.

The year passed rapidly and Holes in Face grew ever more proficient in the skills that were important to the Indians. He was skillful at horse stealing and never lacked for good horses, and with the rifle he had traded his furs for, he became invaluable as a hunter when game was scarce in the winter months. The gun was far more accurate at longer distances than his bow, allowing him kills otherwise impossible. When not occupied with horse stealing or hunting, he trapped with the most skilled of the band and the pelts filled the lodge in expectation of Malcolm McDonnell's visit in the spring. The prospect of a gun for furs made the least ambitious of the village brave the cold of winter to trap in hopes of trading furs for that valued possession.

When the trader finally came in the spring he was welcomed enthusiastically by the whole village and dancing and feasting went on into the morning hours as furs were traded for guns and powder. Abigail got her supply of life-saving medicine and the promise of another bottle in a year, plus all the voluble trader's news. He was hardly out of sight before she was looking forward to his next visit.

The fever hit her in late summer and even with the medicine

she had a hard time controlling it. It finally relinquished its hold on her after several days, but she was more tired than usual and in poor condition. However, the Great Spirit favored them with a fairly mild winter and Abigail saw the first signs of spring come, feeling better than she had for quite some time. Ross was fourteen and so much involved with the affairs of the band she rarely saw him. He had been invited to join one of the young men's akicitas—a society of militarylike organization designed to further the training of the young men in the skills of war and policing duties for the band. His prestige as a hunter, horse stealer, and singer had grown until there was little doubt in Abigail's mind that he would be everything Snow Cloud wanted him to be, but she missed him terribly and neither of her other two children began to fill the void Ross left in her heart.

As the time to move camp approached, Abigail watched with increasing expectation for Malcolm McDonnell to come. He was now her only link to her past and her husband, and she didn't realize how much she had counted on him until the day the men of the village came escorting a trader into camp and it was not Malcolm McDonnell. With disappointment so great she almost cried, Abigail watched the strange white man approach with her son and Snow Cloud, followed by the suspicious warriors of the village.

Ross spoke first. "This man comes in trader McDonnell's place. He tells us trader McDonnell is dead."

The thin, nervous-looking man smiled at her uncertainly and she turned her full attention on him and didn't like what she saw.

"Howdy, ma'am. What this Injun says is true. Malcolm died this last winter. I knew about his tradin' with you and hoped you'd let me take his place. My name's Selby. How do they call you?"

"I'm called Little Yellow Bird. The boy is my son. Tell me how Mr. McDonnell died?"

He shifted his feet and blinked while he answered, "Well now, I wasn't with him, but those that found him said it looked like he'd been killed by Injuns."

Abigail let out a soft, disbelieving, "Oh?" and asked, "Were you a close friend of his?"

"Well now, I reckon I was close as anybody." He laughed shortly. "Otherwise how'd I know about his tradin' with you here?"

Abigail nodded, unconvinced, but having no other choice she offered, "Well, come inside, Mr. Selby, and we'll see what you have to trade for our furs. Did you bring my medicine?"

The squinted eyes widened in surprise. "Medicine?"

"Mr. McDonnell was to bring me medicine. Surely if you knew him, you knew that was his reason for coming here?"

He stammered, "Oh, yeah. Is that the stuff in the little bottles that tastes so bad?"

"Yes. Did you bring it?"

With returned composure he answered, "You bet. Got it in the pack, there."

Abigail turned away and went into the lodge, feeling the man was somehow lying. They soon settled themselves and Ross brought in the furs he had to trade for the medicine and gunpowder.

When the trader handed him a decidedly smaller amount of powder than McDonnell had given them, he asked, "Is this all? McDonnell gave us more."

Curtly the man answered, "Sorry, but prices are goin' up."

Abigail spoke up. "Mr. McDonnell didn't tell us prices were going up. Our deal with him was to be the same."

"Sorry, ma'am, but I can't give you no more than that for what you got here. These pelts ain't the best quality, you know."

"That's ridiculous!" Abigail was beginning to see red. "These pelts are the best quality."

He shrugged. "Take it or leave it. I can get better out of any of the other bands for less. I'm doin' you a favor because of my great likin' for Malcolm McDonnell by even comin' here."

Ross whipped out his knife and grabbed the man's shirt front before Abigail had time to stop him. His quick savagery startled her, and his voice was coldly commanding before she could speak.

"You lie, white man."

"Ross!" she blurted out, "for heaven's sake, let him go."

"Not until he trades fairly with us."

Selby demanded, "You let me go, you young savage, or you'll get nothing."

Ross flicked the knife closer until the gleaming point nicked the man's adam's apple and a drop of blood oozed onto the sharp blade and Ross softly said, "You trade fairly or you'll get nothing, and we'll take it all and your hair, too."

The man tried to pull away but couldn't and gasped, "All right. All right! You dirty redskin. They told me you was the worst thievin' bastards of the whole bunch. Have it your way."

Ross let him go and Abigail sat in stunned silence at his display of violence. Snow Cloud's reaction was completely opposite, and the looks of approval passing among the spectators seated around them were not lost on Ross or Abigail. The disgruntled trader grudgingly gave the Indians a fair trade, and though it was late in the day, he left the camp at a gallop. Abigail felt they would not see him again.

A few weeks after the Sun Dance gathering was over, Abigail learned Ross was preparing to seek his vision. Abigail was heartbroken at the news. According to everything she believed this ritual was the last complete step into paganism and the step she was sure would forever separate her son from her God. She tried to talk Snow Cloud into not letting him go but the proud father could not deny his son, even though Abigail suspected he had second thoughts of his own. Abigail found little consolation in the fact that one of the best men and the closest friend of Snow Cloud, Buffalo Horn, was going with Ross to the sacred hill.

He left during the hottest days they had yet had and with him went Abigail's reason for living. The little determination she had left for living, which had hinged so greatly on Malcolm McDonnell's visits and her son's concern for her, now vanished. The fever struck with a **vengeance** while he was gone and it was only because Spotted Fawn took care of her that she took the medicine at all. Strangely, even the medicine didn't bring her out of it this time, and Spotted Fawn with Wind Woman's counsel decided to double the dose they gave her. Finally she began to respond, but the medicine was gone. It was then Abigail knew she had been the victim of trader Selby's trickery. It was obvious he had diluted the medicine in hopes of getting more furs from them.

Ross came to see her and it was the first time she remembered him being there since he had gone to seek his vision, though Spotted Fawn had told her he had come back with his vision and had been to see her. As always, his presence brightened her spirits. He sat down on Snow Cloud's couch and, forsaking modesty and respect, looked at her keenly.

"How are you feeling now?"

"I'm much better."

"Spotted Fawn tells me the medicine didn't help you as it did before. She suspected there was something wrong with it. It didn't smell as strong to her. Is this true?"

"Yes," she admitted and saw the quick anger in his eyes. Afraid of what he might do she added quickly, "But what is done is done. You mustn't seek vengeance."

"The white trader was a liar and a cheat. It would not be vengeance but justice."

"Ross!" she said sharply. "My God is a just God. Mr. Selby will be dealt with accordingly. I don't want his blood on your hands. That is not the Christian way."

With a mask of stoicism settling over his face he said, "I am not a Christian. I am an Indian and I will seek justice in the Indian way."

Abigail knew it was no use trying to change his mind. She had not wanted to believe her teachings were lost to him but now she realized how minor her influence had really been. She looked down at her trembling hands and said, "I am sorry. You must do what you feel is right."

He stood up and she heard him leave the lodge. Tears filled her eyes and prayers filled her mind.

Winter came early and harshly to the vast, windswept prairie hunted by Snow Cloud's band, and Abigail felt it more intensely than ever before. It would be another winter of starvation and Abigail knew she could not survive it. The years of extreme heat and cold, the fevers and miscarriages, had robbed her of all vitality and, even more important, her son was no longer her son, but Snow Cloud's son. They hunted constantly to keep supplies of food in camp, but the time came when the food ran out and her children sat cold and hungry in the lodge while a blizzard kept the hunters in camp. Abigail waited for what she knew to be inevitable and prayed.

A hunt was organized as soon as the storm let up and Ross came to see her before he left with the rest of the hunters. This time, at Snow Cloud's insistence, the party included Brown Hair. Weakly she sat up as Ross came into the lodge, always uplifted by his visits. He seemed thinner but he stood tall and straight and lithe, more handsome, she thought, than his father, with the softness and charm her features had lent him. He was taller than his father and not as broad through the chest and shoulders and probably never would be, but if her husband had been Apollo then surely their son was Adonis. She smiled weakly but warmly at him.

"We leave now. I have brought you some food to keep you until we return."

Slow Water reached for it and Ross held it away from her, saying, "You may have your share, Slow Water, but my mother and my sisters must get theirs first."

She grunted and snatched the parfleche filled with pemmican

and tore it open. Spotted Fawn rose from her couch and came forward and took the bag from Slow Water, who was already chewing hungrily.

Spotted Fawn stood with downcast eyes and said, "I will see that they eat and I will tell you if they got their share when you return." She flicked her eyes to Slow Water.

Holes in Face said, "Good, my sister. I know I can rely on you."

Spotted Fawn smiled demurely and turned to give Morning Star a piece of the dried mixture of tallow, meat, and berries. Ross turned to leave and Abigail hadn't even said a word to him. She rose on weak and trembling legs and followed him to the lodge opening and stepped into the bitter cold. He was already running after the men with his snowshoes in his hand. She stood with tears freezing on her cheeks, knowing she would never see him again.

The men stopped at the edge of the village to fasten on their snowshoes, and for some unexplicable reason Ross turned and looked back. He dropped the snowshoes and came running to her, and before she could protest he took her in his arms and held her briefly.

Before he released her he said in English, "May your God keep you safe while I am gone."

She answered tearfully, "May the Great Spirit guard you, my beloved son."

His lips were cold against her cheek and then he was running toward where the men stood watching with amazement, which would no doubt turn into laughter and ridicule once he was with them. Abigail didn't wait to see their derision and hurriedly retreated to the fire inside the lodge. But the warmth filling her was not from the fire. Was it possible she had not failed after all? She ate her pemmican and, calling her daughter to her, lay down with Morning Star cuddled warmly against her and slept.

PART II

16

A CAPTIVE IS
RELEASED

Laden with elk and venison, a tired and cold little group of hunters approached the hollow where their lodges stood warm and welcoming. Holes in Face looked back to see if his brother, Brown Hair, was coming. The youngster doggedly struggled to keep up, uncomplainingly. Holes in Face waited for him, feeling both pride and sympathy for his younger half-brother.

The boy caught up with him and lowered his slab of frozen meat and wiped the freezing perspiration from his forehead. "Are we almost there?"

Holes in Face smiled. "Yes, little brother. Rest a bit."

"The others aren't resting. I will be shamed."

"No. I will tell them I had to stop to fix my snowshoe and needed your help." He squatted down and motioned his brother down and pretended to relace his snowshoe.

In a few minutes, when he felt the chill begin to dull his mind, he rose and pulled the younger boy up and helped him shoulder his load again and, with a gentle pat on the younger boy's shoulder, he led off again after the rest of the hunters, now disappearing into the head of the hollow where the band was wintering.

Before he and Brown Hair cleared the trees surrounding the camp, he heard the hideous death wail rise from the unusually silent village. A cold apprehension filled him. Not knowing how he knew, he knew it concerned him and he drove his legs faster in the sluggish snow, forgetting about Brown Hair.

By the time he burst through the trees and into the outer lodge circle, the whole camp was echoing the death wail. Snow Cloud stood in the center of camp, his knife dripping blood in his hand and his voice strained in the death cry, as blood ran down his arms and legs and colored the snow where he stood. He labored on to the lodge, the people of the village wailing in sympathy as he passed them. He dropped the meat on the snow and tore off his snowshoes before ducking into the lodge. His mother's couch was empty.

Spotted Fawn stood with downcast eyes, her hands over her mouth, waiting for him to speak. He asked hoarsely, "How long?"

Sadly she answered, "Not long after you left."

Their words brought a soft sniffling from his little sister's couch and he glanced at the grieving child trying to control her tears. It was against custom for him to comfort her but it was difficult for him to see her small body quivering in sorrow and not want to try.

"Where is she?"

"On the hill across the water."

"Take care of my sister's tears."

Spotted Fawn nodded and he turned to leave as Brown Hair came in, his face contorted with grief. Holes in Face held the younger boy in his arms wordlessly, his own eyes close to spilling over. The desire to see his mother was so great he knew he had to go to her. As soon as Brown Hair was quiet he left the lodge and, ignoring the wailing procession trudging with Snow Cloud through the camp, he ran to the river. Carefully he crossed the ice to the other side and made his way up the hill, aware darkness was closing fast over the small valley where the village was camped.

His mother's scaffold stood desolate against the sky, the wind whipping the robes lashed about her and rattling the charms eerily. He stood still with his young heart in his throat, the hair at his neck prickling with fear of the spirit world. But he would not turn back now. She had told him there was nothing to fear about death. There were no spirits lurking in graveyards, only those in the imagination. With breath coming fast, he labored to climb upon the scaffold and squatted, breathing hard, frosty breaths as he looked at the robe-wrapped form lying on the platform. All her possessions were lined up beside her. Her awls and the scraping tool she used with its handle dotted in red and black for the hides she had tanned using it, her knife and paint pots and a parfleche of food.

With trembling fingers he undid the wrappings and carefully folded them back until he saw her face. He put his hands over his face then and the tears that had not yet been shed came rushing from his eyes and the voice that had not wailed, wailed bitterly into the onrushing night. In a few minutes his grief could be controlled and he fought to clear his eyes, wanting now desperately to see her. He wiped the freezing tears from his cheeks and peered at the painted face, remembering the day she had washed the paint from her face and the grease from her hair and he had seen how she really looked. His hand went to the scar on her cheek and before he realized what he was doing he started to wipe away the paint hiding her pale skin, whispering in her language, "I'm sorry, Mother. I'm sorry. I wanted to take you back to your people but I couldn't. If only—" His voice broke and he forcibly withdrew his hand from the frozen cheek with the ludicrously smeared paint. Moaning with misery, he carefully replaced the wrappings and tied them securely and sat with head bowed beside her until it was completely dark and he was numb with cold.

An owl hooted close by and startled him out of his numbness, and he knew he had to leave her or become her permanent companion. Stiffly he swung down from the scaffold and his mind began functioning for the living once more. Morning Star and Brown Hair were alone now, and it would be up to him to provide for them. Slow Water's indifference would border on neglect no matter what Snow Cloud ordered. Snow Cloud would not abandon them, he was sure, but they needed someone who cared for them to look after them, especially Morning Star. Spotted Fawn was the logical choice and he would ask her if she would stay with them, or if she should marry now that his mother was dead, if she would take Morning Star with her. He and Brown Hair could live by themselves if they needed to.

He didn't go to the lodge of the society where he had been living but returned to Snow Cloud's lodge. He could offer his sister and brother his presence, if nothing else, until he could talk to Spotted Fawn in private. He entered the lodge and Snow Cloud rose to greet him, a look of concern on his strained face.

"Are you all right, my son?"

"Yes."

"I am relieved. I feared for you."

"There was nothing to fear there."

The relief left Snow Cloud's face. "Then you have your mother's power?"

"No. Only the power of her words."

Even more concerned he asked, "You spoke with her?"

"No. But she told me there was nothing to fear from the dead. It is only our own fear we must be afraid of."

Snow Cloud sank crosslegged to his couch in relief. "Your mother was very wise. Even I would be afraid to walk among the dead at night. A man who can do these things could be a great shaman among his people." He paused and looked intently at Holes in Face, trying almost successfully to hide a deeper concern. "Do you have your mother's powers of healing? Do you want to become a shaman?"

Holes in Face sat down opposite Snow Cloud. "No. I have none of her power. I do not wish to become a shaman."

Snow Cloud smiled. "That is good. I was afraid you would, and time is short for me to prepare a son to take my place as chief of my people. Already the younger men are beginning to be dissatisfied because I am not as reckless as they. Soon, I'm afraid, they will want to test my leadership and I am not sure I can hold on to it until you can be elected in my place."

Holes in Face dropped his head lower, feeling even more of a failure. He had been too young to save his mother and now he was too young to save the inheritance Snow Cloud wanted so desperately to be his.

"I am sorry."

"It is no fault of yours that my sons came not in my youth as a strong warrior but at an age when I should be joining the old and wise Nacas."

Holes in Face knew it was true but it made him feel no less guilty. Tears were welling in his eyes and he fought desperately to keep them from spilling over and uncovering his immaturity to his shame.

Snow Cloud picked up his pipe and filled it and, after lighting it and taking a few puffs, he handed it to Holes in Face. "Here, my son, we have not yet smoked together as men. Our grief will have to be our own but this I can share with you."

Holes in Face glanced quickly at Snow Cloud's gently smiling face, seeing understanding and compassion there, and his hand gratefully closed over the ornamented pipe stem. He touched it to his lips and drew in the hot, pungent smoke with a feeling of pride. In the lodge of the society that had invited his presence, he had learned to smoke with the other younger boys and now the accomplishment made him feel more grown up than anything he had so far done.

After several puffs he handed it back to Snow Cloud and said, "My father honors me."

"No man can honor what does not already have honor, my son."

Holes in Face was too filled with Snow Cloud's praise to speak and sat in happy, embarrassed silence until Snow Cloud passed him the pipe again. Before they could say more Spotted Fawn came with Brown Hair and Morning Star, accompanied by Wind Woman, and all serious conversation was ended as Brown Hair sought the company of his brother and Morning Star clung to Snow Cloud. Spotted Fawn quietly set a cooking bladder to boil and busied herself with tidying up the lodge. That Slow Water was present was hardly noticed. She sat as unobtrusive and stolid as always in her place, neither speaking nor attempting to offer assistance to Spotted Fawn. The bulk of the conversation was now between Wind Woman and her son. Holes in Face helped his half-brother with the new bow the boy was making, and after they had eaten and the women had eaten, Wind Woman left for her own lodge, Holes in Face took his mother's couch, and everyone settled down for the long winter night.

For a long time Holes in Face lay awake, watching the fire make flickering shadows around the circular lodge. His most urgent need was to talk to Spotted Fawn and the only way he could think of doing so would be to join the line of courters that came, when the weather permitted, to wrap her in their robes. He wished there were some other way of seeing her alone but Slow Water would not permit it since he was not a blood relative and now old enough to be considered a suitor. Tomorrow evening, if the weather permitted, he would come and join the men who courted her.

The other thoughts troubling him all concerned his youth and inexperience. He had done well for his age. His ability as a hunter was being proven constantly by his skill with bow and arrow and the gun. That he was unafraid was also known. He had several stolen horses to his credit and had even had the good fortune to touch an enemy in a horse-stealing raid even though he had not killed an enemy yet and had not taken a scalp. He would have to do more in order to gain the confidence of the older warriors and the task seemed almost too great for one of his limited experience. He would have to make his own experience if he wanted to take Snow Cloud's place and he would have to begin doing so immediately, no matter how overwhelming it seemed. But sleep overwhelmed him first and his young, tired body thought no more.

A weak sun awoke the camp in the morning but the day stayed mild and though there was still the quietness of recent death lingering in the camp, the people were otherwise busy gathering wood and taking care of the horses while the weather permitted. Even the cold wind that sometimes whipped off the prairie and found them in their sheltered hollow remained but a softly stirring movement in the tops of the leafless and gray cottonwoods along the river. Holes in Face spent the day playing with his brother and sister, hoping to take their minds off the loss of their mother, and found it helped him as much as them, abandoning for the present the brother-sister taboo. He took them sledding and when they were tired of that, they spun tops into holes in the river ice.

As the early falling winter sun began to disappear, Holes in Face prepared himself to court Spotted Fawn. He bathed and put on his best shirt and painted his face in the most attractive way he could in the lodge of his men's society. As one of the youngest of the lodge, he was teased unmercifully by the older members, knowing full well there were among those teasing him one or two who would also be standing at Spotted Fawn's lodge door.

Not wanting to be first to see her he deliberately waited until those he knew were going out to court that night were long gone. Them amid the snickers of his peers he left the lodge and walked slowly with his robe held tightly about him toward Spotted Fawn's lodge—Snow Cloud's lodge. He felt nervous and pulled the robe tighter about him as his nervousness made him shiver. At a respectful distance from where he could see the dark shape of two people in a robe against the glow of the lodge, he stopped and waited with two other of the village hopefuls. One of them was from his own society.

"So! Holes in Face courts Spotted Fawn, who is like a sister to him."

He nodded in stiff agreement. He didn't want to discuss it. Especially with Big Tree. Of all the young men in the village, Big Tree intimidated Holes in Face the most. From the time he could remember joining the other boys in play, this boy had been the biggest, roughest, and most malicious of all the boys. Five years older than Holes in Face, he was head of their society and undoubtedly one of the men Snow Cloud considered a threat to his leadership. He was tall and strong and had a cold-blooded ruthlessness that had gained him one honor after another. It almost made Holes in Face decide not to wait and avoid being subject to the other man's wrath, but he had come too far now to back down and when Big Tree learned he was not a serious rival for Spotted Fawn, perhaps he would laugh the whole thing off.

But Holes in Face hadn't foreseen Spotted Fawn's reaction to his being there. Politely she excused herself from the man she was with and in quick succession bundled briefly with Two Tails and Big Tree in all too obvious a hurry to be with him.

When she cut short Big Tree's prolonged embrace, he passed Holes in Face with a murderous look and threatened, "You had better beware of where you walk from now on, Holes in Face, or you might step on a snake."

Bravely he answered, "I will watch."

He walked with shaking knees to where Spotted Fawn stood with a shy smile on her lips. He clumsily tried to throw his robe around her as he had seen the others do and she giggled at his

awkward attempt. With quick and adept hands she helped him fold
her into his robe until she stood against him, pressing against him
until he could feel the soft warmth of her. A strange sensation
sprang from some unknown and unexplored sense in him and he
tried to back away from her, but the robe was too secure. He
couldn't move away and her arms went around him and held him
even tighter.

"Spotted Fawn," he began in a shaking voice, "I have to talk to
you about my mother, and this was the only way I knew we could be
alone."

She smiled up at him and nodded and he could feel her warm
breath on his cheek as she said, "I too have wanted to speak with
you but did not know how. I never thought of this and thought for
a moment you were seriously seeking my hand in marriage. Big
Tree will be hard on you, you should have told him."

"No. He'll know soon enough."

"I will make sure he does, so he does not hurt you."

Her concern embarrassed him more and he said crossly, "Spotted Fawn, I can take care of myself."

She giggled and snuggled closer to him and he felt as if he
would smother with the presence of her. Struggling hard for
composure, he asked, "Tell me about my mother. Did she say
anything to you?"

"Yes. It was so heartbreaking to watch her die but she seemed to
welcome death. She told me to tell you she loved you and not to
forget all she had taught you and she gave me her ring to give to
you." She wormed one hand between them until she could pull a
leather thong from her neck and place the ring in his hand.

"Is that all?"

"No, there was one other thing she said. She told me to tell you
her death was not caused by the white trader but by her illness. She
didn't want you to seek revenge by killing him but neither should
you trust him."

He nodded solemnly. "I will respect her wish. I will not seek
revenge for her death. Is that everything?"

"Yes."

"Now I must ask something of you, Spotted Fawn. I am worried
about Brown Hair and Morning Star. Slow Water will not be a good
mother to them. If you marry now I am afraid she will purposely
neglect them whenever she can. I could take a lodge of my own for
myself and Brown Hair, if necessary, but Morning Star would be
better off in your care. Can you take her with you?"

She looked up at him, her large eyes unreadable. "I do not intend to marry yet. I will take care of Brown Hair and Morning Star."

"I will provide for you then. You are the best sister anyone could have and I will bring you the best."

She tightened her arms about him disconcertingly and softly whispered with lips against his neck, "I don't want to be your sister, Holes in Face."

He felt suddenly hot and uncomfortable by her closeness and pulled the robe free and stepped away from her. "I must go now. Thank you, Spotted Fawn."

He turned to leave but she called his name and he stopped. She came beside him and placed a hand on his arm.

"Be careful of Big Tree."

"Don't worry about me," he said sharply, embarrassed by her concern.

She dropped her hand and murmured, "I'm sorry. I keep forgetting you are not the little boy I took care of."

He grunted and said shortly, "You had better go in. It is cold."

"I was hoping you would stay and talk more with me. It will not be good for you to come again and I miss you."

"What would we talk about? We are not lovers."

"Do we have to be lovers to talk? You could tell me about your hunting or your horses."

He stiffened with rejection. "That is not something to talk about with women. Now you'd better go in."

Before she could say more, Slow Water came to the opening of the lodge to call Spotted Fawn back to where she could see what was going on. Spotted Fawn answered her and gave one last glance at him and said, "Maybe someday you will not be so bashful."

He watched her run quickly inside the lodge and pull the door across the opening, and her slender figure fastening the door flap shut against the chill was silhouetted before the lodge fire. He felt confused and uncertain and very much apprehensive of what waited for him at the hands of Big Tree. He turned and ran toward the warrior lodge shivering with cold. He squared his shoulders and entered the lodge, prepared to fight. The other members of the lodge were lounging around the fire, joking or gambling—all except Big Tree, who sat smoking sullenly. He looked up as Holes in Face entered, and the voices of the rest of the men silenced immediately.

Twists the Grass, a boy a year or so older than Holes in Face and the one who had become his best friend, asked, "Well, how was it, Holes? Did she keep you warm enough on this cold night?"

Holes in Face glanced at Big Tree and saw the smoldering look in his malevolent eyes. He had been a listener many times to the bantering between the men and near men. Sexual fantasies filled a good deal of their idle time and he was well aware from listening to them that a laugh was much better at smoothing over sensitive areas between them where the women were concerned. With a confidence he didn't know he had, he answered, "Yes, but only half of me at a time. She is too like a thin blade of grass. I will find a plumper woman to robe with next time so both halves keep warm."

They laughed raucously at his misadventure and another, older, more experienced warrior, called Bull Heart, quipped, "You didn't put her hands in the right place. Every *man* knows all he needs to keep warm is his balls."

There was another burst of riotous laughter, fading only when Big Tree stood up. With a malicious grin he said, "Maybe she couldn't find them."

The two of them looked at each other across the fire while the rest of the lodge members howled with laughter. Big Tree pushed past Holes in Face and went out of the lodge. Twists the Grass looked after him and then at Holes in Face and smiled. Holes in Face smiled back and went to his couch and rolled into his robes with relief. He had been prepared to fight but he had not had to. With good fortune this might be the last he would hear about it, but he doubted it.

The weather still held, however uncertainly, until sunup the next day and the scouts who had been sent out the day before came in early with the report of buffalo not too far distant. Quickly a hunting party was organized, with each society picking its best men to participate. It was only natural that Big Tree would be the first chosen to go but when he picked Holes in Face to be the other one from their lodge to go, Holes in Face felt uncertain as to the meaning of his choice. But he could not decline the offer or he would be considered a coward, and his own desire to achieve was greater than his apprehension. Quickly he greased and painted his body to protect it from the biting winds of the plains and shouldered his bow, arrows, and rifle, and with a pack of food and his snowshoes he went to join the others gathering to leave.

Soon they were on the trail the scouts had made coming in and moving at a rapid pace. Big Tree was leading them and Holes in Face knew Big Tree could endure more than any of the rest of them. His own body, not yet fully hardened or developed, would be one of the first to have to fall off the pace. It occurred to him, then, that this was why Big Tree had chosen him. What better way to humiliate him than by making him seem inadequate as a hunter. He made up his mind he would not be the first to fall back.

Miles were covered as the hunters followed the wide wallowing path of the buffalo, and one by one the hunters slackened their paces until only Big Tree was left with Holes in Face a few hundred yards behind. He didn't know whether it was exhaustion or disgust with Big Tree's pace that had made the rest slow down. All he knew was that his own body ached for rest and each step felt like his last, but his anger and determination wouldn't let him quit. The other hunters were lost to his sight as the trail dipped toward a river valley. Holes in Face slowed, his breath coming in great aching gasps. It was time to think about the buffalo and not his anger with Big Tree. The buffalo could very well have stopped in the thickets along the river to rest and eat in shelter from the howling prairie winds, and he would be worse than a coward or a quitter if he stampeded them before anyone was close enough to kill any. His legs were shaking badly and he had no choice but to sit down and rest. He found a sheltered spot out of the wind and blowing snow and sank to the ground.

Too late he realized it was just the kind of opportunity Big Tree might need to finish him, if he sought revenge. He reached for his knife but Big Tree burst from the trees and stood over him with a mocking smile.

"So! The sucking pup has finally had to stop and rest."

Holes in Face said nothing, just looked without fear at the towering Indian.

Big Tree squatted down and said in crisp, guttural tones, "I could leave you here and as tired as you are you would, unfortunately, freeze to death before sunrise and no one would know the difference, but I think you will be smarter next time and not court my woman."

Impetuously he retorted, "She is not your woman. She is no man's woman until she chooses to marry."

A viselike hand closed around his throat. "I am the man she will marry and I want you to remember it!"

"What about the others? Why don't you tell them?"

He smiled coldly. "They already know. She has refused them but I let them come so she may know how much better I am than any one else she has to choose from."

Holes in Face sneered at him, "Then why do you fear me?"

Big Tree released his hold and stood up laughing. "Afraid of you! Should the eagle be afraid of the rabbit? Never! But a woman sometimes feels sorry for the rabbits."

Before any more was said, the first of the hunters came into the hollow and they waited in silence while the rest of the men caught up. When all of the hunters were squatted in a circle, Big Tree picked two of them to scout the valley to see if the buffalo were sheltered in the trees while the rest of them waited and regained their strength.

The buffalo were still in the sheltered valley and just before dark the hunters were able to surprise the small herd. With his usual skill, Holes in Face brought down two of the big animals before they were able to escape the slaughtering Indians. Jubilantly, the hunters butchered one of the animals and had their own feast and each man had a warm cavern of a dead buffalo to sleep inside for the night.

Early the next morning Big Tree sent Holes in Face and one of the other hunters back to camp to bring more men to help pack in the buffalo carcasses. It was a time of celebration for the village. The cooking fires all sizzled with fresh buffalo meat and the hunters were praised and honored with the choicest cuts. There was singing and dancing and Holes in Face was one of the honored hunters, but he took little joy in it. His pride still hurt from Big Tree's words and he knew only one way to regain his pride.

It was near his fifteenth birthday when he again bathed and painted his face and put on his best shirt and carried his robe to Spotted Fawn's lodge. Big Tree was already there, waiting for her to come out into the mild night filled with stars and clouds wafting across the moon in rapid succession. Spring would not be long in coming, and Holes in Face was old enough to begin feeling the urges springtime brought to all things as she breathed life into the land and turned it green under the gray and dying snow.

Big Tree faced him angrily. "I thought I told you not to bring your robe here again."

"You did, but I decided I was an eagle, not a rabbit. Eagles must fly and rabbits must die. I am not ready to die."

Big Tree whipped his knife out and stepped close to Holes in Face, the knife point pressed low against his breechclout but he didn't move.

"I will cut the manhood from you and you will die, rabbit, or you can run, like a rabbit."

"Stop it!"

They both turned and saw Spotted Fawn standing in the doorway of her lodge. Her eyes were filled with anger and her voice shook as she said, "How dare you come to court me in such a manner. I will never accept you, Big Tree. Leave and do not come back."

Holes in Face stood his ground while Big Tree angrily strode away; then he turned to leave, too, angry with her for interfering. Spotted Fawn caught up with him and grabbed his arm.

"Wait! Didn't you come to court me?"

He faced her and glanced briefly into her anxiety-filled eyes, not understanding why she should feel fear for him, and it made him even angrier. "Don't you want me to leave, too?"

"No. Now come back to the lodge."

"No," he refused angrily.

"I see," she whispered and her hand dropped from his arm.

Immediately he was sorry. She turned away but not before he saw the glint of tears on her cheek. He caught her arm and said, "Not to court you but we can talk if you wish it."

She stopped and he folded her inside his blanket and she turned to him and he felt the little thrill of excitement at the touch of her body he remembered from before.

"That was a very foolish thing to do. Now he has every excuse to kill you. Don't you know that?"

"Yes. But if I am to be a man and take Snow Cloud's place, I can let no man tell me what to do."

Her arms went around him and her breath was hot against his neck. "You are far too young to start challenging the strongest of the young warriors. I am afraid for you."

"Don't be. I did not see death for me in my vision."

"And what if your vision was false?"

"How can it be. Already the first part has come true. My mother has died."

She sighed and looked up at him. "You have the mind of a contrary horse. I told Big Tree why you came to see me and he seemed satisfied. Now you do this. How can I save you from yourself?"

"I must do these things in my own way. You can't protect me forever, dragging me away from the fire as you did when I was a baby."

Her hand caressed his neck and he twitched at the touch. She said teasingly, "To me you will always be my little brother and need protection."

He stiffened and said angrily, "I will not. Feel my body. Isn't it the body of a man?"

Her hands slid under his shirt and her fingers caressed his chest. Before he realized what was happening to him he had erected and was pressed against her.

She giggled and said, "Yes, I can feel you are a man."

Her hand slipped toward his groin and in embarrassment he broke away from her and, yanking his robe from her, ran as fast as he could toward the river. Howls of laughter followed his progress through camp as the people of the village, out enjoying the mild night and always aware of what was going on, guessed at his discomfiture. A cold plunge into the ice-strewn river helped him recover his poise, but he didn't go back to the warrior lodge that night, preferring to sleep outside than to be the butt of the men's jokes.

REVENGE

The snow melted and the grass sprang vivid green from the warming earth. It was time to repair lodge skins and make ready for the constant moving of the summer hunts, and also time to tap the box elders for their sweet, sugary sap. When this was done the sheltered hollow was abandoned for the higher ground and the work of gathering food began. The women gathered roots, vegetables, and herbs while the men made the first major hunts of the year. Holes in Face was glad for the change. For too long he had been the camp joke and he was tiring of it. It seemed even Big Tree had chosen to let him off with humiliation instead of violence, for which he should have been thankful but somehow wasn't, as his humiliation grew.

He vented his frustration during the hunts and could boast of more kills than even Big Tree but it was little satisfaction to him. To Holes in Face the matter was still unsettled. Spotted Fawn had saved him from a fight with Big Tree but his pride demanded more. He had not gone to see Spotted Fawn again and avoided meeting her whenever possible. He had to deal with Big Tree daily but he was wise enough to know he was not yet a physical match for the more powerful and experienced man and therefore his only recourse was to be the best at what he could do. He determinedly made it his goal to run faster, jump higher, throw harder, and shoot straighter than Big Tree. He was coming closer all the time. This first large hunt at least proved his competence and the status gained for being the honored hunter increased his confidence in his ability.

The white trader located their camp early in June. The scouts brought him in and Holes in Face felt nearly uncontrollable anger as the heavily laden pack horses trudged by him. He had no proof this man was responsible for his mother's death or that he had lied about the trader McDonnell's death, but seeing the sly face with shifting eyes reinforced his suspicion. He followed the last pack horse to Snow Cloud's lodge, trying to think of some way to trick the white man into admitting his guilt. Holes in Face stepped to Snow Cloud's side and turned cold eyes on the white trader.

"Howdy. Where's your mother? I brought her medicine and"—he laughed nervously—"a few other things you might be needin'."

Holes in Face interpreted to Snow Cloud, "He has brought the medicine and other things to trade with us. What do you want me to tell him?"

"Tell him we want only weapons. We need nothing else and we do not wish him to return again."

Holes in Face faced the trader, his mind seeking the right words. It had been months since he had heard the white man's language and he was surprised how quickly he had forgotten it. "Snow Cloud wishes to trade for guns only. Then he wishes you to leave and not come again."

The man shifted his feet uncertainly. "You tell him he is deprivin' his people of a lot of good things. And where will he get powder and ball for his guns if he don't let me trade with you again?"

Holes in Face spoke to Snow Cloud. "He says we will not have powder and balls for the guns if he doesn't bring them."

"Tell him we know where to get them."

He said in English to the trader, "Snow Cloud knows where to get powder and balls."

The trader stroked his greasy mustache uneasily and shrugged. "Well, guess that's his business. But what about your mother? Ain't she goin' to need her medicine?"

Coldly, Holes in Face answered, "My mother is dead."

Selby's eyes shifted and he seemed to pale a little. Holes in Face watched him intently. Selby cleared his throat and murmured, "Sorry to hear that, boy." Holes in Face could see realization flash through the other's eyes even before Selby said a little too happily, "Then you're the only one here who can speak English?"

"Yes."

Selby's smile was big. "Well, now, guess we'd better get on with the tradin'. You goin' to invite me in? I brought somethin' for all your braves to try. A little present from trader Selby to you."

Holes in Face spoke to Snow Cloud: "He is ready to trade and wants to go inside. He says he has a present for all our braves."

Snow Cloud grunted agreeably. "Tell him to come to the council lodge and we will smoke."

"Snow Cloud says to go to the council lodge and he will smoke with you."

The trader smiled broadly. Turning to his first pack horse, he unfastened a canvas and loaded his arms with several bottles filled with a dark liquid before following Snow Cloud into the council lodge. Inside the larger council lodge, Snow Cloud seated himself in the chief's accustomed place and Holes in Face took his place next to Snow Cloud as the lodge filled with the ranking members of the band and anyone else who could find room.

The pipe was smoked first, then Snow Cloud told Holes in Face, "Now we are ready to trade. Ask him how much he wants for his guns."

Holes in Face relayed the message, his English coming easier as he remembered more of the words.

The trader grabbed one of the bottles he had brought in and said, "No need to be in such a hurry. Here. Have the chief take a little drink of this and see if he likes it."

Holes in Face took the bottle and held it to Snow Cloud. "He asks that you take a drink of this before we trade."

Snow Cloud took the bottle and sniffed at its contents. "Ask him what this stinking water is."

"Snow Cloud does not know what this is."

Selby laughed. "It's a white man's drink. It'll make him feel good. Tell him to try it and if he doesn't like it he don't have to drink it."

"It is a white man's drink. He says it will make you feel good."

Snow Cloud grunted and tipped the bottle to his lips, took a mouthful and choked. Concerned and threatening whispers filled the lodge as every man reached for his knife, but Snow Cloud caught his breath and looked at the bottle thoughtfully while they all watched. He raised it again and took another swallow and this time didn't choke. Holes in Face looked from Snow Cloud to the trader and saw a satisfied grin on the shifty face. He didn't like what he saw. Snow Cloud raised the bottle again and took a long drink. With a smile, he handed it to the man next to him.

"It is good. It warms the belly." He rubbed his abdomen and there was a ripple of laughter around them.

Selby opened more bottles and eager hands reached to try the white man's drink. He passed one purposely to Holes in Face and said, "Go ahead and try it. It won't hurt you."

Holes in Face tipped the bottle and took a small mouthful and swallowed, coughing as the liquid burned all the way down. It reminded him of the bitter medicine his mother took. He had touched his finger to the white powder once when she was mixing it and remembered the awful taste of it. He passed the bottle on to the next man and was aware of the increased conversation among them, with outbursts of laughter, and knew something was happening they weren't aware of. The quiet seriousness of the meeting had turned into something else, and Holes in Face felt a prickle of apprehension as he recalled something his mother had told him about a certain drink of the white man.

When the empty bottles were being handed back to Selby for filled ones, he laughed and told Holes in Face, "You tell them I'll give them more after we have traded."

Holes in Face relayed the message to Snow Cloud, who raised his hand for quiet, then sat blinking uncertainly with a foolish smile on his face. "Tell him we are ready."

Holes in Face turned to Selby. "They are ready to trade. How many skins for each gun do you want?"

With a face suddenly shrewd, the trader answered, "Fifty for each gun with powder and ball."

Holes in Face looked at him with surprise. None of them had nearly that many skins. He told Snow Cloud, "He wants fifty skins for each gun."

The smile left Snow Cloud's face. "We gave only twenty last spring. How can this be?"

"Snow Cloud says you asked only twenty skins last spring for each gun. None of us have that many skins."

Selby shrugged. "Can't be helped. Prices is goin' up. The big traders from the mountains has brought in so many furs they ain't worth nothin' no more. Got to have more in order to pay for the guns."

"He says the traders from the mountains have brought in so many furs they have gone down in value. He needs more to equal the same amount."

"Tell him we have no more. He will trade for what we have or we will kill him and take the guns anyway." An enlightened smile crossed Snow Cloud's face. "He has no choice."

"Snow Cloud says you must take what we have in trade or you won't leave here alive."

Selby looked uncertainly at Snow Cloud's dark and angry face. "You tell him if anything happens to me the U. S. Army knows where I'm at, and they'll wipe him out if I don't get back. Now I'm tryin' to be fair with you. I have to give equal to twenty-five skins for those guns. I've got other expenses, too. It costs money to buy mules and horses to bring 'em in here. Besides, I got other men to pay, and that ain't countin' the powder and balls. I'll let you have the guns for forty skins each and that's the very lowest I can go for you." He stood up. "Now I'll go get some more of that drink for you while you talk it over."

Holes in Face told Snow Cloud what Selby's offer was and the warning and added a warning of his own about the white man's drink.

Snow Cloud laughed. "You are being an old woman, my son. There is nothing wrong with the white man's drink. I have never felt better."

Holes in Face said no more. Snow Cloud hadn't seemed to be too ill affected by the drink. He had certainly showed force when it was necessary with the trader. Perhaps he did worry needlessly.

Selby returned with the bottles and the men who had been less than quiet before resumed their excited comments as the firewater circled the lodge. Selby urged Holes in Face to drink, and he did take another swallow and passed the bottle on and felt a little lightheaded. Something was happening to them and he was sure now it was because of what they were drinking. He could feel the effects of it and had only had two swallows. He would take no more. His mother had warned him not to trust this man and she had been right.

Selby urged him, "Have them bring in their skins and let's see what they got. I got other things to trade besides guns."

Holes in Face had to lay his hand on Snow Cloud's arm to get his attention. "He says to have the men bring in their skins. He has other things to trade if they do not have enough for the guns."

The liquor had done its job. Snow Cloud was beyond caring or command. He waved the men quiet and told them to bring in their skins. Staggering and laughing, the men stumbled outside and soon they came back with the pelts and skins of a winter's work. Unable to do anything to stop them, Holes in Face watched with sickened heart as the men traded their best furs away for worthless goods and, even more incredibly, for all the white man's firewater.

As the bottles circulated freely, the women began to sample the burning liquid and soon the whole camp was turned from an orderly village into a riot of laughing, screaming, gambling, and fighting people. Holes in Face went to Snow Cloud's lodge with the feeling that disaster was in the air and he wanted to be where he could protect his brother and sister and Spotted Fawn. It was the first time Holes in Face had been in his mother's lodge since the days after her death. It was the first time he'd been in Spotted Fawn's presence since he had folded her in his robe and made a fool of himself. Slow Water was gone but Spotted Fawn sat with the two younger children in frightened silence. He felt embarrassment as she glanced at him but he ignored her and sat down on Snow Cloud's couch and watched the door.

Not waiting to be acknowledged, she asked, "What happened to them? Did the white man poison them? I'm afraid."

Without looking at her he answered, "It is in the drink he gave us. It turns a man's mind to spinning like a top."

"Will they die?"

"No. My mother mentioned something about the bad things the white men did that she didn't want me to do. This thing is one of them. It does not kill but she said it takes a man's reason away from him and makes him do things he wouldn't usually do."

"Will you stay with us?"

"Yes."

Relieved of that concern, she became hostess and mother again and prepared a cooking bladder of food and hung it over the fire. Her eyes glanced at him and she said, "I have missed you. I am sorry you were shamed."

"It is not important now."

"It is to me."

He gave her a reproving look and she turned away and he asked Brown Hair, "How is the bow we made last winter working?"

Now that he had been given the signal to talk, Brown Hair was bubbling with questions for his older and idolized brother. "It is the best one I have ever had. I have killed more rabbits than anyone else. Will you take me on the next hunt with you?"

Holes in Face smiled. "We will see. Maybe you and I can go alone and I can see how well you do."

Brown Hair's eyes sparkled with delight and expectation but Morning Star dropped her head even lower, where she sat halfheartedly spinning her wooden top. She had not forgotten that once he had ignored custom and had comforted her, too. But he was getting used to breaking customs. Hadn't he just let Spotted Fawn speak as an equal to him? He got up and went to where she was playing and picked up the top. She looked up at him with expectation and he seated himself crosslegged before her and she was all smiles, beautiful smiles which looked so much like his mother's.

"I will bet you I can make the top spin longer than you can."

She laughed. "And what will you give me if I win?"

"Oh, no, little sister. It is what will you give me?"

She looked thoughtful for a moment. "I will make you a necklace."

He smiled and nodded and she produced a second top. With all her strength, she sent it spinning and he did the same. She giggled and groaned as the tops spun and faltered crazily and spun some more until his keeled over and came to a bumping, hopping stop. She clapped her hands gleefully.

"I won! I won! Now what will you give me?"

Before he could answer, the door was filled with the staggering figures of Snow Cloud and the trader. Spotted Fawn gasped in fear and Holes in Face rose to his feet, his hand on his knife. Snow Cloud was hanging onto the trader and when the trader let him go near his couch, he sat down heavily, his head rolling.

"Think you better get him something to eat, little lady. A little food helps straighten 'em out. I could use some myself. What you got cooking there?"

Spotted Fawn looked questioningly at Holes in Face. He knew she understood English almost as well as he but she was rightfully letting him handle the situation. He ordered her, "Feed them." She nodded and went to offer the contents of the cooking bladder to Snow Cloud first.

Selby looked keenly at Holes in Face. "Too bad you ain't out there enjoyin' yourself with the rest of 'em. Saved a bottle for you if you want it."

"No. You can eat and then I want you to leave."

He helped himself to the food Spotted Fawn offered him, and Holes in Face didn't miss the admiring look he gave her. Snow Cloud sat eating in gross gluttony, totally unaware of anything around him. He tossed away the last of his food to the begging dogs and fell back on his couch with heavy eyes, the juice from his meal running from chin to breechclout.

Selby laughed and commented, "He'll have one hell of an achin' head tomorrow. Maybe you'd better keep this bottle for him. He'll need a little snort to get his head on straight." He held the bottle out to Holes in Face.

In anger Holes in Face knocked it from his hand and the bottle went flying across the lodge, struck a lodge pole, and broke. Through clenched teeth he warned, "It's time you left, white man."

Again the nervous laughter. "Hey, you don't need to be so pushy, son. I don't mean you no harm. In fact, I was thinkin' of askin' you if'n I could spend the night here? It's too late to travel now."

"No. You leave now."

"You know, most Injuns I trade with are friendlier. They let me spend the night and even provide me with a bed partner. Now I'd even give you a gun if'n you was to let me spend a night with that little squaw there."

His control broke and his voice rose. "No!" He pulled his knife from his belt and held it threateningly at the man. "Leave. *Now!*"

Selby rose slowly, a twisted smile on his face. He reached for the pack he'd brought in with bottles of whiskey still in it and when he straightened he flung the pack with all his strength at Holes in Face. Holes in Face sidestepped the pack and lunged at the trader, but Selby had drawn a pistol and it went off so close to Holes in Face he was blinded by the flash and a searing pain tore along his side. He saw the trader leave in a blur and struggled to his feet, groping his way toward the lodge opening but Spotted Fawn caught him in her arms.

"No! Do not go after him. He will kill you. You are already hurt."

His legs were unsteady and his vision still blurred, and he knew he was at a disadvantage. He let her lead him to her couch.

"Lie down and let me see your side."

He obeyed and lay down with closed eyes while she laid sponges of buffalo wool dipped in cold water on his side.

"It is only a slight wound. Is it feeling better yet?"

He opened his eyes and saw her face frowning with concern. "It is better. Are you sure he left?"

Brown Hair, standing in the lodge opening, confirmed it. "Yes. He has taken all his horses and is gone."

Holes in Face sat up. "I'm going after him."

Spotted Fawn gasped, "No! You must not. He will kill you."

"And if I don't kill him he will come again and do this to our people. He has already killed my mother, and I think he killed the trader McDonnell, too. He does not deserve to live."

She was kneeling beside the couch and she put her arms around him and buried her head against him, crying, "Please, don't go."

He felt the warmth spring to life within him and felt again the powerful urge to discover the secrets of her woman's body. The village had become quiet as most of the Indians had by now passed out or fallen asleep. Slow Water had not returned and Spotted Fawn was in his arms. With a heart pounding with expectation he said, "It would be better if I rested and left at sunrise."

He lay back down on her couch and she looked at him with her large, black eyes, lips parted expectantly. She released her hold on him but he reached for her hand and held her. Without hesitation she lay down beside him, trembling and breathless with anticipation. He slipped his arm around her and they lay pressed together, afraid to move.

Brown Hair surveyed them and said disgustedly, "I thought you were going after him."

Holes in Face answered without taking his eyes from Spotted Fawn's suddenly lovely face. "I can find him more easily in the morning. And what if I should leave you and he should come back? Who would protect you? There is not a man left with sense enough to know the trader is our enemy. I will stay until sunrise. Now go to bed."

Morning Star looked at them happily and asked, "Does this mean you will be married?"

Anger did what reason could not and quenched the fire of his body. He relaxed his hold on Spotted Fawn and she giggled. "No. Now go to your bed."

"But it's not time to go to sleep. I'm not tired."

Spotted Fawn giggled again and Holes in Face was temporarily beaten. He closed his eyes and felt Spotted Fawn snuggle down beside him. Without meaning to, he fell asleep.

Much later he awoke and felt her body against his and was instantly aware of her warmth and softness. The fire was out and the deep even breathing of the other occupants of the lodge told him they were all asleep. He touched Spotted Fawn's arm and felt her stiffen as she awoke to his unfamiliar presence. He slid his hand down her arm and rested it on her slender hip. He heard her little gasp of indrawn breath and felt her tremble. He slid his hand on down her leg until he felt her bare knee and brought his hand up under her dress and she tensed. He caressed the soft flesh of her thigh as her hands touched his chest and the warmth and delicate tracing of her fingers across his body only made him more excited. Eagerly, and almost uncontrollably, he pulled her dress up and rolled on top of her, his excitement rendering him breathless and dizzy. Her arms went around him and pulled him to her, and he trembled as his body found hers and filled her in reckless abandon. She gasped and moaned, trying to pull away from him. Her sobs brought him back to his senses, and he pulled from her in sudden realization of what he was doing. If anyone learned of this he would be shamed and lose his honor forever. She was crying, but he was too concerned with his own guilt to comfort her. He picked up his knife and quickly left the lodge. Drunken Indians lay where they had fallen and he passed them with growing remorse and hatred for the white trader.

He went to his society's lodge and gathered up his weapons and some food and went to find a horse. In a matter of minutes he was trailing the white trader's tracks across the prairie. When dawn provided the light, he mounted the horse and followed as fast as he could the well-defined trail of the trader. By midday he came within sight of the trader and slowed his pace. He would wait until the trader had camped for the night and was most vulnerable. He kept out of sight until dark, not breaking his fast, and slowly moved up on the trader's camp, led by the small glow of the man's camp-fire. He lay down and rested, praying to the protector given to him in his vision—the white eagle—while he waited. When he was sure the trader slept he applied new paint and stripped off all clothes except breechclout and mocassins. The fire was almost out now and he crept cautiously forward.

The horses would signal his coming, so he worked toward the camp with the wind in his face. When they gave the alarm he would have to be ready to make his move. He was within view of the sleeping trader. He pulled his legs under him and rose in a crouching position. The nearest horse saw the movement and snorted. Holes in Face sprang forward with his knife raised and a blood-curdling cry rushing from his lungs. The horses lunged away in fright as Holes in Face fell on the blanketed figure on the ground and drove his knife into it. Instantly he knew his victim was not made of flesh and blood and threw himself backward away from the bundle just as the trader's rifle exploded. The ball was so close to him he heard it whistle and felt the shower of dirt it tore up as it plowed into the ground. He sprang toward the crouched shape of the trader a few feet away, behind a tree. The trader rose and, using the rifle as a club, swung at him. The blow knocked him off-balance and he was only able to grab the man's pant leg as the trader turned to club him again. He yanked and twisted the leg and the man came lurching across the top of him. He drove the knife into Selby's back and pulled himself free.

Selby lay groaning on the ground, pleading with him, "Please don't kill me. God! I didn't mean it. It was a mistake. Don't kill me!"

Holes in Face looked down on the sniveling man with contempt. "Why? You had no mercy for my mother."

"Oh, God! I'm trying to tell you. That was a mistake. I didn't know what that stuff was. I thought it was some herb or somethin'. I tried to sprinkle it on my meat and damn near died from the taste of it. I didn't know it was medicine until your mother asked for it. Then I knew, and I'd already wasted some of it. I didn't think it'd make any difference if I added a little something to it to make it look like it was all there. Believe me! Help me. I'm bleedin'!"

Holes in Face squatted in front of the groveling man and grasped his shirt front and twisted it unmercifully. "And you lied about McDonnell, too. He would have told you about the medicine if you really were a friend of his."

"Honest," he squeaked, "I told you the truth."

Holes in Face was unconvinced. There was one way to get the truth from the man. He was not unaware of how the Indians tortured their enemies. Though he had not yet seen his people use torture, the old men told of it in their stories from the days when the Sioux were constantly at war with the Chippewa, when they had lived farther east. He bound the man hand and foot and found a shovel in the pack gear and started to dig a trench. It would be light soon and he could build the kind of fire he needed without it being seen and the trees would diffuse the smoke.

Selby whined, "What are you going to do?"

"My mother suffered from the fever. You will know what it is like."

The man sat with tears running down his cheeks, blood oozing from his back, pleading and praying, while Holes in Face's contempt grew in proportion to the man's pleading. He had not wanted to do what he was doing. He had only hoped to scare the man into an honest confession, but the man's continued lying and total cowardice was bringing him to his ultimate death from a boy trained to respect only the brave. He cut wood and lined the pit with stones and wood and lighted it. When the wood was burned down to red-hot coals, he placed a thick layer of green cottonwood branches complete with leaves over the whole pit. He dragged the screaming and struggling trader to the pit and rolled him in. He had to stuff a handful of leaves into the man's mouth to keep him from screaming and tied him securely spread-eagled to the four corners of the pit before laying more branches of cottonwood over him and then shoveling the dirt on top of him until just his head appeared above the ground.

"Now, white man, how does it feel? Do you think now you can tell me how the man McDonnell died?"

Selby nodded his head vigorously and Holes in Face removed the leaves from his mouth.

"The part about me bein' his friend ain't true. But it was Injuns that killed him. I found his body. They hadn't took nothin'. Just left everything! 'Course I took it. Believe me! Get me out of here! I'm dyin' of the heat. Oh, please, get me out of here!" His voice rose to a scream.

"You keep quiet, white man. Now once more. How did McDonnell die?"

"I told you!" he screamed. "God's truth!"

Holes in Face took his knife and grabbed the man's stringy dark hair where it whorled on the back point of the skull. Here was where his enemy's power lay but he doubted he would gain much power from this sniveling man. He slit the screaming man's scalp and heard his voice beg, "All right. All right! Don't scalp me. Oh,

God! Don't kill me. I'll tell you. I done it. He wouldn't share his trade with you with no one. I done it! I done it!"

Holes in Face kept cutting as the man screamed himself into unconsciousness. When the circle of hair was neatly lifted, Holes in Face went to the river and brought water and threw it over the man's bloody head. It revived him. Holes in Face squatted next to the roasting man and said, "I will leave you now. If you are lucky someone will find you and save you. If you are unlucky you will roast like the dog you are. Maybe some other Indians will come by and watch you roast and when you are done they will eat you as dogs are eaten. If you live, white man, and I see you again, I will kill you."

Holes in Face, with bloody scalp at his belt, rounded up the white man's horses and loaded them with the furs and hides taken from his camp along with the valuable trade goods that were left. Every bottle of whiskey he found he set around the roasting pit for the man buried there to see and, mounting the trader's horse, rode out of the wooded river valley and up the bluff to where his own horse waited. He heard Selby's screams and kicked the horse into a gallop until he could hear them no more.

HONOR AND GLORY

Holes in Face came within sight of his camp the next day. He stopped before he was within detection of the camp guards and prepared himself for his entrance of victory by painting his face black and mounting the scalp he had taken on his lance. His entrance must be grand as befitting the honor due him. He had earned several coups in the Indian tradition of keeping track of a man's deeds. He would earn one for each horse he brought in and

one for the scalp and the most honored coup for touching his
enemy in bare-handed battle. His confidence and pride in himself
were the highest of his young life, and the reaction of the village
would only add to his self-aggrandizement. His excitement was
high as he mounted his horse and, leading the trader's four horses,
dashed with triumphant yells into the midst of the startled camp.

As the people realized what he had done, the whole village
turned out to hear the recitation of his deeds in the council lodge.
Young dogs were killed to feast him and after dark the fires were
built high and the women came to honor him in the scalp dance.
Morning Star was the only one to come from his family lodge to
carry his scalp pole and sing his praises, and the joy he felt in his
victory was diminished. He had expected Spotted Fawn to come
but realized when she didn't how deeply he had hurt her. If anyone
found out he had violated her virginity, Snow Cloud would no
longer be able to acquire the bride price set for her. But that was a
lesser shame to the stigma she would have to bear all her life of not
being a virtuous woman. No longer would the cream of the village
warriors be at her door, and she would have to content herself with
a husband of lesser quality, if, indeed, any would have her. His own
situation was little better. He could brag of his accomplishment
among his peers and gain a coup honor, but if the elders learned of
his indiscretion it could cost him the eligibility for the chieftainship
of his band. No one must ever know, and he had to tell Spotted
Fawn no one would ever know from him and for her to pretend it
never happened.

It was days before the celebration of his deeds was ended and
his evenings were free to do as he pleased. He took his robe and
went directly to Spotted Fawn's lodge. There were no men waiting
and she was not outside. He sang to her through the side of the
lodge and his voice cracked horribly. He cleared his throat and
tried again but the same humiliating croaking resulted. Thoroughly disconcerted, he resorted to blowing on the love flute he carried,
made from the bone of a bird wing. Still Spotted Fawn did not
appear and he slowly realized she would never accept his courtship
again. He stood uncertainly outside and finally, in frustration,
threw down his robe and stalked into the lodge. She was there but
kept her head down.

Snow Cloud greeted him with a smile. "So, the mighty warrior
returns to the lodge of his family." He winked as Holes in Face
settled down across from him and continued, "I am glad you were
not discouraged enough to leave before we could talk. I have much

to say to you." He lit his pipe and, smoking it briefly first, handed it to Holes in Face. "I am very proud of you, my son. You have earned the right to the name of your protector and your voice will be heard in council. I will have Slow Water turn the tipi for you now the scalp dance is over. My pride does not extend to the rest of our people, however. I am very ashamed of what happened. The white trader's firewater was very bad. I do not understand what happened. You have your mother's wisdom. Do you know what happened?"

"I was told the white man had this drink and that it relieved men of their wisdom."

Snow Cloud smiled and nodded. "I should have listened more to her. She was very wise. I am just beginning to know how wise she was, and I suffer all the more for being too proud to listen to what she could tell me. She tried to warn me about the white man. But I let my pride convince me we had nothing to fear from the white man. Now I know we do. We must never taste the white man's drink again. If at all possible we must not deal with him in any way."

From the corner of his eye Holes in Face saw Spotted Fawn rise from her couch and go quickly out the door. It was still another blow to Holes in Face. Slow Water, protective of her interest in Spotted Fawn, rose and shuffled after her. The younger children were already outside playing in the warm night and would play until they were too tired to play more before they came to bed.

Snow Cloud looked at him intently and said, "I do not understand this. First she refuses your suit of her and now she leaves your presence. How have you offended her?"

Keeping his eyes respectfully down, he answered, "She did not want me to go after the trader. She still sees me as a little boy in need of her protection."

Snow Cloud laughed. "I can believe she did not want you to go but I can not believe she thinks you are still a suckling child. You are old enough to take a woman and have the honors now to be accepted by one. Are you serious about Spotted Fawn?"

The question brought him confusion, but he answered steadily enough, "No. I am not ready to marry."

They sat in silence then, passing the pipe between them until Snow Cloud said, "We will have to journey to the pipestone ground to get you a pipe now. Perhaps if the fall hunt goes well we will have time."

Holes in Face nodded. It was getting late and he knew as long as he remained in the lodge Spotted Fawn would not return. He stood after he had emptied the pipe and said, "It is late and the celebration has left me tired."

Snow Cloud nodded and Holes in Face stepped into the night. Brown Hair and Morning Star were coming toward him and he waited for them. With childish adulation they greeted him, and he talked with them for a little while before he left them and went to the lodge of his society.

As Snow Cloud promised, Slow Water turned the lodge covering inside out in the morning, signifying he was giving a feast. From past experience he knew the laborious work of winter that went into robes, shirts, moccasins, and all the trappings of the Indian culture would be lavished on everyone in the band, and Snow Cloud would be left in poverty from the feast honoring Holes in Face as he received his new name.

All day Spotted Fawn and Slow Water prepared food for the camp, slaughtering young dogs and bringing out treasured stores of delicacies in his honor. By night the camp was gorged on food he had helped provide his family and every family of the camp had their share of gifts. Holes in Face would now be known as White Eagle. Songs were composed and sung in his honor, and the maidens of the village danced for him.

When he finally returned to the lodge of his society, he had little doubt as to his ability and superiority. His vision had shown much glory and honor, and his first taste of it had gone straight to his head.

In the morning the camp prepared to move on to the meeting ground for the annual Sun Dance ceremony. White Eagle looked forward to the reunion. It would have special meaning for him this year. As the most honored young man of his band he would be his band's representative in the ceremonies preceding the dance. The first few days of the reunion were spent in feasting and visiting with friends and relatives not seen for months. As one of the treecutters selected by the council of elders in the first few days, White Eagle was required to fast and be purified, and he gloried in the attention. Too long Big Tree had been the one who carried his band's honors and now it was his turn. He had no illusion about why Big Tree had invited him into his society. How better to keep an eye on the enemy than to have him in your company. It was evident Big Tree was angry over White Eagle's honor and selection in the sullen silence of the older brave.

The cottonwood tree chosen for the center post of the Sun Dance lodge was treated with all the respect of a great warrior. The treecutters, painted black as war parties were painted, went to the selected cottonwood—always a cottonwood because its leaves were shaped like the Indian tipi—and danced the war dance. The tree was cut after all the proper ceremonies were completed and never allowed to touch the ground as it was cut and carried to the place of honor in the center of the large area designated as the place for the lodge to be erected. After another round of purification in the sweat lodge, the tree was planted and the men who were to dance were selected and their purification rites began.

White Eagle had almost offered himself to dance to the sun, but something made him hesitate. Despite all the ego building of the last few days he didn't feel he had gained enough honor or was certain enough about his manhood. Changes were taking place in him that told him he was not yet what he would be. His voice betrayed these changes most of all. No longer did he sing since his voice had lost an octave or two the night he had sought to court Spotted Fawn. His face was erupting in strange rashes and he kept it painted completely to hide the embarrassing pimples. The drying paint was as good as anything for the condition but was no help at all for the unwanted fuzz that stiffened with the paint and stuck out ridiculously on upper lip and chin. The urgings he had felt while holding Spotted Fawn became more intense, and he was desperate to culminate the act he had barely begun with Spotted Fawn. In all these respects he was little different than any of the rest of the younger men in his warrior akicita. And like them he was overjoyed at the prospects of a variety of women to court when Snow Cloud decided they would spend the rest of the hunting season with one of the other bands.

When the Sun Dance gathering finally broke up the two bands moved slowly in search of the buffalo, and the young men had several evenings to spend in courting the new girls. But if any of the maidens became infatuated with a tall, handsome brave named White Eagle, she was soon to be disappointed because he never came a second time to enfold any of them in his blanket. The physical contact with the girls did to him what it did to all the virile young men but none of them had had the vision he had. None of them knew the woman he chose to be his wife would die carrying his child, and that knowledge was enough to restrain any attraction he might feel for any of the maidens.

The buffalo were located and the camp site selected beside a stream as close to the herd as possible where wood would be plentiful to help dry the buffalo meat. The hunters were chosen and early one hot morning in July the hunt began. Snow Cloud and the chief of the accompanying band presented their plan and each hunter knew his duty and performed it. White Eagle never had better luck than this day. His arm was strong and his arrows were true. More than a dozen buffalo bore his exclusively marked arrow and he delivered more than a ton of meat to the lodge of his brother and sister and more to the old, sick, and poor of the camp. As the hunter with the biggest kill, he was honored by everyone and the maidens of the large combined camp brought him every choice morsel while Big Tree sulked in anger. He shared with the rest of his lodge companions and they ate well that night and enjoyed the songs and dances of the celebrating camp. The next day they would start the tedious task of drying the tons of buffalo meat killed and for days the camp would stay by the river.

So far things had gone surprisingly well for the bands. The society White Eagle belonged to had been chosen as camp police-men when the Sun Dance had broken up and they had done an admirable job. They had been alert and strict, and the organization was due mainly to White Eagle. He had his mother's ability, and with his increased popularity among the members of his lodge, he was able to use his influence in a way that was totally lacking in most Indian undertakings. Big Tree was losing some of his power in their akicita and it made White Eagle all the more confident.

But good luck didn't last forever, and it chose to change on a hot night when White Eagle and his hand-picked assistants were guarding the horse herd on the prairie above the river valley. They were alert enough, but the dark night, made darker by the thunder clouds boiling across the sky, deceived them. At any moment the stillness could have been shattered by enough lightning to roast a herd of buffalo and the horses were restive and the guards a little nervous, fearing the thunder gods more than human danger. Therefore they discounted all the horses' snortings and whinnies as caused by the thunder spirits. The attack came so swiftly and so unexpectedly they were overpowered before they had time to get help. The raiders swooped down on them and made off with a good number of horses, and White Eagle knew it was no use to follow. In dejection he ran into camp and awoke Snow Cloud and told him what had happened.

The members of the council were called, and soon the old men and the warriors were seated in the council lodge to decide what course of action to take. Excitement was running high and no one was more excited than White Eagle at the prospect of a battle in which to test himself in his quest for supremacy. A war party was picked and White Eagle accepted the invitation with pride. The medicine men of the two bands performed their ceremonies to protect man and horse from their enemies and by dawn the war party, headed by Snow Cloud and his honored warrior friend, Buffalo Horn, and the warrior chief of the other band, took to the prairie to find the marauders' trail. Their group wasn't large because they felt danger might fall on the camp if too many of the warriors were gone, leaving the women and their hard-won winter's supply of meat in jeopardy.

They found the trail and followed it to a camp site not many miles from their own. From the evidence at the camp the interlopers numbered two to three times Snow Cloud's group of men. They weren't more than a couple of hours ahead and Snow Cloud knew they would stand little chance against so large a party in daylight. He decided not to pursue the raiders any farther at the moment. The enemy scouts would be watching for any pursuit and could be watching them even now. In a tactic designed for deception, Snow Cloud led his men back the way they had come and when he thought the enemy would be confident they had given up the attack, he turned his men back in a parallel line of march.

At nightfall he turned his men more directly toward the enemy line of travel. His years of experience did not fail him. It was one reason no man had yet been able to prove Snow Cloud was not capable of being chief. They found the broad track of the raiding party and followed it. Before dawn their scouts brought back word the Indians were camped ahead in a swale. The weary men stopped to rest and prepare themselves for the attack which would be executed at dawn. Fresh paint was applied to man and horse and all the charms and potions sent to protect them were brought out now as they begged assistance from the Great Spirit and members of the animal world revered for their powers. White Eagle took the powdered ashes of the white eagle feathers and sprinkled them on himself and on his horse, blowing them into the horse's nostrils to ensure his endurance and strength in battle. They led the horses until all bladders and bowels were emptied, before they mounted to wait tensely. Snow Cloud gave the signal and they charged the sleeping camp of enemy warriors. Their main intent was not so much to kill the enemy but to retrieve their lost horses. White Eagle as a virtually untried warrior was one of the men chosen to drive off the horses while the more experienced warriors held off pursuit. It was a good plan and Snow Cloud executed it perfectly for the first few minutes as he kept the Indians contained, shooting down their tethered mounts while White Eagle and four others got away with the loose horses. But the raiders had guns and as soon as they were able to use them Snow Cloud suffered. He called off his men when the first man was wounded. They could not afford to lose anyone. Their hope now was that the Indians would be some time in rounding up enough horses to come after them.

By afternoon they knew they were being pursued. There was no place to hide or defend on the open prairie, and White Eagle wondered what Snow Cloud would do. They could abandon the horses and possibly escape, but to lose the horses again was the last thing Snow Cloud wanted to do. Ahead they saw the dust of a herd of buffalo and immediately Snow Cloud turned toward it. When they were close to the herd he stopped and explained what he wanted done. The strongest horses were to get out ahead of the slow-moving herd and turn them back toward where Snow Cloud would wait with the rest of the men. They would bunch the buffalo and kill as many as possible to provide a barricade against the attack of the pursuing Indians.

White Eagle and the boys with the horses would go on and come back with help if they reached camp safely. White Eagle had little choice but to agree and, taking charge of the horse herd, he urged them on at a faster pace. He kept them moving after dark in his urgency to get back to Snow Cloud. They reached camp and answered the challenges of the guards, and without stopping to rest, he summoned the warriors left in camp to follow him back to the others. Mounted on fresh horses, they made fast time to the battle area and arrived just before dawn. They heard the guns of the attackers and charged together at the circling Indians. Each man was on his own and yelling savagely as he kicked his horse forward, ready to fight.

White Eagle's heart was in his throat and beating so hard his voice sounded weak in his ears but he was no less eager to test his skill against the enemy. It was the ideal battle for an untrained warrior. The enemy, tired, thirsty, and running low on arrows and rifle balls, quickly abandoned the battlefield in face of the oncoming warriors. Few shots were fired and fewer still found any mark as the enemy Indians fled with only a few of Snow Cloud's men in pursuit. White Eagle rode directly to the buffalo fortress, more concerned for Snow Cloud than the fleeing attackers.

His anxiety was quickly relieved as Snow Cloud stood to greet him. He was keenly aware of Snow Cloud's age when he saw the tired, lined face and the silver streaks in the black hair which seemed more prominent than before.

Snow Cloud's smile was no less weary as he said, "My son has returned more quickly than I had hoped possible. I don't know how much longer we could have lasted."

"Did we lose any men?"

"Yes. Two dead and several wounded. But we scored more on the enemy. Unfortunately we have no scalps to show for it. But there will be another time."

White Eagle surveyed the battlefield and knew what Snow Cloud said was true. A few dead horses lay scattered but the dead warriors had been carried off by their companions. Their own men were now scouring the battlefield for anything of value.

Triumphantly, they returned to camp. But even though they had won for now, they knew their victory would not last until the enemy had been completely vanquished. They had lost horses and men and so had the enemy. Revenge would keep the war going until one side was entirely subdued. White Eagle felt excitement at the prospect of a continued war in which to show his supremacy. From childhood they were taught it was good to die young on the battlefield like a man before one grew old and dependent, and with the first flush of victory warming his heart, he was eager and ready to test that wisdom to the fullest.

When Big Tree proposed they plan a secret raid to find the enemy and seek first revenge, White Eagle eagerly accepted Big Tree's invitation to join those who were sent invitations in secret to join the war party.

They left in the middle of the night, telling no one of their plan, for Big Tree knew the older and wiser men would have forbidden such a reckless undertaking. If they were successful, they would return to honor and glory. If they weren't, they would sneak into camp at night like stray dogs in the same way they had left.

They traveled all night and at daybreak stopped to rest and nap and eat. By the time the sun was at midpoint in the sky they rode on. They passed the rotting buffalo and horse flesh of the previous battle and found the faint trail of the enemy. It was as Snow Cloud suspected, a whole village of northern Cree Indians moved south to encroach on their hunting grounds. The only way to preserve their hunting ground was to drive the interlopers back north.

They scouted the camp at night and found the camp well guarded and the guards alert. There would be little chance to steal prize horses kept close to their owners' lodges during the day, and a night raid would be only a little less dangerous. White Eagle suggested taking only the horse herd which grazed outside the camp but Big Tree sneeringly refused to consider anything less than the bravest of deeds—that of taking the prize horses tethered close to the lodges. White Eagle could go along with the plan or leave. It made little difference to the rest of them. But if he left he would be named a coward.

They rested and fasted and prayed several miles away from their target during the day, and by night they donned their paint and performed their rituals. When all were ready, they walked with their horses toward the enemy camp, leaving their horses when close to the enemy, planning on each man's capturing at least one horse to ride out. On hands and knees and bellies they wormed their way into the darkened camp, barely daring to breath as they passed the outer camp guards. Once close to the camp they would have to abandon stealth for quickness. One barking dog would alert the camp that intruders were about. Each man had picked the animal he was to capture and each was to crawl as close as he could to that goal. The signal for action was the first bark of the camp dogs.

White Eagle felt the sweat on his face as he tried to keep his pounding heart quiet. He was afraid to breathe and felt light-headed. He stopped and pulled the knife held between his teeth and gulped air and wiped the sweat from his eyes. The first sharp betraying barks of a dog paralyzed him for a few brief moments. A guttural Indian voice calling the alarm released him and he was on his feet and running toward the horse he was pledged to steal a few yards ahead of him. A shot was fired somewhere and more voices rang out in surprise and anger as the camp came rudely to life. The horse he was to steal was whinnying and dancing as it shied from his strange smell. He reached for its rope as the horse's owner raised a lodge skin and fired at him. The ball was close enough to whistle as it passed him. He leaped on the horse as the owner made a flying leap after him and gripped his leg with hands of steel. He slashed downward with his knife, raking the man's forearms deep-ly. The Indian fell away and he kicked the horse as another figure dashed to intercept him. He yanked the horse in a pivot and man and horse met with a bone-jarring crash. The horse staggered but White Eagle held him and plunging over the downed Indian they raced free of the camp. The guards had had time to mount and were now charging in from the herd. He saw another horse and rider clear the camp and be pursued by one of the horse guards.

Yells and shots filled the night and he rode low on the horse he had captured, urging it faster and glorying in the power the animal had as he easily outdistanced whatever was behind him.

He looked behind him now and saw nothing pursuing him. He pulled in the horse and turned to watch, another idea forming in his confident mind. The horse guards had abandoned the herd to protect the camp. He could possibly capture the whole herd if he worked quickly and was lucky enough to meet another of his group to help him. He kicked the horse into a gallop and rode toward where the horse herd grazed. He kept a sharp eye for another of his party and saw two more riding his way.

He waved his arm for them to follow him and slowed his horse until they caught up with him and called to them, "Let's take the herd."

Immediately they kicked their horses after him. The herd was nervously moving ahead of them and men were coming out of the village toward them, running to catch horses with which to chase the raiders. They had to act quickly or their chance would be lost. He let out a piercing howl and charged at the milling horses, trying to turn them away from the camp. He rode breakneck along the outer edge, turning them with his yells. The Indians opened fire with their guns and he saw one of the men with him topple from his horse. He swung low to the side of his mount and turned into the herd, flailing at the driving rumps with his rope as they sped away from the camp. He saw more of his own riders coming to join him and felt the thrill of victory only slightly dampened by the knowledge that one of the men he had led had been either killed or wounded and left to die at the hands of the enemy.

Their escape was complete, and they rode with no little fanfare into their own camp several days later, driving a good-sized herd of horses. The cheers of praise turned into wails of mourning as three families discovered their sons and husbands missing. Amidst the honors and feasts held for them there was also the undercurrent of disapproval from the elders. White Eagle held himself aloof from criticism, feeling it of little importance in comparison to what they had accomplished. He basked in honor and glory and was justly proud of his achievements.

When Snow Cloud requested him to come to his lodge he went eagerly, expecting praise. He prepared himself carefully for the visit, knowing full well Spotted Fawn would be there and wanting none of his new importance lost on her. With all the dignity of visiting royalty he paraded to Snow Cloud's lodge and entered.

Spotted Fawn was busy quilling and her eyes never left her work as he glanced at her slight figure. He settled himself opposite Snow Cloud and waited for the ceremony of the pipe to be completed.

At last, when they had both smoked, Snow Cloud said, "White Eagle has brought much honor and pride to the lodge of his father. Your medicine has been good and your heart full of courage, but I am sad to say your head has been lacking wisdom."

White Eagle looked up in surprise. The vain lifting of his shoulders as Snow Cloud had praised him suddenly sagged, and he whispered uncertainly, "You are not pleased with what I have done? I don't understand."

"I am very pleased with what you have done, but I am not pleased with the way you did it. I know your blood runs full with the vigor and confidence of youth and you see my days of power drawing short and you are trying hard to be the man I want you to be, but I would ask you to decide if you think that a few horses were worth three men's lives?"

"They knew there would be danger. We all knew there was a chance we would be killed but we did it to avenge the loss of our horses."

"I appreciate that. But that is not what I wish you to understand. We have not survived by being reckless and taking chances. We have lived because my grandfather and my father were wise. They took no unnecessary chances. They knew for this people to be strong the strong would have to live, not die. The wise leader considers his people first. He knows you do not expend men for glory and tempers his courage and desires with wisdom. Three of our best warriors have died. That is three fewer men to feed us and protect us when real danger is near. If you do not understand this then you are not worthy to be chief of this people."

White Eagle dropped his head even lower. Everything Snow Cloud said was true. Snow Cloud himself had set this very example many times and he hadn't been wise enough to realize it wasn't because his father was growing too old to lead but because he knew the value of men's lives. All vanity was gone as White Eagle said, "I have not been wise. I sought honor and glory and forgot about wisdom. I will remember your words." He stood then, feeling guilt and shame, and was embarrassed because Spotted Fawn had witnessed his comedown. He hurried away from the lodge, his mind making impossible promises in memory of the dead men without reasoning that it was not entirely his fault they had died. Later he would realize this and later he would return to the lodge of his society and win every man's support of his pledge that the families of the dead men would be provided for by them. Big Tree didn't dare oppose the idea or he would have been subject to disapproval and further loss of influence.

19

A BOY BECOMES A MAN

After a month in the Black Hills the Follow the Wind people returned to their range and roamed the dry, windswept prairie hunting buffalo to procure the prime winter robes and otherwise gathering food for the long winter months. They lived in constant fear of an attack from the northern Indians they had so foolishly provoked and kept scouts and guards posted day and night. Suffering from disapproval of their actions and because Big Tree had been the leader, their akicita lost prestige and was no longer honored with duties for the band. They were once again alone in their wanderings, the other band having gone their own way when they returned from the hills.

White Eagle took it upon himself to ensure that the camp was protected. Every day he scouted on his own for signs of enemy riders. Long hours were spent in watching the vast open prairie from any rise of ground he could find. But he couldn't watch night and day, and one night when the alarm was sounded he knew with certainty what he had been dreading was about to happen. He raced from his lodge ready to fight with the others, but their enemy did not ride horses but rode the wind. They were camped by a river in a thin grove of trees and the fire was on them before they knew it. Frantically they tried to break camp and save what they could, but the fire racing down the slope and through the trees waited on no man and most of the people barely escaped with their lives as they tried to save food and clothing.

The main horse herd was across the river and the few horses tethered in camp for the men were used to ferry women, children, and the old people across. White Eagle went immediately to Snow Cloud's lodge and put his brother and sister on his horse while Snow Cloud brought his own horse for Slow Water. Spotted Fawn swam, holding to the tail of Snow Cloud's horse. The cry of those left behind was hideous to hear and they quickly unloaded their horses to swim back for more people and whatever food they could carry. A few of the women had round bull boats made from the hides of buffalo, and they were loaded as full as possible and paddled across.

In the midst of the confusion the raiders swept down from the opposite side of the river and, catching the panicked horses and guards completely by surprise, made off with a good share of the horse herd. Busy with trying to save their people and a winter's supply of food, they watched helplessly while their horses were driven away. The women wailed and the men stood in frustrated anger as the fire engulfed their lodges and consumed their parfleches of food. White Eagle stood apart from the rest of his family, feeling deeply responsible for the disaster that had just happened. The feeling of isolation that had engulfed him after his mother's death came back even stronger. He had wanted to leave then but hadn't been old enough. He wondered if he should leave now to punish himself for what he had brought them by his lack of wisdom and knew he couldn't because now, more than ever, they would need every man to hunt. Winter was coming soon and many of them would die if food were not gathered to replace what was lost.

In the morning they returned to the ashes of their camp and searched for anything salvageable but the effort was almost futile. Little had escaped the raging fire. There was nothing left to do but take what they had and search for buffalo. White Eagle went with them.

Scouts found a small, straggling buffalo herd and they immediately surrounded them and endeavored to kill every one. They needed not only food but lodges and robes against the winter cold. There were some already sick from the cold nights spent in the open without protection. With the immediate need of food and temporary shelter to protect them from the cold solved for the moment, Snow Cloud sent out men to search for the other bands.

Those who had relatives in the other bands could find homes for the winter; those who didn't would have to ask for shelter with friends or anyone who would take them in. The bands were located and one by one families were dispersed to winter with friends and relatives. What remained of Snow Cloud's people were taken in by the band that had hunted with them earlier. White Eagle and some of the other unmarried men were invited to lodge with the societies of the band. He and Twists the Grass were both taken by the same lodge.

White Eagle spent every possible hour the weather permitted in hunting, going out even when the others would not. His skill and stealth increased from desperation and he consistently brought in something, even if it was only a rabbit or something equally small. Often times he went hungry when his only game was barely large enough to provide for his brother and sister. He learned much about stamina and endurance that winter and even more about himself. The reckless and egotistical boy of summer was gone and in his place a thinking, caring man was emerging. No more impulsive actions for the sake of glory were attempted as he steadfastly braved cold and every adverse condition to bring in food.

By the time he turned sixteen he was shaving with the razor his mother had had the trader McDonnell bring for him, and his voice had decided to settle temporarily into a husky baritone. He was lean, hard, and strong but withdrawn and rarely joined in with the other young men in their fun and games.

Spring came and White Eagle was the first one to find buffalo and bring fresh meat in. He was determined to provide the hides and meat necessary so the Follow the Wind people would be able to live as a separate band by the Sun Dance gathering.

The time came when the bands were to congregate, and as the scattered remnants of Snow Cloud's band were reunited, there were many tears of happiness as the new lodges went up and the Follow the Wind people were once more a band of the Yanktonai Sioux. It was the kind of joy that was infectious and even White Eagle lost some of his melancholy as his name was praised among his people as one of the greatest hunters of all time and the provider of much of what they now had. Snow Cloud wanted him to offer himself to the Sun Dance but still he declined. He did not yet feel he should have the honor attached to this most religious of ceremonies for the bravest of warriors. One obstacle stood in his way and that was the complete surrender or extermination of the Indians who had almost made Snow Cloud's band extinct.

During the first few days of celebrating, White Eagle used his voice again. He joined in the singing and was relieved to discover it didn't crack anymore though, singing with the other men, he didn't really have an opportunity to hear how it sounded. He was even more surprised when he was asked to sing during the Sun Dance ceremony and tried to turn down the honor, uncertain as to the quality of his voice, but the council would not let him refuse.

Snow Cloud told him sternly, "You can not cut yourself off from the people without giving them any opportunity to honor you. Are you ashamed of what you have done for us?"

"Yes. If I had had any wisdom at all I would have stopped Big Tree from going on that raid."

"That is not what I mean. No one has worked harder than you to bring us back together. If you refuse this honor you will turn the people away. I want you to be their leader. Let them follow you or you will lose them."

And so he sang and was surprised and pleased with the quality of his voice. He caught many a maiden's glance as he sang the sacred songs of the Sun Dance and the emptiness he had felt so long was slowly replaced with hope. He even saw Spotted Fawn, with his brother and sister, in the crowd watching the ceremony and he kept looking at her hoping to catch her eye, but she never looked at him.

The day after the Sun Dance was over the bands prepared to part. The band that had hunted with them the previous summer was not deterred by their bad luck—indeed, they had had the best winter possible due to the combined efforts of the two bands—and wanted to hunt with Snow Cloud's band again. For White Eagle the alliance brought mixed emotions. He didn't want any trouble to befall this innocent band, and yet their men would double the number of warriors available to more than a hundred. If trouble did come they would be strong enough to combat it.

White Eagle's soldier society under Big Tree's leadership had been given the police duty as a sign of approval once more, and they carried out their duties with zeal. While the rest of the unmarried men courted the maidens of the other band and vice versa, they steadfastly kept guard. White Eagle watched with envy as the men and near men lined up to court the most attractive maidens and felt a pang of guilt as he saw the line form outside Snow Cloud's lodge for Spotted Fawn and sing and play the love flutes, undoubtedly charmed by the medicine men in order to work magic on the reluctant girl. He saw, too, that they invariably gave up in futility. Spotted Fawn never came out.

In a few days they located the first large herd of buffalo and set up camp. All frivolity came to an end. No one was allowed out of camp any farther away than to get water. All activity was under total restraint until the buffalo were killed. With suppressed excitement, White Eagle came in from his guard duty to get a few hours' sleep before the buffalo hunt began.

He was awakened shortly after going to sleep by the camp guards racing through camp, shouting an alarm. Immediately he and those who slept with him were scrambling to gather their weapons and crawl under the rolled-up lodge covers to answer the call. Fully awake now, they could hear what they hadn't before—the ominous thunder of stampeding buffalo. Mounting their horses tethered behind the lodge, they charged out onto the prairie to meet the stampede with the other men, not immediately concerned with the safety of women and children. They could see the dark mass against the lighter background of drying prairie grass and whipped their horses forward to meet and turn the herd if they could.

Other shapes were visible now with the herd—the shapes of men on horseback—and White Eagle knew their enemies, the Crees from the north, had returned. He fired his single-shot rifle at the nearest Indian as the buffalo swept past him. The man reeled and fell under trampling hooves, and White Eagle turned his horse to run with the charging buffalo, using his rifle as a club now as he tried vainly to turn the outer animals inward. Ahead of him Twists the Grass raced his horse, jabbing his sharp lance into the lunging beasts. Shots were barely heard over the grunting, thundering mass and White Eagle had little hope, with the guns and Indians urging them from behind, of being able to turn so large a herd.

He saw Twists the Grass's horse stumble and one of the wild-eyed buffalo swung wicked horns toward the pressing horse, and the horse was caught off balance and went down. Between White Eagle and Twists the Grass ran a ragged wedge of buffalo already cut from the main herd by Twists the Grass. White Eagle whipped his horse unmercifully trying to keep the stragglers from cutting back in across Twists the Grass but there was no time. The horse jumped to his feet only to be knocked down by the smaller bunch of buffalo as they lunged back into the main herd, and when White Eagle pulled his horse down at the mangled body of his friend's horse he also saw what was left of his friend. Just then something struck him with such force he almost lost his own seat. Dropping his useless gun, he rolled to the side of the horse and clung there momentarily stunned. He felt a hot wetness flow down his arm and realized he had been shot. He pulled himself upright and lay along his horse's neck, keeping low as he swung his horse around to meet the enemy. The Indian was almost on top of him and he pulled his knife as the other Indian lunged at him across the back of his horse. They fell to the ground with the other man impaled on his knife as the last of the stampeding herd thundered by.

Quickly he pulled his knife free and reached to retrieve his gun as another Indian came galloping at him with lance ready to pin him to the ground. He grabbed the gun up and rose swinging it as the Indian drove the lance at him. The lance broke across the gun barrel and the force of White Eagle's swing knocked the Indian from his horse. White Eagle fell upon him with his knife, but the other man was just as quick and caught his hand at the wrist. White Eagle's left arm was weak from the wound and the man was able to throw him off, and he rolled away in an attempt to gain his feet and use his knife again. The other man was prepared for his move and leaped after him, landing on top of him again with knife upraised. White Eagle threw up his arm to ward off the blow and bone smacked against bone as their forearms collided. His weakened left hand grabbed for the other's neck, pushing upward with all the strength he had left to dislodge the man. The man didn't move and White Eagle felt a hopeless sweat spring from every pore as he saw death glinting above him. Suddenly the Indian slumped, his knife falling from his hand and creasing White Eagle's neck as the blade slid past him. He looked up to see Big Tree standing over him, pulling his lance from the body covering his, an evil smile on his face.

"I should have let him kill you, but I want the pleasure of doing that myself. Now get up. We are needed in camp."

White Eagle pushed the dead body away as Big Tree reached to take the Cree's scalp. He found his own knife and quickly cut away the hair on the Indian he had killed. His horse stood nearby and he mounted with difficulty, growing weaker by the minute from loss of blood.

Camp was a disaster area. The buffalo had missed none of it. Most of the lodges were knocked down and those still standing had lodge coverings torn away. White Eagle looked at the scene of devastation with anger consuming him. Men who would do such a thing as these had done to them, not once but twice, didn't deserve to live. The people were beginning to return to the camp now from where they had run to escape the buffalo, and wails of distress at the sight of their belongings filled the air. He hadn't had time to think if anyone might be hurt until this moment, and he urged his horse along the groups of returning people until he found Spotted Fawn with his brother and sister. He slid from his horse and held out his arms to them and they ran to him.

Spotted Fawn saw the blood coming from his arm and gasped, "You're hurt! Let me see."

Snow Cloud came up with Slow Water and immediately took control. "Slow Water, take Spotted Fawn and get our lodge set up. Brown Hair and Morning Star, find something to get water in." He turned to White Eagle and, removing his headband, cut it and wrapped it around the bleeding wound. "Can you get back on your horse?"

He nodded weakly, feeling less certain than his answer indicated. With Snow Cloud's help he mounted and was led into camp. Snow Cloud helped him down and he lay on the ground while Spotted Fawn and Slow Water put what was left of their lodge up. It took more time to find some scattered pieces of robes to make a bed but at last he was inside on a comfortable couch. Water was brought and Spotted Fawn carefully bathed his wound. The ball had fortunately gone through the soft inside flesh of his arm, missing the bone. He had lost blood but there should be no other complications. Tenderly, Spotted Fawn bound the wound for him and he watched her bent head, wanting to speak to her, but he knew he could not with Slow Water present.

As soon as she was done he pretended to sleep, hoping Slow Water would leave and he could talk to Spotted Fawn alone. Snow Cloud was already helping to organize the camp, and his brother and sister were looking for lost belongings outside. He was not to be so lucky. Snow Cloud and the children returned with the disturbing report that Wind Woman had not been found. In the morning they could make a more thorough search but for now her disappearance left them all anxious. Eventually everyone slept from sheer exhaustion but for White Eagle there could be no sleep. He lay suffering as much from emotional shock as physical shock. He had seen his friend Twists the Grass killed. Wind Woman, beloved by all, was missing. And he had almost been killed himself —would have been killed and dead now if Big Tree hadn't saved

him. No longer did he feel as invincible as he had. He was still
learning, still growing, and adding new values to those he had
thought complete. The tempering was beginning.

How long he lay awake thinking he didn't know but was finally
aware that everyone slept. He heard the soft deep breathing of his
brother and sister, the occasional snore of Slow Water and Snow
Cloud. He looked toward Spotted Fawn's couch but she was turned
away from him and he couldn't tell if she slept or not. Very slowly
he rose from his bed, feeling the pain in his arm as he moved it. He
crawled the short distance to her couch and placed his hand over
her mouth and her eyes flew open at his touch. As her eyes
discerned his face, she relaxed, and he removed his hand and bent
to whisper in her ear.

"I have to talk to you. Will you come with me?"

"No. I have nothing to say to you."

"I will speak of it here then and they will hear."

She sighed and rose quietly and followed him outside. Holding
his arm tightly to his side, he motioned her to where the horses
were tied and moved between them to use them for a disguise if any
of the camp police should pass by. She came beside him and stood
with head lowered in subjection.

"I have not told anyone what happened the night the trader
came."

"Does it matter?"

"Yes. No one knows but you and me. No one will ever know
from me. You can act as if it never happened."

"That is easy for you to say. But it did happen and I will always
know and if I did pretend it hadn't happened, you would always
know. How can I be sure you would not someday claim I was not a
virtuous woman. No. I will bear the shame always. I can never
marry."

"You have my word that I will never speak of it."

"Do you think that will change anything? Can I ever accept the
honor of the virtuous woman or belong to the society of one man
only? If I did these things in a lie, would not the Great Spirit punish
me and punish our people by withholding the buffalo from us?"

It was hopeless. Her shame was too great, even greater than he
had imagined. He offered as a last resort, "I will leave then. If I am
not here you will not need to worry that I will tell."

"No! You cannot go. It is I who must go. As soon as Morning
Star is married I will go."

His concern deepened. "But where? You have no other family."

Her shoulders shook slightly. "Does it matter? I know where I must go."

He drew in his breath sharply as he realized what she meant. "No! You cannot! You must not!"

She looked up at him and he saw tears in her eyes and on her face. "What is left? No man will have me. I am a dishonor and a curse to my people."

"That's not true. The buffalo are here and I have seen many men before your lodge."

"Yes, the buffalo are here but are you forgetting we have almost lost everything twice? And if I should choose a husband, would he not know I am not a virgin the night of our wedding? Surely you know that?"

But he didn't know. He answered, "No. I know only what I have heard and don't know how much of what I have heard is true." Still the tears rolled down her cheeks in silent anguish as she looked expectantly into his eyes. He put his hand on her shoulder in a tender gesture, not knowing what else to do. "If it is possible to know the truth from any man, I will know it for you." She looked down, then, and he added, "And also I promise you by the Sun Dance that no man shall hear from my lips that you are not a virtuous woman."

She looked at him again with great pain and stifled a sob and ran for the lodge. He looked after her in bewilderment. What more could he do? Women were difficult. He shook his head, feeling a twinge of guilt and also growing weak from standing so long with the pain throbbing in his arm. He walked with weak legs to the lodge of his society and rolled himself in a tattered robe he found and slept in exhaustion.

In the morning the total of the night's destruction and death was known. Death wails were heard from every corner of the camp as bodies were found and brought in. Wind Woman's body was found, too, and their own voices were raised in sorrow over the death of a truly wise woman. White Eagle felt her loss deeply and the rage within him grew, not only for the Crees but for the part he had played in bringing about her death. The day was spent in building scaffolds for the dead and trying to find articles unfound in the darkness. By night the grim elders of the two bands were ready to hold council and decide on a plan of action against the enemy. White Eagle was in attendance.

Snow Cloud was the first to speak. "My brothers, my heart is heavy. Many of us have suffered at the hands of the enemy. What is even more sorrowful is that our innocent brothers have suffered for being with us. The curse we have suffered has also fallen on them. Now is the time for us to decide what we shall do. If our brothers wish to join us we would be honored but this fight is not theirs. By the impetuousness of our young men we have perpetrated this disaster. If they do not wish to follow us, we shall avenge their dead for them and understand. What say you, my brothers?"

White Eagle sat with his eyes down, feeling the reprimand in Snow Cloud's words. He gathered, too, that for his own people's sake he would hesitate to go on a mission of revenge but his honor and the honor of his people dictated he must avenge the deaths of the innocent band's people. The lessons White Eagle was learning were bitter but he knew what made Snow Cloud the trusted leader he was.

The war chief of the other band rose in solemn determination. "Snow Cloud has spoken well and I say his name with honor. But no man would say my name with honor if I did not pledge my people to take up their weapons and fight with Snow Cloud. No man lets another avenge him and still calls himself a man. Where Snow Cloud leads I will follow."

There was a chorus of approving grunts from every man. White Eagle stood and was recognized. This was his first time to speak in council though he had won the honor when he had brought back the trader's scalp. "My father has said we have brought this trouble upon ourselves. He has taken the blame for those of us who are responsible. My father is wise and we were not. I hope it is not too late for me to be wise but I wish to say to you that every man who wishes to follow Snow Cloud and me into battle must be prepared to fight for as long as it takes to destroy this enemy. This fight must be a fight to the finish. We cannot strike and run this time, for they will only strike harder. Treachery is in their blood. I know Snow Cloud will disapprove of my words, and he is right to disapprove. It is better to make peace with our enemies than to fight. This he has shown us in all he has done and he has been a good leader for many winters. But I do not believe peace is possible with these people. To show you I believe in my words I will volunteer to go to them with a proposal of peace. If I do not return you will know my words were true."

White Eagle sat down and heard the grunts of approval echo throughout the council lodge.

Buffalo Horn, leader of Snow Cloud's most experienced warrior society, stood and was recognized by the elders. "What White

Eagle says is true. I, too, agree peace is better but I believe peace with these people will be impossible. I pledge myself to fight to the death."

The words of agreement were getting louder and more enthusiastic as one after another of the most respected warriors stood and pledged themselves to fight. White Eagle sat with bated breath as a feeling of pride warmed him. At last Big Tree stood, powerful, confident, and not to be outdone.

"The words of the men here are mighty, just as their deeds have been mighty, and I honor all those who have spoken. I, too, pledge my life to save my people and I will follow Snow Cloud and Buffalo Horn until the enemy is nothing but food for the vultures. White Eagle took blame for what has happened but I claim the greater blame. It was my plan and I was their leader. Because of this I pledge to you that I will stake myself to the ground and fight to the death."

Big Tree sat down amidst overwhelming approval. White Eagle saw the look of triumph on his face. They all had been schooled to believe the man daring to rope himself to his lance on the field of battle was deemed the most courageous of men. Once having committed himself he was doomed to fight and die where he stood and could be released only by another man of his society. It was the grandest of gestures and one White Eagle would try to prevent.

The next few days were spent in ceremony and purification rites and dances to supplicate the powers in their behalf. It took four days to prepare every man, not because the ceremonies were long but because a man had to abstain from intercourse for four days before going to war or be exceptionally vulnerable to arrows and rifle balls. When everyone was ready White Eagle went to Snow Cloud's lodge to see his brother and sister and perhaps get some encouragement from Spotted Fawn before he left.

Brown Hair was gloomy because he was too young to go. White Eagle tried to make him feel better by saying, "It is more important for you to be here. You are old enough to hunt and you will have to provide food while we are gone. You may even have to kill buffalo. You and the others left behind have to protect the women and children. If we took you and you were killed, where would our hunters and warriors of a few winters come from?"

Brown Hair gave a wan smile. "How can I be a warrior if I have no chance to be one? If it is more important to be here, why don't you stay and I will go?"

"You are right, Brownie. But you are also unwise. The impor-

tant thing is to live. Those of us who are going may die. The least
capable will die the soonest. I do not want that for you. You would
rush in without experience, perhaps without killing any of the
enemy. That would be a waste. We fight so that we can live. Your
day will come, but not now. Know you are doing what you are most
capable of doing, living, growing, and gaining in wisdom so some
day you can fight to live, not die."

Brown Hair looked at him with awe. "I understand, my
brother."

White Eagle stood and went to where Morning Star was bead-
ing a headband under Spotted Fawn's instruction. She kept her
head down but still he could see tears on her cheeks. He squatted
down and said, "This is very good, little sister. May I have it to
wear?"

Tearfully she replied, "But it isn't finished."

He smiled. "No one else will know that. I want to wear it. I want
to have something of you close to me."

She looked at him then, quickly, and he saw happiness replace
the sadness briefly as she handed the band to him. He said, "Put it
on for me, will you?"

She stood and took off the band he wore and replaced it with
hers and set his feathers in place. He stood and smiled at her and
turned to leave. Spotted Fawn had neither said anything nor
looked at him but now she got up and followed him. Slow Water
grunted in disapproval but Spotted Fawn ignored her and followed him outside.

With eyes discreetly lowered she said, "I will pray for your
safety."

"Maybe you should pray for my death."

She shuddered. "Do not say it! I have never wanted you to die."

"Then what do you want?"

She looked up at him in anguish. "Don't you know?" she
whispered.

"How can I? You will not talk to me. You will not tell me."

She put her hands to her face and ran crying into the lodge.
Feeling frustrated and angry, he went to gather his weapons and
joined the other men preparing to leave. In a short while they were
mounted and riding out of camp to the encouraging songs of the
women. Spotted Fawn was not there to sing him encouragement
and he frowned in total lack of understanding.

They rode for days, following every trail they crossed that could
be the track of their enemy, fasting and praying and getting more

discouraged as each trail they followed turned out to be a false trail. Snow Cloud held council after several days on the trail to see if the discouragement among them was bad enough to undermine their morale. It was taking too much time and the buffalo would not wait forever to be killed. They agreed to look for two more days and if they found nothing they would return to their village and proceed with the hunt before taking the war path again.

The last day of their proposed search they found a fresher sign of a large party. The war party camped and scouts were sent to locate the group making the trail. They came back at dark with the report that it was the enemy camp they were seeking. Morale quickly lifted and medicine men renewed their efforts to protect the warriors. From the information the scouts brought, the enemy were in the midst of drying their winter buffalo stores—buffalo that rightly belonged to the Nakota. This helped fan the fire of revenge.

As White Eagle had proposed before the council, he offered himself to go as a peaceful envoy. There were many who did not wish to delay any longer and wanted to fight but Snow Cloud finally prevailed, and it was agreed White Eagle would go alone under a flag of truce.

At first light of dawn White Eagle was sitting his horse within view of the enemy camp, naked except for breechclout and moccasins, no paint, no weapons but a knife and the lance on which he carried a bleached buffalo hide, not even his shield to protect him. He heard the cry of the guards as they saw him and moved his horse slowly forward. His face showed no fear but his heart was beating hard despite his grim determination not to be afraid. Behind him, hidden in the grass but close enough so they could see all that took place, were some of his own people.

Before he covered half the distance to the circle of lodges, a line of warriors appeared out of the camp, guns raised and riding at full gallop toward him. Instantly he knew his life was in danger. There would be no talk of peace, only his death at the hands of the warrior reaching him first. He hurled the lance with all his strength into the ground and yanked his horse around and kicked it viciously into a dead run as a volley of shots rang out behind him. The echo of the shots, he hoped, would be heard by his own army of warriors just out of sight of the camp. If the shots weren't heard, the men he left behind on the prairie could be easily found and killed.

He turned his horse away from where the men lay in hopes of protecting them and led the enemy straight toward where the rest of his party waited. Bullets still whizzed by him as he rode lying along his horse's neck, a hard target to hit. His horse was hit and fell and he leaped clear and started to run. His own men came charging toward him and he looked back to see if the enemy were giving up their pursuit. They weren't and he ran harder. Snow Cloud and his men swept around him and he fell to the ground to catch his breath. The battle raged furiously for a few minutes until the enemy decided they were too few to match the strength of Snow Cloud's warriors. They abandoned the battlefield and retreated toward their camp with Snow Cloud and his men following in force.

White Eagle got up and surveyed the dead and wounded left on the abandoned field. He caught a loose horse and helped the wounded back to camp and, with two of the less critically wounded men, carried in the two dead warriors from their own party.

Armed and on a horse once more, he rode out to join the battle he could hear and now see as he galloped to join Snow Cloud. He saw an enemy ready to cleave one of his own from behind and raised his rifle to fire, his bullet hitting its mark. He took time to pour another charge of powder into the rifle but before he could finish the load another Indian charged him with lance upraised and he caught the blow in the center of his shield and was unhorsed. He hit the ground on his back as the other rider came at him with lance ready to drive through his heart. He fired the rifle point blank into the horse's face and the flash of powder startled the animal and he reared, throwing his rider's aim awry. White Eagle rolled to his feet and pulled his hatchet free and flung it with all his strength at the other man as he wheeled his horse around for another try at spearing him. The hatchet caught the man between the shoulders and he pitched off his horse. Quickly he used his knife on the fallen men and caught the bloody scalps to his belt.

His own horse stood steadfastly nearby and he retrieved his gun and hastily loaded it as the battle moved away from him momentarily. He leaped onto his horse and charged into the thick of things. Reinforcements were coming from tne Indian camp, but the warriors of Snow Cloud's party didn't waver and held the ground they were on. It was a savage battle marked by the bitterness of the enemies and noteworthy for the tenacity with which they fought. No hit and run here, hoping for a coup and escape without blood. White Eagle saw a man fall and lunged his horse over the fallen man, cutting his assailant down with his hatchet. The rifle was of little use in close combat; the knife and ax, and less often the lance, were making their mark as guns lay scattered on the ground without time to reload.

The dead and dying littered the ground and it was difficult to ride a horse without fear of stepping on a downed man. White Eagle stood his ground and slashed out to the right and left at any man brave enough to come close. More and more of the men on both sides were falling back and soon only a few knots of hand-to-hand combat remained. White Eagle saw Big Tree bloodied and staggering in his circle of movement defined by the thong that tied him to his lance. He was battling two men and couldn't last much longer. White Eagle rode close and heaved his lance into one of the assailants as Big Tree cut down the other and fell to his knees, with blood running freely from many slashes on his body. White Eagle, his own body fairly untouched except for bruises on his back, leaned off his horse and cut the thong tying Big Tree to his death and pulled the lance from the ground and held it out to Big Tree.

"Do you mock me, White Eagle?"

"No. Now get up behind me."

Still the man stood stubbornly. "Why? I am pledged to die."

"Not today, Big Tree. The war is not won, only the battle. We need you to fight again."

Big Tree smiled wearily and bent to scalp his victims. White Eagle dismounted to collect his own trophies and then helped Big Tree to mount a nearby horse. Snow Cloud and a few of the men were watching while more men cleared the battlefield of the dead and wounded. He smiled as White Eagle rode up and they turned together and followed their men to camp, away from the trampled and bloodied battlefield.

They bandaged the wounded and built scaffolds for the dead and rested. The scouts rode in and reported the Indian camp was being abandoned. Snow Cloud immediately called for his men to mount and ride in pursuit of the escaping Indians, and all who could answer the call rode after him. White Eagle rode at his side.

They came within sight of the fleeing Indians and were met with the same furious attacking warriors as before. Tireder and more grimly they fought, savagely giving blow for blow. White Eagle received a lance wound in his side as he bent to scalp a warrior he had just killed. He pulled the lance from his side and whirled, heaving it into the neck of the man who had thrown it, who had stayed close expecting to scalp a victim and instead was killed with his own lance. Another man leaped on his back with knife slashing at his throat and drawing blood. He broke the man's arm across his knee with such force the bone pierced the skin and blood sprayed his face and he was suddenly sick. He turned away, unable to kill the man and left him moaning with pain as he ran to pull another Cree from Snow Cloud. His arm locked around the man's neck as Snow Cloud's knife released his life from his body. He let the man fall and turned away, his stomach trying to retch and too empty to.

He felt Snow Cloud's arm around him as his knees began to collapse. They were standing thus when Buffalo Horn and the chief of the other band brought the chief of the Cree Indians to Snow Cloud.

Snow Cloud asked, "Are there enough of them left for another battle?"

Buffalo Horn answered, "No. What shall we do with him?"

"I will talk to him. Maybe he will listen now." Trying the several dialects he was familiar with, Snow Cloud questioned the Cree. He stood stubbornly resistant and defiant, spitting in Snow Cloud's face. Anger gave White Eagle his strength back for a moment and his fist bloodied the defiant Indian's mouth and sent him sprawling to the ground. Buffalo Horn's lance plunged through the man's body and White Eagle turned and staggered a few feet away and fell.

Later he awoke in camp. Food for victorious warriors was being served in great quantities, and the smell revived him as his empty stomach growled. Snow Cloud saw him move and came quickly to his side.

"Does my son wish food now?"

"Yes. What happened?"

Snow Cloud smiled and handed him a hunk of steaming, juicy buffalo meat, undoubtedly taken from the fleeing Indians. "We have vanquished our foe. They are on the trail to the north and will not return for fear of their lives."

"That is good. You were right. Peace is better than war."

Snow Cloud smiled knowingly. "And my son has become a warrior among warriors but his stomach has become a coward among cowards."

"I am ashamed. I don't know what happened to me."

Snow Cloud's hand rested on his and he felt a warm reassuring pressure. "Do not be ashamed. It was your first day of battle and a day not many men have experienced with such intensity. I would be disappointed if it had not sickened you. Only a man with compassion can lead wisely. You have today felt compassion. I am proud of you, more proud than I have ever been in my life, my son."

20

THE SUN DANCE

The weary warriors arrived at their home camp silent and serious but custom dictated the display of victory, and they adorned themselves according to their honor and rode into camp amid cries of joy which turned to wails of mourning as expected men didn't appear. They had won the war but they had lost more than a quarter of their manpower. Many more were wounded and some would yet die of their wounds. But life had to go on, and to live they had to find the buffalo and prepare meat for winter. Despite the mourning the hunt began and also the days of scalp dancing in honor of the returning warriors. The first night of celebration, Morning Star came to dance and carry his scalp pole and she carried it proudly. Few men had more scalps than White Eagle. He was disappointed when Spotted Fawn didn't join in the dance, but by now had resigned himself to the fact she would never honor him. But he was wrong. The second night she came and carried his scalp pole and sang a song of praise for him. He watched her, hoping she would look his way, but she kept her eyes down, and when the dance was over for that night she disappeared to Snow Cloud's lodge and didn't come again on any of the following nights.

The first day of the hunt took its toll on White Eagle. His wound, barely closed since the battle, opened and bled. He needed help and asked Brown Hair to join him in the next day's hunt. The boy eagerly accepted. White Eagle was surprised at Brown Hair's inherent ability. He rode close to the boy, coaching him in the hunt, and was more than pleased as he saw the boy's skill and confidence develop. Between them they killed a fair number of buffalo, ensuring they would have plenty of meat for the long winter ahead. But the hunt, even if he didn't pull a bow or butcher the buffalo, was still too strenuous for White Eagle, and by the time the hunt was over he had lost enough blood to make him weak. He had been taking care of himself and wore his shirt to hide the bloody wrappings. When he rode in the last day with Brown Hair, carrying the choice meats of the day's hunt to Snow Cloud's lodge, Spotted Fawn saw his condition immediately.

"You are not well, White Eagle. What is wrong?"

He tried a weak smile. "My wound bleeds a little. It is nothing."

She came to him and demanded, "Let me see." She lifted his shirt and saw the scarlet-soaked bandage and gasped. "Brown Hair, help me get him to your couch."

Too weak to resist, he let them take him into the lodge and he willingly lay on Brown Hair's bed and let Spotted Fawn take over. Snow Cloud came in and reprimanded him. "Why didn't you tell us? Only a fool dies when there is no need."

"It was time to hunt. I can heal now."

"And you will—right here where I can watch you and make sure you do nothing foolish. How bad is it?"

Spotted Fawn answered, "It will heal if he will let it, but he has lost blood."

Snow Cloud grunted and looked at White Eagle sternly. "These people need you alive. Consider them before you do anything more that is foolish."

"Snow Cloud is right."

Snow Cloud smiled then and placed a gentle hand on White Eagle's shoulder and left the lodge with Brown Hair to finish bringing in the meat.

White Eagle said to Spotted Fawn, "I saw you at the scalp dance. Have you forgiven me?"

"No."

"Then why did you come to honor me?"

"It was the only right thing to do. Snow Cloud told us of your bravery, and since I am considered a member of your family, it would not be right if I did not honor you."

At last he thought he understood. She hated him and he didn't blame her. "To keep the people from gossiping. I had hoped you really wanted to honor me. I will understand if you do not come again."

She finished wrapping his wound in tight-lipped silence, on the verge of tears, and hastily left to continue slicing buffalo meat with Slow Water. He lay weakly on the couch with eyes closed until Morning Star came in to see him. He heard her footsteps and opened his eyes, smiling at her.

"Will you be all right?" she asked, concern creasing her young forehead.

"Of course. But will Slow Water be angry with you for coming to see me?"

"No. I was caught up with them. Spotted Fawn said I could come for just a little while until they had more meat for me to lay on the racks. Will you be staying here for a while?"

"Yes. Until my side heals."

She smiled and he saw the strong resemblance she had to their mother. "I'm glad. It will seem like I have a whole family again."

He held out his hand to her and she took it. She missed her mother more deeply than either he or Brown Hair ever could, and he realized it now. He smiled at her. "I had thought of letting Brown Hair sleep at my lodge. He has done well and deserves the honor."

She thought about it a moment and said with a sigh, "Yes. I don't see him much anyway. We cannot talk. Why is it you will talk to me?"

"I have learned things from our mother about the white man's customs. They do not think it bad for brother and sister to talk. Otherwise I would not. But remember Brownie and you were raised to follow the Indian way. Because I choose to break this custom does not mean you should."

She nodded and smiled. "I'm glad you talk to me. I would be lonesome if you didn't, but I will remember not to speak unless you speak to me first. I had better go now."

He released her hand and she darted out the door and his thoughts turned to Spotted Fawn. Their every encounter only left him more confused and frustrated as to what he should do to help her. There hadn't been much opportunity to seek the answer he wanted to give her, or even to know whom he should ask. Who would tell him that he could believe? Could he rely on anyone or should he seek his own experience, knowing full well the consequences of such an undertaking? He closed his eyes and slept.

It was several days before Snow Cloud let White Eagle return to

the lodge of his soldier society. Brown Hair was reluctant to give up
the bed and company of the older boys of the society, but he still
was not experienced enough to be asked to join. The days passed
swiftly and soon the camp was on the move again, hunting and
gathering food for winter. The accompanying band did not go its
own way at the end of the fall hunt, preferring to stay with the
Follow the Wind people for security. Both bands had suffered in
power in vanquishing their enemy, and it was only wise to remain
together for protection and to try to rebuild their bands by hoping
the young men from each band would take members of the other
band for wives.

White Eagle and Brown Hair spent a good many days hunting
together, the older brother teaching the younger all the skills he
had himself learned. The bond of friendship and respect grew
deep between them, and White Eagle's pride in his younger
brother grew as Brown Hair mastered the arts he was being taught.
But not all the learning was about hunting. Brown Hair had other
questions and White Eagle answered them even when the questions were about their mother. Brown Hair had been old enough to
realize White Eagle was special to their mother, and when he felt he
dared ask White Eagle about it he did.

They were riding back to camp after a successful hunting trip
when Brown Hair asked, "I remember our mother leaving us with
Spotted Fawn while she took you away from camp. What was it you
did? Was she teaching you as you are teaching me?"

"Yes."

"About the white men?"

"Yes."

"Why? Why didn't she teach Morning Star and me about the
white men, too?"

"Because I am not Snow Cloud's son. I am the son of her white
husband, killed by Snow Cloud."

Brown Hair looked at him with startled eyes. "Then you are not
my brother?"

"Only half. We have the same mother but not the same father."

"Oh. Now I see. What was the name she called you? I have
forgotten."

"Ross. It was my father's name."

"Ross." He rolled the unfamiliar sound off his tongue. "May I
call you that when we are alone?"

"I do not wish it. It is best forgotten now."

"Ross," he said again tentatively, and White Eagle knew his

brother had no intention of forgetting. "Do you want to be a white man?"

"No."

He smiled then. "Good. Maybe you can teach me what she taught you. I remember a few of the words, I think."

White Eagle laughed shortly. "I'm not sure I can remember enough to teach you. I'm not sure of the words anymore myself. I will forget them all before I see another white man."

Brown Hair frowned in disappointment. "That is too bad. But maybe you can try?"

"No, Brown Hair. She did not want it and I have forgotten too much. I want to forget it all. This is my life and I want no other."

Brown hair said no more and they continued into camp in silence.

The cold winds and first snow of winter came and the combined bands moved to a sheltered river valley to make camp for the winter. Leisure hours were spent inside while the snow fell, making new weapons and enjoying the companionship of other men. Gambling and storytelling filled much of the time and try as White Eagle would, he came no closer to finding an adequate answer to the question of whether any man could tell if a woman was a virgin. He made Brown Hair a new bow and arrows and took him hunting whenever the weather permitted. It was not an exceptionally hard winter and they lived without fear of starvation.

Spring came quickly and White Eagle passed his seventeenth birthday. Except for the problem of Spotted Fawn, he was untroubled and confident. This year he would participate in the Sun Dance and he looked forward to the honor eagerly. He had no doubt in his mind he would be welcomed into Buffalo Horn's warrior society as Big Tree and one or two of the other older boys had been.

The snow fled before the warm prairie winds, and it was time for the spring hunts to begin. With zest White Eagle threw himself into everything he did, feeling the exuberance for life throbbing in his every vein. The longest day of the year came and when the next waxing moon turned the nights almost as bright as day the bands of the Yanktonai known throughout the Sioux nation as Nakota gathered for the annual Sun Dance ceremony. The reunion was as gay and noisy as ever, and the feasts and gifts abounded. As one of the young men offered for the dance, White Eagle was especially honored with gifts and choice meats from all the young maidens of the gathering. He responded by an intense round of courting,

which only served to remind him of Spotted Fawn and the shame
between them. He was glad to see the time come when the religious
part of the Sun Dance ceremony began and all contact with women
was forbidden as they underwent purification and instruction.

When his petition to dance was honored he was at once filled
with joy and uncertainty, and the uncertainty grew as the instructions continued in earnest for those men chosen to dance. He chose
to sacrifice his body for the people of his band, sending up a silent
prayer for the redeeming of Spotted Fawn's virtue.

One of the most noteworthy of maidens was chosen to repre-
sent the deity who had brought the sacred calumet pipe to the
Sioux, the White Buffalo Cow Maiden, and she stood in ceremonial
regalia outside the sweat lodge with the sacred pipe, waiting to lead
the dancers to the Sun Dance lodge. The painting of their bodies
began with the hands and feet of all painted red and each wearing a
scarlet cloth across their loins. White Eagle's shoulders were
striped in blue, denoting his chosen sacrifice, and he wore anklets
and arm bands of rabbit fur and a symbolic sunflower medallion.
They emerged from the sweat lodge wearing wreaths of sage and
carrying sprigs of sage in their right hands. The White Buffalo
Cow Maiden led the way, singing the sacred chant, and the people
gathered around the open lodge where the dance was to be held
echoed her chants as they walked in the gray light of predawn.

The shaman in charge of the ceremony carried in the skull of a
buffalo and performed the ritual on the altar built for the purpose.
As the sun's rim appeared on the horizon, the drums began, and
each dancer, accompanied by two men attendants, went to his
designated position. White Eagle would dance around the center
pole and he stood before it, his eyes on the rising sun, while the
men pinched the skin of his chest and slit it with a knife. He gritted
his teeth against the momentary pain and stood stoical as bone
skewers were thrust through the slits and he was tied by stout
leather thongs to the center pole of the Sun Dance lodge. The
tempo of the drums increased, and with eyes transfixed on the
rising sun, White Eagle began to dance to the rhythm, exerting
pressure ever so slightly against the bonds that held him. He knew
it was expected of him to dance until sundown before tearing away
the flesh in the symbolic tearing away of ignorance. Each man had
women members of his band crying encouragement, and White
Eagle thought he heard Spotted Fawn's voice along with Morning
Star's.

During the day there were intermissions in the dancing for

other ceremonies and songs, giving the sacrificed men a chance to rest. The first intermission came and White Eagle stood still, his breath coming fast from his efforts. To his surprise Spotted Fawn came with Morning Star to wipe away his sweat and blood and bathe his body in cool water. He stood with eyes fastened on the sun, feeling her gentle touch on his body and smelling the scent of the sweet grass swabs she used to wipe away his blood, burning them in the fire in what was a symbolic act to ensure constancy in love. It was enough to bring a smile to his lips. One more time, as the last song was being sung, she wiped his face and neck and dampened his lips. Gratefully he licked the moisture as the singers finished and the drums began again. He had little time to think about her action, usually associated with lovers, as he began dancing again.

By the second intermission he had to kneel on the ground to rest and again Spotted Fawn and Morning Star attended him. This time she brought him more water and his parched throat welcomed the cool refreshment as the hot summer sun beat down on his head and burned his tortured eyes, making him almost blind and aware only of Spotted Fawn's voice and touch. He wanted to ask why she was doing this—why she was acting like a maiden in love with him when he knew she was not—but now was not the time.

By the last intermission he was on the verge of exhaustion and sunstroke. The water revived his body but his eyes were beyond help, and the agony there exceeded the agony of tortured body and exhausted arms and legs aching for relief. He kept telling himself it would only be a short time and his suffering would be over. Already the sun was dipping toward the western horizon and he would be released from the self-inflicted torture, and when the drums began again he danced on with leaden legs and burning eyes.

As the sun's fiery rim touched the horizon, the agonized men began to pull free of the thongs holding them. White Eagle was one of the last to break free as the sun disappeared from view. He lunged backward violently, throwing all his weight against the thongs secured through his resisting flesh, and tore the strips of skin from his chest. He was only dimly aware of being carried in triumph from the lodge amid shouts of congratulation. He was taken to Snow Cloud's lodge and laid on a couch prepared for him. They were all there with him, praising his courage, and Spotted Fawn, with Morning Star's help, washed his bloodied body and stopped the bleeding of his wounds. He slept from physical and emotional exhaustion.

When he awoke the lodge was quiet, but the dancing and singing of the celebrating camp went on outside. He was thirsty and tried to rise. A figure moved from out of the shadows and Spotted Fawn brought him water. He drank gratefully and lay back, still blurred of eye and aching.

"I have some dog meat ready for you if you want it."

"Not yet. In a little while. Why did you come today? I told you you didn't have to."

"I wanted to."

He misunderstood her intention and said bitterly, "To see me fail?"

She sobbed and kneeled beside him and took his hand, crying, "No! Not to fail. Don't you know yet? Can't you guess why?"

He couldn't see her clearly and raised his hand to her face and felt her tears. "How can I? Every time I talk to you you cry."

She held his hand against her cheek and he felt her lips against his skin. "I love you, White Eagle. I have always loved you. Why do you think I let you lie with me? I hoped you would love me, too, and want to take me as your wife."

He pulled his hand free from hers and cried, "Don't! It isn't possible."

She sat beside him and he felt more than saw her large eyes boldly on his face. "Why isn't it possible? We are not blood related. I could never love another."

He turned his head away as the truth dawned bright as the sun before his blind eyes. And he had been blind. But the blindness was not because he had not found her attractive. He realized now just how much she did attract him. His blood was always stirred by her. But the specter of his vision had shackled him to bachelorhood and celibacy. In a tortured whisper he said, "My vision prophecied that the woman I take will die."

"I am not afraid of death. I have wanted nothing else since I gave myself to you. To live without you is death. To live with you is life beyond my wildest dreams, though I would die."

"No!" he cried but didn't get a chance to say more as her lips covered his. He couldn't resist her. His arms went around her slender, warm body, so yielding to his, and he kissed her until she broke away and he felt her tremble with the passion of her desire.

"Can you deny that you want me, White Eagle? Can you refuse your heart what your body so desperately desires?"

"I must. I cannot have you die by my body." Tears, soothing and cooling, washed his eyes and she held his head against her while he clung to her and heard the voice of his vision repeat the words, "Do not try to alter the events of your life. All these things must happen for your vision to be fulfilled."

When he opened his eyes again he could see her, although the outline of her face wavered in a halo of gold from the effects of the sun. Her eyes were large and lovely as the eyes of the doe of his vision, the lips parted expectantly below the delicately boned nose and high cheekbones. He couldn't deny any longer that she was the doe of his vision, but he couldn't accept the edict that he had to marry her and bring her death. He would not do that. He touched her face with gentle fingers and she smiled at him. "You are the one in my vision. I know it now, but I love you too much to bring you death by my seed."

"Tell me of your vision. I have never heard it."

"It showed my mother's death and my growing in honors and deeds. It showed me you and your death with my child in you. Then it showed me going to a white eagle's nest. What happens there was not clear and I do not yet understand why these things must happen."

"It is indeed strange. But I am not afraid. It did not show which child of yours I died with, did it?"

"No. But it makes no difference. I don't want you to die at all."

"But what if it is a child conceived when I am very old? We may have fifteen or twenty children. We could live long and be happy. Don't you see it doesn't have to mean I die with your first child? And even if I did, we would have some time together, no matter how short. That is all I ask—to be loved by you—to be your wife."

He let his hand slide down the bare, slender arm where she took it in hers. "No. Never. I would cut my manhood from my body before I would let it kill you."

The tears came to her eyes again. "Please, don't say that. Give me hope. Tell me you will consider it. I have nothing to live for if you tell me my love is doomed to die without having been given to you. Please don't tell me no." She pleaded with tears running down her cheeks and her body shaking.

He put his arms around her and pulled her down to him and stroked her glossy head, whispering, "All right. I will consider it. I will pray. I will go to the sacred hill again if I have to and see if my vision changes. Anything you wish I will do except that which brings your death."

She raised her head and smiled and he kissed her. She heard voices outside and stood up quickly and retreated to her couch but not before she signed to him that she loved him.

Snow Cloud came in with Slow Water and came to his son's couch. "How are you, my son?"

"Well, Father."

"Have you eaten yet?"

"No. I have been resting. I will eat with you, now."

Snow Cloud smiled and Spotted Fawn rushed to heat again the tender young dog meat she had prepared for White Eagle. When it was again boiling White Eagle sat up and she served him, pressing his hand in a way that wouldn't let him forget the promise of her body and he felt the warmth flow through him. They ate and smoked while the women ate. At last Brown Hair and Morning Star came in and again he was exalted by their praise. He was quite wrung out of emotion, so much had happened, and shortly after basking in glory, he slept.

21

T O U C H E D   B Y   T H U N D E R

Morning found him strong again and ready to assume the responsibility of helping to organize the breakup of the Sun Dance gathering. The other band moved with them almost as normal procedure now and it was becoming more and more evident the two bands would meld into one eventually. Several marriages had taken place, tying the two bands even closer through the bond of family as well as friendship. Which band would be the dominant one was yet to be decided. Both the head chiefs were of an age to be replaced. It would be only a question of who died first or who had the most influence on the combined councils when it came time to elect a new chief.

Once the summer hunt was completed the two bands crossed

the Missouri River, moving toward the Black Hills to spend the hottest weeks of summer and to continue their food gathering and hunting. Once they were encamped in the cooler, pine-clad canyons of the Black Hills, White Eagle was formally initiated into the warrior society, a position he accepted with pride. Snow Cloud declared it an occasion for a feast, and he made it the most lavish ever in approval of his son and heir. White Eagle, too, was obliged to give to the fullest of his wealth, and when the night was over he had but one horse left, the breechclout he wore, and his knife and bow. But a man who was not generous could never achieve status, even though his generosity left him destitute of every possession. He could soon build his wealth again. The Black Hills harbored wild horses among its many canyons, and in the course of hunting deer he would soon learn where they were.

Hunting occupied much of the young men's time in the following days. They found a few wild horses and spent several days breaking them in the quick Indian fashion. It was not only great sport but fun for the lusty young men and yet another way to prove their superiority. Three feet of the unbroken horse were hobbled together and the animal was turned loose to buck until it was exhausted. A buffalo robe was then put on the horse's back and when it no longer had strength to buck the robe off a man would mount. When the horse accepted the man, which usually didn't take long, the man had a broken horse. White Eagle gained a few horses this way but he needed more if he was to pay the bride price for Spotted Fawn, provided he decided to take her as his wife. To gain more horses he would have to raid some enemy camp and at the moment he welcomed the idea of getting away from camp. Time was becoming heavy on his hands and Spotted Fawn's attention to him was wearing down his resistance. He wished, at times, they had not declared their love for each other, for now, instead of shunning him, she was everywhere it was proper for her to be in his presence, making him increasingly aware of her. She even discovered when he bathed and would come to bathe at the same time. He was sure someone was conspiring with her, for he tried to bathe at different times and she always seemed to know. Even though Slow Water was in attendance, she made no attempts to conceal her body from him, enticing him almost beyond his own good sense.

His idea of going on a horse raid was accepted wholeheartedly by the bored younger men in camp. Even Big Tree did not refuse when White Eagle invited him to join him and his closest friends. He decided to take Brown Hair with him, too. The boy was old enough, and it was time he had the opportunity to test his confidence and courage. Brown Hair was ecstatic at the invitation.

The evening before they were to leave, White Eagle went to the sweat lodge to be purified and to seek the prevailing spirits in his behalf. From the sweat lodge he ran to the river, naked, in the cover of darkness. He dove into the cool, spring-fed water and delighted in the solitary swim until Spotted Fawn's slender, naked shape stood silhouetted on the river bank. She dove into the water as silently as the streamlined otter she resembled and swam to him. He stood angrily, waiting for her to reach him, but when she surfaced with the water streaming from hair and breasts he had little anger left and hungrily took her in his arms and kissed the cool wetness of her mouth until he felt he could no longer be sure of his control. He pushed her away roughly.

"You shouldn't be here. I have just come from the purifying ceremony. Do you wish the spirits to turn against me?"

She smiled at him. "No. I just wish you to take me as your wife. Can you deny that you want me?"

"No. I don't deny it. But you told me to consider it. I am considering it, but you make it hard to think of anything else but you."

She laughed. "That is how I want it. I want you to think of me, not of death and dying, but living with me, your body springing to life in mine. Do you not want it as much as I?"

He sighed in hopelessness and stalked from the river. He didn't dare stay. Where *was* Slow Water? He must speak to Snow Cloud about keeping a closer watch on Spotted Fawn. He went straight to the warrior society lodge and without a word to anyone there went to his couch and pretended to sleep, though sleep didn't come easily with so many vivid pictures of Spotted Fawn crossing his mind.

In the morning the small party of men left the camp with the encouraging songs of the women cheering them on. Spotted Fawn was among them and came out of the crowd of young women to hand him a good luck charm, openly declaring her love for him by the act. He felt embarrassed and a little angry and took her gift without a word or look of appreciation. The joy on her face quickly turned to hurt but he did not dare stop to right the matter now and rode on, feeling even more angry.

They rode southward, intending to visit with the related Teton Sioux bands, known as Lakota among the related tribes, along the way, eventually hoping to find an enemy camp of Arikaras, or some other, to raid. It was not all serious. The weather was hot and the game plentiful as they traveled through the golden prairie grasses, waving in the hot summer winds like billowing clouds. White Eagle was teased unmercifully because of Spotted Fawn's rash act and he could not take the teasing well but tried to pass it off, however ineffectually. That it bothered him was apparent and only made the teasing more intense. Even Brown Hair's eyes sparkled with mischief at his discomfort.

They spent some days with a band of Lakota and heard many stories of white encroachment and of the great amounts of furs and hides being transported across the prairies from the Shining Mountains of the west to the white population centers on the banks of the mother of rivers to the east. White Eagle and the rest of his party found much to disturb them in the news and with troubled hearts continued their journey south.

Far south of their Black Hills camp they rested their horses on top of the bluffs overlooking a broad river valley. Moving slowly along the wide river was a caravan of heavily loaded horses and men. White Eagle immediately turned his men away before they were seen and rode quickly out of sight, a plan beginning to form in his mind. Here was such a caravan of white traders as the Lakota had spoken of, their pack animals loaded with furs and hides headed east. Already angered by the tales of waste and destruction caused by these white men, their cheating and debilitating of the Indians so evident in the camp they had visited, the men and women both drinking the white men's liquor, White Eagle needed no more excuse than the sighting of this caravan to know the white men must suffer for their deeds.

Safe from detection, he slid from his horse and the rest of the men followed, squatting in a circle around him and gave their attention to White Eagle.

"I have a new idea. The Lakota told us of the white traders taking their loads of buffalo hides and furs to the east, and it made me sick at heart to learn the very thing we depend on for our life is being squandered in such a way. We have seen, just now, a caravan heading toward the rising sun. We could stop this caravan, brothers, by taking their horses. Why steal from the Indian when we can steal from the whites who are stealing from us?"

They grunted in agreement in unison, except for Brown Hair, who remained respectfully silent, and Big Tree, who asked, "What is your plan?"

"We will wait until dark and sneak into their camp and take all their horses. Without their horses they can't carry the furs. When we reach a village of our brothers we will tell them where to find the hides and furs. The white man will have to trade again to get them back."

Chuckles came from nodding heads as the men saw the humor in this, but Big Tree wanted more.

"I say we kill the white men and take everything."

One or two nodded in agreement, but White Eagle remembered too well the lesson he had learned in their war with the Crees. "No. If the white men are killed it will bring trouble to all the Indians. We don't want retaliation against any of our people. The white men will be less inclined to seek revenge if we take no lives."

Others nodded in agreement with his words and one of the older warriors said, "White Eagle is right. Once we were unwise and we paid dearly for our lack of wisdom. There must be no killing or we would be tracked down and killed likewise and all our people would suffer. White Eagle's way is the only way."

Two Knives' words were enough to sway every man's opinion to White Eagle's side, except Big Tree. He sat frowning sourly, but unwillingly agreed, "It is as White Eagle wishes."

They spent the rest of the afternoon eating and resting and at dark they mounted their horses and rode to the edge of the bluffs, found a trail down to the river valley, and picked up the broad, well-defined track of the fur traders. They saw the glow from the traders' campfire after riding a number of miles in cautious silence. Leaving their horses with Brown Hair to guard and bring when they had the stolen herd moving, they crawled closer on hands and knees and finally bellies, in the tall, rustling grass that was all the cover they had. The traders had camped next to the river, using the river as one side of their corral. The other three sides were made up of their packs and gear. Inside this confined area the horses were hobbled and tethered. White Eagle hadn't foreseen difficulty like this. They would have little chance to get the horses in such a confined space, if any chance at all. He motioned his men back and they moved back to where Brown Hair waited.

Big Tree sneered at him. "So! What great plan do you propose now, White Eagle?"

White Eagle was not intimidated. "Patience, Big Tree. We must have patience. This is the first time we have raided a white man's camp. We need to learn their routine. I say we watch for the right time to take their horses. Surely it will come if we are patient. Do all of you agree?"

There was a chorus of grunts from all but Big Tree, and he stated, "We are fools to listen to White Eagle. I say we ride in and overpower them. You will never have any better chance than now."

Two Knives loyally said, "No. We must have patience. I say we wait and see what happens tonight and tomorrow. If by tomorrow's moon we have not seen our chance, then we will do it your way."

Every man grunted approval and Big Tree was the first to take up his weapons and start back toward the traders' camp.

White Eagle told Brown Hair, "Take the horses out of sight. If the sun rises before we have attacked, they will be seen."

Brown Hair nodded silently and gathered together the lead ropes of the horses and moved away with them. White Eagle ran to catch up with his warriors and they moved silently toward the camp, crawling when they came close enough to be detected on the broad grassy river bottom affording not even a tree to hide behind.

They lay watching the camp and skillfully camouflaged themselves with the grass and weeds available until they would be virtually undetectable in daylight. They saw the campfire dwindle and the traders turn into their beds with two of the men remaining awake to keep guard. Still no opening was apparent to take the horses.

At first light of morning, White Eagle was awake and watching the camp. The cool, crystal-clear air magnified the sounds of the waking camp and the coughing, throat clearing, and other noises of men waking came distinctly to White Eagle's ears. The cooking fire was built up and men began to move inside the barricade of packs. The voices sounded good-natured as the white men talked and laughed but White Eagle couldn't define any words.

Then, in totally unexpected good fortune, the opportunity they sought materialized. The men were untying the horses and driving them outside the protective corral to graze. By sheer luck they were headed straight toward where White Eagle and his five companions lay. Every man held his breath and lay still as the traders scanned the vast open landscape in which nothing moved. Assured that nothing was within miles of them, the traders turned back into the camp and the horses came grazing in their direction. They lay so still the horses only snuffled curiously at their smell and continued grazing until White Eagle and his men were lying in a grove of hobbled horse legs. Slowly they began to move among the horses, cutting hobbles and speaking in soft reassuring tones to keep the horses calm.

The traders were eating and the smell of their food came

drifting tantalizingly to the hungry Indians. White Eagle's stomach growled loudly, and a skittish horse threw up its head and whickered suspiciously, sidestepping away from him as he reached for it. The neigh alerted the traders and they turned heads in unison to see what was bothering the horses. One of the men rose to take a better look and White Eagle knew they would be discovered. He looked quickly around and saw one of his men standing and heard the traders exclaim as they saw him, too. The camp became a confusion of noise and shouts as the men jumped to their feet, casting aside tin plates as they reached for their guns. White Eagle leaped up and caught the offending horse and slipped a rope over its tossing head and bent to cut its hobbles. Shots exploded the silence and the horses began to mill nervously. White Eagle leaped onto the back of the shying horse he held and saw the rest of his men doing the same. More shots whizzed into their midst as they circled the frightened horses and lashed out at them, yelling to scare them into the direction they wished them to go.

White Eagle saw Big Tree on the opposite side of the herd, still on the ground as he struggled with a panicked horse. One of the traders was running toward him while the rest stopped to reload their guns. He saw Big Tree gain the back of the frightened horse and urged his own horse after the running herd.

They herded the horses along the steep bluffs marking the edge of the river valley and kept them going until they found the trail they had used coming down the night before and chased them all the way to the top. All the run was gone out of the horses, and they slowed down and were easily turned to where Brown Hair waited. The other four men could handle them now, and White Eagle rode back to the rim of the bluff and looked for Big Tree. He was coming up the bluff.

Big Tree gained the top of the bluff, and White Eagle saw a fresh scalp dangling from his belt.

Angrily he confronted him. "There was to be no killing."

Big Tree grinned wryly. "It is as you wish, White Eagle. I only took his scalp."

"Where is he?"

"I left him down there." Big Tree turned his horse and pointed down the bluff and White Eagle saw what he had missed before in his concern for Big Tree. The dark figure of the man lay at the bottom of the bluff.

Without another word to Big Tree he urged his horse back down the bluff to the prone and bleeding man. He slid from his

horse and bent over the man's body. Blood pulsed from the circular wound on the crown of his head. He turned the man over and
held his ear to his heart. The heartbeat was still strong and he
would live if he didn't bleed to death before his companions found
him. But not here—he was too far away. White Eagle cut the sleeves
from the man's new-looking shirt, made a thick pad, and tied it
snugly over the neat incision. Then he lifted the man onto his horse
and rode, holding him, along the trail to the trader's camp.

When he was within sight of the camp he stopped his horse and
helped the man to the ground. He stirred and opened his eyes and
started in fear. White Eagle held him and pointed toward the
camp, and the man, too much in shock to fight, looked with
frightened eyes where White Eagle pointed.

Weakly he questioned, "What're you doin'? What're you wantin' me to do?"

White Eagle pulled the man to his feet and turned him toward
the camp and released him. The man sagged weakly, and White
Eagle had to hold him to keep him from falling. The man would
never be able to walk the distance to the camp. He raised his head
and cried out in perfect imitation of a wolf to attract the attention
of the camp. The man he held trembled with uncertainty, and he
lowered him gently to the ground. He mounted his horse and
circled the spot several times as he watched the traders come
cautiously out of their camp with rifles held ready. He turned his
horse away from the wounded man and set it at a gallop along the
trail toward where his party waited.

He found them on top of the bluffs, rode into their midst, and
said, "I am ready now. It is time to go."

Each man took his string of horses and headed at a trot northward, reaching their camp in the Black Hills after a few days' ride,
arriving in triumph. The trip had taken less than two weeks and
White Eagle felt a strange excitement at the thought of seeing
Spotted Fawn again. He tried to repress the feeling, but when he
saw her among the crowd waiting to welcome them as they rode in
with their herd of horses, it was impossible to ignore his desire for
her.

They held a scalp dance celebration for Big Tree, and the
camp, eager for something to relieve the tension of waiting for
their men to return, turned out in force to honor Big Tree. Several
maidens sought the honor of carrying his scalp pole since he had
no wife, but his mother refused any girl the honor and they had to
be content to dance and sing.

White Eagle, not approving of the act of taking the man's scalp, didn't attend the scalp dance and stayed in the warriors' lodge. He sat smoking quietly, thinking, until his thoughts were interrupted by Spotted Fawn's call. He moved to the back of the lodge, which was out of view of the people gathered for the dance, and raised the lodge cover.

Spotted Fawn kneeled on the ground and asked in a whisper, "Are you alone?"

"Yes. But you shouldn't be here."

Her answer was to put her arms around him and raise her lips to his. His body responded instantly to her touch and he kissed her long and well. Breathing heavily, he finally pushed her away. "Now go, before you are seen."

"No. Not until you tell me if you will marry me."

"I haven't decided yet. I will not decide until after I have gone to the sacred hill again. Now go!"

"I love you," she whispered as she rose.

White Eagle groaned in agony and let the hide fall, cutting off the sight of her, but he couldn't forget the feel of her and placed his hands over his groin until his breechclout lay flat and smooth again. He had to end this torment. As soon as the fall hunt was over he would have to seek his vision again.

The bands broke camp the next day and started the long journey back across the Missouri to their own hunting grounds for the fall hunt. With relief White Eagle took charge of his duties as his warrior society was picked to supervise and police the trek home. It was the escape he needed, and when the first herd of fat, thickly robed buffalo were sighted, the camp was quickly chosen and the work of slaughtering additional winter food began. In the days following the first sighting of the buffalo, White Eagle had little time to think of Spotted Fawn, but when the hunter's work was done, he went to the medicine man's lodge and entered. He was bidden to sit and smoke in the time-honored ritual.

When the ritual was over the shaman asked him, "You are troubled, White Eagle. How can I help?"

"I wish to go to the sacred hill again. I need to seek a new vision or verify the old vision."

"Ah! You doubt the Great Spirit brought you a true vision?"

"No. But I want to make certain the vision I have has not changed."

The old man looked intently at him. "Why?"

"My vision foretold of my wife's death in childbirth. I wish to take a wife but can not if I know she will die bearing my child."

The shaman looked thoughtful. "Yes. I remember now. It was a strange vision. One we thought was perhaps not a true vision. It is not against custom to go again to seek your vision. Come with me. We will begin preparations."

He followed the shaman to the sweat lodge, stopping long enough at the warrior lodge to ask Two Knives if he would accompany him. They stripped off what clothing they wore outside the sweat lodge and entered completely naked and sat in respectful silence while the shaman proceeded with the purification rites. When the fire was finally lit, White Eagle and Two Knives rubbed themselves with pungent sage to purify themselves while the shaman prayed to the deities.

By afternoon, White Eagle and Two Knives were able to leave on their journey to the sacred hill where they would stay until White Eagle received his vision. When they reached the hill they made camp, and White Eagle made further preparations to climb the steep and rocky hill. When he was at last ready, he left Two Knives behind and, naked, without weapons, food, or water, he climbed the hill.

He found the place where he had lain more than three years before and settled down to wait and watch, taking in everything happening around him. Everything was important in vision seeking. Even the flight of a bird or the squeak of a cricket held meaning, and he must remember everything. Unlike the first trip to this hill, the weather was not warm. He was barely warm enough during the day when the air was warmed by the sun, but at night the bitter cold wind blew across the hill and he spent hours walking or running to keep warm.

Without food and water his strength failed quickly and he wondered if death would come before his vision. The more he suffered the more he wished it, until he was convinced the symbol of the eagle's nest in the first vision meant death, and he lay cold and wretched, waiting for it with his eyes wide open, praying for an end to the torture of his body.

The wind increased and he felt the icy chill knife through his already cold body and he shivered violently. Black clouds raced across the sky and the first terrifying bolt of many bolts of lightning struck the hilltop with thunder crashing deafeningly before the light of the bolt had disappeared. Huge hailstones, as large as grouse gizzards, pounded his body, bruising him with wind-driven force of hard-thrown stones. He crawled agonizingly to a rock where a wolf had dug a den at one time and crawled into it as the earth shook with the thunder and lightning playing tag on top of the hill.

A bolt struck so near it blinded him and he held his hands over his seared eyes as the power and fury of it surged through him, making his skin tingle, and he heard the voice coming as it had come before, from the wind and thunder. The chill left his body as the voice commanded, "Open your eyes and see the vision you seek."

He slowly dropped his hands and out of the blackness came the bright piercing light. He kept his eyes on it until he saw it take shape and come as it had come before in the form of a doe and consume him with the feeling of love and contentment. He cried when the vision faded, but the voice reminded him, "These things must be. Look again."

He looked and closed his eyes against the blood-bay mare with the death's skull head. The tears ran down his face as he shouted, "No! Whoever you are, whatever you are, no!"

The voice filled his ears again. "These things shall and will come to pass. It is written in your life. Do not try to resist them. Do not try to change them. Go now and do what I command is to be done in your life."

The blinding light faded and he saw only the faint blue luminescence of his own skin, glowing strangely, frighteningly. He crawled from the wolf den on hands and knees and found the trail leading down from the hilltop as the storm moved off the hill and crossed the plains like a dark veil. He reached the bottom of the hill, shaken and weak. He called Two Knives and stood leaning against a rock for support.

Two Knives came hesitantly toward him and stopped a few feet away, terrified. "What happened, White Eagle? You look strange. Look how your skin glows like frost fire. Are you all right?"

"I'm all right. It is the fire of the thunder god on my skin. I felt it go through me."

"Can you walk? I'm afraid to touch you."

"I'll try." He let go of the rock and took a step and sagged to his knees. Two Knives bent to help him as he tried to push himself up. He raised his hand to Two Knives and as their hands touched, sparks flew and Two Knives jerked his hand away with a cry.

"It is true! The fire of the thunder god is in you."

White Eagle looked at his body and the strange blue glow was gone. He said, "Look, it is gone. Your touch released the power of it. Help me."

Reluctantly, Two Knives reached again to take White Eagle's hand and this time no sparks flew. Assured, he lifted White Eagle to his side and helped him into camp, wrapping him in a heavy robe before the fire while he fixed food for him to eat.

After a good night's sleep, White Eagle felt strong enough to start back to the village. He didn't want to wait longer. It was cold and miserable and every day would only make the weather more unbearable. They reached camp and White Eagle went immediately to the sweat lodge to repeat his vision to the shaman under the oath of truth. The ritual was done and the questioning began as several of the wise men of the village witnessed his story along with the shaman and Two Knives.

"Did you receive a vision, White Eagle?"

"Yes."

"Was it the same vision as before or a different vision?"

"It was the same."

"How do you know it spoke true?"

"I don't know. I have no proof except my eyes and my ears. The voice was the same. The symbols were the same. It was as it was before."

The shaman turned to Two Knives and asked, "Do you believe he saw a vision?"

"I think he speaks true. When he came down from the hill he glowed with the fire of the thunder god. When I touched him the fire went through me. Truly he has been touched by the thunder god."

The men looked at each other and at White Eagle with widening eyes. This was something so magical they would have to speak of it in private but their minds were already made up. They were convinced the man before them had been touched by the thunder god and was therefore to be held in reverence. White Eagle would not know it then, but from that moment he would be spoken of as Touched by Thunder and his life would become legend among them. He would be, indeed already was in their eyes, chief, because he had been chosen by the thunder god.

The shaman asked of the elders, "What say you?"

One by one they nodded in solemn acceptance that his vision had been a true one.

"We have accepted your vision as true. Go now and be at peace. The thunder god guides and guards you."

Two Knives and White Eagle left the sweat lodge and went to the river to cool their bodies in the chill water. Already the camp crier was announcing he had returned with a true vision, and when he and Two Knives returned to the lodge of their warrior society, Spotted Fawn waited with food for them. He didn't want to talk to her just yet. He was still confused and uncertain. His vision had all but commanded that he must take her, yet he hoped for some other way. He took the offered food but said nothing as she stood respectfully silent with head down. He started into the lodge and she touched him. He waited without turning toward her, not wanting to look at her.

Softly she asked, "Don't you want to talk to me?"

"Not now. Later when I have decided what I must do."

"Has not your vision already told you what you must do?"

"Yes. But I'm not sure I want to obey it."

Her hand fell away and he ducked inside the lodge too upset even to eat what she had brought. Tired, cold, and confused, he rolled into his robes while the others ate his meal and talked with Two Knives of their journey, and he slept a restless sleep.

The morning dawned clear and cool, the storm having moved on during the night. White Eagle, still confused and depressed by his experience on the sacred hill, wanted and needed time to accept the truth of his vision. More than anything else he needed assurance that he should follow the vision. Only one man had wisdom to help him and that man was Snow Cloud. He went to his father's lodge to seek help. Snow Cloud greeted him with a smile and after they had smoked, White Eagle made a suggestion.

"You promised to take me to the sacred place of pipestone. I am ready to go now if you can go with me."

Snow Cloud answered, "It is a good time to go. We can leave when the sun rises. Will you stay and have food with us?"

He rose in rejection of the offer, Spotted Fawn's presence too disturbing. "No. I have something I must do. Another time."

In the morning they left camp and rode southeastward toward the Big Sioux River and the area of the pipestone quarry. Snow Cloud had invited a number of men to go with them, Brown Hair among them. They rode without fear, confident they were well armed and strong enough to protect themselves from any hostile parties that might cross their path. It was a trip to enjoy for all of them except White Eagle. While the others laughed and joked, he sat in gloomy silence, wrapped in his own problem.

They crossed the Big Sioux River in a few days' time and

camped near the pipestone quarry and made preparations to walk on the sacred ground. In the morning White Eagle and Snow Cloud went into the quarry while their companions stood guard nearby. Snow Cloud walked among the slabs of rose-colored clay, looking for the exact piece that would make the best pipe. White Eagle followed, and when Snow Cloud found what he was looking for, White Eagle watched as Snow Cloud carefully chiseled the soft rock into the right-sized piece.

"I have something I wish to speak of now, Father."

Snow Cloud straightened from his exacting carving and gave his full attention to White Eagle. "Is it about Spotted Fawn and your vision?"

"Yes. What shall I do?"

"No man can tell you what you should do, my son. No man knows what has happened between you and Spotted Fawn and no man can know, but you, how you feel about her. Pretend for a moment I am you and have just asked you what I should do in the same circumstances. Can you not find the answer?"

White Eagle couldn't answer. It was too obvious to him what he should do. Distressed, he said, "I do not want her to die."

"I have talked to her about this. She is not afraid to die. She would gladly accept death as your wife, so great is her love for you. If you do not take her I am afraid she will take her own life. Is this not so?"

"Yes. She has spoken of it."

"Then you have no choice. Your grief will be great when she dies but I think your guilt and shame if you let her take her own life in dishonor will be far greater. Are you so small a man you would let her die thusly?"

White Eagle turned away in agony. He could refuse her no longer. If he had never taken her virtue it might have been possible to save her, but not now. Snow Cloud was right. He had no choice but to carry out his vision, and he felt a deep and wondering awe at the power ruling his life so strongly that a careless act in his uncertain manhood, seemingly so long ago, had dictated this moment. Truly the most powerful of gods ruled him, and he kneeled on the sacred ground and exhorted the god of thunder to give him strength and wisdom.

He felt Snow Cloud's hand on his shoulder and looked up.

"I have your calumet, my son."

White Eagle rose and ran his fingers over the smooth block of clay which would be so carefully transported back to their camp and so exactingly hollowed into a pipe for him by the pipemaker and sanctified by the shaman. "I am ready to return. I have made my decision."

Snow Cloud smiled with approval. "Good."

The evening of the day they returned to camp, White Eagle took one horse and tied it in front of Snow Cloud's lodge. If the horse was accepted it would be gone in the morning and he and Spotted Fawn would be betrothed. He spent a restless night and was awake early to see if the horse was gone from in front of Snow Cloud's lodge. He walked with uncertain steps toward his father's lodge and stood looking at the place where he had left the horse. The horse was gone. His proposal had been accepted, as he knew it would be, against all hope. He raised the door flap and went in and was greeted by Brown Hair and Morning Star with unconcealed delight. Spotted Fawn sat in shy, trembling silence, her face glowing. Snow Cloud asked him to be seated and they smoked.

When they both had smoked, White Eagle asked, "How many horses do you wish in payment for Spotted Fawn?"

Snow Cloud responded with, "How many do you think she is worth?"

White Eagle looked up to see if Snow Cloud was serious and saw a sly wink. He smiled and answered, "I can not place a value on her in horses." He heard Spotted Fawn's soft gasp.

"Neither can I, my son, but I would ask of you five horses to give to the most deserving among our people. When you have done this, you may have her. Will you live here?"

"No. I wish us to have our own lodge. This winter I will bring her the hides she will need to make our lodge cover and the rest of the things we will need. After the Sun Dance, when we move to the Black Hills, I will take her when we will be able to cut the poles for our lodge." He heard Spotted Fawn's muffled sob and knew she was not happy with his decision. He rose to leave and went to stand before her and touched the top of her bent head with his hand. "I will talk to you tonight, Spotted Fawn."

He came back after sundown with his robe over his arm and blew his love flute outside Snow Cloud's lodge. Spotted Fawn came immediately and he led her away from the lodge and any curious onlookers. Contrary to most Indian courtships, he wanted what he did and what he said unwitnessed. When they were out of sight along the river bank, he unfolded his robe and put it around himself, holding out his arm to take her in close and cover her, too, but she stood with head down, resisting, even though the night was cold.

"You are unhappy because I wish to wait until summer?"

"Yes. I want to be with you now. I would not mind living in Snow Cloud's lodge."

"I know. But if my vision is true and I believe it is, we do not have much time to be together, a year, maybe less. I want us to be alone and free to spend all our time together without interference. I do not wish to share you or our love with anyone."

She came into his arms then and he enfolded her in the robe. She shivered against him and raised her face and he kissed her. "I love you so very much it will be hard to wait, but now that I know the reason I can be patient. I will have much to do."

"I will start hunting tomorrow."

She hugged him tighter and he felt a deep, warm contentment. The urgency of his need for her was still there, but he had no trouble controlling it now. The wind picked up, its cold chill soon penetrating even the thick robe, and Spotted Fawn shivered again.

"We had better go in now. Do not be unhappy if I do not come often. We have long to wait, and holding you makes the waiting difficult."

She nodded and whispered through chattering teeth, "I understand."

He kissed her again and, not altogether willingly, walked her back to Snow Cloud's lodge.

22

SPOTTED FAWN

The months passed as White Eagle hunted and trapped, bringing almost everything he caught to Spotted Fawn. He saw her only at the times when he brought something to her and only at these times did their hands touch or their glances of love tell the other the hardship of waiting they were feeling. Spring came and White Eagle felt his eagerness grow with the greening of the plains. He welcomed the mild days when he could be gone hunting with the other men for days at a time, involving himself totally, purposely leaving him little time to think about Spotted Fawn.

The Sun Dance celebration was the most difficult time of all. The gathered camps reuniting in complete abandon made it all the easier for him to see Spotted Fawn and the desire he had kept reasonably under control became almost impossible to restrain in an atmosphere where everyone was doing whatever they wanted. He had numerous opportunities to see Spotted Fawn alone, but knew avoidance was the only possible way to keep from taking her before he was ready. When the first days of reunion were over he was once again in control.

When the Sun Dance gathering broke up he could hardly contain his joy, but as the camp hunted before moving slowly toward the Black Hills, his joy turned to anxiety. When they finally made camp in the Black Hills he had to force himself to take his horses to Snow Cloud's lodge and help Spotted Fawn pack the household goods she had been making all winter for their own lodge. Her excited laughter as she carried things for him to pack only added to his depression. At last they mounted their horses and, leading two heavily laden pack horses, they left camp amid cheers, giggles, and jests, most of which were obscene.

He led her for over a mile up the canyon until it was a narrow, secluded defile, thick with pines and cool between high rock walls. Snow Cloud would see that they were guarded and not disturbed. While Spotted Fawn unpacked, he selected and cut trees to make poles for their lodge and brought them in until they had enough for a circle large enough to support the cover she had made. Together they fitted the hides over the poles and raised it slowly toward the top, adjusting it as it required, until their lodge was complete. With unconcealed happiness, Spotted Fawn quickly and efficiently arranged her lodge, saving the bed for last. He tended the horses and, too tense to sit idly, he brought wood.

When Spotted Fawn had everything ready she came to the lodge door and asked demurely, "Would my husband like to eat now?"

Nervously he went inside. The fire was laid but unlit, their belongings neatly arranged, new mats and robes on the ground, and a large fur- and robe-covered couch stood waiting. He went to it and sat down, sinking deep in its soft comfort. He had never seen a better-made or more finely decorated set of household furnishings than Spotted Fawn's. Fear and uncertainty were replaced with pride at her accomplishment. She stood expectant and shy at the door and he looked at her for the first time, taking in every detail of her elaborately decorated white doeskin dress and jewelry, all painstakingly done for her wedding. He hadn't even noticed them before.

With a catch in his voice he said, "You look very lovely, Spotted Fawn. You have done well with what I have brought you. I have never seen more beautifully decorated things than these. I am very pleased."

"I am glad you are pleased, my husband."

Still she stood and his uncertainty returned as he looked at her, taking in her slender beauty, feeling desire filling him. He asked, "Did you wish to eat now?"

"No, my husband."

He was torn with wanting her and fear and sought delay with, "I am hungry. Would you fix me something?"

She sprang to life then as if released from some strange enchantment, lighting the fire in the darkening lodge, and brought out some choice pemmican for him. She served it to him with a variety of fresh and dried fruits and sat across from him waiting to do his every command. He ate a couple of bites and found his appetite gone. It was no use. He would have to consummate their marriage sooner or later and delay only added to his tension. He set the platter aside and she looked up in dismay.

"It does not please you?"

"It pleases me but I cannot eat now. I torture us with delay because I am afraid. I know what I do will bring your death and I wish I could delay forever but my body cannot wait."

She came to him and kneeled on the soft fur robe spread beside the couch, her arms going around him. "I am not afraid. I do not believe I will die for many winters. I will bear you many sons before I die. Do not be afraid for me. If I die, I will die proudly and happily, for I am your wife and am the envy of every maiden in the Sioux nation."

He raised her head and looked into the large black eyes so filled with love for him and brimming with emotional tears. He kissed her and her body pressed against his with desire. He helped her remove her bridal dress and she kneeled before him, firelight dancing on her slender, supple body. His lips touched her small, firm breasts and every fear and doubt was swept away by erupting passions as they came together in fierce, suffocating desire, which quickly consumed him and left them both only a little less inexperienced than they had been before.

In the next few days their knowledge grew as they spent days and nights in undisturbed and complete absorption in discovering the delights of each other. But when the first intense and totally selfish, self-indulgent physical demands were finally becoming satisfied, a remarkable transformation began to take place in White Eagle. With increasing consciousness of what would be the ultimate result of their physical love, he became more and more concerned with her every response to him, finding little gratification in his satisfaction if she was not also gratified. His love turned outward, wanting to give to her all the happiness he was capable of giving. He took more time with her, controlling his own desires, seeking her approval in all he attempted to do to please her. At first she was reticent, completely subjugated to his dominance over her life, and anything he wished was her command, but he persisted and she finally became more candid about her desires, instructing him as she had when he was a child. Ineptness turned to art and a love that had been founded on physical attraction and the circumstance of close association became a rapport of mind and body, needing no words, so intense was their awareness of each other's needs and desires. The rewards were greater than White Eagle had thought possible. The contentment and love he felt were far more over-whelming than he had felt during his vision.

The time came when Spotted Fawn, by custom, should be returned to the main camp and be isolated in the women's lodge, but he didn't take her, ignoring the taboo of contamination her condition was supposed to bring to his sacred objects and weapons, and insisted she share his bed as they would have little time to be alone left. Their wedding moon would be over shortly after her menses ended. When that day came, they loaded their horses with regret and returned to the camp of their people.

They were welcomed back with no less enthusiasm than when they had left. Spotted Fawn set up their lodge next to Snow Cloud's and they became part of the band once more. For White Eagle it was a very trying time. He wanted to be alone with Spotted Fawn, and his lodge suddenly became a meeting place for the camp as everyone came to see the new lodge and to admire the quality of Spotted Fawn's handiwork. Out of sheer frustration he went hunt-ing to keep his anger from erupting at the intrusion of his privacy. Spotted Fawn consoled him by assuring him interest in them would soon wane, but it lasted far longer than he liked.

Soon it was time to start the journey back to their hunting grounds, and White Eagle was relieved to be moving and took part in policing the move with the men of his warrior society. The relief was only temporary as he found too much of his time had to be spent away from Spotted Fawn. He could have refused his duty but he had too much sense of responsibility to do so. He grew even more unhappy with the night guard duty but accepted it, promis-ing himself it would be the last time. Too precious was their time together to be wasted in separation.

He even resented the buffalo hunt which began shortly after their return to the plains, knowing each animal he killed would have to be taken care of by Spotted Fawn. He killed with a vengeance and brought a minimal amount to his own lodge, giving most of his kill away and spending the greatest part of the day waiting for her to finish her tasks so she could be with him. He remembered, then, what his mother had told him about his father. He wanted to be the kind of a man for Spotted Fawn he visualized his father had been. He had not understood her meaning then, but he understood it fully now and, defying all custom, he went to help Spotted Fawn. She looked at him with shock as he joined her with his knife and began cutting strips of buffalo flesh to be dried.

"What are you doing! You shouldn't be doing this! What will the people think?"

He kept right on working and answered, "I do not care what the people think. My happiness is being with you and sharing my life with yours for the time we have. Does it matter what we do as long as it is together?"

She smiled at him warmly. "No, my husband, but you will be the joke on everyone's lips."

He looked at her and asked, "Is my manhood so suspect that I need worry?"

She giggled and met his eyes. "No, but you do not take joking well, I have heard."

He smiled at her in agreement. "No. But I am not afraid to defend my honor."

In the days and weeks that followed, he helped her. She had no old mother to save her hands from the acid mixture of brains and urine used to tan the hides, so he did it for her, and together they taught each other the skills needed to turn out the soft robes and skins their life depended on. He became the laughingstock of the camp and the butt of much vicious gossip. At first he was asked to join in the men's hunts but as he refused, they stopped asking. He didn't let it bother him, finding far more reward in being with Spotted Fawn and sharing their every moment. When Brown Hair began to shun him he realized more was involved than just his honor.

He followed Brown Hair to the river one day and sat down beside the quiet boy. "I am sorry I have brought you shame, but you should not feel shame for what I do."

Brown Hair's face twisted in anger. "Do you know what they say about you? The man who was to be chief! And you do nothing about it! Even Snow Cloud's honor is tarnished. I am ashamed that you are my brother!"

The bitterness of his words shocked White Eagle but he kept calm and asked, "What do they say? I have not bothered to listen for it has been of little concern to me."

Brown Hair looked at him in disgust and turned away in rejection of the man he had once thought perfect. "They say you are a woman. That you have lost your manhood and should wear a woman's dress."

"And you believe this is true?"

Brown Hair's eyes came back to him, wavering in their uncertainty. "I do not know what to believe. I see the same brother I loved and honored, but I see him do woman's work."

"I do a woman's work not because I am a woman but because I love Spotted Fawn and want to share everything with her. You know the prophecy of my vision. She is to die with my child. We may have a little time together or we may have a long time, but I want to make what time we have together filled with happiness for her. Can you understand that, my brother?"

Vehemently he answered, "No woman is worth losing your honor for."

"Who says I have lost my honor? I have not changed. I have only grown to know some things are more important than saving honor. Would you choose honor over giving life to someone you love? I don't think you would. Now, do you wish to test my manhood, brother?"

Brown Hair was silent for a long while, staring unseeing at the water until White Eagle saw tears roll down his cheeks. He stood abruptly and ran along the bank away from White Eagle and White Eagle watched him go with a heavy heart. It was possible he was wrong in what he was doing but he didn't believe he was. He rose and walked back to camp.

Spotted Fawn greeted him with a smile which quickly changed to concern. "What is wrong?"

He sat beside her and put his arm around her. "I have just spoken with Brown Hair. It seems I have not only shamed myself but have brought shame to my brother and father, also."

"I know. The women speak of little else."

"You should have told me."

"I knew you would hear it soon enough."

"Are you ashamed, too?"

Her hand came to his face. "I am not ashamed of you. I know what you are. But I feel shame for you because you humble yourself for me in front of everyone and I feel shame for letting you do it, even though I know why you do this for me. If I could convince you I was in no danger and get you to stop, I would, but your vision is more powerful than my words and I have not wanted to beg you to stop because then I would destroy the very thing that has made your love the greatest love of all. There is no other like you."

He took her hand and kissed it, and she pressed into his arms. "I would not change what I have done but somehow I must give my family back their honor."

"Perhaps we should go live among your mother's people. Do they not look differently on these things?"

"I understood so from her, but I have no desire to live with the whites. No. We will stay here and I will win this in my own way. And I will also promise you that if you bear our first child without dying I will stop bringing you the shame of my help in front of our people. Now I think I must see Snow Cloud."

"Surely he understands?"

"I think he does but I would like to talk with him about it. His wisdom is greater than mine." He kissed her and left the lodge and went directly into Snow Cloud's.

Snow Cloud greeted him but there was no happiness in the older man's face. "Sit, my son, and we will smoke and perhaps talk?"

White Eagle sat and when the first ritual smoking was done, he said, "Brown Hair has told me I have dishonored my family. Do you feel this way, too, my father?"

"Brown Hair is young and has idolized you. It is hard for him to understand what you are going through. But to some extent what he says is true. I do not doubt you are still worthy of honor, but the young men who would be chiefs are causing much talk. I cannot defend you, my son, only you can do that. What is done, is done, but the consequences are perhaps greater than any of us could have imagined."

"Yes. I was thinking only of Spotted Fawn and myself. I am ready to defend my honor when the time comes. I have not changed. I have only found something more important than honor."

A ghost of a smile touched Snow Cloud's face. "I knew it was so but I am glad you have told me. I do not fear for your honor or your manhood. I only fear it will cause the elders to doubt you and your rightful place."

"For that I am sorry. I should have had more wisdom, or at least the wisdom to have asked your advice, but since I cannot change what I have done, I can only prove that what once was, still is. But do not ask me to change what I do, for I cannot. I will tell you what I have told Spotted Fawn. If she lives through the birth of our first child I will try not to bring you shame again."

"I understand, but will the people understand and remember when the young men dishonor your name?"

White Eagle absorbed all the meaning in Snow Cloud's words and knew he was right. The fit leader must think of all the people.

"You are right. Maybe it is a sign that I should not be their leader."

"No! If I thought so I would tell you. Even what you do for Spotted Fawn tells me, more than anything else, you have a greater capacity to lead them justly than any other, for you have the deeper feelings which are lacking in men who want only power. But you must prove it to them."

White Eagle stood. "I will try, Father." He left the lodge and heard Morning Star, who had witnessed the whole conversation, come after him. He turned and smiled at her.

She looked into his face briefly with questioning concern and dropped her eyes. "I am still proud you are my brother."

His hand touched her shoulder in appreciation of her words, unable to find words of his own before she darted back into Snow Cloud's lodge and left him standing alone. He went back into his own lodge and sat down. Spotted Fawn looked at him with questioning eyes.

"Snow Cloud does not doubt me. But I have been thinking of what he said. The next time it is your time to be isolated maybe you should go to the women's lodge and I should join the men."

She threw her arms around him with a little cry of happiness. "It is what I hoped you would do. But what if I don't need to be isolated?"

He frowned, not wanting to think about that aspect of their relationship. "Then I will not leave you until it is necessary."

In a few days Spotted Fawn needed fresh meat and he took her with him to hunt. When they returned with an antelope, he was helping her scrape the hide outside when Big Tree and several of his closest confederates approached. They stood nearby making sarcastic comments until White Eagle could stand no more. Spotted Fawn saw the anger in his eyes and laid a restraining hand on his arm, but he threw it off and rose to face Big Tree.

"If Big Tree has something he wishes to say to me, why doesn't he say it to my face?"

"That is hard to do. We do not know which way you face. You look yet like a man but you do a woman's work. We have brought you a present so we can tell what you are." Big Tree was handed a bundle and as he shook it out laughter accompanied the act. He tossed the dress at White Eagle's feet and said, "Put it on. It becomes you."

White Eagle stood in smoldering anger while the people of the camp rushed to witness the confrontation. Now was the time to defend his honor. He drew his knife and held it before him threateningly. "Do you wish to test my manhood, Big Tree?"

The mocking laughter died as Big Tree drew his knife and said with years of hatred rasping in his voice, "I will prove you have no manhood."

They circled each other warily, looking for an opening, until Big Tree lunged in viciously with his knife aimed for White Eagle's stomach. White Eagle, quicker and more lithe of movement, jumped out of reach and darted past Big Tree, his own knife drawing a thin line of blood as he barely drew it across Big Tree's thigh. Big Tree turned, his face black with anger, and lunged again at White Eagle and he could not elude Big Tree a second time. He leaped backward and to the side but Big Tree was prepared for such a move and their bodies smacked together as the bigger man threw his weight into White Eagle, knocking him to the ground and falling on top of him. White Eagle was already prepared for the lunge and had his legs curled to catapult the larger man away from him. He expected to throw Big Tree on his back with the force of his legs but the larger man was too heavy and landed in a sitting position from which he quickly gained his feet.

They circled one another again and White Eagle knew he was at a serious disadvantage. While Big Tree was slower of movement, his mind was just as agile as White Eagle's. There would be no way to trick him, and Big Tree's strength was greater than his own. His only hope was his endurance and speed. He darted in, feinting a thrust, and Big Tree dodged in the opposite direction. White Eagle swiftly plunged the knife at his opponent, who was caught off balance and fell heavily with White Eagle on top of him, trying for a throat hold. Big Tree's powerful hand gripped his wrist and they slashed at each other with their knives, oblivious to the shouts around them as the crowd of people urged them on.

Big Tree threw White Eagle off, knocking the wind from him and leaving him vulnerable for a brief moment. Big Tree pounced on him only a split second too late or the knife which slid dangerously along his ribs would have been between them. He caught Big Tree's leg and twisted it, using Big Tree's own momentum to throw the man from his own body. He scrambled to his feet, grabbing at his knife, and they met head on, hands locked on wrists and straining to the breaking point. White Eagle kicked Big Tree's leg out from underneath the larger man and they fell heavily, White Eagle capitalizing on the force of the fall to knock Big Tree's knife from his hand as his own knife sliced flesh on Big Tree's other wrist. Big Tree released his grip for an instant and White Eagle pulled free. Big Tree heaved upward with all his strength and dislodged White Eagle, and he found himself the one on the ground, kicking and slashing to avoid the choking hands of his attacker, as he rolled free. Big Tree retrieved his knife and stood with his breath coming heavily, waiting now for White Eagle to dart in again. White Eagle circled, looking for the right moment, trying to determine a vulnerable spot, but there was none. He couldn't let Big Tree rest and lunged in and out in a series of quick feints, trying to lure Big Tree off guard, but the other man was not to be tricked.

For long minutes he thrust in and out at the bigger man, waiting for a mistake and afraid there would be none, as each of their knives continued to nick and draw blood. Big Tree grew tired of the cat-and-mouse game and charged at White Eagle in desperation. He dodged the big man's knife but not his well-aimed knee, which sent White Eagle sprawling and his knife flying. Dimly he heard Spotted Fawn scream as Big Tree fell on him. He met the big man with both hands driving forcefully into the larger man's neck with enough power to stop his breath and make his eyes roll as he locked his hands around the thick neck, feeling Big Tree's knife tear his ear. Big Tree shuddered with eyes popping and lost his strength as his breath remained cut off in White Eagle's desperate grip. His body sagged and went limp. White Eagle forced Big Tree from him. Releasing his grasp, he found Big Tree's knife and held it against his adversary's throat while the crowd screamed for blood. In a few moments Big Tree's breathing returned to normal and his eyes opened to blink at White Eagle. He lay perfectly still, awaiting his death with dignity, the knife point pressed against his throat.

White Eagle rose and threw the knife away. Through clenched teeth he breathed, "You may live, Big Tree, because this people needs brave and strong men." He turned away and the crowd parted for him as he walked painfully to the river, feeling his many bruises and cuts. He waded into the water and felt some relief as the cold water numbed his abused body.

Two Knives, Snow Cloud, and Brown Hair came with Spotted Fawn to see if he needed help. Brown Hair looked at him with unconcealed admiration and he knew he had won in more ways than one. He came out of the water and Snow Cloud was the first to ask, "Are you all right, my son?"

"Yes."

Buffalo Horn joined them, looking at him with respect. "I came to tell you you still have a place in the warrior society."

"I hear your words, Buffalo Horn, and am glad. I will return to my place in time but not just now." He looked at Spotted Fawn and she glanced at him obliquely. "Now I wish to return to my lodge in peace."

They stood aside for him and he walked back along the trail to camp with his well-wishers following him. He went inside his lodge and no one followed but Spotted Fawn. She came to him immediately.

"Let me see how badly you are cut."

"Not bad."

She frowned at him. "That is what you think. Now turn so I can see."

Quickly she explored his body, ordering him to their couch so she could treat him. He obeyed willingly. When she had all the bleeding stopped, she set on a cooking bladder full of fresh antelope meat for him. After they had eaten she closed and fastened the lodge flap against the cold night wind and joined him on their couch.

"Is all the doubt gone now, my husband?"

He smiled. "Do you think I doubted?"

She laughed. "You always doubt, White Eagle. Perhaps that is what makes you different. But never change. Your doubt will save you."

"You speak in riddles. Am I married to a medicine woman?"

"No. I just know what I know."

He kissed her and despite his bruises and cuts he sought the greater comfort of her body, forgetting all but the warmth of her love and losing himself in it.

23

FROM JOY TO SORROW

The first snow of winter fell on the great plains and the two bands moved to their customary sheltered river bottom. It became easier now for White Eagle to spend every moment with Spotted Fawn— he working on new weapons as she quilled and sewed. His contentment was great and for a while he could almost forget their life could not be like this forever.

In February the illusion ended when it became apparent Spotted Fawn was pregnant. His contentment turned to anxiety and he found it difficult to hold her without feeling guilt and the guilt preyed on his mind until he could not hold her at all. She accepted his withdrawal from her with unquestioning patience, for which he was grateful, but it made it too easy for him to forget her needs while he dwelled on his own guilt. He couldn't resume intimate contact with her as the days lengthened into weeks, unable as he was to overcome his fear and guilt, and he took it for granted she understood the depth of his feeling by her silence.

Even though he had not touched her for weeks, they still shared the same couch and she finally put her arms around him, pressing her body against his, brushing her lips against his smooth, strong back and shoulders until he broke from her grasp and whispered in frustrated agony, "Don't."

"Why not, my husband? What is done, is done. If you believe our time together is short, then you are denying me the only thing I have lived for. I need you more than ever now, White Eagle. I need to know you love me, and you have not touched me for a moon."

He turned to her and the anguish on his face was even more pronounced in the flickering firelight. "You know I love you. That is why I cannot love you now. I see you and know it is my love that is bringing your death, and my manhood dies."

"Then give yourself to me. I need you and I want you. Let me try to give you back your manhood."

He lay still and unanswering and she moved closer to him, kissing him, caressing him, whispering tender words of love, and fondling him until desire overcame guilt and his potency returned. When they finally lay at peace in each other's arms, tears filled his eyes and he buried his face against the softness of her breasts and let them come and she held him, comforting him wordlessly with the assurance of her touch.

At last he whispered against her soft warmth, "If only there were some other way. Is there some other way, Spotted Fawn?"

Her hands rested gently on his head. "No. But I do not believe my life ends with this child. Can you not believe that, too? It has to be. I *will* it to be."

He raised his head and gently brushed his tears from her breasts. "I want to believe it. I almost did." He looked into her face, drinking in the delicate beauty of it. "You are the strong one and I am the weak one. I thought it would be you leaning on me, but I see it is I who leans on you, just as I did when I was small. Maybe Big Tree is right. Maybe I should wear the dress of a woman."

She laughed lightly. "Now you know the secret known by all women."

"That women are the strongest?"

"Yes."

It was his turn to laugh. "No man will ever believe it."

"No. And maybe it is good you do not or you would not love us."

He bent to kiss her and she curled close to him and they slept.

The last cold days of winter passed quickly and spring came again. White Eagle had to go hunting for fresh meat. Spotted Fawn's appetite doubled and she craved fresh meat after a winter of dried food. He hated to leave her more than ever now, the bond between them reinforced by his devotion and sense of duty to make every minute between them happy. The day he felt his child move within her filled him with joy but also made him feel more keenly the regret it would never be his to enjoy. He often felt emotional exhaustion from the joy of living and sharing with Spotted Fawn and the dread of what was to come.

The camp returned to the plains and White Eagle had to hunt. They needed food to sustain them, and Spotted Fawn insisted they would need food when the baby was born. He did as she asked, torn between wanting to be with her and the need to believe she was right.

The Sun Dance gathering came and passed, and they moved after the summer hunt to the Black Hills. Spotted Fawn was no more the slender, willowy woman he had married. She moved heavily now as his child filled her slight body to its limit. His love for her increased as his concern for her grew. Gently now, he lay with her, almost afraid to complete the act that gave so much contentment to them both. By the time their stay in the Black Hills ended, their intimacy was also ended. She rode on a travois all the way to their hunting grounds and he refused to leave her to hunt, knowing her time was near. The lovely smile came seldom now as she covered her discomfort with a mask of stoicism. She begged him to go hunting and, finally, he went, finding the activity helped ease his anxiety as he vented his tension with each deadly arrow.

He returned late in the day after killing a good number of buffalo, bringing her a fat buffalo hump, and went straight to their lodge.

Morning Star was waiting for him. "They have taken Spotted Fawn to the women's lodge."

He turned without a word and went straight to the women's lodge, set a little apart. He cast aside more custom and threw open the door flap. Startled gasps greeted him as the women attending Spotted Fawn eyed him with disapproval.

He braved their stolid stares and ordered, "Leave."

"It is not allowed. These things are women's things."

"I want to be alone with my wife. Now leave!"

They went around him and out the door and he kneeled beside Spotted Fawn. A contraction wracked her body and she closed her eyes against it. He took her hand and held it tightly until the pain was gone. She opened her eyes and smiled wanly at him.

"Again you defy the customs of our people."

"You know I would not be separated from you."

"I know. But this is no place for you. I do not want you to see me this way."

"We have shared everything from the beginning. I want to share this with you, too."

She shook her head. "No. This is one thing you cannot share."

Tears came to his eyes as he perceived a deeper, more final meaning to her words. "I will not leave you."

Another contraction seized her and she was isolated from him in her pain and he put his arms around her and held her trembling body, his tears wetting her cheek.

She opened her eyes and brushed the tears from his face with a smile. "Do not cry. Bringing forth life is a happy occasion. Your son will be strong and healthy. You cry in vain. Now please let me do this as our people's custom dictates. The women will help me if I need help."

"I wish to stay but if you do not want me to, I will honor your wish."

"It is how it must be, my husband. Tomorrow I will be with you again with our son. Tomorrow I will tell you I love you and hold you close with our child between us and I will be fulfilled. No woman could be more happy than I am."

He bent to kiss the pale lips and whispered, "I will love you until the sun stops rising, Spotted Fawn. Tonight I will come sing a song for you and for our son. When you hear it you will know my love."

She smiled and as she did another pain seized her and her eyes closed against it. He kissed the hand that touched his face and rose to leave, looking back as he reached the door. She lay tense with pain, her hands pressed against the body that tormented her. He ducked out quickly and went with unseeing eyes to his lodge.

Snow Cloud waited for him as he entered. "I have come to wait with you, my son. Come. We will smoke and talk. Soon my grandchild will be born."

They sat down and lit White Eagle's pipe and smoked, talking of the hunt and of many things until darkness closed out all sight of each other except for the glow of the pipe. Morning Star came and built a fire and prepared the buffalo hump for them but White Eagle couldn't eat.

He stood up before Snow Cloud was finished and said, "I must go sing to Spotted Fawn."

He left the lodge and went to the women's lodge and stood outside, hearing the anxious voices within. He coughed discreetly and one of the women came out.

"How is Spotted Fawn?"

"The baby has not come yet."

"I asked how she was doing?"

"She weakens." The woman turned and ducked back into the lodge.

White Eagle stood in silent despair for long moments, and then with emotion coloring his voice, he sang for Spotted Fawn. He became aware of the noise of the camp diminishing as they heard his voice and were aware of his words and involuntarily stopped to listen. He finished the song he had composed for her and stood waiting for some sign that she had heard but all his ears heard was her muffled, agonized moan. He returned to his own lodge.

Snow Cloud looked up and asked, "How is she?"

"The baby has not come and she weakens."

Snow Cloud spread his hands in helplessness. "Then it is as your vision has shown?"

White Eagle nodded silently. They sat without words for long hours. Snow Cloud rose from his seat at dawn and said, "I will go see how she is. You rest."

White Eagle lay back on his couch and slept fitfully. Snow Cloud returned in a while and White Eagle awoke. "Is she better?"

Snow Cloud shook his head sadly. "No. We have called the shaman to attend her."

White Eagle's body sagged and his face took on a grim, hopeless look. If only his mother or even Wind Woman were still alive. His mother would have known what to do, and he had more faith in Wind Woman's herbs and potions than in the shaman's rituals. He blamed himself for not taking her to the white doctors. He remembered her suggestion to go live with the white man and the memory of his refusal deepened his guilt. He had thought he did not need the white man's ways but now he wished he had not been so stubborn. His own mother's illness was evidence that the white men had more power than the red men. If he had acted soon enough the white doctors could have saved her. It was possible that going to the white eagle's nest had meant taking Spotted Fawn to the white men to be saved. Anger overtook doubt and anxiety and he rose and paced the small area of the lodge in frustration.

The shaman worked with Spotted Fawn for two days before he gave up hope and with his rejection of her the blame was placed on White Eagle for his defiance of their customs. They couldn't have blamed him any more than he blamed himself, and the transference of guilt from the shaman to him only brought him deep and unreasoning anger. The rejection he had felt for the white man was being replaced with a rejection for the superstitious rituals of the shaman.

He went to the women's lodge after the shaman left but the women refused him entrance and Snow Cloud made sure he would not defy them by personally placing himself in the door of the lodge.

"Wait in your lodge, my son. I will bring you any news."

He went and sat in utter dejection on his couch until evening. Snow Cloud came and stood silently before him until he raised his head in acknowledgment. He knew it was over but he still asked, "Is it over?"

"Yes. She suffers no more."

"The baby?"

"It was never born."

He closed his eyes against the shock of it and sat in stiff silence until tears squeezed from between tight eyelids and he was reduced to grief. He pulled the knife from his belt and slashed at his body until Snow Cloud caught his wrist and held it. He cried his grief to the world and the camp heard his wail and became silent with only the wolves feeding on the buffalo carcasses answering his cries. Then, like echoes coming back to him, other voices were lifted in grief over the death of Spotted Fawn, but they would soon be stilled and only his grief would be heard.

A scaffold was built and Spotted Fawn's body was placed there with her most treasured articles, to stand alone on the vast, empty plain. The camp moved on and life moved on for everyone but White Eagle. He sat alone in his lodge within sight of Spotted Fawn's scaffold and cared not that the camp left him behind. For days he sat without eating, wishing his life would end, until Snow Cloud came with Buffalo Horn and Two Knives. When they entered his lodge he looked up with unseeing eyes, hoping it was an enemy who would take his life.

Gently, Snow Cloud said, "The moon of mourning is over, my son. Come with us now."

He made the effort to rise but was too weak and sank back down on his couch. Snow Cloud went through the parfleches and found some pemmican and brought it to him, but when he tried to eat it his stomach rebelled against it and he was sick.

Snow Cloud ordered, "Two Knives, see if you can find a rabbit to make some soup for him. He has not eaten for so long his stomach won't accept anything solid."

Buffalo Horn offered, "I will go with him. Two hunters are better than one."

Snow Cloud sat down to wait with White Eagle and when the two hunters returned with a rabbit they soon had a fire going and the rabbit simmering in a cooking bladder of water. When the marrow was cooked out of the bones and the flesh juices thoroughly released into the broth, they fed him and ate themselves and prepared to spend the night with him until he had gained enough strength to travel.

In the morning he ate more of the strengthening broth and was able to stand. Snow Cloud and Buffalo Horn helped him onto a horse, but when he saw they were going to leave the lodge behind he spoke his first words since they had come for him.

"Bring the lodge."

"You will not need it now. You have a place in your warrior society."

Stubbornly he insisted, "I will not leave without our lodge."

The three men did his bidding and soon the lodge and its furnishings were loaded onto a travois and they rode slowly away from the earthly remains of his beloved Spotted Fawn.

For a while he attempted to return to the life of the camp and become one of them but when the snow fell and they moved into winter camp and the activity of hunting came to a halt for the winter, so did his activity come to a stop. He spent long days in brooding silence alone in his lodge. Days went by without eating and nights went by without sleep. Snow Cloud and others came to try to encourage him but he would only stare woodenly at the fire someone else had built and say nothing. Morning Star came to bring him food and Brown Hair brought him fresh meat whenever there was a hunt, but he ate little, if at all, and only because he didn't want to hurt their feelings. For himself he only wanted a release from the guilt and sorrow he felt.

By the time the snow began to melt he had made up his mind he should die. Because he had shown no interest in keeping himself fed or a fire built to keep him from freezing, Brown Hair had come to stay with him and watched him constantly, trying in every way he could to talk to his older brother and bring him out of his depression, but until White Eagle had devised a plan to bring about his death he remained remote. With Brown Hair in constant attendance and alert for just such an act, he knew taking his own life would be looked for and thwarted. But there was one in camp who would accommodate him. It would mean forcing himself to become a part of his surroundings again but with the goal of his death in mind, he found it easy to begin eating and making the first attempts to take care of himself.

Brown Hair smiled with relief when he realized the change that was taking place in White Eagle. "You are better, my brother?"

White Eagle's voice was tight and almost incoherent from long silence. "Yes."

"I must tell Father and Morning Star." He ran from the lodge with a happy face and returned shortly with Snow Cloud and Morning Star.

Snow Cloud looked at him anxiously. "Brown Hair tells me you are eating again. Is your grief finally over?"

"My grief will never be over, but to sit and wait for death takes too long. I must be strong so I can go find death where it waits for me."

Morning Star gasped with horror and Snow Cloud frowned with concern. "You speak with the tongue of the evil spirits, my son. Shall I call the shaman to come drive them from you?"

"Forgive me, Father. I have thought of little else but death. If I speak of it now it is only because it has been so much a part of me. If it comes I will welcome it, but do not worry that I will kill myself. I meant only that I have decided to rebuild my life and meet death when it is ready to take me."

Snow Cloud smiled with relief. "Then our prayers to the Great Spirit have been answered. Welcome back, my son."

In the next few days, when he was feeling stronger, White Eagle abandoned his lodge and went once more to join the warrior society. They accepted his presence uncertainly at first, but as he forced himself to act naturally and do what was accepted and expected of him, they lost their skepticism of him, and when the first hunts of spring were organized, he was among the men to take the hunter's trail, along with Big Tree and Two Knives.

Snow remained only in the sheltered areas in the woods and hollows, but on the plain the spring of life was everywhere in evidence. Flowers were blossoming in colorful exuberance, made all the more vivid against the emerald background of new grass. The air was fresh and sweet with dew and clouds floated high in the bright blue sky, white and fluffy. White Eagle saw none of it nor felt any renewing of life within himself as he rode. His whole being was occupied with his death and the plan of how to bring it about. He stayed close to Big Tree and when the hunters decided to break up into groups of two and three he elected to go with Big Tree.

They had ridden in silence until they were out of sight of the rest of the hunters and had found a brush-filled hollow near a stream course. Game of some sort was sure to be hidden in the thicket and they needed to plan their hunt and stopped some distance away.

Big Tree said, "I will ride to the other side and wait if you wish to drive them out, or I will do the driving. What say you?"

"Neither, Big Tree. I want you to do me a favor."

"A favor? I don't understand."

"You have always wanted to kill me. Now I wish it to be done."

Big Tree looked at him in surprise. "Then the evil ones still possess you? I wondered."

"No. No evil spirit possesses me and neither does the spirit to live. You loved Spotted Fawn, too. Can you not hate me enough to kill me for bringing her death?"

Big Tree looked concerned. "It is true I have hated you for many things, White Eagle, but you have proved always that you were the better man. You spared my life twice when you could have let me die. Now I give you yours."

White Eagle's voice rose in desperation. "But I do not wish to live!"

"And I do not wish to kill you. You suffer more this way."

White Eagle pulled his knife and lunged at Big Tree and knocked them both to the ground, drawing blood, but he was no physical match for Big Tree after a winter of letting his body live in neglect. They wrestled briefly and Big Tree disarmed him and held him down easily. Tears of anger and frustration blended with the dirt as he lay facedown, struggling futilely. At last he lay still and Big Tree released him and stood.

"Now I have given you your life twice again, White Eagle, and you are in my debt once more." He paused to let the full import of his words impress themselves on White Eagle, then continued, "I will ride to the other side of the thicket and you will flush the game for me."

He mounted his horse and, taking White Eagle's horse, rode away. White Eagle slowly raised himself from the ground and wiped the dirt from his face and sat watching Big Tree with anger and despair. Big Tree was soon gone from sight and the birds resumed their cheerful songs. His eyes were distracted by a little yellow bird that fluttered close, picking the first maturing seeds of a weed. The bird cracked seeds for a bit then opened its beak in beautiful trilling song and cocked its head at White Eagle. He imitated its song and it sang back to him. He picked one of the seeding weeds and held it for the bird and it darted close and snatched a mouthful and hopped away and sang again.

Softly he whispered, "What message do you bring, little yellow bird?"

The bird was startled by his voice and flew into the thicket. White Eagle stood and looked around him, seeing the beauty of the plains for the first time and wondering what he should do. He picked up his knife and walked slowly into the thicket, threading his way through the dense, greening twigs and hearing a deer flee before his prowling. He emerged on the other edge of the thicket and saw Big Tree lifting a small buck onto his horse. He mounted his own horse and the two men rode back to camp in silence.

White Eagle returned to his own lodge and stood, overcome with sadness as he looked at the trappings of the lodge so beautifully worked and looking so unused and forlorn. He touched each article, his fingers tracing the intricate designs of Spotted Fawn's work. Silent tears wet his cheeks as he slowly began to realize there was nothing left here for him. His vision had not shown his death, and he felt restless and wanted to get away from all that reminded him of Spotted Fawn. This part of his life was over and he had to shut it out of his mind. It was time to go in search of the white eagle's nest.

He returned to the warriors' lodge determined to lock his grief and guilt from his mind. He didn't return to his own lodge until the camp broke to go on the first buffalo hunt. He packed it, unwilling to leave her things behind but not knowing yet how to dispose of them. They were still too dear to be given away just yet. He knew he would have to eventually, but that could wait until he made the final break.

24

IN SEARCH OF THE WHITE EAGLE'S NEST

White Eagle turned his horse and looked back at the circle of lodges that had been his only home for twenty years. He was outfitted with the finest his people could give him. On his chest he felt the unfamiliar weight of the copper medallion Snow Cloud had placed there. The break had been difficult, more so for Morning Star and Brown Hair than for himself. It had been hard to leave them, but he had little idea what life held for him and could not risk taking them with him. It was entirely possible he would even return before winter.

Without a definite idea of what he should do, he turned his horse southward. He would be among friends in the Yankton bands of the Nakota and he would perhaps discover from them what it was his life held. He was more alone than he had ever been in his life and felt infinitely smaller in the vast open plain where sky and earth met without interruption in the far distance—where, vulnerable and dispensable, he was but a speck moving slowly across an unchanging panorama of green, rippling grass—yet he felt no fear. Death at enemy hands was not terrifying to him.

He spent a few nights among a band of Yanktons and was disheartened by their declining state from contact with the white men. He tried to counsel them into resisting the white man's encroachment and to stop using the white man's liquor, but they were hopelessly addicted and increasingly dependent on the white man's trade. More than once they tried to make him realize the magnitude of the white man's power.

By the time he left them he had determined to know the white man's strength on his own. If what the Yanktons said was true, there was little hope for his own people. But if he could learn how great or how small was the white threat, then it would be possible to know if they could declare war on the white man and drive him from their land.

He came to the white man's trail along the Platte River and knew sooner or later the white man's caravans would pass him there. He would wait. He made camp in a spot overlooking the river on a barren bluff. From his high perch he could easily see any caravan coming for miles along the river bottom and anything else that might threaten him. He ate nothing but dried food, building no fire and taking his horses down to the river at night for water, keeping as inconspicuous as possible.

Days passed before he saw a long line of wagons, mules, and horses coming from the east, along the river. He gathered his things together and loaded his horses and rode down the bluff without hurry to meet the westwardbound caravan. The forward scouts rode up to him suspiciously and he sat his horse stiffly, feeling uncertain but showing no fear.

The two men eyed him warily and one of them said to the other, "What do you make of him? Sioux maybe?"

"Could be. Know any Sioux dialect?"

"Naw."

White Eagle watched them, hearing the almost forgotten language of his mother, assimilating the words slowly and understanding them. The white man signed to him but sign language was something he had not used often enough to remember it any better than the white man's language. With awkward slowness he signed to them that he had come from the north.

The two men looked at each other skeptically and one asked, "Do you suppose there's a whole bunch of 'em hid somewheres?"

"Could be. Let's take him to Captain Campbell and see what he makes of him."

They motioned White Eagle to come with them to the approaching train but he stood his ground. They sat with him and waited until the slow-moving caravan came up to them. The man they called Campbell came forward with a group of well-armed men from the train, all obviously experienced mountain men.

Campbell asked, "What have you found here?"

"Don't know, Mr. Campbell. He came riding down off the bluffs big as you please and stopped right here. He doesn't seem to understand sign language too good, but I'd say he was Sioux."

"Which bluff did he come from?"

One of the men pointed out the bluff where White Eagle had waited and the man called Campbell sent some of his men to scout the area. They returned after scouting the bluff with a report.

"Been only one man there for several days, captain. No sign of any others."

Campbell turned to White Eagle and said, as he appraised him, "He waited there for us. I wonder why."

With hesitancy, White Eagle signed that he wished to go with the caravan. Campbell looked at him keenly and asked, "What do you think, men? Shall we take him along?"

"Sioux are damned treacherous, captain. Might mean trouble either way."

"You're quite right about that. But at least if we have him with us he won't be bringing any more down on us for turning him away. Watch him, Seth. Let's get moving."

The man called Seth came out of the group and pulled his horse alongside of White Eagle. "Looks like I get to babysit you, Injun."

They stared at each other and White Eagle felt there was something familiar about the man and the man looked hard at him, with squinted eyes, recognition lurking in the distant reaches of his mind. He said, "Say! Ain't I seen you before? God damn me, if you don't look familiar."

The man named Campbell heard Seth and turned his horse back. "Have you seen him before, Seth? Where? It might help if we knew."

"Seems like to me I have, but I can't recollect where." He pulled off his hat and rubbed his fingers thoughtfully over a circular bald spot on the crown of his head.

"Maybe you'll think of it later. Let's move out."

The wagons creaked forward and the man called Seth motioned White Eagle to fall in behind the wagons. He went with the man and they followed the caravan until it stopped for the night. He became the camp curiosity as the men settled around the campfires built inside a barricade made with their wagons and equipment. Some of the men tried to talk to him in some of the Indian jargon they had picked up but he pretended not to understand even the few words of Sioux he recognized. He would learn much more if they didn't think he understood anything they said.

They offered him food and he ate, but when they offered him a drink of the white man's whiskey, which was being passed around the camp for the enjoyment of the men, he refused.

Seth exclaimed, "Well, I'll be damned. First time I ever seen an Injun refuse firewater."

The rest of the men laughed heartily and they speculated on him. He listened intently as the whiskey loosened their tongues and he became more familiar with the somewhat corrupted version of his mother's language.

"I wonder if he'd trade me that thing he wears around his neck for some tobaccy?" one of the men asked.

Seth answered, "Dunno. Wouldn't hurt nothin' to try."

The man began to propose a trade with White Eagle for his medallion but he stared at the man stolidly. When the man grew frustrated he made an attempt to touch the medallion, but White Eagle caught his wrist and held it tightly and forced the hand away.

Seth cautioned, "Better leave him alone, Tully."

The man rubbed the smarting wrist and nodded. "Yeah. He ain't too cooperatin'."

A young man was passing by and Seth called to him, "Hey, Charlie, you on first watch?"

The man stopped and answered, "Yes. Are you?"

"Naw. That's why I wondered if you'd do me a little favor and keep an eye on our Injun friend here, while I sleep?"

Charlie came closer and looked with interest at White Eagle. "I don't know, Seth. I don't know anything about Indians. Is he dangerous?"

Seth and the man Tully laughed uproariously. Seth finally was able to answer, "Well, now's as good a time as any to learn."

Charlie looked uncertain and White Eagle felt sorry for the man. By his clothes and his manner he was obviously on his first trip into the wilderness. He was not too much older than White Eagle.

Charlie asked, "Can he understand English?"

"Naw. But you don't need to worry. I'll tell him he's to go with you. Maybe you can even teach him some."

Seth proceeded to use sign language to indicate White Eagle was now in Charlie's care. They stood looking at each other—the one apprehensive, the other noncommittal. Charlie turned away a little hesitantly and looked over his shoulder at White Eagle and White Eagle followed, while Seth and Tully still chuckled.

They reached Charlie's post at one corner of the barricade and he looked at White Eagle standing with arms crossed and face passive and said with a hopeless sigh, "You might as well sit down there and get some sleep."

White Eagle continued to stand, looking uncomprehendingly at the man.

Charlie murmured, "Oh, God. How do I make you understand?" He attempted to show White Eagle what he wanted him to do and ended up by doing it himself. White Eagle sat down and leaned against a pack, but his guard, uncomfortable by his presence, couldn't keep his eyes from constantly turning to White Eagle, and the sweat of nervous tension glistened on his brow.

When Charlie looked away again, White Eagle pulled out his knife and held it up to him when he looked back, handle first in a gesture of friendship and trust.

Charlie was hesitant to take it from him so White Eagle tossed it to him, and the man picked it up, keeping his eyes riveted on White Eagle. He smiled, then, saying, "It really must show that I'm not much good as a guard. You probably should be guarding instead of me. I bet you wouldn't be as scared of me as I am of you. How old are you, anyway? Bet we're about the same age. God! I bet I sound like an idiot to you, talking my head off and you can't understand a word I say." He paused and looked thoughtful for a moment before he said, "Thanks anyway." He held up the knife before sticking it in his belt and his meaning was clear.

White Eagle closed his eyes and slept, awaking sometime later at the sound of voices. He looked around and saw his guard sleeping soundly a few feet away. He reached out and touched Charlie's leg with his hand. The young man started and looked about in apprehension. White Eagle pointed to the advancing men and Charlie rose to his feet quickly.

It was the relief watch, and in a few minutes White Eagle and Charlie were walking through the tethered horses and mules toward the men's bedrolls. Seth was still asleep and Charlie was clearly uncertain whether to wake the man or not and finally walked on, motioning White Eagle to follow. Reaching his own bedroll, he gave a blanket to White Eagle and they both lay down to finish their night's sleep.

At dawn scouts went out to look over the country. When it was decided no Indians waited to pounce on them, the horses and mules were let out to graze. After a leisurely breakfast, camp was broken and the caravan moved on, hoping to make their customary twenty to twenty-five miles a day. White Eagle, not only liking the young, inexperienced Charlie but also wanting to keep from jarring Seth's memory, rode with the young man at the back of the half-mile-long caravan, eating dust or mud, whichever they encountered.

Charlie took everything in, enjoying the monotonous scenery of shallow, muddy river and treeless valley rimmed by featureless bluffs. He looked at White Eagle often, wanting to talk and knowing it was useless and talking anyway, expressing all the enthusiasm of youth on a great adventure, and White Eagle listened, hearing in this young man's speech the same educated English his mother had taught him and remembering more with each word Charlie spoke.

When they were alone, out of hearing of any other men, Charlie said, "You don't understand me, I know, but I want to thank you for waking me last night. If they'd caught me asleep, I'd be walking instead of riding today."

For days White Eagle rode with them, watching and listening as the caravan followed the Platte River valley westward on a gently inclining plain. He endured with them the heat and cold; the dust and violent storms that left them ankle-deep in water and the hoards of hungry insects that plagued them as their landscape changed from grassy plain to arid sagelands; and the gentle bluffs became rugged hills of spectacular eroded rock with buttresses and battlements like ruins of ancient cities. The water was often bad and so was the travel as they negotiated swollen streams and deep

gullies or crossed deserts of blowing sand where cacti lamed their
animals. At times the tempers grew short, but the nightly ration of
whiskey relaxed the men, and it was a time for reminiscing about
home and the life they were leaving behind as well as the life they
were fonder of in the mountains. There every man became his own
man—suffering cold, hunger, and every deprivation, knowing any
day could well be his last, but willingly doing so for the right to live
unencumbered, totally free of every civil and moral restraint.
White Eagle soon learned the whiskey seldom affected these men
as it did the Indian, and he was beginning to find much that was
worthwhile in these men and their equipment and in their organization, which he admired most of all. He was also beginning to
realize the full scope of their civilization and what it would ulti-
mately mean to the Indian. He was beginning to see what the
Yanktons had tried to tell him—indeed, what his mother had tried
to tell him—and it was all being reinforced and made more mean-
ingful because he was experiencing it.

He was not totally convinced there was no other way but sub-
mission to their overwhelming force, and his mind grew circum-
spect, perceiving they would all be affected by these white men as
by a highly infectious and destructive disease. It only made him
anxious to know more and see more of these people—his mother's
people, his people. He knew then the power behind his vision had
brought him here, and he felt certain he was guided by his god to
these men. There was no doubt in his mind that he was doing what
his vision had meant for him to do.

They were in high country now. Mountains loomed ever closer
and more game was available. Big Horn sheep and antelope sup-
plemented their diet of buffalo, along with sage grouse and jack
rabbit. The dark-haired man they called Stewart was a foreigner on
a holiday in the wilderness. And holiday he made it. He was
everywhere, hunting and exploring and experiencing to the fullest
all the adventure of the trail. He killed a grizzly bear and celebrated
by treating the camp to his private stock of liquor. The camp was
soon noisier than usual with a double ration of firewater.

It was this night Seth rememberd White Eagle as they sat
around the campfire, their tall tales getting taller. Seth was trying
to frighten Charlie by retelling the story of his scalping when he
stopped in the middle of the story and stared openmouthed at
White Eagle as he remembered.

"God damn!" he exploded. "You're the one, ain't you? I'll be go
to hell! I never expected to see you again, you thievin' bastard!" His

look of amazement turned to laughter and he held out his hand to White Eagle. "Injun, I want to shake your hand."

Charlie was the first to ask, "What do you mean, Seth? Who is he?"

Seth answered, "Like I was saying, this bunch of Injuns grabbed off our horses and I, like a damned fool, goes running after 'em. This one big brute was takin' my best horse and before I know'd it, he was takin' me, too. He rode me miles from camp and took my hair and left me to die. Next thing I know is, this Injun, here, was packin' me back to camp. He let me off where the camp could see him or they'd never a found me and old Seth would be one damn dead turkey." He shook the hand again at White Eagle, who took it, and Seth said, "I want to thank you for that, you damn thief."

They shook hands and White Eagle continued to look noncommittal and Seth asked, "Now, where the hell's my horse?"

His companions laughed and White Eagle sat without expression, convincingly uncomprehending, seeing the beginnings of respect light more than one eye around the fire.

The caravan moved on, traveling across ever more forbidding country as they climbed higher toward the distant mountains. The deserts were worse, the canyons deeper, and the scenery more spectacular as they passed tortured hills and were tortured themselves by the sun, dust, and mineral-laden drinking water that made the greenhorns sick. The first-timers carved their names with those of past travelers on a huge mound of soft eroding rock, and in the next day or so they saw the true Shining Mountains. Within another few days they were crossing the pass—a wide, sage-covered plateau—and dropped down into the valley of the Green River and camped with the fur traders and trappers already there, waiting for their supply caravans to arrive, ready with their bales of furs to ship east.

It was a spectacular scene to the newcomer. The very size and grandeur of the mountains surrounding them made even more spectacular the overwhelming number of white men, numbering more than three hundred, with just as many, if not more, Indians there, some of them from western tribes never seen by White Eagle. Spectacular as a group, the trappers in their half-civilized and half-Indian garb were no less colorful as individuals. They wore leather combined with ruffles, bells, and beaded moccasins, bright-colored blankets, and hair as long as an Indian's, sometimes braided, sometimes wild and flowing, as were their beards. Their

Indian consorts and horses were at least equal in adornment, and on most occasions more highly adorned. The women wore every color of the rainbow, in feathers and beads and ribbons. Jewelry was even more in abundance than in Indian camps, and the horses were lavished with every sort of decoration worn by man and woman.

It soon became apparent to White Eagle that the different camps were rivals in the fur-trading business, and as the first hectic days of trading passed, the rivalry was expressed in every sort of activity the half-civilized men could think of. Horse races and shooting matches were the big crowd pleasers and drinking and gambling weren't far behind, as each camp sought to outdo the other. White Eagle was virtually an island in the midst of a swirling, volatile river of men and women. No one kept track of him now and he was free to wander and look and listen where he would, returning usually to be with Charlie, who manned the store, so to speak, for the Campbell caravan because he was the only one sober enough to know what he was doing.

One night he found quite by accident another quiet, sober group of men gathered around a separate campfire, some distance away, while the valley in general was on another bout of noisy carousal. He went to investigate the presence of this new group of men and rode boldly into their midst.

A man near his own height with dark hair and thin face spoke to him in a language he didn't understand. When he didn't answer they talked among themselves for a moment, then the man spoke to him in English.

"Are you lost, my friend? There's no firewater here. What camp do you come from?"

White Eagle stood silent as the man looked him over and waited for him to answer. Getting no answer, the man signed to him and White Eagle pointed in the direction of Campbell's camp.

Another man, larger and bearded, spoke. "That direction of the Rocky Mountain Fur Company, Tom. He no look like fur trader to me. What you think?"

"Could be a spy to find out what we're doing here."

The other man shook his head and chuckled. "Or he be one drunk Indian and can't find his way home."

This brought laughs from the other men seated around the fire, and the man called Tom grinned. "Well, maybe we'd better take him back where he belongs."

The bearded man rose and they motioned White Eagle to

follow them. They got their horses and rode with him to Campbell's camp. Campbell was in his tent and he looked up when they entered.

"Good evening, gentlemen. Mr. McKay, isn't it?"

"Yes. We found this Indian wandering around our camp and he indicated he came from here. Is he one of your men?"

"In a way he is. Did he cause any trouble?"

"No. We thought he was drunk and got lost."

Campbell laughed. "Not that one. He won't touch the stuff."

The two men appraised White Eagle in interest and he remained silent and aloof.

McKay said, "That is a little strange for an Indian. Where'd you find him?"

"We didn't find him, he found us. He was camped near the trail and joined us. He hasn't caused any trouble so we have let him tag along. Did he say anything to you?"

"No. Didn't seem to understand us, so we weren't sure who he was, but if he's your man, we've brought him to the right place."

"Quite frankly, he's not our man. He's just as much a mystery, almost, to us as when we first saw him. He hasn't spoken a word but one of my men says the Indian was one of a band that stole some horses from a returning caravan a couple of years ago and this man saved his life. We think he's a Sioux but we're not sure."

The dark, bearded man chuckled and asked, "Has anyone looked to see if he has a tongue?"

They all laughed and Campbell shook his head. "No, but he has one, I'm sure. Well, thank you for bringing him back. Are you here to sell or buy furs?"

"Neither. We were in the area and came to join the party."

Campbell smiled. "Well, there's always next year. How are things going with the Hudson's Bay Company this year?"

"We've had a fairly good year. Well, Mr. Campbell, we better get back to our own camp."

"Good night, gentlemen."

They turned to leave and White Eagle decided in that instant he wanted to go with these men and followed them out of the tent. They saw him coming after them and motioned him to stay but he ignored their motions and came with them. They took him back to Campbell's tent.

"Sorry to bother you again, Mr. Campbell, but we can't make him understand he's to stay with you."

Campbell shrugged in hopelessness. "I can do no better with

him, I'm afraid. He's been harmless so far, so I doubt he'll bother
you if you can't make him stay here."

The two men looked at each other and then at White Eagle.
McKay motioned to him and said, "All right, come along."

He rode with them to their own camp and they discussed him,
or so he assumed, in the language he didn't understand. They gave
him food and a blanket, and he settled down to spend the night
with these men who didn't drink the white man's whiskey and
weren't joining in the wild entertainments of the rest of the
trappers.

In the morning he followed them as they went among the
trappers and talked, sometimes in English and sometimes in the
other language. They met many men they knew but one man they
seemed to know a little better, and they greeted each other in
English.

"I'll be damned! If it isn't Joe Meek. How are you, Joe?"

"Tom McKay! You old skunk! It's good to see you. I been real
good, and you?"

"Couldn't be better. Do you remember Jacques Broulette?"

The two men, looking a good deal alike, with dark hair and
beards, smiled as recognition dawned. "Sure," Meek said. "How
are you, Jacques?"

"Just fine, my friend."

Joe eyed White Eagle and asked, "Where'd you find him?"

Jacques laughed and Tom answered, "We didn't. He found
us."

Meek studied him and realized who White Eagle was. "Ain't he
from Campbell's camp? I'm sure I saw him there."

"Campbell said he was, but he didn't want to stay with Campbell
when we took him back there and has been followin' us around
ever since."

Meek laughed. "Well, I'll be damned! He's a strange one, all
right. He talk to you yet?"

"Not yet."

"Well what the hell you going' to do with him?"

"I don't know. Maybe he'll find someone else to attach himself
to."

"You going back to Fort Vancouver from here?"

"Yes. You ready to come with us?"

"Not yet. There's still some money to be made here, I think, but
don't know what's going to happen to the Rocky Mountain Company. Things look kinda bad what with Bonneville, Wyeth, and the

American Fur Company hornin' in on things. Guess I'll stick around and see what next winter brings."

"If you change your mind you know where to find us."

"Sure do. Nice seein' ya again. Give my regards to Dr. McLoughlin."

They parted company and White Eagle followed the two men to where the trappers and Indians were racing their horses against one another. His two companions drank a little of the liquor being passed around and placed bets but not nearly with the abandon of the other men around them. Fights broke out when the race was over, and White Eagle looked with disgust at the drunken riot of men around him. Except for the two men he was with, he found the drunken white trappers and the even drunker, more belligerent Indians deplorable.

His two companions quietly exited from the noisy crowd and he stayed with them until they came near Campbell's camp, then left them to get his belongings. He had made up his mind these two men were different from the rest and it was with them he wanted to stay. When he came riding into their camp a little later they looked at him with surprise and dismay. He dismounted and went about unloading his pack horse as they watched, unable to do anything about his staying. He was beginning to see the humor in their apparent frustration and didn't know how much longer he could keep from trying to talk to them.

McKay was visibly at his wits' end and in words and sign he tried to make White Eagle understand. "Now this is going too far! You can't stay with us." His sign language was just as emphatic as his voice. "We live far from your people. You go back to your own people with Campbell. We live far to the west on the big water."

White Eagle stood unblinking as Tom McKay tried futilely to communicate with him, and his men watched and whispered among themselves until they could no longer contain their laughter. McKay was angry now and he drew his knife and waved it threateningly at White Eagle, but White Eagle stood with arms folded across his chest in utter incomprehension. McKay hurled the knife into the ground and walked to the campfire, shaking his head. The men were laughing and he was muttering, "Damn dumb Indian."

Jacques wiped away tears and chortled, "He not dumb. *You* the one not make sense to him!"

This brought on another round of laughter, and McKay glared at the stolid White Eagle. "Well, then, stubborn. Look at him, standing there like stone. Now, what the hell do you do with a stone Indian?"

The laughter rose again and Jacques slapped his knee. "*Mon Dieu,* Tom, I never think I see the day you couldn't handle any Indian."

Tom sat down and dished himself up a plateful of food. White Eagle came and took a hunk of buffalo meat from the fire and sat eating, while the men, over their laughter, watched him with interest.

Jacques finally said, "You know, Tom, he is one damn handsome Indian."

Another added, "Not very old, I think, Jacques."

"*Oui.* But look at the scars on him. He one hell of a fighter, I think."

Tom looked at White Eagle thoughtfully and asked, "How do you think he'd fair against the rest of the lot?"

Jacques shrugged eloquently. "Who is to know. But it would be good times finding out, eh?"

McKay smiled. "That's just what I was thinking. As long as we have to feed him, we may as well get a little money off him."

Jacques frowned. "But McLoughlin would not approve, no?"

McKay sobered. "No. But McLoughlin ain't here and we are."

Another said something in their other language and they all lapsed into it and he understood no more of the conversation. He took his horse and went hunting. If he was going to eat their food, it was only fair he provide something for them to eat. At dusk he returned with a fine deer and they watched with amazed stares as he laid his prize before their leader.

Tom McKay looked up at him and said, "I'll be damned! You ain't a completely worthless Indian at that."

White Eagle rolled into his robe and went to sleep with a smile on his face. In the morning he was the first one awake and lit the fire and set a haunch of venison over it to roast. Tom McKay raised his head from his bedroll and looked in puzzlement at White Eagle. One by one the men awoke and all looked at their strange companion.

Jacques said with a smile, "*Mon Dieu,* that smell good. Maybe we better off to keep him. He cook and maybe win us some money, no?"

Tom shook his head. "How can we enter him in anything? He can't understand a damn thing."

"Maybe we can find a man who can speak enough Sioux to talk to him. It worth a try, no?"

"Well, maybe. At least we can explain to him he can't stay with us."

They ate and set off, with White Eagle following them, to make the rounds of the scattered camps in search of someone who could speak Sioux. They finally found a trapper with a Sioux wife and her daughter, and they began the four-way conversation.

The woman asked him in the Yankton dialect, "Who are you and where do you come from?"

"I am White Eagle of the Nakota. Who are you, and why are you so far from your people?"

"I am Crushed Berry, also of the Nakota. Several snows ago I was given to this white man. You wear the medallion of a chief. What has happened to your people?"

"I am son of Snow Cloud, chief of the Follow the Wind people. This was his gift to me when I left." Mother and daughter both glanced upward at him and he looked at the girl for the first time. She was about Brown Hair's age and quite pretty.

Crushed Berry's husband translated the conversation to Tom McKay, and Tom said, "Explain to him we come from far west of his people and we will not be going east. If he wants to return to his people he will have to stay with Campbell, who will return east."

The trapper translated into Sioux and White Eagle told the woman, "Tell them I do not wish to return to my people but wish to go with them to the west."

When McKay got the translation he looked perplexed. Jacques grinned and said, "Ask him if he will be our entry for the contests, no?"

The question was asked in Sioux and White Eagle answered, "Tell them I do not wish to compete."

The answer was given and McKay asked with a touch of impatience, "Then why the hell is he here?"

White Eagle waited aloofly, with arms crossed, until Crushed Berry interpreted, and he answered, "I am here to learn about the white man."

The answer was given and Jacques laughed and McKay swore, "I'll be damned. What do you make of him, Edwards?"

The trapper shrugged noncommittally. "Dunno. Could be some religious thing. Maybe he had a vision. Do you want me to ask?"

McKay looked thoughtful, sighed, and said, "Guess not. It

wouldn't make much difference. Looks like we're stuck with him. Thanks anyway."

Edwards grinned and the little group split up, with White Eagle trailing McKay and the man called Jacques back to their camp. The other men questioned the two in their language and the looks of disappointment made White Eagle feel uncomfortable. If he had felt more sure of his physical capabilities he would have been glad to compete with the other men. A year ago he would have had little doubt about how well he could do, but the defeat at Big Tree's hands was still fresh and he doubted he had gained back enough strength since then to hold his own in the rough and tumble contests. But he had a fast horse, and it took little effort to be accurate with the white men's rifles.

He formed the white man's words in his mind first and then with studied slowness he delivered them to the silent and gloomy men seated around the camp. "My horse is fast and my aim is good with the white man's gun."

They looked at him in astonishment and Jacques exclaimed, "*Mon Dieu!* He can talk!"

McKay looked at him in disbelief, then anger. "You God damned Indian! Have you understood everything we've said?"

"When you speak the white man's language, yes." The words were coming with less effort.

"The hell!" The shock was over and the humor of the moment set in and they laughed, and White Eagle found himself smiling at their complete enjoyment of the joke.

Finally, McKay sobered and said, "You've got a lot of explainin' to do, Indian. I'd like to hear it."

"I am not an Indian by birth. My mother and father were white. My mother was taken by the Sioux before I was born. I was raised as a Sioux. What the man Edwards said about a vision is true."

McKay asked, "What about your mother?"

"She is dead."

McKay asked the others, "What do you think, men? Does he look like a white man?"

Jacques looked at him intently, "Maybe. With a bath we could tell better, no?" His eyes danced with devilment.

It was just the revenge they sought for the trick he had played on them. He didn't resist as they bodily carried him to the river and scrubbed the paint and grease from his body and hair. He stood before them naked, without the concealing paint, and his hair, loose and clean of the darkening grease, was a dark chestnut, not black.

Jacques whispered, "*Mon Dieu!* I think he tell the truth, Tom. All he need now is his hair cut and white man's clothes, no?"

They all nodded in agreement, and Tom asked, "What was your mother's name?"

"Her white name was Abigail."

"Well, it's not likely you could dream that up. Got any other proof?"

"I have her ring." He retrieved the medicine bag from the ground and opened it, handing the ring to McKay.

McKay studied it and passed it to Jacques, saying, "Well, I'll be damned! Ross was your father's name?"

"Yes."

"We got to have a name for you. Do you want a white man's name?"

"My mother called me Ross."

McKay smiled in agreement. "And what about a last name?"

"She never told me it."

McKay surveyed his men. "What'll his last name be, men? Got any ideas?"

They all looked at White Eagle thoughtfully and Jacques spoke up. "How about we call him Chestnut, for his hair, eh?" It sounded like Cheznut the way Jacques said it.

McKay asked, "How do you spell it, Jacques?"

Jacques shrugged and grinned. "I not good at spelling, *mon ami.*"

McKay took a stick and wrote the name in the mud of the river bank. White Eagle looked at it and knew the first name was spelled correctly. The last name McKay spelled CHESNUT. "Is that okay with you, Ross?"

He nodded. "I do not know how it should be but it will make little difference. It will be as you have it—Chesnut."

Jacques, not overlooking an opportunity, asked, "Did you mean what you said about wanting to compete in the contests for us?"

"Yes. I would do it for you, but I have not regained my strength since winter. That is why I did not wish to do it before. I did not want to fail."

McKay asked, "Do you think your horse can win?"

"He is good, but I do not know how good. There are many good horses here."

"And you say you can shoot a rifle?"

"I had one once. I did not often miss."

McKay grinned. "Well, you better get your pants on and we'll just see how good you are." He turned away, then turned back, puzzled. "Are you going as a white man or Indian?"

"I will go as White Eagle."

White Eagle rode his horse into the throng of people with McKay and his men riding with him. He wore his breechclout and moccasins, and his hair was braided and greased. His face was streaked with fresh paint. They entered him in the race that was about to begin and while the entries were gathering, they went gleefully to make bets with the other trappers.

The race started with a gunshot, and the horses leaped forward on the first lap of a long, tiring race. White Eagle soon realized endurance rather than speed would be needed to win, and he let his horse pick his own speed. He was within sight of the leaders, with two other men riding close beside him, as the last lap of the race was indicated by the judges. He urged his horse on and the stout-hearted animal forged ahead, gaining ground on the leaders. He was running with the leaders as they entered the home stretch, and as he tried to pull his horse around the horse in front of him, he was boxed in and cut off. There was no time left to pull his horse out of the box and around the outside, and he finished fourth.

He rode his horse back to where his unhappy comrades stood paying off their wagers. He said, "I am sorry I did not win for you."

McKay looked at him. "Not your fault. You did the best you could. They boxed you in. Otherwise you would have made it. Can you do better with a rifle?"

"I don't know. Do we have time for me to try it?"

"Be a damn good idea. Come on, let's see what you can do."

They rode back to their own camp and gave him the rifle. Targets were set up for him and he practiced with McKay's rifle, learning the feel and accuracy of it. Soon they were grinning enthusiastically as he became used to the gun and his aim became deadly.

Jacques breathed happily. "*Mon Dieu*, I think we have a winner, no?"

McKay smiled. "You may be right, Jacques. How do you feel about it, Ross? Are you ready?"

"I can try."

They rode back to the noisy, by now drunken crowd gathered

for the shooting contests and entered White Eagle. Bets were made and soon his turn came to challenge the best of the men shooting. He easily outshot the man who was getting a little erratic from too many sips of liquid refreshment. Another man came forward to challenge him, and he easily won again. The word went around that a real marksman was needed to beat the Sioux, and pretty soon a tall, brown-haired man came to challenge him.

He asked McKay, "Is this your man, McKay?"

"That's right. White Eagle, this is Jim Bridger. He's said to be a good shot."

White Eagle looked into the keen gray eyes and held out his hand in the white man's fashion of greeting he had seen used so much among these men. "It will give me pleasure to shoot against a truly good shot."

Bridger grinned and answered, "I'm ready if you are."

The targets were set and the contest began. Bridger was good and White Eagle had to bring all his concentration and skill to bear as they constantly equaled each other's ability. A moving target shot finally won the contest for White Eagle, and his backers whooped in unbounded delight as they collected bets.

Bridger held out his hand to White Eagle and said, "You're a damn good shot."

White Eagle countered, "I had to earn every one."

They shook hands and parted, and Bridger was surrounded by his confederates and moved away. As the big money winners, McKay and his companions were soon being plied with whiskey and invitations to other contests. With money to risk they were swept along, becoming more boisterous as the whiskey flowed. White Eagle felt increasing dismay at his companions' apparent lapse of character, and when McKay suggested to Jacques that maybe two of them should return to camp to relieve the two men left to guard their horses and equipment, White Eagle volunteered and gladly left them to their disgusting pursuits.

He rode toward his camp and saw the young man, Charlie, riding toward him. He hadn't seen Charlie since he had moved to McKay's camp and wasn't aware until now that he missed this white man who was so uniquely sober among so much drunkenness and ribaldry. He waited for him, and as Charlie recognized him, he smiled.

"Hello, my friend. I'm glad to see you. Captain Campbell said you moved to another camp." He stopped and laughed self-consciously and continued, "Here I go again, talking to you as if you understood me." He held out his hand, his face showing his embarrassment.

White Eagle grasped his hand warmly and said in English, "I do understand you, Charlie. And I am glad to see you, too."

The other man looked aghast. "I don't believe my ears! Am I really hearing you talk to me?"

White Eagle smiled. "Yes. I am sorry I did not speak to you before, but it has been a long time since I spoke your language."

Charlie laughed. "Well, how about that! Guess the joke's on me, as usual. But now that you can talk to me, I want to know you better. What is your name? Where did you come from?"

"I am called White Eagle by my people, the Nakota. Your people call us Sioux."

"Well, White Eagle, we've got a lot of talking to make up for. Can you come with me and we'll get acquainted?"

"I have to go to my own camp, but you are welcome there."

"All right, but it'll have to be later. I'm on an errand for Captain Campbell."

White Eagle held out his hand again and said, "Good. We will talk later then."

Charlie shook his hand and smiled and they parted. White Eagle rode on to his own camp to relieve the men stationed there.

By dark the men still hadn't returned, and he built a fire and roasted a slab of venison from the deer he had brought in and sat listening to the sounds of the night. He caught the faint thud of hooves and reached for a rifle and waited in the shadows beyond the firelight for the rider to be recognized. He was surprised when the visitor turned out to be the daughter of Crushed Berry.

He stepped from the shadows and asked in Sioux, "What are you doing here?"

"Your friends sent me to keep you company."

"I do not need company."

"They will not be pleased if I return so soon. They paid me well."

He was instantly angry, his male pride suffering to think she'd had to be paid to come to him. "They had to pay you to come? Then I do not wish you to stay."

"You do not understand. My mother's husband demands payment for me. He will beat me if he has to give the money back to your friends."

He relented. "All right. Get down and we will talk. I wish to hear more about a man who would sell his daughter."

She dismounted and came to the fire and seated herself close to him. "He is not my father. I was small when my father was killed. When the trapper took my mother, he took me, also."

"How long has he been selling your company?"

"Since the last rendezvous."

"And you do not mind that he has sold your virtue?"

She shrugged unconcernedly. "It makes little difference since he has already taken it for nothing."

White Eagle looked at her, his anger mounting again, not for her but for the white man who had defiled her and used her now to make money. "The more I see of the white man the more I find to hate in him. Do you want me to kill this man for you?"

She looked at him in surprise. "You would do such a thing for me?"

"If you wish it. I cannot give you back your virtue but at least I can avenge it for you. It is our way."

She thought about it for a long moment before she answered, "No. It is too late now for us to return to the ways of our people. If you should kill him, then neither my mother nor I would have anyone to take care of us, and we would be but dogs among our own people. Surely you must know that?"

He nodded. "I have never seen it among my people, but it was spoken of. You are still young and beautiful. You could yet find a man of your people to marry you."

"No. The white man has treated me well since he has found I can bring him much from the other white men. Why should I wish to live like a slave as a squaw, when now I need do only those things which keep me beautiful?"

White Eagle didn't answer, feeling disgust and anger. Here was yet another example of the white man's destructive influence over the Indian. Except for the trader McDonnell and young Charlie, he found little about the white man he could honor. He was almost ready to give up his quest for the white eagle's nest and return to his own people. All the respect he had been acquiring was rapidly dissolving into contempt. He had left Campbell's camp because he had thought he'd found better men. That illusion had vanished today, and now this. His discouragement was now complete.

She moved closer to him, until her arm brushed his and said, "I'm sorry what I say displeases you, but it is the truth. If you were pleased with the life you led, you would not be here. Is this not so?"

He felt discomfort from the closeness of her body and the

memories of pleasure her touch brought and tried to put it from him. "No. Perhaps you should leave now."

She began to cry and he was immediately compassionate. He put his arm around her, not quite knowing what he should do about her. She looked at him tearfully. "You said you found me attractive. Were you only speaking false words?"

"No."

"Then do not send me away yet. I could please you if you would let me."

She was in his arms and her warmth was stirring him. He kissed her and for a moment forgot the past and wanted only to know again the warmth and comfort of someone. Desire filled him and he could think of nothing else until he felt her hand slip under his breechclout and his manhood died with her touch as the realization of what he was doing came with swift devastation.

She pulled away from him and looked at him strangely. "What is wrong with you? Have you lost your manhood? Is this why you did not want me to stay?"

With strained voice he said, "Yes."

She stood up and looked at him with contempt. "Now I know why you are here. And you dare to tell me to return to my people and live like a dog? I pity you."

She mounted her horse and was gone, and he sat alone with shattered pride and mounting shame. He wondered if he would ever be able to touch a woman again without fearing his seed would kill her. He prayed to the Great Spirit to release him from his guilt and return his manhood, but knew even as he supplicated the powers ruling him that it would have to be his own mind that released him from his guilt before his potency would return. Still his pride was injured, and he sat in frustrated silence, wondering how to prove himself worthy of the name and badge he wore.

In the morning he announced to his sleepy and hung-over companions, "If you wish, I shall enter in all the contests."

Jacques grinned broadly. "*Mon Dieu, mon ami,* we hoped you would be grateful for our gift, but this is too much, no?"

Before he could answer, McKay added, "You don't owe us anything, Ross. We came here to have fun and we had one hell of a lot of it last night, thanks to you."

"I wish to do this." He turned abruptly and went to the river to bathe and apply fresh paint and ready himself for the contests ahead.

Jacques followed him and asked, "Is there something I can do to help you?"

"No."

"If you do well, my friend, I will send two women for you tonight."

White Eagle didn't look at Jacques, but said, "Save your money, Jacques. I do not wish any women."

The man was aghast. "No women! How can this be?"

White Eagle looked at the wondering face and answered, "Someday I will tell you why, but not today."

The quizzical look left Jacques's eyes and was replaced by warmth and compassion. His hand rested briefly on White Eagle's shoulder. "You do not need to tell me. I have been the fool and fools do not deserve explanations, no?"

"You did what you thought would bring me happiness. I will not forget."

"Will you, then, shake hands with me, my friend?"

White Eagle smiled. He liked this man, in spite of his drinking, and wanted to be his friend. He offered his hand without hesitation.

Jacques grinned back at him and White Eagle's own grin broadened, and Jacques exclaimed, *"Mon Dieu,* my friend, you have *fossettes!* How you say it in English? Le dimple? Never have I seen the Indian with these! But I forget. You are not an Indian. You make the good Indian but I think you make even better white man. When this over, we cut your hair, no, and throw away the grease and paint?"

The smile left White Eagle's face. Jacques saw the uncertainty and was quick to add, "But maybe not all at once, eh?"

"No. It will take time to do. I have never been a white man before."

"Oui. You have all the time you need. And I will leave you to do your preparation. Good luck, my friend."

He watched the big man leave and returned to his preparations, offering prayers to the different protectors he would need to help him through the day. When he was ready, he returned to camp and mounted his horse. Eagerly, the men who had not been unlucky enough to be left behind came with him.

He went from one physical contest to the next during the long, warm day. Endurance and determination were all that kept him going as the sun dipped toward the west. He had been beaten as many times as he had won during the day of footraces and weapon-ry contests. He even attempted to wrestle the camp champion, but he was no match for the big, burly man and doubted he could have won even in the best of condition. But some vestige of pride had been gained as he proved he was as good as or better than most of the men there. The last event of the day was an all-out, free-for-all game of Indian lacrosse. He was a skillful player because of his speed and agility, but he was no match for the bruising bullies seeking to knock him bodily from the game and he finally fell victim to a conspiracy to injure him. He lay bruised and unconscious on the field as the sun disappeared, leaving the playing field in a dusty pall raised by the trampling teams of men. He didn't know his companions picked him up and carried him back to camp until he woke up in his robe.

Jacques was applying cold, damp cloths to his head and saying, "If he does not wake up, we will have to carry him all the way to the White-headed Eagle's nest."

The words penetrated White Eagle's fuzzy brain and he asked, "What did you say about the white eagle's nest?"

"I only make the joke, my friend. How do you feel?"

"I feel like I was caught in a buffalo stampede."

They laughed and McKay said, "Damn near it, anyway, but you did yourself proud, White Eagle."

The name reminded him again of what Jacques had said. "You mentioned the white eagle's nest. Do you know of such a place?"

"It is not a place, my friend, but a man. Why?"

"I had a vision showing me going to a white eagle's nest. It is this place I look for now."

Jacques and McKay exchanged glances, and McKay answered, "My stepfather, Dr. John McLoughlin, is called by the Indians White-headed Eagle."

White Eagle's blood began to pound in his veins. "Who is this man? Where do I find him?"

"He is the chief factor for the Hudson's Bay Company at Fort Vancouver in the Oregon country. If you go with us, you will meet him."

White Eagle smiled in relief. Now he knew why he had come to this place and had been guided to these men. His vision was leading him and he would follow it to the white eagle's nest.

EPILOGUE

Within the pages of this novel are included several historical people and events. Among the most notable is perhaps Daniel Boone, who was so closely associated with Kentucky in history and on television that the reader may be surprised to find him in the Missouri Territory in this novel. Those who know Daniel Boone's whole story know the same drive that led him to Kentucky also led him out of Kentucky and ever westward, for Daniel Boone was truly a man with a wandering foot. If age had not caught up with him there is no doubt that only the Pacific Ocean would have stopped his questing into the wilderness, but the Rocky Mountains proved to be the limit of his travels and he did finally settle and die in Missouri.

Another notable historical character is Dr. John McLoughlin who was one of the most important men in the history of the Pacific Northwest. McLoughlin as chief factor for the British-owned Hudson's Bay Company built a fur trading empire that stretched from the Spanish-held territory of California on the south into the far reaches of Canada on the north and to the Rocky Mountains on the east. A stern but fair disciplinarian, McLoughlin was respected by both white men and the Indians who called him White-headed Eagle. McLoughlin's roots went deep into the Oregon

311